Invigilator

Invigilator

Stephen Geez

Fresh Ink Group
Roanoke

Invigilator

Fresh Ink Group
An Imprint of:
The Fresh Ink Group, LLC
PO Box 525
Roanoke, TX 76262
Email: info@FreshInkGroup.com
www.FreshInkGroup.com

Edition 1.0	1994
Edition 2.0	2012
Edition 2.1	2016

Book design by Ann Stewart

Cover design by Stephen Geez

Cover art by Anik

Cataloging-in-Publication Recommendations: Science Fiction; Military Fiction; Militia Fiction; Aliens (Sci-Fi); Alien Invasion (Sci-Fi); Terrorism (Fiction); Black Ops (Fiction); Cattle Mutilation (Fiction); Black Helicopters (Fiction); Earth Invasion (Fiction); Political Sci-Fi

Library of Congress Control Number: 2012936146

ISBN-13: 978-1-936442-08-9

In memory of

Robert and Doris Sullivan

Curmudgeons I could always count on

Acknowledgements

Thanks to the following freedom-loving citizens:

Team Leader: Ann E. Stewart, Managing Director,
The Fresh Ink Group, LLC

Production Team: Anik, Tom Stockbridge, Patsy LaFave

Content Team: D.R. Wagner, Lucas Cale, Beem Weeks,
Mark Allen North

Support Team: Kent D. Casey, Todd Tessin,
Marshall Shearer MD, Susan Stewart,
Jean Buchanan, Lendia Buchanan,
Vicky Riner, Dillard Greenwell

Member Team: All of *you* who subscribe to the newsletter at
www.FreshInkGroup.com, then discover our
books, shorts, and more. It keeps us going
when you buy our books and spread the good
word.

Chapter 1

You will be captured or killed.

Of course, not being discovered, not having to run, never having to fight—that was the ultimate goal. Eugene Weisman would rather die than be captured, rather be taken down cold than chained up and carted off to some secret cell where—

Russell Watterson signaled him, then started moving again, the younger teen now heading for the creek.

Eugene followed a parallel route, his own movements nearly silent, his method precise to prevent leaving a trail. Russell must have chosen the proximity of swift water to cover their noise, a way to move faster with less risk of detection. Eugene recognized the strategy, but so would the enemy stalking them, the big man who'd sworn to watch them die.

Russell hesitated, then began working his way along the rocky bluff. Eugene tried to calm himself, holding his breath to listen for sounds that don't belong, anything distinct from the restless winds and taunting bird-songs and that splash of creekwater rushing over rocks. But then he got careless and let the taut reins of self-discipline slip, and he tasted the metallic bile of fear as droplets of cold sweat lurched in fits and starts down his back. His leg twitched, then twitched again, his heartbeat now racing out of control, pounding in his ears, distracting him with the sound that *never* belongs.

These defensive drills used to be fun—until the big man announced that go-time had arrived. He'd loaded the weapons with live rounds, he warned, so now even the least mistake could prove lethal. Eugene didn't like to think about the possibility of dying just months after turning fifteen, but he'd pledged to protect the others, even to sacrifice his own life, if that's what it took.

Russell stiffened and pressed his slight body against the jutting bluff. He must have heard something.

Eugene crouched low and peered through razor grass. Smallish even for his age, at least his size made it easier to hide, though flushed into the open it would prove a most serious disadvantage. No way could he take down a grown man hand to hand—not one with skills, anyway—and he couldn't outrun one in a straight line, either. He would have to rely on his own cunning, and on the rigorous training he'd undergone since making a man's commitment at barely twelve. Yes, evasion offered his best odds, there being little chance of Eugene posing a credible threat to *this* adversary.

At least not yet.

You will be captured or killed.

Russell gazed upstream, then signaled Eugene, pointing at his ear, tracking the sound of someone moving their way. Both teens had learned the importance of trusting each other's senses during these missions. Inseparable as long as Eugene could remember, they fairly matched in size and strength, despite a year's difference in age, Russell now just weeks past fourteen. This young pair of woods-rats had been hunting together since they were big enough to carry guns, and they'd been running increasingly dangerous simulations for three years now and counting. They'd learned to think and act as one, preparation that all came down to this moment and three choices: try to escape, remain hidden until the enemy passed by, or make a pre-emptive strike and take him out.

Russell appeared confused, unsure. He must have lost track of their pursuer.

Everything sounded normal.

The water, Eugene thought. *Escape.*

Russell looked over the edge of the rocky bluff, a twenty-foot drop to the surface. Recent rains had swollen the creek, their fishing hole now likely deep enough for a plunge. Should they jump, then head straight for the opposite shore? Getting through that rusty tangle of barbed wire and into the overgrown border of cowpatch could provide fast cover, but it would trap them within firing range, pinning them too close to make their next move. Better to swim straight for the shallow rapids, then risk the unsure footing of that umber-orange chert gravel to run down the creekbed a ways, covering as much distance as possible, at least until trees and bluff-rock obscured their position.

Russell peered about, listened, and glanced toward the water again.

The pounding in Eugene's head filled him with ambivalence. Maybe they should run away from the creek, split up, try to disappear into the woods. Uncertainty heightened his panic, threatening to slow his reaction times.

Trust your instincts, or die with your doubts.

He gestured toward the creek. Russell nodded back.

It would be the water.

Eugene's heartbeat faded amid the rustling of impatient trees, the rumble of an amorous bullfrog, the buzz of boastful cicadas. Making a decision, focusing on the next move, these bolstered his confidence. Right choice or not, this pair of mere boys would live by it or die by it.

Or worse, be captured.

Russell signaled to wait, something's not right.

Eugene gripped his Colt Frontier single-action .22 and stroked the barrel. He'd filed off the sight to practice aiming by hand, earning praise for his proficiency. Not very powerful, but shaped just right for his hand, it would do the job, taking down even the most imposing attacker with a well-placed shot, especially given time to follow with another round, then another.

Or at least it would buy some precious seconds, enough to save Russell, his one true friend in a world the size of these Tennessee hollers, the bus route to school, and the town of Waverly a railroad stop between Highway 13 to the west and McEwen back east. Both boys had lived simple brush-stroke lives in a bigger picture they'd only just begun to imagine—and learned to fear.

Eugene needed to pee—bad, all of a sudden—but dared not take the risk. He wiped his forehead, grimy with dust and perspiration in the humid August heat. His scent would give him away as surely as the whisper of his breaths and the pounding that filled his chest and ears.

Then a twig snapped, and without warning the world fell quiet.

The birds stopped singing, the cicadas paused to listen, and the rush of creekwater faded to silence, a single Tennessee holler hesitating between the briefest ticks in time.

A lone bird next to Eugene cried out.

Then one near Russell echoed the betrayal.

And finally Eugene heard the enemy move, a steady, methodical whisper through the brush, coming this way from downstream.

Russell stiffened again, his instant look of terror hardening into resolve. He gestured one last time toward the creek and held up a . . .

Then nodded and leapt!

Eugene hit the water only seconds behind him. The icy cold seized his

breath, his neck stinging where a branch scraped deep. He kicked desperately, tangling in submerged brush, pushing forward, clutching his gun, his
feet finding gravel as both boys ran for their lives.

Down the rocky bar, across the shallows, up and over a mossy log,
around the bend, then quieter as they shimmied upward through a familiar
crack in the face of opposing rock bluff.

They dared pause a few seconds, scanning the scene, listening. No sign
of the enemy; they must have outrun him.

Russell squeezed himself to the top of the crevice, reaching down to
pull Eugene. They scrambled up and over the edge, then rolled and sprang
to their feet.

And there stood the big man, his 9mm Luger aimed at Russell's chest,
the M-16 leveled at Eugene's face, a beefy finger squeezing the trigger.

Eugene remembered needing to pee.

You will be captured or killed.

"Please—"

Click.

*   *   *

Colonel Chester McGovern, Special Forces CID (Central Intelligence
Division), boarded the Huey for a short chopper flight up the Cumberland
River just north of Erin, Tennessee.

Commanding Major General Ashe adjusted his headset and signaled
the all-clear. The Huey lifted off, escorted by a Cobra gunship from Ft.
Donelson. "We'll be touring the old Cumberland Sanitarium, vacant thirty-
some odd years now," Ashe told the colonel.

"You got numbers for me?" McGovern asked, adjusting his own headset to be heard over the rotor roar.

Ashe tapped his satchel, but didn't open it. It had to be frosting his
butt to report to some 90-day wonder-punk from Washington, especially
on a secret ENAC (Emergency National Action Control) project. Nobody
had offered to tell even a *general* with Ashe's level of clearance why CID
wanted these projections. "Logistics put together a couple plans," he said,
watching the colonel for any hint about what might be in the works. "In
each, there's a trade-off between how fast we can put it together and how
many detainees we'd be able to secure."

"What's the quickest for a basic quarantine?"

Ashe rubbed his jaw. "By deploying MP's around the perimeter, we could start filling it within thirty minutes. Six to eight hours, and we'd have chain-link with razor wire up, fully electrified."

"How many?"

"Depends on amenities and short-term emergency medical needs. The boys put down two-forty, but that means upwards of five hundred if you don't care how comfortable they are, and if it doesn't matter they'll have access to communicate with each other."

"What's the next level?"

"Well, if it's too secret to use civilian suppliers, figure thirty-two hours to bring in full service support, upgrade the water and sewage capacity, and tighten perimeter controls. That'd hold eight-hundred for you, short-term. They won't like the accommodations, but we'd be keeping 'em alive."

McGovern gestured toward the satchel. The general removed a file folder and handed it across. McGovern studied the charts. "I don't see max capacity here."

Ashe shrugged again. "Add a few days and wave one helluva magic wand to get what I need, I'd say it could be outfitted to hold twenty-six hundred, give or take a dozen—but if you're talking full medical quarantine, we'd have to seal the buildings and run tubes or tunnels. Prisoners would be stacked like firewood, so if they got something that'll spread through contact . . ." He watched the colonel, but still got no hints. "Anyway, we don't have to worry about cold weather for another two or three months, so until then we could shoot for holding three thousand."

McGovern closed the file and studied the general, an old-liner at least two decades ahead of this academy-stamped 33-year-old. McGovern figured such an aging desk warrior with a paunch and a pretty pension burning a hole in his pocket would jump all over one last chance for a taste of glory when this mysterious CID project turned out to be more than yet another damned fantasy about terrorists threatening a march into the heartland.

The general grinned. "Of course, we're talkin' August in the Tennessee woods, which means we'll need to drop in a tanker of repellent to keep prisoners from flying out on the backs of big-ass skeeters."

McGovern studied a cluster of houses passing below. "Or contaminating civilians through insect contact," he said without looking up, taunting his superior with the obvious reluctance to offer concrete information.

The general hesitated. "You got any guidelines for this drill?"

McGovern looked him in the eye. "No, sir, except to say it's looking like more than a drill."

Surely the general had fished enough weed-choked ponds in his time to know when a bite or two is the best you're gonna get.

Ashe looked distracted as the Huey dropped in to land on the sanitarium grounds. Yes, McGovern had been put in charge of a very real threat, and he knew that Commanding Major General Ashe better seize this opportunity to make himself look good.

McGovern hated needing to rely on these people, but at least the general and his military pups could be counted on to marshal their capabilities when the big dog finally barked.

And they would never dare question orders.

*   *   *

Misfire!

It's not over 'til you're dead.

Eugene fired.

Click.

Russell stood trembling, staring in disbelief at the Luger still trained on his chest. Eugene was shaking, too, nearly deaf to all but that damnable pounding in his ears, but he cocked and fired again, then again.

Click. Click. Click. Click.

He looked past the rifle barrel, into the eyes of the man who'd hunted him down.

Click.

The man nodded his head, then lowered the M-16 and tucked the Luger into his belt. He reached out and gently but firmly took the nickel-plated .32 from Russell's badly shaking hand, then cocked it and aimed at the boy's head.

Click.

Tears filled Russell's eyes, a tendril of snot kissing his lip even as he struggled to appear unfazed. "But Dad," he said, his voice breaking, "you said *live* rounds this time."

Mr. Watterson nodded, handed back his son's pistol, and studied both boys for a moment. The big man rubbed his square jaw, then stroked his crew-cut black hair. Dressed in heavy camouflage fatigues, he managed to look cool and relaxed, unaffected by the suffocating August heat, by the sheer audacity of hunting down his own son and the boy's best friend, then firing on them—point blank. "That's what I said," he answered, his deep voice carrying through the trees. The birds all paused to listen. "So did you do what you was supposed to?"

Russell glanced at Eugene, then looked off into the woods and began to fidget like a young'n who figures he's in trouble but hasn't yet decided just how much. Eugene had already calmed enough to slow and control his own breathing. Soaking wet, a puddle forming under him, he didn't feel cold anymore, either. He still needed to pee, but that could wait.

"You heard the click," Mr. Watterson prodded his son. "Coulda been a misfire, maybe a mistake. You had time to turn it around. What'd you do?" He leaned closer, eyeing the boy suspiciously. "What'd Eugene do?"

"He fired back," Russell said, sniffing the snot back into his nose. Wisps of steam started rising from his wet shirt.

"And what'd *you* do?"

"But . . ." Russell cast his gaze down at the rocks, at his water-logged sneakers, at an iridescent beetle trundling toward a patch of weeds. "But . . . but you're my dad," he protested, any conviction to this argument already leeched away before he could get the words out.

"Listen, boy," the big man said louder. "I done told you no matter *what*. Did I or did I not say I'd rather see you dead than captured?"

Russell tugged at his shirt, then picked at a burr clinging to his belt loop.

"Eugene!" he barked. "Is that what I said?"

"Yessir."

Watterson reached toward Russell, who flinched but stood his ground. The boy's father wrapped a beefy hand around his skinny arm, then leaned down, looking him right in the eye. "Somebody y'all think you know can be the *most* dangerous. How many times I done told ya that? We're *through* playing games now. If they find you out, first thing they'll do is try to get close, to be someone you get familiar with, someone you trust. They might come a time you can't trust even me, when you can't let even your own daddy catch you, life or death. That time might as well be now. You understand me?"

"Yessir," Russell said.

The big man studied the small teens for a another moment— sizing up the enemy, it felt like—then slung the rifle over his shoulder and turned to leave. "Fall in," he said. "Let's get somethin' to eat."

Eugene and Russell hurried to catch up, one on each side as they walked across the rocks and headed toward the trail through the woods.

"You done a good job, Eugene," Watterson said.

"Thank you, sir."

"You did a good job, too, son, except for when it come time to fire. We'll work on that. It's the most important part."

"Yessir."

Eugene puzzled over how he'd gotten around them, how he'd crossed the creek without being seen, even managing to remain dry. Maybe he'd been there all along, having spooked them somehow into coming right to him. And what was it that made all the animals and even the water get quiet all of a sudden?

Watterson stopped and looked from one boy to the other, then reached out with each hand and clasped their shoulders, squeezing hard and pulling them closer. "They was some mistakes made, but I'm still proud of you boys."

He squeezed again, then started walking on. It made their shoulders hurt, but it felt good, too.

It felt *real* good.

*   *   *

McGovern and his entourage toured a decrepit residence hall in the abandoned sanitarium, stepping around stained mattresses, broken furniture, and crumbled plaster scattered across the floor. They ignored crude depictions of genitalia and the epithetical stylings various intruders had spray-painted along the walls. Late-afternoon sunlight filtered through broken and tar-smeared windows, casting an eerie glow. Once antiseptic, it now reeked of filth, smelling dank and moldy.

This would make an ideal emergency prison.

General Ashe was touting his fort's and troops' capabilities, fine men ready and up for the task, when the RIO signaled an incoming communiqué. "Colonel, a call for *you*, sir!" he announced, proffering the instrument.

"It's time," the old man told the colonel over the phone. "Pick up a brief at Fort Belvoir on the way, your eyes only."

They all hustled to the Huey, then flew to Ft. Donelson where the colonel quickly thanked General Ashe and boarded an F-15 Eagle for the short flight to Virginia. He needed to pick up some classified files and a sealed case from his office before heading to Walter Reed Memorial Hospital for one *very* important meeting.

McGovern ran through contingencies in his mind, most little more than speculation. He did come to one conclusion:

The time had come to make his own move.

*   *   *

Eugene liked it when the Wattersons invited him to eat.

He liked their big old two-story house overlooking Little Richland Creek, too, the weather-worn wood with beveled beams and portico porch built back when boards were planed by hand, the slightest decoration an enormous work of pride. What a contrast to his aunt's shack just up the road, the run-down tar-papered planker with well-pump and outhouse he'd known all his life, the place he'd wound up after his mother died in child-birth and his drunken father ran off for good, never to be heard from again. As much as Aunt Willow's resentment over having to raise him stung, the Wattersons' unwavering acceptance and constant welcome left him feeling somehow safer, like maybe someplace did exist where he truly belonged, where he would always find people to count on, especially when you can't count on whomever you're with.

Mrs. Watterson put the baby in the crib and helped the little girls place big steaming bowls on the table, then sent Russell and Eugene off to wash up. She decided to follow and help Eugene dab stinging red iodine on that scraped neck, children being how that are about medicine that tastes bad or hurts.

The phone rang.

Suspecting Aunt Willow calling for him, Eugene listened from the doorway while Mr. Watterson went to the kitchen and answered it. Mrs. Watterson always had trouble dealing with Eugene's aunt, it being difficult to talk when she had to bite her tongue so much. Willow upset her easily, especially whenever that woman had been drinking or wanted to talk ill of her own nephew.

Mr. Watterson had to pause for a shrill tirade so loud that everybody could hear. Finally, he interrupted, "Yes, Miss Weisman, I understand, but we're having our supper now. I'm sure it'd be okay if he comes home after he finishes eating. Yes. Yes, ma'am. Yes I will. Have a good day, Miss—" He looked blankly at the phone after an audible click cut him off.

Mr. Watterson seldom said much at mealtime. Mrs. Watterson always fussed over the new baby and Russell's little sisters—the older one seven, another barely five—but this time she remained quiet, worry creasing her brow. Eugene and Russell kept watching each other while everybody ate fried ham and cornbread and soup-beans with fresh-sliced onion. Finally, Mr. Watterson broke the tension.

"Eugene!" Even his quiet talk seemed like a bellow. "I'm sorry, son, but your aunt seems to been drinkin' heavy this time, and she's mad as a hornet now. I'm afraid you're gonna have problems when you get home—something about not cleanin' up good enough to suit her."

Eugene looked as his lap. "Yessir." His cheeks burned. Everybody had stopped eating, watching him now. He hated that, not that he blamed them.

That's when Mr. Watterson did something unusual: he kept speaking. "Listen, son. The kinda talk I been hearing outta that, well, out of your Aunt Willow's mouth—I'm thinkin' maybe she's about to start causing you bigger problems than you might be ready for. I just want you to know—we just want you to know," he added, glancing toward Russell's mother, "that we got us plenty room here, and you're always welcome if you need a place to stay."

Mrs. Watterson hastened to add, "Just like when Jolene come and lived with us—to help with the new baby? Really, she came here mostly 'cause she was expecting a child of her own, and that didn't sit none too well with her daddy." Eugene had liked the black teenage girl from the old-town area out by the tracks, the part of town you could look down on from the High-way 13 bridge. Still, she'd mostly kept to herself during those four months at the Wattersons' before she moved north to live with relatives. "Some-times young'ns," continued Mrs. Watterson, "they can't make it work at home, so they need 'em a safe place. I know your aunt's been making noises about you bein' old enough to move on, but truth is, you're still just a boy—"

"Now, he's old enough," Mr. Watterson uncharacteristically inter-rupted, "to take care of hisself, and plenty smart enough, too." Then he turned to Eugene and added, "But even so, you need to stick with family whenever you can—"

"And we like to think of ourselves," she finished, "as your family."

"Thank you," Eugene said, still too embarrassed to look up, though it wasn't his anger at Willow he wanted to hide, but rather how much the Wattersons' words meant to him.

Russell interjected, "You can move in *my* room. Ain't like I got no brothers or nothin' to share with."

"Ha," Eugene said with a sidelong smirk. "You snore and wet the bed."

"I ain't never snored!" Russell protested, ignoring the other charge.

Mr. Watterson cut in again. "Whenever you think it's come to that, Eugene. It was a big responsibility you took on, and that includes all of us lookin' out for each other even more than just bein' family." He waved his fork to cut off further discussion.

"Yessir."

As they ate, an uncomfortable silence slithered here and there, uncowed by the clink of forks on plates, the chewing and burps and mumbled excuse-me's. Unspoken, everybody's thoughts couldn't help but dwell on Eugene having to deal with his drunken aunt when he got home. He wanted to tell them it was okay, that he'd made the commitment, and he knew how to stay focused. If problems from Aunt Willow had to be tolerated along the way, so be it. He could handle things. After all, he always had.

Too soon, it seemed, the time came for Eugene to walk up the gravel road. Mrs. Watterson fussed over him, examining the scrape on his neck, straightening his scraggle of blond-brown hair, brushing imaginary lint from his striped crew shirt and faded jeans. Like some little 4-H girl sending her favorite calf off to slaughter, she struggled to maintain her composure.

Mr. Watterson simply nodded at him and walked away, moving to his gun cabinet in the front room, then removing several weapons and his cleaning supplies. He turned for a moment and said, "You remember what we said, son."

"Yessir."

Russell walked with him until they neared the Weisman place. Eugene tried to hide his apprehension. He wondered which stage of drunkenness Willow had reached by now: *mad, mean,* or all the way to *maudlin.* She always started out angry at the world and everybody in it. Then she would lash out, seeking revenge, trying to hurt people. Finally, she would start feeling sorry for herself, ultimately breaking into sobs as the guilt set in, then trying to be affectionate with her nephew, no matter how she'd just treated him.

Maudlin, he could deal with easiest. He hoped she'd already got there. If not . . .

His voice low, Russell said, "Dad wants to do live rounds tomorrow, this time for real."

"I'll be there," Eugene whispered, too close to home now, a sense of

Willow hanging in the air, best not disturb her.

"See ya then," Russell whispered back, his words meant to reassure, Eugene knew. And like a wisp of fog, the Watterson boy faded into the night.

Eugene looked toward the lights at Willow's place, then squared his shoulders and walked ahead, passing through the broken gate and on up to the house. He hid his Colt Frontier in the "tater" box on the porch before going inside, knowing that by now Russell had cut through the woods to circle around the back and watch through that door that Willow always kept propped open.

It didn't matter that his friend was out there seeing and hearing it all as Willow launched into a screaming fit, slurring her words, then grabbing him by the hair and yanking his head back and forth as she whipped him mercilessly with a worn leather strap. He knew Russell would understand that no matter how long he held out, he would eventually cry because he simply couldn't help it.

And because that was the only way to get her to stop.

No, it felt good knowing Russell wouldn't leave until it was over, that his best friend would be clutching his own .32 and biting his lip, never really intending to intervene but ready if given no other choice.

Then as Willow supervised Eugene performing whatever chore had put a burr in her sock, doing again whatever he'd already done but could never do right, Russell would run toward home, reduced to his own tears by the time he arrived. He would slam the door and rush upstairs and disappear into his roan. Mrs. Watterson would be rocking the baby, her own eyes glistening but never saying a word. Mr. Watterson would pause from cleaning his guns, then heft one for a moment, sight down the barrel, and get that far-off look in his eyes before shaking his head and resuming his task.

Eugene tried to stay out of his aunt's sight for the rest of the evening. Forbidden to go out, he sat on the floor behind his cot and waited for her to drink herself beyond maudlin and into benign stupor. He worried over a bleeder on his left arm that hurt especially bad, but the rest of his welts and bruises appeared to be the kind that would fade in the coming days.

When it looked like she'd settled down for the evening, Eugene eased up onto his cot and dozed lightly.

He had a vague sense of Willow up and moving around, then recognized the sizzle of pan grease like she'd decided to cook breakfast this time of night. He heard the door open and close, sounds on the porch, but by the time he realized she was rooting in the tater box she came bursting into the house, screeching and waving the gun in his face, accusing him of planning to shoot her in her own bed. "Yer plannin' to *kill* me, you no good li'l sumbitch!"

Up on his feet now, he started to back away, pleading, "Come on, Aunt Willow, put it down. You know I'd never do nothing to you." He realized backing away wouldn't help, that maybe he should try to ease closer and wrest it from her.

She swayed uneasily on her feet, glancing back and forth between him and the weapon clutched in her twitching hand. "Y'all is planning to *shoot* me, you and that nasty boy from down the road!"

He inched closer, noting that at least she hadn't cocked the loaded pistol.

"The gun's for *huntin'*, Aunt Willow. And for protecting you and me from prowlers. You know that."

"Y'all is *evil*," she snarled. "Has been from the beginnin'. Devils is what you is!" She cocked the gun.

Eugene moved closer.

Her hand tightened on the grip. She raised it and aimed.

He lunged.

Pop!

*   *   *

Flying from Ft. Donelson to Virginia, Colonel McGovern tried to admire the spectacular Appalachian scenery—the obstinate mountains and patient valleys, splay-fingered lakes and rapids-tugged rivers, threads of blacktop highway lacing small towns through ragged-fringed forest—but the need to formulate a career-propelling strategy kept distracting.

Except that he simply didn't have sufficient information to come up with one.

When the brass suddenly pays attention, something is definitely happening, and that's when opportunities present—for the smart ones who recognize and exploit them. Even when the attention leads nowhere but to situation status quo, it's a man's status that can change, if only just a bit.

A quick landing at Ft. Belvoir, then an aide appeared. "We have lift ready to take you to Walter Reed—as soon as you're ready, sir." Yes, people would adjust to the whims of McGovern's schedule now. The shift had begun.

McGovern entered the administration building, then used key codes, retinal scans, thumb-print reads, and voice-activation to work his way underground to a hallway of numbered and lettered suites, most of them various headquarters for CID programs and special projects. He entered one marked *IVG*, the ID for *Program Invigil*, where he surprised his aide, a youngish man kicked back in a chair, his feet on the reception desk as he read about the travails of some heroic bassmaster in a fishing periodical.

The aide stumbled his way to attention and saluted. "CID communications, sir," he explained. "I'm to arrange for telecon at your earliest convenience." Again, at the *colonel's* convenience. McGovern could get used to this.

He accepted a sealed courier pack and glanced toward the door to the inner sanctum. Using his thumb print to open the lock, he scanned the contents, aware of the aide's longing glances toward the largemouth bass on his magazine cover, that look of a teenage boy gawking at some staple-naveled beauty.

"Ten minutes," McGovern announced, startling him from his reverie. He headed to the inner suite, closed the door behind him, found nothing new on the message readout, then took the papers to his private restroom. He hated to waste the unavoidable time spent perching on a toilet, preferring at least to read files in order to make efficient use of those precious seconds.

Taking care of business left him four minutes, during which he keyed access to the wall of file cabinets and removed nearly a dozen folders per the list in his satchel. He'd already read a couple, but the rest exceeded his clearance, a line he never considered crossing, even had the file system not been set up to record every access with full details of who, what, when, how long, and especially what hadn't yet been returned.

The communications lieutenant led him to a sweeper portal opening into the conference room, a series of devices checking him for contraband. No amount of clearance would bypass this requirement, not when somebody else could have planted a listener or tracker in, say, the colonel's clothing without his knowledge.

Alone in the room, he watched the big screen link him audio-visually with secure data transfer to the Pentagon where numerous under-officers stalled him for another ten minutes until the Army's four-star appeared—one of the Joint Chiefs.

"Colonel," the superior acknowledged with a nod. "Your security clearance is hereby increased one level, putting all of *IVG* at your disposal, including all national security designations and any non-military ops. In many ways, your unfettered access to information now exceeds the president's."

McGovern nodded, hastily adding a "Yes, sir."

Looking grim for the briefest moment, Four-star also pointed out, "That means you're eligible for purge, too."

"I understand, sir," McGovern acknowledged, feeling rather powerful in being recognized as somebody who would soon know so much he might have to be killed were it in the best interests of the country—or of its latest administration. "A necessary precaution."

Four-star waved him off. "You are hereby assigned to the position of Commanding Officer, *Program Invigil.* You will be briefed by your antecedent, but effective immediately you will report directly to me."

"I will do my utmost to fulfill your expectations of me."

"Listen, son," the old man said, leaning close to the camera, "This is likely a dead-wash, but it might just turn out to be the most important operation we've ever run. Either way, keep it tight and you'll be in line for promotion in a few years, possibly one of the youngest generals ever. Keep in mind that several of the Chiefs don't believe much in *IVG*, except for its one major supporter. Me, I'm down the middle. I don't expect we need to do much more than be ready, just in case. That'll be your job, and you have all federal departments at your disposal, in particular the FBI and all the upper levels of state. Remember, when you walk the dog, our butt's hanging out."

"I have much to learn quickly, sir. Will the general's health allow him to provide support?"

"He's had a stroke," Four-star answered. "Doctor says rehab would help some, but we really don't expect him to pull through. You need to learn what you can from him right away."

"Yes, sir," McGovern said, understanding that he was being told the general would not survive, regardless of his medical prospects. Better to go quietly than to linger and risk becoming a problem who can't think clearly about how his mouth might compromise a confidential operation.

"By the way, Colonel, he's the one recommended you."

"I will endeavor to live up to his confidence in me." Cripe. So practiced at acting deferential, he found it difficult to speak to superiors as one of the boys instead of someone still outside the club.

"Tell him I said Godspeed, and assure him Army'll look out for his loved ones." The general nodded and stood, the meeting over, then glanced off-screen and said, "Wait." After a moment, he added, "I've been told you'll need to bring another file that's not already on your list."

"That is?"

"It's marked *Waverly, Tennessee.*"

*   *   *

Eugene wrested the gun from Aunt Willow, who backed away and stood there blinking stupidly at the bullet hole in the wall. Without a word, she turned and headed for the kitchen area, falling into a chair and cradling the bottle of bootleg whiskey she'd befriended earlier in the day.

After a few minutes, her head started bobbing, the first time leading to another, then finally pulling her forward into a slump that resulted in snores and intermittent whistling.

Eugene slipped out the back and hid his pistol in the woods, then returned and draped a shawl over her shoulders. He stood there and tried to summon even a small measure of hatred toward her, but the best he could muster was a creeping, shuddering awareness of his fear. Sure, he felt sorry for her, this life of hers no way to live, but she never made any effort to change it, or to help him better his own circumstances. Instead, she resented and despised him, always making sure he knew it.

Exhaustion crept over him, so he moved to his cot and stretched out, fully dressed, a sheet pulled up more against persistent skeeters than any hint of chill in the hot, humid air. He buried his face in the ratty remnant of pillow and tried to work up feeling sorry for himself, but failed miserably. He did manage to summon a few brief surges of anger, but the more he tried to hide them, the faster they would buck and throw him back into his own fear. He just wanted to feel safe, but Willow had slowly taken even that from him, and the more Mr. Watterson prepared him to protect himself from any kind of outside danger, the more vulnerable he felt in his own home. He began trembling, feeling cold now despite the heat, wrapping himself tighter in the sheet until he finally drifted off to sleep.

Waking after a while, not sure how long he'd drowsed, he heard somebody moving around the kitchen. It had to be Willow, the only one he shared the place with—not like the Wattersons, a big family, everybody looking out for each other with enough goodwill to share some extra with the pest of an orphan boy down the road. Being Russell's big brother would have been so cool, a lifetime of somebody covering your back, full entitlement to Mr. Watterson's time and, well, attention.

And having a mom, especially one as good as Mrs. Watterson.

He rolled over and buried his face again, trying to make Willow's place disappear, pretending this ramshackle shack in Willow's corner of the woods had never existed.

The movements stopped, a cicada chorus through the screens rousing into an encore performance.

The floorboard squeaked right behind him. Mr. Watterson had drilled him and Russell on situations like this.

Ready your defense; plan your escape.

His pistol still in the woods, he had no other weapon handy, not even a knife. The layout offered only two ways out: past his attacker to the front door, or through the screened window on the other side of his cot.

Identify the enemy.

Surely it had to be Aunt Willow, except that she'd passed out drunk. Could it be the real enemy, the one Mr. Watterson had been training them against these past three years? He couldn't look, still feigning sleep to catch the stalker unprepared.

Once you move, commit.

Another squeak—

And he bolted, hitting the screen with both hands and diving through. He turned for a glimpse as he dropped to the ground.

There in the dim light, surprise in her face, stood Willow with a butcher knife poised in the air. She'd come to eliminate her demon nephew once and for all. She'd belittled and shamed him, beaten and whipped him, and now she wanted him gone so much she'd tried twice in one night to kill him.

You got your wish, Aunt Willow. Ain't never coming back.

He retrieved the pistol and his last box of ammo from nearby brush, filled his pockets with loose bullets, then found a small scrap of rag and wrapped the Colt before shoving it down the front of his briefs, his shirt hanging loosely to hide the lump. He headed along a path in the woods that would lead him to the gravel road about a quarter-mile down the creek toward Wattersons'. Before the first turn, he paused and looked back at the shack, but couldn't detect anything moving in the murky, moonless dark, Willow probably asleep again, his aunt dreaming of new ways to hurt the only person in this godforsaken world who even came close to, well, loving her.

Nausea tickled his belly, then spread in waves until he had to kneel in the tall grass, trying not to vomit. Sobered up in the morning, would Willow even remember what happened? Would she know why he'd fled, this time for good? He pictured her standing there with the knife in her hand, but the image turned to those times she'd used it for slicing the homemade birthday cakes she'd baked him in the early years; or cleaning their catch clear out to Kentucky Lake back when she had that beat-up old Chevy and would take him bream fishing as the willowflies swarmed; the two of them hoeing and planting their meager garden, then canning the bounty and stacking carefully labeled Mason jars on the shelf; even crawling into that foam-shedding chair with her to read and tell Bible stories on quiet nights, every now and then. He hated the whiskey and what it did to her, just as he wanted to rage against his father for turning out no good, and his mother for dying on him.

He pushed on until he found himself in front of the Watterson place, the familiar house now just a hulking shape, a series of shadows against the dark woods, sanctuary guarded by the murmurs of night sounding the all-clear.

Mr. Watterson slept in there, the stern man who cared more than he showed, but did show it with a simple shoulder squeeze, or that look in his eyes when you'd done right; and Mrs. Watterson, always fussing and cooking and cleaning and full of so many hugs she just had to keep giving them away, no way she could ignore the scrape on a boy's neck even when nothing could be done to make it better; and Russell, as close to a brother as any kid could want, all tough and cool, yet still wetting the bed and embarrassed that anybody might find out except for his own family, Eugene included; and the girls, always crawling into his lap and wanting to hear stories; and the baby . . . that nice house, a safe place, even that mission he didn't really understand, though it didn't matter because they'd accepted it together and everybody trusted Eugene as much as if he'd always been one of them.

He wanted to call out, to wake them all, to see them come out and carry him inside, a swarm of Wattersons welcoming him and checking that scrape on his neck and seeing if maybe he might want something to eat.

But he couldn't find his voice, and his feet wouldn't take him any closer, and he knew he could never wake this family, disturb their rest, rouse the baby, prove Willow didn't want him and that he had no place else to go.

He lowered his head, rubbed his eyes, and moved slowly down the road, eventually picking up the pace, his steps deliberate.

After nearly a mile, just shy of Highway 13, he came across the little patch of fenced-in cemetery where his mother lay buried. He climbed over the rusty wrought iron and moved through the tall grass to her grave, its small stone crusted with fresh moss and grime. He stirred the grass to roust any snakes, then pulled the ammo from his drawers, keeping it and his pistol tucked under him as he lay down next to the marker. He rested for a minute, then rubbed his face and sat up to study the mossy stone.

"Mama," he whispered like he had so many times before. "Mama, Willow still ain't heard none from Daddy, and it's got to where I just can't live there no more." Ashamed now, he explained, "It ain't 'cause I've not been good, but mostly 'cause she's drinkin' so heavy again, which is just about all the time now. She gets to where she's thinkin' all kinda things ain't true and—" He lowered his head. "And I'm afraid she's gonna hurt me, or that I might have to hurt her from defending myself."

He paused, then lay back in the grass, the humid air crawling up his bare arms—and a spider, too, but not big enough to matter as long as he didn't make it want to bite.

"The Wattersons said I could live there with 'em, if I need to."

Of course, she didn't answer him. She never did, but he always felt better after talking to her, like instead of keeping it all to himself he could tell her without worrying what anybody else would do with it.

"See," he said, lowering his voice, "I never told you this, but when I turned twelve Russell said I could join their cause, and I wanted to, so Mr. Watterson held his hand against my chest and said something was inside me now. It didn't hurt none, and I don't know if he was just havin' fun with me, but he said him and Mrs. Watterson and all the kids got it, too, and he's been real serious about protecting it ever since, so it sure seems like it must be true. He calls it a mission sometimes, lookin' out for each other and what's inside us, teachin' us how to protect ourselves 'cause there's bad ones'll come capture or kill us if they ever find out.

Each of you got it in you to bring salvation.

Whispering now, he explained, "I never said nothin' because he said anybody who knows is in danger. Now I think something's about to happen 'cause he's been hurryin' so much to make sure we're ready. I wanna stay there with 'em, but not if it's just 'cause of the mission. And if it's true what he says, then it's better we not be all together where they can get us."

She did want him to move on because it might be safer that way, he knew, but only the cicadas answered his words.

Don't you worry 'bout me, Russell. I'll come back someday.

Peering around to make sure nobody could see, he let himself cry just a little, then closed his eyes and wiped his face.

And for the third time in this most important night, he drifted off to sleep, thinking so many thoughts about an uncertain future they seemed to be canceling each other out, leaving only a teenaged boy with no place to go, surrounded by the indifferent call of cicadas in the hot, humid darkness.

I will protect whatever's inside me, no matter what.

*   *   *

As Colonel McGovern waited to see the seriously ill general, he pondered what he'd been reading about *IVG* the past few hours, now that he finally had access to all those files that used to taunt him from their sealed cabinets. What struck him most was just how long the program had operated. He thought it fairly new when he received the assignment some five years earlier, but the file covered more than sixty years, except that the name *Invigil* seemed to date just short of three decades.

An aide showed up and escorted McGovern to a private room in what appeared to be a security area: sealed doors, barred windows, sallyports at every turn. The general lay in a typical hospital bed, leashed to various machines on small carts.

A practitioner of sorts, probably a physician, hovered over the old man, then turned to McGovern and, without introducing himself, said, "You have fifteen minutes, and I mean *only* fifteen minutes." He gave him a PPD, presumably in case he needed to call for help, then left through a glass door that shifted to opaque upon sealing with an audible whir and click.

"Congratulations, Chet," the ailing general told McGovern, his speech slurred. For such a serious old coot, he finally looked relaxed for the first time since the colonel had known him—almost relieved, if that could be possible. "I'm glad they went with my—recommendation." He had to speak from one side of his mouth, and catching his breath seemed to be a problem. One eye had been taped shut, likely unable to blink, very much at risk of drying out. The other eye studied the young protégé.

"Oh, uh, thank you, sir. I'm sorry about your—"

"Quiet now," the general said, trying to wave his arm but failing miserably. "Too much—to cover. Sit here." He tilted his head slightly, apparently indicating a spot on the bed right next to him.

The room offered no other seating, so McGovern pushed aside several tubes and wires and sat, antsy about the uncharacteristic proximity, then flinching when the general grabbed his arm with the good hand and held tightly. "Of the five operatives—my five good men—you knew the least. But your—your role—was most important. Now you know—it really was—infiltration by aliens . . ."

"An invasion, sir? From someplace beyond this planet?"

"Still don't know yet—just proof they exist—maybe came here—maybe here before us. Expect evidence soon—but don't use it right away. Program's been allowed—to wither on the vine. They think we got them all—decades ago—when it first . . . I know better, though. I know. You prove they're still at large—and parlay that into more—into more power—then do what you must—but don't be quick to reveal—their true nature." Panting from the exertion of holding his head up, he lay back, still clutching the colonel's arm.

"Will the files explain all this, sir?"

"Some of it, but not all—and you need to figure how—to use it."

"To use the information?"

"With the proof you already have—civilians would panic. The enemy is like—some damn kiddie movie-invaders living inside humans—growing inside their hosts. Parasites—but more than that. Most was destroyed—what's left is handled by bio-med—by Doc Aggeous. He thinks if they live—long enough, they might can learn—to control their hosts."

"We have some of these, um, aliens in custody?"

The general nodded, his head lolling sideways. He winced from the pain. "Everything you ever heard—the conspiracy buffs—they don't know a lick of real truth. We've never had—any kind of leak." He chuckled at the irony.

"You're saying we have living aliens—in custody?"

"Second—second generation." He smiled lopsidedly, drool running down his chin. "They can spread."

"Have they?"

"Joint Chiefs say no—but I think they have—just no proof yet—but getting close. *IVG* is set to watch—see if they spread—or more comes."

The colonel finally understood his previous role. "I was preparing to round up and detain large numbers of people in case we obtained proof—"

"Suspicion, even—" the general interrupted. "Can't risk—can't take a chance—"

"How do we detect them—I mean, in human, um, hosts?"

"Aggeous is working--on that. Bigger problem—how do we test people—without explaining why—or causing panic. Hell, can't even take DNA samples—from eighty-some percent—without civilian court orders. We was setting up—mass drug testing—tax rebates so employers would—a way around Bill of Rights rulings—but then backlash against—police powers—politicians crying *terrorism* too many times—" He gasped, then caught his breath and shuddered before resuming. "Health threat is best excuse—mass vaccination for something else—then taking samples same time—plus legislation for—for emergency sweeps to penetrate—private health care—"

The colonel could only watch as the general wheezed and winced from the pain. Most of their fifteen minutes had already passed; they would be interrupted soon.

The general squeezed his arm with a ferocious grip. "FEMA!" he blurted, meaning Federal Emergency Management Administration, the agency where appropriations of very large sums often wound up channeled through untraceable accounts controlled by special programs. "Juggle your resources—and play on fear—create threats and be ready to move—however you detect—can't waste—waste . . ." He trailed off, mumbling, "Don't let 'em—don't—"

The general's grip tightened to the point of pain. The colonel tried to pull away, but the old man clawed frantically and grabbed his wrist, drawing blood with a fingernail scrape.

"I should call the doctor," the colonel said.

"No! He's the one—killing me—for CID. Gotta tell you—gotta . . ." His mouth worked furiously. "Detection—containment—eradication." He gasped and looked at the younger man, fear now showing in his exposed eye.

"What? What else should I know?"

"You'll see—you'll—"

Several machines sounded alarms as the grip on McGovern's wrist loosened and fell away. The door turned transparent, then opened with a click and a whir, the same man entering, no rush, almost casual. He looked at the machines, but didn't register surprise. "I hope you had enough time," he said, noticing where the colonel rubbed his wrist. "Do you need medical attention?"

McGovern shook his head and headed quickly for the door.

No, he hadn't had enough time. He needed to learn a lot more. His new job had turned out to be either a complete joke or a mission more important than he ever suspected. He needed to get back to Ft. Belvoir and go through the files, call in the other operatives, recommend a replacement for his old position, then figure out how to save his country from a conqueror he couldn't comprehend, a threat that would earn him a roll of the eyes and a look of pity if he tried to convince any sane man on the street that this threat merited serious concern.

The dying general never got to finish the briefing, but he'd managed to say a lot.

Detection, containment, eradication.

*　　*　　*

They moved down the gravel road just after 2:00 a.m., the humid air dense and heavy, their pitch-black disguises drifting through the moonless night. Sporting gas-protector face masks with infrared projector-scanners and thermal-imaging, both worked along the high weeds marking the gravel road, cradling dark cases that could pass for bowling-ball bags.

They paused to listen and study the scene, then moved a ways and paused again, each time picking out places to duck and hide, routes of escape. They spied an opossum mama crossing the road, young'ns clinging to her fur; then a big chicken snake in the grass; and plenty of field mice, their eyes eerie green flashes in the viewfinders before they disappeared into the brush. The interlopers listened for distinctive solos amid a cacophony of insect noise and the syncopation of riffling Little Richland Creek. They wrinkled their noses at the swirling pockets of odor, manure and rain-soggy fields and rotting vegetation. Pause, then move, then pause again.

They detected no perimeter defenses during their approach to the old Watterson house. Moving close, they listened outside several of the latch-hooked window screens, the last line of defense against determined insects and spiders. They moved around back and eased up onto the rear stoop, then sliced a corner of the screen, unlatched the door, and slipped inside.

Removing foot-long, finger-thin wands from thigh holsters, they split up, one positioning himself at the back of the first floor, just outside the big bedroom, while the other covered him from a vantage point adjacent to the front-room gun cabinet. Just as Jolene had described, Mr. and Mrs. Watterson slept in a big oak-headboarded bed, the baby in a nearby crib. The big man snored quietly.

One careful step, another, then another, and the intruder stopped beside the bed. He extended the wand toward Mr. Watterson's face and squeezed off a short *pffft* of gas. Mrs. Watterson opened her eyes and looked reflexively toward the crib just before a short *pffft* knocked her out.

Two steps to the crib, *pffft*, two steps to the doorway, and the other intruder quietly opened the gun cabinet to remove the box of cleaning supplies. He opened it, lifted out a tray, and found the object concealed underneath. Shaped like a slightly oversized deck of cards, it appeared solid, its surface a dull black. The intruder nodded, then slipped it into the compartment in his bag.

Both removed small aluminum pony tanks from their bags, the scuba regulators replaced by facial breathers that looked like oxygen masks, then positioned themselves either side of the big bed. Gripping the devices carefully, they placed their fingers on activator buttons, then waited another ninety or so seconds for signs of waking. They wanted their victims' excess sleep-gas to breathe off, but not enough to give them a chance to wake and create signs of struggle.

Just as Mr. Watterson's eyelids started to flutter, the intruders placed the breathers over both faces and pressed the buttons. A potent brew of carbon monoxide, by-product gases, and sooty ash invaded unwary lungs. Two breaths, three, and the gasping started, then coughing and a bit of squirming—but not too much. Five gasps, and she stopped breathing. He managed six before falling still, the rhythm of their quiet snores disappearing from the sounds of dark summer night.

The baby proved quick and easy. She only gasped twice before dying.

They targeted Russell next, moving quickly to his room. Alerted by furtive sounds, he was reaching under the bed for his weapon as a wand hit him with a triple blast of the sleep-gas, making him drop the pistol and slump quickly to sleep. One of the intruders carefully returned the .32 to its box and slid it back under the bed while the other moved to the girls' room and dispatched two efficient *pffft*s followed by life-choking blasts from his tank.

It took nearly five minutes for the boy's extra-large dose to begin wearing off, his wiry briefs-clad frame twitching once, then again. Russell looked so much like a pint-sized, slightly freckled version of his father that there could be no doubt Watterson really had become a family man, his wife and children just everyday country folks living everyday lives, enjoying the simple pleasures, appreciating each other, never suspecting that this hot August night would be their last. Russell gasped five times, filling his young lungs with poison, then gave one final shudder. The ammonia odor of urine filled the air as a dark stain spread across his shorts and onto the fitted sheet.

The intruders removed small devices from their bags, palm-sized apparatuses with long silver needle-rods projecting outward. They plugged them with interchangeable cylinders, making them look like ominously dangerous asthma inhalers, then moved from victim to victim collecting samples, a new cylinder for each body. They opened one dead mouth after another, inserting a rod up through the back of the throat and nasal passages directly into the cranium, then pressing a button that caused a faint *pssst* sound as it filled the chamber.

The collection complete, they replaced the devices in their bags and quickly arranged the scene: both little girls arrayed on the floor, bedsheets twisted around the younger one's leg as if she'd gotten tangled while crawling frantically toward the doorway. Several blasts from a tank left the undersides of their gowns sooty.

Russell's body wound up just past the top of the stairs, fallen in front of his sisters' room, felled too soon by the smoke and heat, unable to breathe, unable to save the little girls.

Mr. Watterson, a heavy sleeper according to Jolene, apparently never made it out of the bed. Mom had snatched the baby from its crib and crawled toward the foot of the stairs, probably calling out to alert the other children, desperately trying to save her family. The poor woman suffocated too quickly, the baby dying in her protective arms.

Several more blasts painted in the minutiae that rendered this job a work of art.

The intruders packed their tanks and searched the first floor for a suitable electrical outlet. They located one in the parlor next to a stack of newspapers where peeling wallpaper revealed a slatted, unplastered wall. An old lamp was plugged into the socket.

This one would be easy.

One man reconnoitered while the other removed a small electrical device from his bag. He plugged it in and flipped a switch, triggering a barely audible hum that increased in pitch until a tiny green light glowed. The other man returned and watched the first press a button that sent a surge of high-amp voltage into the house wiring. He yanked the device from the socket just in time to avoid a shower of sparks.

Flames quickly spread to the newspapers and raced up the peeling wallpaper, setting the entire wall afire.

The men watched for a moment, then exited through the back door and hurried up the road, pausing only long enough to pull black bicycles from the brush. Their bags clipped to the rear, they quickly rode the couple of miles to Highway 13, one activating a tiny transmitter strapped to his vest.

A beat-up red pickup wheezed along and pulled over just long enough for them to slip their bikes under a tarp in back, then climb into the bed and pull the tarp over themselves.

The pickup headed north, away from Waverly, and disappeared into the night.

*   *   *

Barely awake, Eugene sat very still and watched as two men clad in black slipped quietly into a pickup, its lights off, and drove away in darkness.

He smelled smoke, wisps creeping through the woods and into the old cemetery patch. Racing to the Watterson home, he found impenetrable curtains of flame. He rushed from door to window to door, but the heat drove him back, no way inside, thick smoke steadily widening the perimeter.

"Russell!" he cried. "Mr. Watterson!"

Randy Caruthers and one of his younger farm hands roared up on an ATV, the boy shouting into a cellphone. Before they could see him, Eugene faded into the woods, trembling and sick as the fire hissed and squealed delight over its feast. A siren cut down the open roadway, the first fire truck roaring up to the scene.

Eugene moved closer to the creek and climbed a tree to watch, flames slowly yielding to the play of water, another truck pulling up, an intake hose now run to the swimming hole.

Stench and smoke swirled around the tree, even long after the flames had died. More vehicles arrived, a reporter, police, investigators, gawkers. Time started moving faster and faster, too quick to grab a hold.

Dawn broke over the horizon, and they brought out the first body bag. Then another, and several more. Nobody had survived.

A reporter managed to pull a deputy off to the side, not far from the tree. Eugene froze and held his breath, afraid he would fall if he tried to hang on another second, yet too afraid to climb down.

An awful tragedy, the voices agreed. Might have been faulty wiring, but arson hadn't been ruled out. Somebody had been down to talk to the Weisman boy, but he'd run away last night after trying to shoot Willow Weisman during an argument. There'd be a warrant for the boy if he didn't turn up soon. Too early to speculate on the record, but maybe there'd be a connection between Weisman suddenly attacking his aunt and somebody setting this deadly fire.

The conversation moved away from the tree when a couple of hearses pulled in for the body bags, so Eugene quickly climbed down and began sneaking his way upstream. He never slowed until he'd passed Willow's place and started working his way up a rock bluff to the east, a route that temporarily exposed him—if anybody had been around to watch.

He slipped into a crack between boulders and tried willing himself to stop trembling, finally pressing his face against the mossy rock in a futile attempt to stem his tears.

Not only had he lost his best friend and the only "family" who ever loved him, but he'd watched the answers to all his questions die, too.

Mr. Watterson had been telling the truth.

Each of you of got it in you to be salvation.

They'd all accepted a greater responsibility than he ever imagined, one he didn't fully understand, against an enemy he couldn't comprehend.

You will be captured or killed.

Now Eugene was the only one left.

Chapter 2

"Watterson was infected, all right," Dr. Calem Aggeous confirmed, "but get this: so was every member of his family." He dropped himself into the chair opposite Colonel McGovern's desk. Fat, oily, unkempt, he didn't bother to posture the least bit of deference to the newly installed commanding officer of *IVG*.

McGovern bristled at the obvious lack of respect, but reminded himself that this bio-medical research specialist worked under contract, not commission, and still enjoyed the same very high level of security clearance as the colonel. He studied the man for a moment, then allowed himself to relax and sit back. "You're sure?" he asked, suspecting even as he said the words that Aggeous would have explained any doubts.

The doc looked across the tops of his glasses and cocked his eyebrows, refusing to dignify the question. "General got screwed out of his trophy," he observed, referring to the previous commander. "Spent his career hunting aliens; then by the time it got to where we started understanding them, he dies before he can finish the job." He started picking at his fingernails. "Or maybe it was just luck, all those years with a cushy job, playing bigshot with no real crises to manage, and he's outta here in time to hand the shit-work to someone else."

"He played an important role in our national security."

Aggeous snorted. "Truth is, he hollered *The sky is falling* so many times that not many took him seriously anymore. Turns out the sky *is* falling, and he deserved more respect."

"You were with him from the beginning?"

"No, but close. He brought me in after securing the first landing site."

"I'm finding lots of gaps in the files," McGovern said, loath to admit ignorance but needing information.

"He didn't trust anybody but me and a couple other members of the team. He figured if something happened to him, better one of us bring the new guy up to speed than leave paperwork around that might fall into the wrong hands."

McGovern leaned forward, eager to learn everything. He would correctly document it all this time, creating a proper, classified military record.

Having to trust the accuracy of whoever does the talking could prove sloppy and dangerous. "I expect to be fully briefed."

Aggeous snorted again. "Listen, Chet. He said he recommended promoting you over the others because this threat is breaking wide open now and you're so tight-assed Army you'd be able to impress the brass to pull together whatever resources we need, but he also warned me to tell you only what you need to know; otherwise you'd piss away your time trying to write it all up, creating possible security risks and keeping you at a desk when we need you on the front line."

"You're planning to withhold information?" McGovern practically gasped. So much for trusting this one.

"No," Aggeous said, allowing a hint of smirk. "But it just might be I got a bad memory—unless and until things seem, you know, relevant. Course, now it's lookin' like maybe we got a full-fledged invasion going, and you need to be ready."

"Off the record," McGovern said, projecting all the authority he could muster, "tell me what else I don't have time to glean from the files, plus what's missing. *Now.*"

Unfazed, Aggeous leaned out and looked toward the cabinets of secured documents, then shook his head, this mountain-climb difficult to sum up with a short hike. "I'll give you the bottom line: so-called UFO sightings are everyday business, but the old man never believed in any but those first two, just a couple months between 'em more'n twenty-five years ago, just a mile or so apart south of Camden, Tennessee."

McGovern pulled a folder from his desk, then removed several photographs showing a sort of bloated boomerang shape, its finish a dull or scuffed obsidian, about four times longer than a Jeep parked behind it. Tossing the photos on his desk, he asked, "This is the first site?"

Aggeous nodded, then resumed picking at his nails. "Higgins took 'em before I arrived. He was still second lieutenant back then, sent with a couple MP's to check out a radar flash. By the time they started setting up a quarantine perimeter, the ship sort of melted, then evaporated right before their eyes. Higgins said it left four what-he-called *stick critters* there on the ground, but within minutes they melted and disappeared, too. One of the MP's up and dropped dead right there on the spot. Then I arrived to assess the danger of contagion just as the second MP dropped dead. Did a thorough autopsy on both and found no explanation. Been studying them bodies ever since, and still ain't found nothing."

"You and Colonel Higgins experienced no symptoms?"

"None—but we sure walked on egg shells for weeks, and I had to talk us out of having to quarantine ourselves. So the upshot of landing number one: a handful of photos, no ship recovered, no aliens captured, two dead soldiers, and a story that sounded like UFO conspiracy at a time when half the population believed in alien abductions."

"The percentage hasn't dropped much over the years."

Aggeous snorted. "It has among the military brass, but back then it was enough to get Higgins his star, budget, staff, and a secret program. The only reason IVG is still around today is because he's been working one supporter on the Joint Chiefs."

Not so much interested in the politics, McGovern asked, "Were any black boxes found at the first landing site?"

Aggeous shook his head, then struggled to his feet and performed a little dance to increase the circulation in his legs. "Two come from that farmer who found the second ship. What he described sounded like what Higgins saw, except that when the ship dissolved only two aliens disappeared, leaving two behind that looked hurt but still alive. He loaded them in his truck, then fetched those boxes out of the grass and headed up to the house. Wasn't 'til next day we enhanced the photos and spotted a third box over by some trees. He says he never saw it, and we couldn't find it."

"You had his house searched?"

"We had every inch of his whole world searched."

"The other two are still in Huntsville," McGovern said, referring to the arsenal complex in Alabama. Growing weary of having to ask questions, he found himself beginning to dislike everything about the civilian researcher.

"Yeah, one still intact, the other having been scanned and blasted and electrified and dissected and even sent up for some zero-gravity testing on one of the shuttle missions, all to no avail. Everything we can learn says it's just a slice of pressure-stressed carbon, not quite as hard as a diamond, with no moving parts. The old man was obsessed with finding the one we recovered from Watterson, hoping all three together might cause something to happen, but he eventually gave up on the idea, figuring we needed to find it if only to see if anybody else was infected."

"The general told me you have a specimen."

"You can see it when you're ready for the full bio-med briefing in Huntsville."

"We're talking about one or both of those the farmer rescued."

Aggeous picked at his thumbnail. "Well sort of, but not exactly. See, they didn't live more'n a few minutes at the house, then disappeared like the others, but the farmer eventually admitted they left behind a sample."

"What are you talking about? What's it look like?"

"Well, it's one you can't see—not yet, anyway." The doctor studied the colonel across the tops of his glasses.

"Why not?" McGovern demanded, exasperated by this prolonged game of twenty questions.

"It's living *inside* that old farmer."

*   *   *

Food.

Next time, food—and some toilet paper sure would help, too.

Three days Eugene had been working his way eastward. He'd pilfered from gardens and raided a feed-corn bin, but unripe and raw got old fast, and the hunger kept coming. At least the creeks provided water, and the weather had kept dry and warm enough to sleep at night. Without toilet paper, though, washing in the ice-cold creeks had proved a serious, bum-chilling nuisance.

Still, some hot country ham and a big bowl of soup beans with a slice of fresh onion just like Mrs. Watterson used to make . . .

Time to keep moving. Surely by now he'd passed McEwen, more than a day spent following Trace Creek toward Duck River, the location a blur in his mind when he tried to picture that map Mr. Watterson . . .

He avoided moving along roadways, except where he could count on fast cover if a vehicle approached, but working through fields and woods, especially at night, left him disoriented, unsure of his bearings, and sometimes even, well, scared. He would pause and will himself to calm, then study the sky, the terrain, anything offering a clue. Sometimes it all seemed too much to handle, though, and he'd wake from a nap trembling, east blending into west, morning no different from dusk, up every bit as dangerous as down . . .

Make your plan, prepare contingencies, execute.

Ashamed of himself, Eugene knew he should be formulating a better plan. Mr. Watterson had tried to prepare him for this, yet already the lone survivor had proven less than up to his responsibilities. He simply didn't know what to do.

Or where to go.

Or whom to trust.

Trust nobody, he decided. Used to be, the Wattersons could be trusted, even counted on, the only people who ever proved how much they trusted in Eugene. Was it that kind of trust that got them killed?

Eugene would be next, this he could count on, unless he quickly learned how better to rely on himself. How does one do that without knowing the enemy? Is it the government? Invaders? Rivals of Mr. Watterson? *Anybody who might find out Eugene's sworn life-or-death secret?*

Mr. Watterson had long shown suspicion of police and any other kind of government official. "They's just dog-shit people, too," Eugene had heard him say once, "but they's the most *dangerous* kind of dog shit. You step in it—even by accident—and it'll climb right up your leg to bite you in the ass."

Eugene's own butt felt kind of sweaty right then, but he cringed at the thought of getting bit, especially by some dog-shit government people—the kind he couldn't trust.

He spotted a sign out along the blacktop county road giving five-mile notice of Dickson straight ahead. He worked his way behind a farmhouse set amid hundreds of acres of fields and woods and red-earth cattle ponds and chert creekbeds. Scared and feeling dishonest, he let hunger get the best of him, so he raided a smokehouse to find venison jerky drying on strings, plus some dried pork wrapped in paper and stacked on a box. He took what he could reasonably carry, stuffing it into a brown paper sack, then headed for the woods and sat by a creek for water while eating. Stiff and salty, the cured meat nevertheless tasted wonderful. His belly full, he lay back in the tall grass along the bank and closed his eyes, wiping grimy perspiration from his face several times as his mind faded in and out.

He tried to listen to the animals, especially the birds, separating their sounds from the riffling creek. He jumped when a lizard darted across his leg, which meant he had to get up and do a thorough snake rustling before he could relax again and close his eyes.

Several birds sang nearby. Something scurried, maybe another lizard, maybe a field mouse. Breezes rustled the leaves, insects buzzing to fill the lulls. More birds joined in, so many birds . . .

A twig snapped!

Another!

Somebody or something big must be coming closer—maybe more than one of them. They moved slowly and methodically, now trying to keep quiet, not the way people would act when out for a casual stroll. It must be hunters hunting—but for what? Squirrel or rabbit or something out of season like deer?

Or Eugene Weisman, the fugitive teen . . .

He reached for his waistband and cradled the Colt Frontier tucked there under his shirt. He listened, trying to pinpoint the location of these potential adversaries, the direction they moved, how many had come to get him . . . but his heart started pounding until the noise drowned out all but the loudest sounds.

You will be captured or killed.

Why did he always panic when he needed to stay calm? Mr. Watterson had warned it's okay to feel scared—*later,* after the danger passes.

If you survive . . .

And haven't been captured.

Find your zone.

He'd been *there* more than a few times: in his zone, perfectly calm, tuned in, hypersensitive, poised for action. He found it exhilarating, like becoming omniscient, taking control, coiling to strike, everything coming in slow motion, reaction times the briefest lightning flashes against a back-drop of infinite time.

He could hear movement again, coming from the direction of that farm he'd raided, closer now to the creek-bank. He eased over onto his side, staying low in the tall grass, and peered up the slope, considering his options. He could roll backwards and land in the creek, but the water flowed mere inches deep here. He'd have to spring up and run fast with unsure footing to follow that route.

He turned the barrel of his .22 toward the movement and poised his thumb over the hammer, reluctant to cock it lest the click be heard.

Aiming and watching. Another step. His heartbeat faded into the breeze, all senses trained.

Nothing else existed; he'd found his zone, and it felt good.

A face appeared, peeking around a tree, now gazing up and down the creek, looking for something . . .

A girl! A teenage girl with long brown hair hid behind that tree, but he couldn't guess her age, not without seeing her more clearly.

He started to relax, hearing the birds again, and the riffle of the creek, but then he saw it: she carried a rifle, a Winchester model "94" 30-30 Carbine with lever action and 13-round side slide. He'd targeted with one just like it, Mr. Watterson's present to Russell for turning twelve. It didn't look right, a *girl* carrying it, but the way she held it did seem sort of natural, even balanced in a way, like it had become a part of her.

Stepping into the open, she craned to see up the distant bluff, and she looked pretty, more beautiful than any of the girls at school—at the school he used to attend. The breeze danced loose strands of her hair, a slash of dappled sunlight making it shimmer. He wanted a closer look, but Mr. Watterson had warned him the worst enemy can appear harmless, even like a friend.

He pressed his thumb against the hammer, watching, waiting.

She moved quickly into some scrub and disappeared. After a minute, she eased left, then back to the right again, gradually working toward the creek without looking his direction.

Sixty yards, fifty, forty, she kept coming, vanishing sometimes, then appearing again. No way could she see him, a single unmoving eye peering from between tufts of grass.

Thirty yards, twenty, fifteen, then even closer.

She froze, then looked straight at him, but didn't register his presence. Should he reveal himself? Confront her, order her to drop her weapon, let her see he's armed?

Or just open fire?

Ten yards, no time left. His heart started pounding again, panic rising. He must make a move, now—

"Set the gun *down*," a voice said quietly, a man directly behind him.

Eugene tried to turn and see, but a rifle barrel hovered inches from his ear.

"*Now!* Set it *down*."

"Who—?"

Click.

*   *   *

The escorted Huey set down inside Redstone Arsenal at Huntsville, Alabama, an area known for its aerospace industry, the Air & Space Museum, and the ever-popular Space Camp for burgeoning astronauts of all ages. Dr. Aggeous conducted his research underground, his lab complex burrowed into the side of one of the rolling hills overlooking the missile-

and rocket-vibration towers in the sprawling complex.

Dozens of checkpoints and security verifications later, the only two men in *Program IVG* with sufficient security clearance to access the entire site found themselves in a hallway with more than two-dozen doors evenly spaced. A man in uniform wordlessly opened one for them, then closed and sealed it after they stepped inside.

The doc paused to wheeze, then dropped himself into one of the low, overstuffed chairs arrayed in the carpeted room, gesturing wordlessly toward the interior glass wall. McGovern stepped up to the transparent barrier and studied the enclosed space on the other side: light blue walls; straight-backed chair and simple desk stacked with paper, pens, and several paperback books; shelf above it lined with more books and dozens of DVD movies, all recent titles; TV/DVD player on a wheeled stand; low food table with a tray of partially eaten cafeteria-style rations; stainless steel prison-style toilet/sink in the corner; plain old-fashioned oval rug in every shade of brown on the tile floor; and military-issue bunk with an apparently napping old man propped against several pillows.

"Richard Kilbourn," Aggeous offered. "Late of Camden, Tennessee; now what you might call a long-term resident of northeast Alabama."

Mr. Kilbourn wore a light-green jumpsuit—worn and frayed around the edges—white t-shirt visible at the neck, and white socks shoved into beige shower sandals. He could still pass for an old farmer except for looking unnaturally pale, a man who'd not seen the sun in more than two decades.

The geezer opened his eyes long enough to size up the visitors, obviously recognizing the doc, only mildly interested in the new man sporting Army dress-greens. He closed his eyes again.

McGovern considered what it must be like confined to such a place. It certainly looked more comfortable than a military brig, cleaner and safer than a county jail or state prison, but the lonesomeness just in the few minutes he'd stood there watching the old man already felt palpable. The cell showed no links to the outside world, no antenna or cable jacks, no radio, no internet access, not even a phone. Standard voice-activated speaker-mikes had been mounted next to the bed and over the desk. A similar pair showed on this side, one next to the glass, one over by Aggeous, except that these included talk and listen buttons. Mr. Kilbourn need only speak to be heard, but his captors could control when and if he could hear them talking back. Looking up, McGovern confirmed the presence of one recessed blind that could be lowered to cover the glass, another that appeared only semi-transparent from this side, probably a one-way mirror.

His back still to the doc, McGovern asked, "The alien is *inside* this man?"

"That's how it works." Aggeous proceeded to wheeze, then fart twice for emphasis.

"Where?"

"All through him, near as I can tell. I've opened him a few times, took two of his fingers—" McGovern noticed the man's left hand had lost its last two digits. "Those tests proved it, but the *best* proof has been the animals."

McGovern turned and faced the doctor.

"Take a load off," Aggeous said, gesturing toward the other chairs. "You're making me tired just watching you."

McGovern sat stiffly, tugging his uniform into position. "What animals?"

"We been releasing critters into his cell for years, mostly lab rats and gerbils. Then we catch 'em and test them, including dissection. Couple years ago, we started finding aliens in the ones that were in there long enough for the old coot to have physical contact, like a pair of rabbits he picked up and petted."

"The alien is *procreating?*"

"I'd say the one in Watterson was, too. That's why the boss resumed trying to run down everybody who ever so such as *knew* this old man. The missing black box had been the goal, but once we figured out they spread, he became obsessed with making sure no more was out there, plus coming up with a way to identify infection—though I never liked that word, *contamination* being more accurate, maybe even *impregnation.*"

Mr. Kilbourn opened his eyes and shifted up onto his elbows to stare blankly at the visitors, then appeared to grow bored before dropping back into the pillows and closing his eyes again. He stroked absently at his face several times, then seemed to be trying to shoo invisible gnats with his gnarled, liver-spotted hand before letting it fall leadenly. His whole body twitched until he began to snore lightly.

"Doped up," Aggeous explained. "We keep serving him goodies in his food. Keeps him docile, lowers his resistance. Haven't bothered him lately, though, so if you want to question him, we'll need a day to pump him into blind submission. You won't learn anything we don't already know, or that the alien don't want him to say."

"The file indicates that he is the one who gave up Watterson," the colonel observed, pausing to await an explanation.

"Had to ask the right question. He kept insisting he'd not seen or talked to anyone between finding the landing site and us showing up. Then one day the interrogator asked him who he talked to *before* finding the site. It turned out to be Watterson, somebody he'd known from being in the same good-ole-boy militia some years before. Said it was Watterson who called and told him where to find the site, and to keep his mouth shut about it. So Kilbourn had been telling the truth, but it sounds like *Watterson* was the first one to get there, if only briefly."

"What do we know about Watterson since then?"

"Ain't my area," Aggeous wheezed. "That's between you and them files the old man left you. Me, I got a live geezer, pieces of two dead MP's, samples of dead alien, several live specimens, and all the research data. It's on *you* to sort it out and save the world." He farted again, waving his hand in the air to dispel noxious fumes.

McGovern found himself growing annoyed with the doctor. More than showing a lack of respect for high-ranking military officers, it seemed like he refused to take the alien threat seriously. Complacency after decades of believing it had been contained might be understandable, but this past week had proven otherwise. Could it be confidence in the new commander—or believing that these invaders proved no real threat? Or was it something else entirely? McGovern tended not to trust *anybody*, and Aggeous was losing credibility fast. "This man," he said, "has been in *that room* more than twenty-five years?"

"Except when I sealed him out for surgeries and, well, lab work."

"Besides testing with animals, what else goes in and out?"

"Food and consumables in, waste bio-sealed and straight to the incinerator. Cleansers in for him to do his own housekeeping: new linen and clothes whenever he puts the old ones in the waste packet—though he settled into that jump-suit some years back and doesn't seem to care it's not clean anymore. Air is pumped through the exhaust feeding an incinerator."

"Visitors?"

"This man doesn't even *exist* anymore." Aggeous grinned. "His wife told everybody who'd listen that he'd been taken by aliens, and she believed it right up 'til cancer got her about ten years ago. They was a few thought the U.S. Government kidnapped him." He smirked. "Can you imagine?"

"National security—"

"Yeah, yeah," Aggeous said, struggling to his feet. "Burn the house down to protect it. C'mon, you've seen the geezer. Now the labwork."

On their way out, McGovern turned for another look at Mr. Kilbourn. The old man watched him intently, but quickly closed his eyes.

They moved to another underground section and found the lab in a sealed chamber marked *IVG*. McGovern almost retched when Aggeous slid out a large drawer to reveal the liquid-sealed remains of two thoroughly dissected men, probably the MP's.

"Nothing exciting here," the doc said, hacking for a moment. "No change after all these years. Dead end." He closed the drawer, then opened several cabinets to show rows of jars and cases and slide racks and various odd containers. He lifted a glass container down and set it carefully on the table, touching a button to brighten the room lights. "There's your alien—or one of its offspring, I should say."

McGovern hesitated, then leaned closer, but at first it appeared to be nothing more than clear liquid. He looked even closer, and finally saw it slowly coming into focus. Shaped like a starburst or flower, the simple pattern of gossamer threads appeared finer than wisps of spiderweb. McGovern studied it while Aggeous set up a slide under a microscope.

"Protein nucleotides linked by silica—like a chain," Aggeous explained, gesturing toward the scope. As McGovern peered at the slide, the doc explained, "except they create patterns that look kinda like handwriting. No two samples are the same, though—like snowflakes, I guess. The crypto-boys can't make anything of it. Every time they upgrade their computers, I run it through again, but we still can't find a pattern."

"This is what infiltrates the, um, the *host* body?"

"Follows the blood lines. That one took me weeks to get out of a gerbil after it'd been allowed to grow nearly a month." Gesturing toward the samples in the cabinet, he continued, "I found several strands in one of Kilbourn's fingers at the four-month mark. I waited ten years to take the second finger and found it as complex as the skin's system of capillaries, no way to get it out intact. He passes strands to the animals through his hands, but I figure by now touching any part of his body would do it."

The simple beauty of that thread under the scope fascinated McGovern, the way it refracted light in shifting hues without letting him focus on any single link for very long. Eventually he straightened up and started eyeing the various containers in the cabinet.

Aggeous continued, "Dissection has to take place *in* the preservative. Contact with air, and these babies melt until they evaporate. Or if the host dies, they evaporate right through the skin. In all cases, I can't capture anything but a shift in the light spectrum, no trace of any gases or elements except what would normally be there."

"Then how do you—?"

"Live dissection, partial submerge, oxygen pump, fast expose, then slow extraction. Lucky I did Kilbourn's first finger that way or I'd have missed the strands."

McGovern disliked the very idea of live dissection, especially with a human subject . . .

"We can fool 'em, though. If we extract a piece directly into fluid, then maintain bio-homeostasis, they'll last a while. That's how we saved the Watterson-family samples 'til we got 'em here."

"Are the strands alive when you do that?" McGovern reached for a jar and examined it, noticing how the doc flinched, there being a bull in the researcher's china shop.

"Naw. Once they're cut off, they appear to be dead, though how they procreate seems to be their little secret. Rodent testing over the years suggests it takes a couple decades to reach maturity for that—for the ability to spread viable pieces on their own, I mean. It's been tricky enough just preserving them to have a look-see."

McGovern worked his way through the vials, holding them up to focus on strands, sometimes singles, sometimes splits. "You have live specimens other than what's in Kilbourn?"

"Yes," he said, putting the jars back into the cabinet. "Only because I finally figured out why the rodents were dying after a few months: it takes *two* hosts."

"Two? How can it live in two animals at the same time?"

"Not the same time. The hosts are sequential. See, if I put another animal in before the ones he handled died, the first would initiate physical contact, then die immediately. Within hours I could find highly developed versions in the second animal. Now I got a cat and two dogs acting as second hosts. I could take you over to see them, but they don't look like anything special. Soon I'll kill one and cut off part of another for a closer look." He locked the cabinet, put the scope away, and said, "Of course, you're in charge now, so say the word and consider it done."

McGovern watched him check the MP's again, then seal the drawer. "In short, then, it takes twenty-some years to begin procreating, spreading pieces into hosts that—for lack of a better word—gestate them a few months, then pass them to a permanent host, all with no obvious effects on the original carrier."

"But there is an effect," he said, pulling a logbook from a drawer, noting the date, making a note, then returning it to its place. "It infiltrates the brain, too. Kilbourn's aware of his: I could tell after just two or three years. He used to act like a caged animal 'til one day he calmed down and started watching me, sometimes even smirking like he knew something I didn't. Used to be he was barely literate, but now he can go through a paperback in thirty minutes. I mean, just look at him and you can see something is going on in his head. Still, he won't tell us a thing, and no kind of interrogation can make him talk."

"So why didn't the alien inside him have to spend six weeks in an interim host?"

"My best guess is that it wasn't a new generation, but rather the mature one in the stick critter. I figure it shed all those little filaments and transferred itself, which is why the alien it left died right away."

"But it took decades to achieve reproductivity."

"Had to grow its network again, enough to have tiny passable filaments in the hands. Let's get out of here," he added. "I need to take a leak."

"So what we *don't* know," McGovern summed up, "is whether or not Watterson contaminated anybody else."

Aggeous dimmed the lights and headed for the door. "In fact, the old man believed Watterson was too smart not to spread it to at least one person outside his family—people he could trust with something like that. But hey, my job is to understand them. You're the one who has to worry about containing them."

McGovern glanced at the *IVG* plaque inside the door and wondered if the old sanitarium would be big enough to isolate however many more might be out there. "At least all that's left are second generation," he said as the doc reached for the door, "which buys us at least a decade or more."

Aggeous stopped and turned. He studied the colonel a moment, then snorted and spread his hands. "But what if somebody else got infected same time as Watterson more than twenty-five years ago?"

"But why would—?"

"Remember, by the time Kilbourn arrived at the site, they was already *two* stick critters dead."

*   *   *

Smack!

"Answer me, you li'l prick!" Marshall had worked himself into a rage. He grabbed Eugene by the hair, yanking his head back to glare at his face.

The young teen strained against the duct tape that twined him to the wooden chair.

"Answer me! Who are you? What are you doing here?!"

Smack!

Eugene's lip bled onto his chin.

"Who sent you?"

Smack!

Eugene coughed, bloody spit dribbling from his mouth.

"Stop it! Stop! He's just a kid!" Licia cried. The pretty teenage girl with long brown hair stood in the corner, wringing her hands, tears in her eyes. She'd been biting her lip until it, too, started to bleed.

Eugene looked up at the sound of her voice. She'd been the only sorta-friendly looking face among the group of three there in the kitchen with him. He'd heard only first names, but the man hitting him looked like he must be her brother. She looked about sixteen, he a good ten years older, with similar hair, only cut short and parted on the side. He occasionally fingered what must be dogtags jingling under his shirt.

Marshall and his buddy, Jake, had wrestled Eugene to the ground and wrapped him with duct tape. Marshall had shouldered the slightly built captive and bodily carried him back to the farmhouse.

Jake stood off to the side, covering him with a pistol Eugene recognized from photos Mr. Watterson had used to teach the boys, an ominous-looking M1911A-1 Colt .45 with 6-round box mag. Jake looked to be a few years older than Marshall, a handsome fellow with short, sandy hair and bushy brown mustache. His arm never wavered from his ready-to-fire stance, his eye studying Eugene carefully. No emotion, nothing. Just watching, impassive, ready to blow away the little guy there to spy—or who'd maybe come just to find something to eat.

Smack!

Still no reaction from Jake. No sympathy there.

"Marshall!" Licia cried. "Stop it! You hear me? Stop it now! This ain't workin'," she pleaded. "You're *hurtin'* him."

"Hurt ain't what he needs to be worryin' about." He glared appraisingly at Eugene, announcing, "He should be thinkin' about being tied to a cinder block and sinkin' to the bottom of Kentucky Lake—*after* we beat his ass and break all his bones." His glare turned to a grimace—a grin maybe?

Eugene had no trouble believing him. *You will be captured or killed.* Killed would be better, of this he was sure.

"He's just a runaway—afraid he's gonna get in trouble, is all," Licia pleaded. "Ain't that right?" she asked Eugene, desperation in her voice. "Tell him. You're just passin' through on your way somewhere else!"

Eugene had no plan, saw no imminent escape. Watterson had warned him the enemy was everywhere—when you least expect them—and could look like anyone. He squeezed his eyes closed. If they'd just kill him and get it over with . . .

Persevere, no matter what, and wait for your chance.

Talking would be a risk—either buy some time or stop this all at once. At least if he said something . . . *anything,* maybe it would quell Marshall's rage. His captor was growing dangerously close to losing control.

Buy some time, Eugene. Say something.

Identify the weak link, look for your ally, plant seeds of dissension, grow a friend.

Watterson had spent too much time teaching him to avoid capture, not enough on survival or escape.

He squeezed his eyes closed and felt them brim with tears. He didn't resist crying anymore, seeing a possible advantage. Licia was sympathetic. It was all he had.

Besides, the tears were anything but fake.

Raising his face, opening his eyes again to look directly at the girl, he let his voice quiver as he nodded and confirmed, "You're right. I run away."

Marshall snorted and started to pace the room. Jake finally let emotion creep into his expression, softening with—what? Relief?

Tears spilled down Licia's cheeks, too. "Don't worry; we don't care none about that. What's your name?" she asked, moving closer.

Marshall reached for her arm to hold her back, but she pushed his hand away.

She knelt before the young teen taped to the chair and reassured, "It's okay, we won't give you up. You can tell me your name."

Eugene looked just briefly into her eyes, then lowered his head and looked at his lap again, tugging gently as if to test his restraints. He glanced up toward still-pacing Marshall, then Jake, then looked down again, shaking his head just perceptibly side-to-side.

"Put the pistol away, Jake," she ordered, trying to sound friendly, relaxed. "He's not goin' nowhere. He ain't here to hurt nobody." She forced a smile. "I'm Licia," she offered. "What do you want me to call *you*?"

Eugene glanced toward Jake again.

Jake shoved the Colt into his waistband and leaned against the wall, trying to look nonchalant.

"I'm a fugitive," Eugene whispered.

"Not here, you're not," she said soothingly. What a sweet voice, so soft, quiet but confident. She seemed pleased that he was starting to trust her.

"Eugene."

"Weisman?" Jake asked, surprised some, but maybe not so much.

Marshall stopped pacing and stared at the captive, so tense he was ready to explode. Eugene looked at the men, back at Licia. She nodded slightly; it would be okay to admit who he was.

"Yes, sir." Anticipating a reaction from Marshall, he cringed, helpless to defend himself.

Licia's older brother just . . . *smiled!*

"He can tell us what happened!" Jake exclaimed.

Marshall furrowed his brow in thought, looking concerned again. Turning to Jake, he wondered, "How do we know *he* wasn't the one give 'em up?"

Licia started to argue, but Eugene interrupted, "Because it was my *best friend* who died—and the man training me and the best family of people you ever known—" His voice was getting louder, his fear and pent-up feelings fighting their way to the surface. These people had captured and hurt him. Somebody else had killed his friends. Now even *Eugene* was a suspect.

He grew mad—*furious.* The more he thought about it, the scene he'd imagined for three days—his best friend Russell, coughing and choking, crawling desperately through the house trying to save his family, overcome by fumes and smoke and flames, snuffed out of existence the very year he'd vowed determination to kiss his first girl . . .

His nose was dripping, his vision blurred by tears. He felt ashamed, but too mad to care.

"Get 'em off!" Licia demanded, grabbing shears from the kitchen drawer, snipping determinedly at the layers of duct tape.

As Marshall reached for her again, this time the other man stopped him. He shook his head no. "Don't try to run, son," Jake warned. "We're not here to hurt you," he added quietly.

Eugene believed him. He trusted Licia. He was afraid of Marshall, but he understood all three of them were on the same side. Maybe Eugene would be, too . . .

His hands free, face down out of embarrassment, he felt his busted lip, his stinging face, the scabbed-over scrape on his neck that had started bleeding again after a vicious deflected slap. He used the front of his soiled t-shirt to wipe his face, then Licia gave him a hand towel.

"Get him some water!" she barked.

"Don't you be tellin' me—" he started to protest, but she cut him off, clearly mad as a hornet.

"You done *enough* already. Get him something to drink."

"Aw, Licia, I didn't hurt him none. He's a tough one—" Marshall was protesting while filling a glass at the sink.

"And get him something to eat. No *wonder* he's stealin' food—he's been runnin' for his life from the ones killed Wattersons." She pulled a chair over in front of him and sat down, gently reaching out to tilt his face up. She gingerly touched the split lip, the scrape-scab. "Gene, honey, my name's Licia Emery. That's Jake Coleman, and the cow-pie there—" She glared at Marshall. "He's my brother, Marshall Emery. You all right?"

"*Eu*gene," he corrected.

Licia grinned. She looked *very* pretty when she smiled.

Marshall proffered the glass and set about making ham sandwiches with fixin's from the fridge.

"Why don't we sit at the table, *Eugene*. You need to use the bathroom or something?"

He did, but it could wait. He moved to a chair at the table and drank half his water, wiping his face again with the towel. Suddenly, it became very important to regain his composure, to appear in control, to look like a man in front of Licia. He wanted to come off confident, something that would be a lot easier if not for those waves of trembling still sweeping over him, his heart pounding just a little too loud for comfort. She didn't seem to notice.

"I'm gonna call Marty Varne," Marshall announced, placing a platter with seven or eight sandwiches on the table.

"Don't get him fired up," Licia warned, noticing Eugene's interest in the food but hesitation to take any. She grabbed one and took a big bite, pleased with the flavor. "You *can* make a sandwich," she jabbed at her brother. "Least you can do *some*thing right." She gestured toward the sandwiches and looked satisfied when he took one and started to eat enthusiastically.

Marshall returned after using a radio in the other room to call Marty. "He'll be by in a few hours—soon as he can get away without attracting attention. He said he's coming to the meeting in the morning. Even Durbett will be there."

Over the next few hours, Licia ministered to Eugene's injuries, washed his clothes while he took a long, hot bath—embarrassing the daylights out of him when she slipped into the bathroom to leave him her terry-cloth robe—kept him busy talking about school and TV and stories and who-all he knows, scrupulously avoiding thinking about the Wattersons, all while Jake and Marshall made dozens of radio contacts in the other room. She apologized for her brother but asserted that his intentions are always good. She explained how her father had died the year before, leaving the farm to the two of them—Marshall becoming legal guardian for the fifteen-year-old now-turned-sixteen. "Marshall and Jake and them—and sometimes me, too—they think Daddy was *killed*. They think *ever'*body in the militia's a target."

Eugene mostly remained quiet. He felt somewhat at ease, but still couldn't help but wonder what his future held—where he'd go, what he would do. *Hitting the road* had proved much more grueling than he'd expected.

"You can stay here for a while," she offered, seeming to read his mind. "If you want."

Sheriff's Deputy Marty Varne showed up and scrutinized the interloper. They all sat in the front parlor, the officer pulling off his heavy uniform shoes and loosening his tie. He took off his mirrored shades and looked closer. A tall, brawny man with scraggly brown hair and beefy face, he kept sucking his teeth and rubbing his nose. "Yeah, it's Eugene Weisman," he decided. "I run down his ninth-grade school pitcher. What do you know about the Wattersons gettin' killed, boy?"

Eugene wasn't sure what to say.

"Some thought you started that fire, you know."

"No sir, it wasn't me."

"Somebody *did* start it, then—weren't no accident?"

"I didn't see 'em do it, but I saw two men dressed in black leavin' there—"

"Where was *you?*"

"In the cemetery."

"Where they's buryin' the Wattersons tomorrow," Deputy Varne clarified.

Of *course*, that's where they'd be buried. He'd not thought about a funeral—the finality of his best friend sealed in a box and lowered into the ground. Sometimes it still felt like Russell would be outside waiting in the woods for him . . .

"Keep him here tonight—" the deputy announced, grunting to his feet and putting his shades back on. He looked over his glasses toward Marshall, adding, "Secure. We need to hear the whole story tomorrow, but let Durbett question him. I can't be involved. We'll decide what to do then." The deputy started to leave, but remembered something he'd forgotten to say.

Eugene Weisman would spend the night on a makeshift pallet, locked in the bathroom, fussed over by Licia before she'd leave him there for the night. He had mixed feelings, but the ones he least expected were profound grief. Even with the facts laid before him, he was surprised at himself, confused that he could hate somebody and—dare he think—like her, too. A thousand memories, mostly bad, but more good than he'd realized washed over him as he drifted into fitful sleep. Deep inside, somewhere in the back of his mind, he'd thought his choices, his actions, all were something he could somehow undo. But no more.

"Sorry to tell you this, son," the deputy had said. "But your Aunt Willow was found in the house. She'd got drunk and fell and hit her head. Woman who'd come to collect some money Willow owed her found her there. She was already dead."

Everything in his life had changed, his past gone, his future uncertain. Trying to sleep, to find confidence all would turn out okay, Eugene tried to look ahead. Nothing made sense. It all scared him—a lot.

And there was no going back.

*   *   *

Colonel McGovern had never been inside the Pentagon before. He could have felt excited about it if he allowed himself to. Summoned by his contact on the Joint Chiefs, it was time to see if he was passing muster, to find out how he was handling the job. There would be questions to answer, but he had a few to ask, too—if he had the balls to ask them.

The job was too important to be a pussy about handling his superior. If military life had taught him anything, it was that as long as you play your hand smart, your balls can't be too big.

Or hang too low.

Four-star finally came into the conference room where McGovern was waiting patiently. Neither had any files, no paperwork of any kind. No way to take notes.

"You got a plan together yet?"

"No, sir."

"Good. You don't know enough—haven't had enough time. Can't afford for you to run off every direction half-cocked."

McGovern nodded. Best to let the ranker talk first.

"Was that good-ole-boy in Tennessee infected?"

"He and his entire family."

Four-star rubbed the corners of his mouth. He wasn't surprised. "Could be others, too, then."

McGovern nodded, then added, "Yes, sir." He needed to slip a few sirs in early.

"Got anybody else in mind?"

"Haven't worked on it. Too many blind alleys on the good-ole-boy—Watterson's his name."

"Like what?"

"Traced him far as CIA, then hit stone wall. He worked for *us*, didn't he?"

"He free-lanced for some time, yes. Retired, took the money, supported a family, laid low. Turned down offers to reactivate—not even short and simple assignments."

"He was involved in something personal, wasn't he?"

"Don't know. He had favored status—done us a lot of good. We didn't care how he played out his personals. Would be surprised if somebody like that *didn't* have his fingers in at least something. That's the kind of people they are."

"The kind of people we turn them into," McGovern added.

Four-star just spread his hands. "Takes all kinds."

"Am I going to learn more on him?"

"That's not *your* turf."

"I thought my turf was everywhere."

"Forward, not back. What about Watterson's black box?"

"It's safe now—with the others."

"Oughta be the last of them."

"Oughta be."

Four-star seemed satisfied with that. "You met with the team yet?"

"Only Aggeous. All five will be at Belvoir tomorrow. I wanted to talk to you first."

"It's tough starting out when everybody knows more than you."

"I can work with it."

"Keep it straight and simple. Most of them don't fully know what the others are doing. International's monitoring for *all* kinds of alien reports, captured technology or rumors thereof, zanies and crackpots and crop circles and news-hounds and such. It'll bore you to tears, but let him run on for hours if necessary. Don't know what you're looking for, but hopefully you'll recognize it when you see it. Throw him at least one bone, something he can run down for you, even if it's a fake—it keeps him sharp and committed."

"So far nothing outside the U.S.?"

"Far as we know. So far nothing outside of those two in Tennessee. How'd you get as far as CIA on Watterson—was it your domestic-info/coordination guy—who's it, Dunkin?"

"Yes." No *sir* this time. It went by unnoticed. "He checked in yesterday to see what-all I wanted for the meeting. I had him do a fast one. Look, what's *this* guy worth to me?"

Four-star smiled. "You'll come to depend on him a lot. His people *found* Watterson in the first place. They can tap anybody or anything—especially FBI for *your* purposes—and do it faster than you can get a phone number by calling the operator."

"Except CIA?"

"Well, you have to respect turf. CIA, NSA, FBI, SS, even FEMA—everybody's got secret projects going, and when you butt up against something they need to keep secure, that might be as far as you get. I'm the only way you can crack the last level—and you'll need to sweet-talk me real good to convince me."

"General, why is this thing Army CID? Shouldn't it be National Security Agency—or even FBI or CIA-Domestic?"

Four-star studied the colonel for a minute. It pushed the limits of questioning authority, but both understood it was a fair query. McGovern had to wonder if project control might shift elsewhere now that the threat had been revived, had to be concerned how much cooperation or resistance he could expect if he needed to mobilize mass resources and rely on people whose feathers might be ruffled over not being in charge, to contend with the fact that CID probably wouldn't command the respect he would need in a crisis. Sure, CIA had fallen into *dis*respect over scandals and revelations—but that had only been recently. Back when *IVG* was set up, CIA was extremely powerful. NSA was probably the logical choice—those boys certainly had the connections and clout, not to mention it was right up their alley. Hell, they could run FEMA out of their *back* pockets with both hands in their cash-laden *front* pockets.

"This one's different," Four-star finally answered. "CID was first on-scene—your predecessor, in fact, and the doc that reports to you now. Oh, and apparently Watterson, too, but not in an official capacity. He was doing CIA at the time and apparently never reported anything to them—not that he should have. NSA's been capturing and studying alien technology since the '40s. They're running massive research and testing projects in New Mexico and Arizona including the big one under White Sands. Nothing they have seems related. We figure it's all come from somewhere other than these parasites *you're* tracking. They've got nothing alive—and what they *do* have aren't body infiltrators."

"But this still sounds like it fits right in with what they're doing."

"Frankly, they'd had a series of screw-ups back when this was first set up, especially mismanaging public information, and they were too big with too many people on need-to-know. When this first-ever actual *invasion* started—especially considering the nature of it—the president agreed to leave it right where it was in CID, separate from everything else going on, and keep it no bigger than necessary. It had to be contained. If *anybody* ever let on that aliens were out there taking over human bodies, the panic would've torn the country apart—still could, though the public wouldn't be so quick to believe it these days. It seemed to be cleaned up right away, and there was no technology left to study except those boxes—which doesn't seem to be anything but raw material from what we can tell—so we kept it close to the vest, set up *Program Invigil* to watch for more, and left it at that."

"Why so worried about getting that third box back?"

"Mostly because wherever *it* was, there was probably another alien. Then when we found out they *could* procreate, finding it got more urgent. Lucky, possession of the box was what helped our mole ID that Watterson really *was* a suspect."

"And we had him and his entire family *killed* without even being sure?"

Four-star grinned. "You don't know Watterson. If we'd tipped our hand, there's no way we'd have had a chance to confirm. Quick and dead was the only way. Turned out to be a good thing, huh?"

McGovern ignored the question. "Dunkin used FBI to recruit the local, that black teenager named Jolene Carter, and move her in to check on Watterson. But then he passed her back and had them move her out under witness-relocation. I don't understand this—"

"Witness relocation?" Four-star was surprised. "He should've just *taken* her out. Higgins seemed to get soft there right toward the end—we should've put him down sooner."

McGovern noticed the nonchalance about essentially having another general executed once his health was too bad to do his job. "Now she's a loose end."

"Then tie it up. Look, your job is to eradicate every last one of them. You have no good way to ID them without killing or capturing and mutilating the hosts—after which you can't ever let them go anyway. You can't afford to leave any maybes on the streets. Do what you must."

"Look, sir," McGovern started, wording his question carefully. "This is a lifetime commitment for me now—nothing else matters. I need to know—if this thing blows up, is it going to NSA or somewhere else? Am *I* in control all the way down?"

Four-star nodded. "It's you and me, *Colonel*—by the way, we'll get your rank taken care of soon."

"Thank you, sir. But, what if the public becomes aware?"

"They won't."

"But—"

"Look, it stays tight and *never* gets acknowledged. I don't care what it takes or what you call it. If you have to round up half the civilian population, if you need mass eradication, if you have to work the agencies, we'll hide it behind the war on drugs or RICO or terrorism or kiddie-porn rings or internet cyber-threats or whatever. You keep *me* informed and we'll work it. Your *second* job is to keep it under wraps."

"And my first job?"

"To keep it under control."

"No matter how?"

"Whatever it takes."

Chapter 3

He could hear her outside the door several times during the night. She never said anything, just crept down from her upstairs bedroom, tip-toed to the bathroom, paused and listened. After waiting a moment, apparently assuring herself that all was okay, she would ease back up the stairs again. Eugene wasn't sure how many times she checked on him; eventually he slept so deeply that he quit waking at the slightest noise.

The sound of a flush, water rushing through the pipes from upstairs, voices in the other room, must mean morning already. With no window, he couldn't be sure how late he'd slept. He was stiff from the pallet—at least it'd been more comfortable than the ground where he'd slept the three previous nights.

Aunt Willow—*dead*. Sad reality rushed back in on him. *Russell. The other Wattersons.* Locked in the bathroom of a house full of strangers, running from invisible boogeymen, some kind of alien or something supposedly inside his body, a mission to save the world.

Well, *maybe* on that alien part. On the mission part, too.

Why did he want to tell Aunt Willow he was sorry? Sorry he'd been so much work for her, had made her life so difficult, had made her mad so many times. *Had driven her to drink.*

Had never said, "I love you, Aunt Willow—no matter what."

She was dead and it hurt more than he could imagine. He kept pushing the feeling down, but it would fight its way back. So he pushed harder until finally it seemed to fade. It didn't go away—he just put it somewhere else to deal with later . . . after he had come to grips with more-pressing matters.

He could hear Licia stirring around near the door, guessed she could hear him using the toilet. When he flushed, she spoke up.

"Finally got up, *huh*, sleepy head?" She unlocked the door with a key but didn't push it open, apparently remembering his reaction when she'd walked in while he was in the tub.

"Mornin', Eugene," Jake Coleman greeted, taking another sip of strong-strong coffee. His trademark cowboy-style fedora with blue-jay feather sat beside an egg-gooey plate on the table. Marshall and two other men nodded. Licia was already breaking eggs into a sizzling frying pan.

"You been eatin' berries and bugs too long," she kidded. "Time to fatten up your skinny little hide." In no time, she had several pans sizzling with hash browns, country ham, scrambled eggs, and pancakes. She used the ham grease and too much flour, corn meal, and milk to make way too much white gravy. She'd already placed a platter of buttermilk biscuits covered with a dish towel on the table.

Nobody said much while Eugene ate more than he thought he could but not as much as she'd served. She was hovering around, poised to cook more if he so much as hinted like he had room for it, but he was forced to leave just a bit. That was okay; he'd learned from Mrs. Watterson that, to a southern mom, eating everything on your plate meant she hadn't cooked enough. He figured there would be some grateful dogs out back waiting for his scraps. He was right.

It was past 9:30 already. Another half-dozen men showed up, plus a pretty blond woman in her twenties named Tracey who set about helping Licia serve more coffee and biscuits with jam before tackling the kitchen for clean-up.

Eugene was politely introduced by name only, no explanations offered, none asked for. Licia kept watching him, but she always smiled sweetly whenever he looked up. He noticed everybody dressed much nicer than he would've expected—even Marshall and Jake wore ties and starched shirts.

The funeral. The Watterson services were just hours away. With too many things to think about—people to meet, a new situation to assess— he had to be on his toes, needed to make plans, had to worry who might be a threat . . . yet through it all, his grief kept dragging him down, clouding his thoughts, leaving him feeling scared and helpless like he was sinking, that belly-drop that happens when you swing out of a giant tree and plunge into a deep hole in the river. He'd thought grief was what he felt over losing the mother he never knew, but this proved so much more. Did it ever go away—or would it be like this from now on?

Licia smiled and telegraphed her reassurance as Jake and the others led Eugene out to one of the outbuildings, leaving the women to finish up in the kitchen.

What looked on the outside like an old storage building adjacent to the smokehouse he'd been foolish to raid the day before turned out to be elaborately built and comfortably furnished inside—with weapons cached everywhere! Under the floor, in the wall, in disguised boxes and furniture. Marshall was passing them around, working himself and most of the men into an exuberant fervor, locking and loading and clipping and closing and breaking down and setting up and calibrating and sighting. They wanted to get outside and blow something away.

Or some*body*.

Jake remained impassive, calm, somehow above it all. He kept their enthusiasm dampened, reined in. It was funeral day, not the appropriate time to blow off steam that way.

Marshall was also showing off his collection to Eugene, quizzing him to see what he'd learned from Watterson, handing him things and getting tickled at how competently and confidently the youngster handled artillery.

Eugene discovered that admiring, then handling each piece with the awe and respect such fine weaponry deserved won him approval from the group. It was a rite of passage, maybe even a test, a display of attitude that spoke volumes without him ever opening his mouth.

They accepted him right off; *he* was one of *them*.

Several more cars and trucks arrived; then rose a flurry of excitement when Flynn Durbett pulled up in his extended-cab, bed-capped pickup. Jake and Marshall went out to talk to him before calling Eugene to join them as they walked to the house. They agreed that Durbett shouldn't appear at the funeral, that he'd lay low, staying with Eugene. He didn't acknowledge young Weisman's presence until they went inside and sent the women out to keep the fellers in line.

All four sat around the kitchen table. Flynn began, "Eugene, I'm Flynn Durbett. Do you know me?"

Eugene looked him over. Durbett looked older, more like Mr. Watterson's age, pushing forty—if not pulling it—mostly bald on top and white-haired around the sides, excellent physical condition, muscled and trim, deep tan, piercing hazel eyes. He seemed somehow both relaxed and poised to pounce. Despite the heat, he wore a suede vest loosely tailored to conceal what Eugene later discovered was a custom .357.

"No, I don't know you."

"Watterson never mentioned me?"

"No, sir."

"Don't call me sir, son, and I won't call you son. You don't have any reason to respect me yet, and I'm not your daddy."

"Mr. Watterson never mentioned you, Mr. Durbett."

"I'll let the *mister* go, seein' as you're young, but when you're ready, call me Flynn. Eugene, do you trust me?"

"No," he replied, just like that, surprised at his own cheekiness. Truth was, he didn't. Had no reason to yet.

"Good, Norm trained you right."

"*You* knew him?"

"We go way back. I understand your aunt raised you and now she's dead?"

"Yes."

"Sorry to hear it. No father—no other relatives?"

"No."

"Wattersons was like a family to you, wasn't they?"

Eugene looked down toward the table. He hesitated, then quieter, answered, "Yeah."

Durbett had a bit of the drill-sergeant's bark when he spoke, but he softened, adding, "Norm Watterson was a good man—one of the best. I'm sure his family was, too. He had a son about your age?"

"Russell was a year younger than me." Eugene was still looking down. Damn, this was hard to talk about.

"Your best friend?"

Eugene nodded wordlessly.

"Russell was lucky, then. Good father, good best friend." Durbett paused until Eugene looked up again, then continued, "I need to ask you some things. First, let me tell you, you *can* trust me, though I don't blame you if you don't yet. Me and Norman go back to when we was not much older than you. We've worked together and done saved each other's ass many a time. We kept in touch every now and then, even though he retired after—well, we'll talk about that later. I promised him if something happened, I'd look out for whoever was left to carry on his mission. Eugene, I'm wonderin' if that might just be you."

Eugene nodded. This man obviously knew something. Of course, Watterson had warned the boys that people who know a lot are either the ones to trust or the most dangerous.

"Who killed 'em?" Just like that, Durbett asked.

"At least two men, dressed all in black. They was wearin' funny masks and carryin' black bags."

"On foot?"

"On bikes, then in back of a red pickup that stopped when they got to Highway 13. They went toward Erin."

"Did you go back to the house?"

Eugene nodded, looking down again.

Durbett apparently decided against pursuing that. The result was already known. "Eugene, who do you think they was that killed 'em?"

Eugene looked him right in the eye, almost startling him with the intensity of his gaze. "The enemy," he pronounced, a hint of guttural growl in his voice.

"*Who?*"

"Government."

Durbett looked at the other two just as Marshall Emery made a fist and slammed it on the table. Eugene jumped, startled.

"*Why* was they killed?"

Eugene didn't want to lie and say he didn't know. "I don't wanna say."

"Good man," Durbett encouraged. "I understand how important it is to keep secret. I'll tell *you* a secret not many know—just us three—" He motioned toward Marshall and Jake. "—And several others. We was all committed to helping Norm protect something he thought was *inside* him." He was watching Eugene carefully for his reaction, but found no surprise on the young man's face. Maybe there was even a hint of relief. "He said he was protecting an alien."

Eugene still said nothing. Jake nodded. Marshall's face betrayed a hint of skepticism, but he nodded, too.

"If he was training you to help protect it, then you musta known about it, too." Just like that, not a question, just a statement.

Eugene didn't deny it. "That's why they killed him," he finally said.

"Did he put an alien in Russell, too?"

"In *all* his kids," Eugene answered, taking a chance, "And *Mrs.* Watterson, too." *Take a chance. Trust your instincts. Sometimes they's all you got.*

"That means they'll think it was spreading," Durbett said as much to the other two as to Eugene. "Who else did he put 'em in?" The other two couldn't help but lean forward in anticipation of the answer.

"I don't know of anybody else," Eugene stated evenly, staring back at Durbett resolutely to dare the older man to prove otherwise.

Flynn Durbett sat back and relaxed. He looked at the others again, then back at Eugene. Very quietly, he said, "It's good he could pass others along before they got him—" Still watching, even quieter, almost a whisper,

"—but that means you're the only one left."

Eugene knew Durbett saw it in his eyes. He was trying to project composure, defiance, determination—but deep inside, the young feller was confused, afraid, wanted help.

"I want to help you," Durbett said.

"Me, too," Jake echoed.

Marshall nodded.

Eugene looked down again, finally breaking eye contact. He whispered, his voice cracking, "I can't let 'em capture me. I can't let 'em kill me."

"We won't let 'em," Durbett assured. "All right you stay with the Emerys for a while?"

Eugene nodded.

"You need more training. We're gonna need some time. We got some things to accomplish. You'll be okay."

Eugene kept his face down, reaching up to wipe a tear from his cheek. Damn, where did that come from? Nobody seemed to notice.

Durbett told the other two, "Don't tell anybody Norm was killed until after the funeral—until they get back here. We can't have somebody gettin' worked up and letting on we know. They'll be watchers there."

Eugene looked up in time to glimpse Licia as she stole quietly away from the kitchen window and slipped out to rejoin the others. Durbett smiled like he'd already known she was there.

Once everybody had left for the funeral home in Waverly, Durbett backed his truck up to the outbuilding. He had Eugene help him unload a very impressive arsenal, quizzing the younger guy and looking impressed with his knowledge. Granted it was book info, photo IDs, but it was fun to see such artillery right there, to heft the various pieces, to ask intelligent questions.

Eugene was amazed at the variety of international sources. He knew the British rifles: two RA1 500 .50-caliber snipers (the "Fearsome," Watterson had called it) and an MK1 .303-caliber jungle carbine with 10-round box mags. Eugene aimed that one toward a hay bale in the distance.

"Farther than that," Durbett urged. "We're talkin' a good four-hundred meters or more."

Durbett showed a Swedish selection: a Carl Gustav model .45 submachine gun, plus another machine gun, the Stoner 63 MG3A1, a 5.56-caliber with range comparable to the rifles. He boasted four Swedish shoulder-fired rocket launchers, L14A1s similar to the Soviet Grail or U.S.

"LAW"—the standard Light Anti-tank Weapon. At first, Eugene thought it *was* the Grail until Durbett unpacked one, the SA-7, with different kinds of rounds, including concussions for both. "These are like the U.S. Stinger, but not as accurate. Even though they're easier to buy, I still get at least $10,000 for each one."

"Both are illegal," Eugene offered matter-of-factly.

"So's the Stoner. That's just *one* reason these good-ole-boys—even though they're on *your* side—would still kill you where you stand if you start runnin' your mouth."

"I got the *most* to hide."

"That you do. That you do."

They unloaded some more, packing artillery into the various hiding places. Eugene started to feel more comfortable with the older man, reminded a lot of Mr. Watterson—firm and confident, attentive, understanding. Even respectful.

The grenade launchers surprised him. He was starting to see weaponry beyond what Mr. Watterson had taught him about, including two each of the 40mm standards: the M-203 and M-79, both with up to 300-meter ranges.

Durbett showed him how to mount the 203 on both the M-16 and AR-15, then taught him how to operate the slide breech. He had him break it down, obviously pleased and impressed with how quickly he learned. "Not like some pussy," the older guy mumbled. "You'll be able to take care of yourself." Eugene was proud.

The last thing they unloaded was another rocket launcher, the new generation of LAW M-72, with cases of E4 deep-penetration warheads, one case of E5 general-purpose moderates, and a case of E6s for behind-armor effects. Eugene wanted to learn how to set up and operate one, but Durbett seemed to be anxious to get them put away before people started coming back from the funeral. "You'll get your chance."

With everything packed, Durbett suggested they walk the perimeter to check for signs of infiltration while they waited for the others. Mid-afternoon by this time, it was hot and sticky. Eugene kept wiping sweat from his forehead, wondering how this older guy seemed so cool and relaxed. "How did *you* know Mr. Watterson?" he ventured.

Flynn walked along for a minute before answering. "We did operations together. We was what you call freedom fighters—mercenaries. We went on and joined the French Foreign Legion, intending to make our fortunes and retire to some tropical isle, but, well, things happen. We spent some time in Tunisia, got disillusioned with the kinds of jobs we was doing after a while, then emigrated to Uruguay and changed our names. CIA offered us some big bucks to do a job in Central America, plus witness relocation back in the U.S., so we took it."

"Relocation?"

"Where they set you up somewhere with a steady income under your new identity. Anyway, Norm was sweet on Ethyl ever since she was a kid—never forgot her. He tracked her down and married her and moved to Waverly and decided he was through fightin' for good. I was gonna move on again, but decided to stick it out here in the U.S. I could pick up big-pay jobs from the CIA or NSA every now and then with the under-standing that they'd clean up the mess if I ever got busted runnin' illegal guns, so I opened a dealership at Victoria, Texas—between Corpus Christi and Houston. Let's just say I have ways to acquire toys that are hard to come by."

"And you sell to guys like these?"

"That's my customers. Private citizens who believe in the right to bear arms—and think they *need* to keep personal arsenals—mostly members of militias like the one Jake Coleman runs. They got hundreds of people in several states, some with a lot of money, most with a lot of determination and a healthy dose of paranoia."

They stopped to examine the footsteps and drag-marks where Eugene had been subdued. "Sloppy—shoulda covered the tracks," Durbett mused.

"Do you care how weapons are used—or who you do *jobs* on?"

"Didn't *used* to. Norm got his conscience first. His family became what *he* cared about—then of course, that alien he believed in. I got to where I understood more and more how our own government preys on and de-ceives its own people, supposedly for national interest that really ain't nothin' more than somebody-in-power's personal agenda. I try to stay neu-tral as much as I can, but I *do* give advice to my customers and, well, I owe Watterson my life and now I owe it to *you* since you're carryin' on his mis-sion." He paused and got a faraway look, whispering, "Of course, con-science can get you killed." He walked on, Eugene keeping up.

"If Mr. Watterson retired, then how did—?"

"He got a call—fast emergency job right there just a few miles from Waverly, somethin' for CID—that's Central Intelligence Division of the U.S. Army. It was years later before he told me he'd found an alien that was now inside him and needed protection. He said he had some kinda black box, too, that he'd need to use when the time come."

"Use for *what*?"

Durbett shrugged.

"When *what* time comes?"

"Can't be sure what he meant."

"Well, what did the alien *look* like and how'd it get inside him?"

"He said you couldn't really see it. Far as how it got in him, somethin' about transferring right through the skin. He didn't understand it much at first, but some years later he told me it was gonna try to have young'ns, but he needed 'em growed in somethin' else for a while before they could be put in humans."

Eugene thought about it for a minute, distracted by Durbett's interest in twigs and branches and mats of pine needles and dead leaves and mossy rocks and spider webs and all manner of things. What was he looking for? "He butchered them cows," Eugene concluded.

"What cows?"

"He was raising cows—seven of 'em—kept 'em in the low pasture where the pond is. When we all said we'd help with the aliens, we went out there and he spread a coupla big tarps and cut five of 'em open one at a time. He had each of us reach inside one and get our hands all bloody, then sent us all to wash up while he bled 'em and got 'em ready to take in to Wanamaker's for processing. He butchered the other two a couple of years later and done it with the baby. After that, he didn't have no cows no more. Didn't farm much, either—just a garden. He told us we had the aliens inside us and spent most of his time trainin' me and Russell and readin' all kinda books and stuff."

Durbett was leading him back to the house without remarking on the revelation. Eugene had suspected the cow-killings had something to do with passing the alien—especially since even the baby had to get bloody like that, but Durbett's explanation had filled in the gap. He'd pressed Watterson at the time, but his mentor had told him, "Best you don't know nothin' until it's time, then you'll understand without nobody havin' to tell you."

Marshall and Licia, plus Jake following in his own truck, were first to return from the funeral. Durbett and Eugene met them as they pulled into the long, gravel drive leading back to the farmhouse.

Durbett reminded Marshall *not* to distribute any weapons until after he'd gone. "I'm gonna stay here tonight—me and the boy got some unfinished business. Look, I know you need to have some kind of meetin'—but keep it short. People's worked up right now. You're gonna have to tell 'em Wattersons was killed—they already think so, anyway, but you need to keep this alien thing close to your vest for now. A lot of 'em won't buy into that. Besides, it don't matter *what* people believe. Fact is, Wattersons was part of us and they was killed because *somebody* thought they was a threat."

A caravan of vehicles descended on the premises—more than forty or fifty people in all. Deputy Varne was patrolling the area in his car. Carrying concealed weapons, two men talked briefly with Jake, then started walking the perimeter. Flynn Durbett and Eugene Weisman faded to the outskirts of the crowd gathered in the open air behind the house, everybody waiting to hear Jake Coleman speak. Eugene was surprised when they started by pledging allegiance to a U.S. flag flying at half-mast on a rusty pole.

"What's the greatest country in the world?" Jake shouted.

"America!" several shouted.

"What are the principles we are sworn to uphold?"

"The Constitution! The Bill of Rights!"

Jake eyed the crowd. "America is corrupt!"

Everybody shouted agreement.

"The *government* is corrupt!"

Louder, more exuberant assent.

"Our own government—*by* the people and *for* the people—has been infiltrated, taken over, destroyed by outsiders!"

"Take it back!" somebody bellowed. More agreement.

"The day will come—*soon!* Norman Watterson held the key—and for that, they *killed* him! Him and *every member of his family!*"

Murmurs, curses, growing rage. "How do you know for sure?" somebody asked.

"I can't say yet. The solution is safe—for now—but to speak before we are ready is to risk losing before the battle begins."

"What do we do?"

"What we've *been* doing! Training, arming, preparing our loved ones, practicing survivalism, anticipating a holocaust like hasn't been fought on American soil since the Civil War!"

Eugene thought of the issues of slavery, states' sovereignty, federalism—concepts he'd learned about in school. He noticed several black men, a dozen women, an Asian among the group.

"The day will come, but right now we are vulnerable. Go back home, recruit those you can trust, prepare. We will communicate through the usual channels with our brothers and sisters in the north and out west. We will come to you with our plan. We *will* be victorious!"

"And pay back for Norm Watterson and his family!" someone shouted.

"Payback! Payback!" several dozen started to chant before Jake Coleman shushed them. Eugene tried to picture the images lingering in everybody's minds: six coffins—right down to the little baby-sized one—hearses borrowed from Erin and McEwen, six graves . . . those that knew Norman Watterson must be both sad and furious, the others simply enraged. They didn't have to know the man to understand what he symbolized, why he'd given his life, a casualty in the battle that soon would erupt into full-scale war.

"Please go home now—it is not safe for us to assemble right after the funeral like this, to be unarmed and unprepared, to be so vulnerable to the killers of Watterson and the destroyers of the American way of life. I *promise* you we will prevail!"

Eugene was reminded of the preacher who'd once held a tent revival in the field by the cemetery—alternately whipping the crowd into a frenzy and bringing them back down to ponder ideas, to reflect, to vow change and envision a better future. For such a low-key man, Jake Coleman had some very passionate feelings about his politics—and the people who shared those ideas. Just like that preacher.

The meeting was over, but the crowd didn't disperse very quickly. They mingled, sharing and talking, visiting old friends, some venting, others speaking in hushed tones, reflecting on the funeral, making secret plans. Marshall circulated, occasionally talking business and making arrangements for weapons deliveries to commence the next day.

Durbett and Eugene eased around to the front and slipped inside. Licia was busily making sandwiches, listening to the crowd through the kitchen window. She set out cold sodas and snacks as they pulled up chairs. All three ate in silence. Durbett peered out the window several times, then motioned Eugene to follow him into the parlor. They stretched out on recliners and watched country-music videos for a while, still not speaking. People started to leave, the crowd dwindling to the last dozen or so still talking quietly with Jake and Marshall. The sun was going down, mosquitoes starting to swarm, lightning bugs winking here and there, hovering indifferently.

"Mr. Durbett?"

"Call me Flynn, Eugene, if you want."

"Yes, sir." He hesitated, then blurted, "Do you really believe I got a alien?"

Flynn shrugged. "Watterson thought so and *he* wasn't stupid. I don't rightly know, Eugene, but I'm not sure it matters. The government seems to believe it—and is willin' to kill over it. It's just one more reason they's dangerous to private citizens who got a right to be left alone. I used to work for government—still do on occasion if I got no problem with the job—but Norman bein' killed . . . and Ethyl and them kids . . ." He trailed off, that faraway look in his eyes again. "Eugene, aliens is like religion. Don't know the truth, don't know a good way to prove it one way or the other, and people's gonna believe what they want."

Eugene thought that over, more perplexed than he'd been before he asked. "I don't know *what* to believe," he concluded. "I don't know what's true."

Durbett looked him over, then rubbed his bald pate and snorted. "Eugene, I stopped believin' in truth a long time ago. They's truth and they's reality. Most of the time you ain't gonna know the truth, so you best stick to reality."

Eugene thought he knew what Durbett meant, but he was still unsettled. Quietly, he asked, "And what's reality?"

This time, Durbett looked very serious. He studied the young teenager's face, seeming to think that over. Finally, he answered, "It's where you are *now* . . . what these people is gonna *think* of you . . . and what's gonna *happen*."

"What *is* gonna happen?"

Durbett smiled again, using the remote control to flick off the television before standing up. "We'll just have to see." He left Eugene sitting there while he went outside and conferred with Marshall and Jake.

Most of the people had left, so they came back inside with the only two remaining men. All five set about arming themselves. Marshall retrieved Eugene's Colt Frontier from another room and gave it to him with a box of ammo.

About Eugene's weapon, Durbett commented, "We'll do better by you, Eugene, but for now, stick with what you's comfortable with." He patted under his left arm for emphasis.

"We're goin' to the cemetery," Marshall explained to Licia. "Be gone two hours or so."

They loaded into two trucks and a car, then drove backroads toward Waverly. Eugene rode with Durbett, Jake with Marshall, the other two in the car.

As they rounded the bend and climbed slowly toward where Willow lived—used to live—Eugene felt his stomach dropping again. Durbett slowed down as they passed—he seemed to know Eugene would be curious. The house was dark, no sign of anything amiss. "There'll be time later—not tonight," Durbett said, almost whispering. Eugene looked, then quickly looked away.

Durbett slowed again as they passed the burned-out shell of the Watterson place. The outbuildings lurked as spooky shadows in the faint light of crescent moon. They glanced for a moment, then stared straight ahead as Durbett pulled away. Eugene noticed in the side-view mirror that the other vehicles had fallen farther behind. Durbett turned off his headlights and slowed, the sound of gravel-crunching tires competing with the familiar insect noises of the night.

He stopped just short of the cemetery, shut off the engine, put a hand on Eugene's arm to keep him from trying to step out, then waited. After a few minutes, the other four appeared outside the vehicle. Marshall and Jake headed straight for the area where wreaths stood on wire frames—obviously the new graves—while the other two split up and disappeared into the darkness. After a minute, Jake came back alone and stayed to guard the vehicles while Flynn and Eugene walked to the gravesites. Marshall stood off to the side, cradling an M-16, scanning every direction.

Eugene noticed the six burials, all side-by-side, but was startled to see a mound of dirt near his mother's grave. He walked over and saw boards covering another fresh-dug hole. *For Aunt Willow.* Of course. He wondered what kind of funeral was planned—if any—and who was making the arrangements. He wanted to attend, frustrated he could not because he was a fugitive.

Eugene looked over and noticed Durbett was standing adjacent to the first grave—a mound of red-orange soil and gravel, blanketed by arrangements of flowers, a small foil marker jutting up proclaiming, "Watterson, Norman." As Eugene walked over, he saw the older man reach down and press a steel-tip rifle shell deep into the soil. "Ammo for my friend," he whispered. "I don't know where he is, but *now* he's armed." It sounded corny, but it was a heartfelt sentiment.

Eugene looked away. He stared at his mother's grave for a moment, then at where his aunt would be laid to rest. He looked at the moon, at Marshall standing off to the side. He strained to see where the other men providing ground cover would be patrolling. He looked everywhere but at the Watterson graves. He felt that sinking feeling again, the mad rush of dropping into the water, the sudden fear that maybe it wasn't deep enough or unseen obstacles lurked just below the surface—the inescapability of commitment.

He was falling, his heart pounding, feeling overwhelmed and scared.

His throat hurt, his eyes blurred, his nose runny . . . Mrs. Watterson, the girls, the baby. He forced himself to look at the other foil markers.

Russell's was the third mound, smaller than the first two, the boy who'd wanted to grow up faster than his body would allow, a simple guy who just liked to hang out with Eugene doing whatever crossed their minds.

His best friend.

He stared and he stared and he stared, but nothing changed. It was dirt in the darkness, some wilting flowers, a damned foil marker.

Durbett's arm was around his shoulder. He tried to look up, but everything looked too blurry. It wasn't safe to stay. He felt himself being gently led away.

Eugene stopped, turned to look again, then tugged away from Flynn Durbett and walked back to Russell's grave for the last time. He pulled his Colt Frontier from his waistband and opened the chamber, removing one shot.

He bent down and pressed it deep into the soil, then straightened up, satisfied, ready to go.

He just *couldn't* leave his best friend out there unarmed.

*   *   *

"I don't understand. I thought we were going to meet—"

"That has been changed," Colonel McGovern said matter-of-factly. That was more explanation than he felt obligated to give Dr. Aggeous. He continued to walk, anxious to get underground, to get to work.

Aggeous wheezed, hurrying to keep up with the colonel. "I'm not prepared to go to Huntsville right—"

"You will *not*—!" McGovern whirled and faced the doctor. "—continue to discuss your assignments out here in the open. I will brief you under secure conditions." He hurried on.

Aggeous wheezed some more, still trying again to match the colonel's gait, mumbling under his breath.

They followed the usual security routine on their way down to *Program Invigil.* The doctor looked annoyed about having to use his *own* thumbprint and voice recognition, plus punch in his own codes—like the colonel didn't trust anybody.

"You will commence experiments to see if our Mr. Hall will—or even *can* transfer his alien into another human host."

"But I have other—"

"Look, I don't know what else you might be working on, but inform your other superiors you would like to be relieved—or *I* will. *IVG* is your priority now. This is a national—a *world* crisis. You will report exclusively to me or you will be replaced."

Aggeous started to sit, but the colonel remained standing. It was going to be a *very* short meeting.

"But how can I get Mr. Hall—?"

"Start killing him, *slowly*, leaving no question in his mind that his life is coming to an end. Put an expendable man in the cell with him, then monitor and record his actions. I want *every* type of analysis from radiation readings to changes in the light spectrum to electro-static, gasses in the air, other possible by-products of the change—*all* physical transformations in the old host *and* the new—whatever it takes. You're going to *force* a transfer and learn everything there is to know about it."

"But what if it doesn't—?"

"*Figure out* how to make it happen, Doctor."

Aggeous seemed to be thinking it over, frustrated, perplexed. "I need a couple of days to—"

"You'll go *now* and get it started. If you need tomorrow to clean up some other business, do it, but I want results by the end of the week. Two and a half decades of not understanding the threat has screwed us out of being prepared now that we're in the middle of an invasion."

"You still want me to keep the black boxes away from—?"

"Those have already been removed from your control."

"What?!" The doctor got red in the face and slammed his fist on the desk. "But you can't—"

"You're bio-med, Aggeous. If you convince me with solid evidence that you need them to further your work, we'll cross that bridge when we come to it."

"But where *are* they? What are you—?"

"Don't question me, doctor. You're on a need-to-know basis and that's not your area."

"But I have the security clearance—"

"*If* and *when* I, the project commander, deem it necessary. Your ride is waiting," he added by way of dismissal.

"But where am I supposed to be getting another host?"

"He will be waiting for you."

"Did somebody volunteer for this?"

"It will be against his will. He will have no foreknowledge of what is to happen. You will record his impressions, monitor to see if and when—and how much—he becomes aware. I'll be curious to see if and what Mr. Hall decides to tell him, too. Figure the old man will know he's being monitored, so expect him to communicate as much as he can but actually say as little as possible."

Aggeous stared the colonel down for a moment, then flinched. "I'll get it set up. I'll be gone tomorrow, but will commence with the exposure the following day." With mock deference and a slight bow, he added, "Feel free to monitor my progress at your leisure, *Colonel.*"

"Report to the transportation office on your way out. You leave immediately."

As Aggeous started out the door, he turned and added, "By the way, I recommend you bring the new guy down in the next few days and let me give him a thorough physical—like I've done with everybody in the project. Don't know exactly what I'm looking for, but I'll feel better having looked—even if it's just to establish a base-line. This threat is too great to risk infiltration of *our* team." He was gone before the colonel could respond.

McGovern called down the hall to the aide controlling the conference centers, telling him to hold three of the four men waiting to meet with him. He wanted to see his domestic-information specialist first.

"Colonel," the man greeted, going through the motions. Lt. Col. Dunkin appeared only a few years older than McGovern, a stocky man with jet-black hair and deeply tanned, ruddy complexion.

"Sit down," McGovern instructed, taking his own seat. "Tell me what you've learned."

"Well, sir, we've pushed the boundaries with our limited sources. Best we've had going are existing FBI investigations and current monitoring. I've used them heavily, but I sure hate to stir up as many layers as they got over there."

"I'll take care of that. In fact, I'll want several agents assigned to your efforts exclusively. After we've decided our course of action, you let me know what else you need."

"Yes, sir." McGovern nodded for him to continue, so Dunkin explained, "Watterson was a retired free-lance operative, mostly CIA in the '60s—this we've known. I've got *nothing* that says he's done any jobs since, and I can't determine how he came to be on-site at the Camden landings."

"He was called by my predecessor," McGovern filled in. Files *can* be useful. "His perfect record and proximity made him ideal for fast containment. He turned it down, though, before it could be explained—apparently understanding that if he listened long enough to hear the details, he'd either have to take the job or be considered a security risk."

"And now we know he went after all," Dunkin concluded. "It seems his aunt was married to Mrs. Hall's brother, so he must've recognized something—either the name or the address or whatever. He must have shown up just out of curiosity, or to protect his kin."

"That figures—down in those hollers, they're *all* related to each other somehow."

Dunkin allowed himself to smile—but only briefly. "Other than that, his history is uneventful. He bought that place north of Waverly, got married and, some years later started his family."

"No regular employment?"

"Nothing documented. If he did odd work around town, there's no record. He used his savings, paid cash for everything, and apparently squirreled away the rest of what surely must have been a tidy sum. He used his special IRS exemption codes from then on, exercising his option to control his assets without any scrutiny from the feds or the state of Tennessee."

"Associations?"

Dunkin nodded. "Seems he's associated all through those years with a group of good-ole-boys that are part of a loose-knit cadre of militias in seven states—real low-profile, mind you. He's done training a few times, mostly for small, hand-picked groups learning guerilla tactics. Most of *those* guys are Northeast Alabama and Central Tennessee."

"FBI got a good database going on these militias and the various members?"

Dunkin smiled. "*I* was impressed. It's where I got all this."

"Step it up—data collection and analysis, membership infiltration, investigation of their histories, squeezing informants, arrests that can lead to forfeitures and deal-cutting—even some abductions if necessary, but only on the fringes at first. We can't afford to stir up the hornets too fast; we're not ready yet."

"*Abductions?*"

"Coordinate with Rawley; he'll be setting up several detention centers. What about their communications?"

"Most is open. Short-wave, newsletters, meetings, and so on. There have been interceptions in writing, mostly tic-tac-toe code too short to decipher." Dunkin hesitated, then added, "They can change the code on that for nearly every message."

McGovern nodded. "Plus word-of-mouth," he concluded.

"That is the biggie. Good-ole-boys talkin' to good-ole-boys."

"Mass monitor," McGovern instructed. "Tap every phone on the list and have a team compile and analyze."

"What kind of channels you want followed?"

"Full privilege. Just do it—no record, no warrants or other agencies involved."

"That's kind of risky—"

"Only if we're planning to use the information through a public venue—like criminal courts—where we might have to explain how we found out something. Trust me on this, we'll not be using anything that can come under scrutiny later. Full privilege."

"Good then. My guy hinted from here to Sunday that FBI was already doing that, but he backed off on the admission."

"Good for him. That's who you want workin' it. When you come at him with full privilege, you're hanging it on CID and he'll open like a clam. Then he's got no reason not to show you *all* his pearls."

"Probably be right *proud* to show what he's done, too." Dunkin grinned. McGovern was getting him to relax, starting to reveal a guerilla disposition despite his dress-greens.

"I need a public-info campaign, too. What's the best way?"

"How far you going?"

"I want to push civilian backlash against the militias—paint them as domestic terrorists, make them unpopular, start scaring some old ladies. In the long run, it'll help pass legislation and so forth, but for our purposes, I just want the less-committed to lose confidence in their organizations, to be afraid of what might be coming down when the shit hits. And if we goof up and let our asses show once or twice, it'll help to make sure the general public doesn't mind."

"Then FBI's got the biggest organization, but they've screwed some up *bad* these past few years. I really don't trust some of the people I'd have to work with—and don't think the others are up to it. No . . ." Dunkin trailed off, rubbing his jaw and thinking. "I'd say FEMA and NSA are your only two viable options, low-key and competent, already set up and running."

"FEMA may have to play a different angle down the line," McGovern said.

Dunkin was obviously pleased to see him strategizing out loud rather than just ordering. It started giving him insight into how the man thought—something that can be very helpful when you have to think for yourself, fast and furious in the thick of things—trying to anticipate the reaction of the man who'll get the report when it's over.

McGovern directed, "Use NSA, but string my privilege as far as it'll go. Reveal *nothing* about the alien angle. Play it that we got reason to figure these militias are going to be even more dangerous than they've been. NSA and FBI already know they're after the political structure and have a lot of local law enforcement in their pockets, but you pushing on behalf of CID will give the impression that the U.S. military is threatened. That'll be big enough for them."

"I know how to play it," Dunkin added, stressing his confidence.

"There's another angle I want to explore. Line me up the right man at ATF to talk to. These militias depend on weaponry, most of it illegal. I don't want ATF knowing a damn thing except that we anticipate handing them some gold feathers when the time is right. They'll eat that up. Most of the upper-brass over there are jokes, so we can't risk trusting them, but they'll play our way when we want to put them out front." Dunkin smiled, simply nodding. McGovern grinned back. "They'll jump on the chance to take credit when we *really* want 'em in case there's blame."

They both sat there for a moment, McGovern giving the lieutenant-colonel time to ponder, to make sure his questions were answered.

Finally, Dunkin stated, "There's two things I'm worrying about."

"We *need* more worrying," McGovern said evenly, his way of inviting the underling to continue.

"Turncoats on our side is the first one."

"Yeah, I figure they're everywhere you go—especially when it moves down to troop levels who might jump sides in the fracas, but that's okay for now. Play it very close and keep knowledge of aliens out of it. We're after militias, far as anybody's concerned."

"That's my second worry. All this is gonna be felt. I mean, these guys are gonna know something's going on. Aren't we tipping our hand?"

"That's what we want. It's like setting fire to peasants' huts—eventually they'll run out where you can get a bead. These militias feel enough heat and they'll expose themselves. Any members wound too tight'll cut loose. The rest will step up recruitment and exposure in the face of this growing threat, giving your undercover guys more entrées."

That covered, McGovern called down to have the other three sent in. Majors Rawley and Salisbury and Lt. Col. Dunkin already knew each other. Lt. Col. Poole was new.

"Gentlemen, I've moved Rawley to logistics and control—my old job. Major Salisbury, you will still handle international, but your focus will shift to gathering data on foreign support of domestic militias and sources of weaponry. Leave somebody monitoring the crop circles, but don't expect that to lead anywhere. I need you on the real deal. Rawley, start coordinating with Major General Ashe out at Ft. Donelson in case the old Cumberland Sanitarium might be needed for containment. Proceed with that, ready for up to several hundred with *full* support, though I anticipate the numbers will be more like a dozen or two over the next few months. Just be *ready*."

He paused and studied each man's face for a moment, then quietly explained, "Look, the emphasis has shifted from watching to preparing for confrontation. We've got proof the aliens have been at large, procreating and taking over human hosts. We've already eradicated a half-dozen and must assume there are more—most likely members of one or more militia groups. Lt. Col. Poole, you've come aboard to plan various invasion and assault contingencies, and to coordinate if we have to make our move large-scale."

They all seemed—even Dunkin—to be trying not to breathe.

"Questions or comments?" McGovern asked.

Everybody waited, then Poole ran his fingers through his stubby, flame-red crewcut hair and pronounced, "We're gonna wipe them aliens off the face of the planet."

"But they live inside citizens," Dunkin pointed out.

"You can't have a war—" Poole started, spreading his hands.

McGovern finished for him, "—without casualties."

*   *   *

He tried to slip out of bed, but Lena reached over and took his hand, tugging gently, urging him back. "Come on, Joe, we still got time," she whispered.

"I have to get to work," he objected, checking his watch again.

"You said four—I gotta be out by three-thirty." She pulled the sheet down to reveal taut breasts framed by bikini tan-lines, fingering her nipples with her free hand. She smiled, her pink, glossy lipstick setting off pearly white teeth, the tip of her tongue . . . "You know I gotta let it out—'specially the way *you* help." She licked her lower lip, then shifted down under the sheet with a low, audible sigh, still tugging at him.

He hesitated, one knee on the side of the bed, his body crisscrossed with Venetian-blind slashes of refracted sunlight, moving closer. She stroked down his naked chest, continuing lower, a light feather-touch. He found himself slipping under the sheet, felt her arms encircling him, her breasts pressing close, her hot breath on his neck and face, her lips.

He hurried, pressing on, working hard; she held off, shifting away, changing her rhythm, surprising him sometimes, shifting again, checking the clock on the wall. He got more forceful, straddling her, keeping her in place, working even harder . . . She squirmed, gasped, pulled free, then gave herself back to him again—just long enough so he had to start over. She sighed, wiggling away, pushing him back down and climbing on top, sliding back to find him but not staying quite long enough . . .

3:00, 3:10, 3:15 . . . She stayed with him, let him rise, then rolled under and clung tightly, moaning and gasping her pleasure, thrusting back with all her strength, an award-caliber performance.

"Gotta rush," she whispered. "Rest a minute." She hurried into the bathroom, lingering an instant to smile nakedly from the hallway.

Joe glanced at her phone on the end-table. He could hear the shower running, but decided to wait. The water stopped, a hair dryer, drawers opening and closing. He got up and slipped into the bathroom. She was working on her make-up. He smiled, caressed her a moment, then stepped into the shower.

"Gotta go, Hon. Can't be late—he'd as soon fire my ass as grab it for a feel. See ya in the morning?"

"Don't know what time," he responded loudly, competing with the shower. "May have to work extra—I'll get here soon as I can."

She smiled, answering, "Lock up on your way out." As an afterthought, she added, "Love ya, Sweetie—look forward to the *next* time."

He peeked out the shower curtain to admire her caboose as it sashayed out of the bathroom.

He dried and dressed quickly, then went to her phone, checking his watch. He couldn't be late; not this night, not after all this time. He dialed a number, then said quietly, "Joe Pennington. Confirmed this morning. It'll be somewhere along the San Antonio River—don't know exactly, but we're taking 181 to 72 and heading up. Don't take 'em until *after* they leave the river area. Remember, I'll be in one of the vehicles, so watch out for me." He paused a moment, then answered, "Yeah, supposed to be already fitted, at least four cases. Be at least two vehicles, maybe a third. I won't ID until the last second, maybe have to ride out with 'em if they get away. Yes, I will."

He hung up, checked to make sure his hair was combed, then pulled his boots on. He examined his snub .38 and tucked it down close to his ankle. He walked out to his 4X4 truck, strapped on his underarm holster with a .45, then opened his glove box and lifted a panel from the bottom, concealing his ID and wallet. He locked it, checked his hair again in the mirror, then pulled away from the curb and headed south toward Victoria to keep a very important appointment. After months of moving boxes with questionable contents around South Texas, he'd been offered a chance to make some serious money on a bigger job.

*   *   *

Lena was watching from a coffee shop on the corner as Joe passed through the town of Inez. Satisfied, she walked around back, climbed into her compact car, and headed home. She parked one street over, then cut through her friend's yard to her own house. She went to the end table, opening its door with a key, and pulled out a small digital box, noting the phone number appearing on the LCD display. She pressed a button on another device and listened to the phone call Joe had made.

She dialed a number, waited, said, "Yes," played the recording, then read the number off the display. "Is that what you needed, Hon?" she asked. Pausing, she added, "No, I'm just pussy to him; he thinks there's no reason to worry about me. He ain't *told* me nothin', either. Good."

She paused again, then smiled. "Any time, Flynn Honey. I do appreciate the money, but you *know* I'd do anything for *you.*"

*   *   *

Flynn Durbett hung up the phone and took one last look at the monthly list of electronic fund-transfers to a bank in Georgetown, Grand Cayman. He memorized the total, then flash-burned the document. He nodded at Marshall Emery.

Eugene Weisman was fidgeting on a low couch, watching Marshall inspect several modified sub-machine guns. "Who owns the shop?" he wondered. The lad had grown bolder about asking direct questions since the long drive from Tennessee to Texas, delivery detours along the way.

"Technically, it's mine," Marshall offered absently, "but it weren't *my* money." He was impressed with the modifications, commenting how the new Chinese artillery would sell well *and* be effective when needed.

"Wouldn't be smart for *me* to own nothin'," Durbett explained. "So I make mine and have it sent out, and my buddy here gets a thriving business and lots of legit profits out of the deal."

"All four dealerships?"

"Well, yeah, but the bigger money is in the distributorship, licensed in seven states."

"Don't get *too* far into what he don't need t'know," Marshall cautioned.

Durbett grinned while putting away the paperwork. "Why? Don't want them aliens knowin' our business?" He laughed at himself.

Eugene didn't. Neither did Marshall. Durbett noticed and stopped.

"I still don't think he should go," Marshall argued. "It's too risky. Let's leave him here, or send him off with Lena for the night. Let her jump his bones. You ain't never had no pussy yet, have ya, Weisman?"

Eugene didn't answer.

"I want him close," Durbett concluded, standing to put on his vest and methodically arming himself to the teeth. There, no more argument about it. Of course, Marshall—if anybody—wouldn't let up until he was satisfied.

"He'll learn how you work it. You already risk letting runners ID you if the shit ever hits the fan—I thought that was why you used to stay clear of the transfers."

"First, I don't know what'll go down tonight, but even if it runs smooth, it's *my* get—always is. Don't never trust nobody else for the serious stuff. Second, if the boy's gonna live with you, pretend to be old enough to stay out of public school, learn to take care of himself—he's gotta be an asset, not a liability. Work him. You don't do that keepin' him on the out."

"Yeah," Marshall said. He'd given up.

As all three went outside to load into a 4X4, Durbett added, "Besides, his life may depend on handling himself in the *deep* shit. He needs to get used to the smell."

Durbett at the wheel, the smallish teen between him and Marshall, they left for the rendezvous.

Marshall nudged Eugene. "Looks like you're about to get your first whiff."

*   *   *

Two choppers lifted into the sky and headed west. They were solid black, their only designations small, glossy-ebony bureau numbers below horizontal stabilizers and on their tails visible only with infrared. The HH-GOA Night Hawk carried four men, the AH-64 Apache hauled six, everybody in black.

They crossed Alabama's I-65 between Decatur and Hartselle, then continued west until they reached a half-dozen miles south of Moulton over patchwork fields of farmland and rolling hills dotted with ponds and small lakes. They set down a thousand meters apart in clearings adjacent to two different gravel roads. Rotors stopped, they waited in the quiet until long after insect noises had resumed.

Two stayed with the choppers; the others moved into the darkness, relying on their night-vision masks. One pair descended on the old, decrepit farmhouse while the rest fanned around the perimeter.

The old woman was the only one home, her nephew and farmhands gone for the night. She woke up, thought she heard a *pffft*, and fell back asleep.

The pair stood vigil inside while two others, on their signal, roused the twelve head of cattle and let them into the small corral. As one man led them one-at-a-time to the pasture, another butchered and a third retrieved samples from their hearts, brains, and livers, mutilating them to cover what specifically had been done.

The pasture men withdrew first, then the inside pair, the perimeter patrol last. The choppers faded into the night sky and headed toward Huntsville.

The old lady would wake up an hour later with a headache, nauseated, groping for her pills in the dark before falling back to sleep.

A young guy driving home from the bar would swear he saw a black chopper lifting off less than a quarter-mile from where *them cows* got found butchered, his report passed along by word-of-mouth until it made its way into a monthly newsletter issued by a militia organization based in Oklahoma City. The story would be picked up and added to a decades-long chronicle of sightings listed in another newsletter out of Muskegon, Michigan.

Aboard the Apache, the overweight man who'd taken the samples removed his mask and, using a pen-light, examined the vials in the padded, black case. He wheezed several times.

Dr. Aggeous was satisfied.

*   *   *

The fishing boat pulled alongside a Japanese-registered supertanker in the Mediterranean, an oil freighter under all-stop ostensibly for a routine check of instrumentation. The smaller craft was registered from Belgium, out on its standard two-week run. A small gantry crane swung over the side from the freighter and hoisted one piggy-back container painted black. Half the size of a railroad car, just big enough to fill a semi-truck trailer, it was packed with enough cases of Belgian FN Mini-mini 5.56-caliber MGs to gross more than $2 million at $2,500 a piece—after expenses—on the black market. Add to that the Soviet SA-7 Grails and German Heckler and Koch 9mm MP-5s already set up for 500rpm, and it would be a $3-million shipment. The piggy-back was lowered into an empty ballast tank and sealed in. The tank was flooded and left full during the voyage to the Gulf of Mexico.

As the tanker passed south of Port Arthur on the Texas/Louisiana border, the captain enjoyed a game of chess with a ham operator out of Corpus Christi—a regular match for the two men, except neither seemed to be very good at it. The captain had to make his moves seem like reasonable responses to the outlandish strategies of his land-bound adversary. The Texan's moves were actually careful signals detailing the status of Coast Guard air-and-sea patrols. Thanks to increasing consolidation, both men knew that whatever the Guard was up to would cover the DEA (Drug Enforcement Administration) and ATF (Bureau of Alcohol, Tobacco, and Firearms).

A salty old seadog with his own 82-foot shrimp trawler, his son and two other hands aboard, was also monitoring the game, amused at the moves, carefully copying down the information they conveyed. Out from the set of small commercial piers adjacent to Victoria called Port O'Connor, their shrimpboat boasted a simple set-up for beheading, sizing, and icing their catch. Just east of Galveston, approaching open water south of High Island, staying near a number of other similar trawlers under cover of night, they pulled alongside the Japanese supertanker as it paused to release ballast before approaching port with crude for the refineries of Galveston. It took less than five minutes to lower the piggy-back to the deck of the trawler.

The shrimpboat pulled away, heading southwest at a leisurely pace. In less than an hour, the piggy-back was unpacked, crates of weapons stored below decks and covered with layers of fresh shrimp. The black container was dropped over the side in four-hundred feet of water, sinking out of sight. They resumed shrimping the next day, working their way almost to the Mexican border by nightfall, about thirty miles out and heading toward South Padre Island.

*   *   *

Joe Pennington arrived fifteen minutes early, so he drove around, killing time, looking forward to the anticipated ambush arrests. He'd spent months undercover, moving small caches of weapons with one other man he didn't know, usually from Port O'Connor or Port Aransas, always in small panel trucks to a rendezvous just outside Corpus Christi. Under new pressure to crack open some militia weapons-procurement networks right away, what he'd expected to be a six-month operation was being pushed by his superior for a fast show-off bust.

The timing couldn't be better. The ringleaders finally trusted him enough to bypass the regular drop-off, to move a larger shipment and make the delivery himself. This was what he'd been working toward—and the map he'd been given directing his caravan to a point along the San Antonio River had made the logistics of coordinating the raid and arrests especially easy. It looked like this might really put as big a dent in the illegal-weapons trade as the bosses had planned to portray it.

He recognized the guy he'd run with before, plus met several others for the first time. The panel truck looked similar to what he'd been using, except this one was all beige with no markings. A balding man he'd never seen before, about forty years old, seemed to be running things, explaining that they'd be taking a detour to pick up more trucks and kill some time. It was a bigger shipment than expected, so they needed to wait for more help. It would be a long night.

What luck for G-man Joe! A bigger cache, more bodies in custody, more people to crack for info, more media attention, a bigger feather in his cap.

Joe and two others climbed into the back, then played cards by battery-operated lantern during what started to worry him was too long a drive. The more he was convinced plans had changed, the more he wished he'd managed to get an undercover partner involved—or had worn a wire so his back-up would know to track him. He didn't consider that maybe he'd been scanned for transmitters as he climbed aboard.

They finally stopped at a secluded warehouse near the Mexican border just outside Brownsville, Texas. Joe had no idea where he was nor if his team had somehow managed to follow. The balding guy directed the others to two more panel trucks, then had Joe ride up front with some teenage kid. It was finally dark out—well after 9:00—as they drove onto South Padre Island. The sign warned that the causeway would be closed from 10:00 until 6:00 a.m.

"We goin' all the way back to the same dropoff?" Joe wondered.

"Eventually," Flynn Durbett said quietly. "We got a lot of work ahead of us first."

Joe nodded. His bust might happen after all. Was he in danger, or had he lucked into an opportunity to trace the source and cast his net even wider? The kid couldn't be older than fourteen or fifteen; surely he wouldn't be around if something dangerous was planned.

They headed up the island for several miles, then pulled off into a sandy stretch of rolling dunes and scrub brush adjacent to a small cove, parking out of sight from the road. The other trucks arrived several minutes apart. The men slung beige netting over all three vehicles, then settled in for a quiet, maddeningly tedious six-hour wait.

At about 4:00 a.m., they unloaded two Zodiac boats equipped with electric motors and carried them down to the water. One man stayed behind to guard the trucks while Joe and the others launched into the dark waters of the gulf.

Young Eugene, Marshall, and Joe rode in the lead boat with Flynn, who was using some kind of signal tracker with lighted display, occasionally whispering adjustments in direction to the man tending the motor. They pulled alongside the shrimp trawler and climbed an aluminum ladder, leaving one man in each boat.

A pair of shrimpers with two more Zodiacs waited on-deck. Using a small gantry, they lowered the boats and started on crate after crate of guns and parts. Joe's role was to carry boxes from the shrimpers to the man operating the gantry. He kept count, thrilled with the size of the cache. Four boats making round trips transported eleven loads in less than ninety minutes. While the twelfth load pushed off into the darkness, yet another Zodiac was unpacked and inflated with a compressor, presumably for the last few boxes and to carry Flynn, Marshall, Eugene, and Joe Pennington back ashore.

As the ATF agent bent down to help one of the shrimpers lift the last crate of weapons, he heard several faint clicks. He froze, barely able to see the barrel of the M-16 pointing at his head from the left, a .44 from the right. Something he couldn't identify pressed against his back. While the shrimpers took his .38 and holstered .45, then thoroughly duct-taped and left him lying in the fetal position, he could see Eugene watching from off to the side. He quit trying to squirm, waiting to see what would happen, understanding that his prospects for survival had grown bleak.

*   *   *

Eugene stood very still, watching as Flynn Durbett squatted and put his face close to Joe's. "They're going to slit the tape holding your arms and drop you in about ten feet of water just off one of the Belize cays. Backstroke and kick like a mermaid and you should have no problem making it to shore—that'll be safer than trying to undo the rest of the tape out there in the current." Durbett slid a box of waterproof matches into Joe's pocket, checking to be sure there was no ID of any kind on the man. "Use these to make a signal fire, but wait until you see one of the scuba boats—could be several days—and they'll pick you up. Better have a good story, *Joseph B. Pennington*, because ATF agents ain't too popular down there. They's only one notch above DEA on the food chain. By the time you get back stateside and file your rather embarrassin' report, we'll be long gone. Notice I've made sure you ain't seen no identifyin' nothin' to help you figure us out."

"Up his ass!" Marshall blurted, no longer able to contain himself. "Drop his ass *now*."

"I've got a rusty engine block," one of the shrimpers offered.

"That'll work," Marshall enthused. "It's a quarter-mile deep right here. Let's make him hurt until he talks. If he lies to us, we drop him and let him drown. If he comes straight, we do him a favor and put a clean shot in his head before we drop him." He spit on the deck for emphasis.

Durbett looked like he was thinking it over. "Normally, I don't like killin' that ain't necessary. I like the idea of Secret-agent Pennington taking back a warning from us—"

"It's a *better* warnin' if his mama don't never see him again," Marshall argued. He pointed the M-16 at Joe's face and fingered the trigger, so worked up that his shoulders twitched.

"It'd be good practice for the kid to put it in him," Durbett mused.

Marshall smiled, his eyes glistening in the moonlight. "Yeah, that'll work. Good practice for when the time comes he ain't got no choice."

"Start shavin' down that *moment of hesitation*," one of the shrimpers concurred, laughing at the thought.

Watching the Weisman lad blow the fed's face off became a popular idea for the evening's entertainment. Eugene watched quietly—except for his pounding heart. He didn't want to kill the man, but he *did* want to please these guys who were on *his* side. Whatever Durbett said . . .

"Bring the block," Durbett decided. "We'll let Pennington here have a say in his own fate."

Marshall wrapped a steel cable around the agent's ankles and tied it to the block. Using the gantry, he hoisted the rusty chunk of iron over the water, pulling Joe right to the edge of the rail.

Eugene could see the man shaking as Durbett peeled away the tape covering his mouth. He motioned Eugene over. "Draw your weapon, sir," he told the teen.

"Blow his kneecaps clean off," Marshall goaded.

"It's *your* call, Penny," Durbett intoned. "My moles done told me more than you think, so you answer my questions with the truth, y'hear? If you lie, I say wrong answer and the boy here'll blow off a piece of you. You tell me what I want and we'll have captain drop you by the cay for a swim. But if you make the boy blow a piece off before you talk, you'll bleed to death before you get rescued from that island."

Eugene knew that Durbett could see he was shaking, too, and suspected he didn't really want him to shoot. Joe stubbornly resisted talking, so Durbett produced a small sheet of paper and read off the agent's mother's address. After that, Joe started breaking down, struggling to avoid tears.

Over the next fifteen minutes, Durbett learned all he wanted to know, including some key names and the rundown of another surveillance project that could impact his operations. He was most interested in learning about the push to take out key players in the militia movement, but was convinced Pennington didn't know where the pressure was coming from—or why. He queried about the alien angle, but the agent didn't seem to be in that loop—didn't even take it seriously.

Durbett retaped the man's mouth. "Swing him over the water," he instructed.

Joe was squirming and twisting as he hung head-down under the rusty block.

Durbett nodded to Marshall, then casually sat on a bulkhead cover and looked at his watch to remind everybody they were short of time.

Marshall grinned, putting his arm around Eugene's shoulder and leading him to the rail. "Take out your weapon, son," he said quietly.

Eugene complied, numb, almost dazed.

Durbett took it from him, turned away to inspect it in the dim light, then handed it back. "Aim for his head—it's a moving target, now."

Everybody looked amused by how Pennington squirmed and tried to watch what was happening even though he was twisting around in circles with no control over the direction he could see.

Eugene aimed, but he was wavering. He drew a direct bead several times, but lowered his arm until his .22 was pointed at the water.

"Give him the sixteen," one of the shrimpers suggested. "Something with more balls."

"He's not been trained with it," Durbett said quietly. "No unnecessary shots out here."

"He's tryin' to get you captured or killed," Marshall said quietly to the teen, leaning in close so their faces were beside each other, still watching the man dangle in the moonlight. "Take him out." Just like that, calm and quiet.

Mr. Watterson had trained Eugene for this. Mr. Watterson had warned him. Mr. Watterson wanted Eugene to survive, no matter what. Mr. Watterson wouldn't hesitate . . .

"Take him out," Marshall whispered.

Twisting and turning, dangling over the water, black all around. That was a man hanging there—one with a mother who loved him.

"No time, Eugene, take him *now*. We gotta go."

Eugene aimed firmly and cocked his pistol. His arm was steady, his grip solid. He sighted down the barrel. Joe Pennington came around again. Eugene could see the fear in his eyes, even in the darkness. The man was crying.

"*Now* Eugene. He would've killed you a hundred times by now. *Do* it," Marshall whispered.

Eugene couldn't hear the pounding of his heart anymore, the waves lapping against the hull, the breeze. He was in his zone.

It was time to kill.

"No," Eugene whispered. He uncocked the hammer, tucked his pistol back into his waistband. "No."

"You'd rather be *dead*," Marshall growled, furious.

"He's not ready," Durbett said. "Leave him alone."

Eugene turned toward Flynn's voice—

Pfoom! Pfoom!

"File your report at the bottom, you son of a bitch," Marshall growled.

Eugene whirled as Marshall waved his arm toward the man at the gantry. The agent's face was blown up, his head split, black ink running down and dripping into the water.

Splash.

The men laughed and high-fived each other—all but Durbett. He was watching Eugene. The teen was shaking, his heart pounding in his ears, nauseated, vomiting over the rail.

Eugene felt Durbett's hand on his shoulder. He was embarrassed, choking and spitting, trying to catch his breath, to calm down.

"You done good, Eugene," Durbett whispered so the others couldn't hear.

Eugene wiped his face. "But—"

"But nothin'. You're gonna *need* to learn to do it *fast*, but it should never be *easy*." He looked over toward the others who were still giddy with the adrenalin-rush of cold-blooded killing. "And it should *never* be fun." Eugene nodded, keeping his face turned away from the group. He wanted to recover before they saw him.

After a moment, the mood subsided. "We gotta go," Marshall said.

As Eugene climbed down to the Zodiac, he heard Marshall grunt as if in pain, Durbett's voice growling something about, "Send a *message*, I said. Unnecessary killin' makes us no better than *they* are." Eugene inspected his pistol and discovered Durbett had removed the rounds. Seemed like that should make him feel better, but it didn't.

Once ashore, Durbett handed him his bullets without a word, so he reloaded and said nothing. They carried the boat to a panel truck and loaded it in the back. The other two trucks had already gone; only one man remained with the third.

"What's that?" Eugene suddenly hissed.

Weapons out! Fanned every direction. Listening and watching. Eugene had his Colt out almost as fast as the others.

Durbett's gaze alternately scanned the area and watched Eugene. The teen was listening, trying to determine what he'd heard.

"It's ringing, like a phone," Eugene whispered.

This way? That way? Durbett was gesturing, trying to determine the source.

Eugene shook his head; he couldn't be sure.

They waited and listened. Nobody else could hear.

"Move out," Durbett whispered. He locked the fourth man into the back and climbed in the passenger side, Marshall behind the wheel, Eugene in between. They drove off the island, no hassle, without incident.

It was a long trek back toward Victoria. Eugene was distracted, Durbett watching him carefully.

"Shoulda killed him," Marshall said to Eugene. The teen didn't respond.

"What'd you hear back there?" Durbett asked.

Eugene shook his head, confused, frustrated.

"Shell-shock," Marshall grinned. "Ain't never seen somebody taken down before. That's all right."

"You think that's what it was?" Durbett wondered.

Eugene shook his head. "A phone ringing."

"A phone?" Marshall asked.

"It's a phone."

"You hear it *now*?" Durbett asked, serious, maybe worried.

Marshall looked amused. "What do we do about a phone ringin' in your head?"

"You need to answer it?" Durbett asked, still dead serious.

Eugene nodded.

"Well, hell then!" Marshall mocked, "Answer the damn thing."

"I don't know *how.*"

Chapter 4

"Nucleotide markers," Dr. Aggeous explained, "—a way we can check later to see if you've been contaminated."

Lt. Col. Poole flinched, rubbing his arm where he'd been injected. "You're *sure* it ain't dangerous—?"

"Naw, we been using it for years. Everybody on the team's been marked. It's classified, though, so don't be talking about it. I mean, if you wanna whisper to one of the others, well, that's between you two—but I wouldn't let the colonel hear you running your mouth. I guess you're already starting to see how tight-assed he is."

Having passed his physical, Poole was getting dressed again. "You got *that* right," he agreed, grinning and wagging his bushy red eyebrows. "But *you* said it—not *me*."

"I've only been able to synthesize a small amount of it so far," Aggeous continued, "and if it ever leaked about its existence, we'd get a run on people wanting it. You have to realize, there's a whole lot of officers over the colonel who'd get *real* pissed if they found out there was a way to verify the alien and they'd not been offered it."

Poole carefully arranged his hat, remarking, "I best get on out of here. I'm due up at Cumberland to work on setting up that detention camp."

Aggeous took a shuttle across the Redstone Arsenal compound and worked his way down to the underground quarantine. He took a seat in the glass room adjacent to Mr. Hall, wheezing as he stretched out in the recliner next to a rack of equipment. He nodded a greeting to the men on the other side of the glass.

The new man was a refugee from Haiti with a long, dark face set off by wide, flat nose and deep-set obsidian eyes. Despite a hint of gray in his short Afro hair, he didn't look to be older than forty. He stood up and moved to the window, glaring both curiosity and hatred at his fat captor. Mr. Hall stared vacantly, only a glimmer of recognition in his face, holding his stomach and perspiring heavily. The old man looked ill.

Aggeous keyed one of the machines to transfer camera and audio recording to a different hard-disk, then punched in instructions to scan for conversation and physical contact between subjects. Over the next few minutes, he watched and listened on a small monitor as several brief inter-changes played out—mostly the Haitian peasant asking questions like when do we eat and do we get to bathe and do we go outside. Mr. Hall usually just shook his head no. There was no clear physical contact between them.

The machine played only one sequence in which there might have been contact—when Mr. Hall got up to urinate, and then when he was returning to his bunk. The men were juxtaposed by the camera angle for a brief mo-ment, but the way Hall shrunk away, it looked obvious he'd scrupulously avoided touching . . . and that he'd not had enough time to, anyway.

"Whar t'be *my* bed?" the Haitian asked through the glass.

Aggeous reset the equipment and frowned, then rubbed his face with one hand while waving toward Mr. Hall with the other. "*He's* layin' on it."

Hall opened his eyes again, cocking his eyebrows slightly in question. "Whar t'be *his* bed?"

Aggeous grinned knowingly. "He won't be needing one anymore. That's right, Mr. Hall. That lunch you had about an hour ago was poison. You see, we're through with you. You're too old to count on keeping that thing inside you alive. You could have a heart attack or something and die on us. We figure we're gonna lose it soon anyway, so we'll either get it over with or give you a chance to pass it along."

Hall sat up, alarm in his eyes. "You stinking *son* of a bitch," he growled.

Aggeous wheezed to his feet and walked to the glass, quietly adding, "Maybe so, maybe so. Either way, you'll be dead in a few hours. Now, what's it gonna be?"

"Wuss he talkin'?" the Haitian demanded, eyes darting back and forth between the two men. "Wuss dis?"

Hall lay back, a look of determination, defiance on his face. He closed his eyes.

Aggeous watched for a while. The Haitian eventually lost interest and started to peruse the shelved videos and books, obviously unable to read but looking in fascination at the pictures. Hall kept his eyes averted, but continued to appear increasingly uncomfortable, even sickly. Aggeous kept rubbing his own temples and shaking his head as if trying to soothe away a headache, looking at his watch, staring impatiently at the men opposite the glass.

Another five minutes, another ten, twenty, Hall starting to squirm from cramps, Aggeous alternately squeezing his eyes closed and rubbing his head, then shaking it. The Haitian was watching them both, obviously scared, bewildered. Death was on its way . . .

*   *   *

The door swooshed open to admit Colonel McGovern, dress-uniform, black briefcase in hand. He walked to the glass wall and looked over the scene, acknowledging the doctor's presence with little more than a glance. "Nothing yet?"

"Naw," Aggeous wheezed. "Not yet." He reached up and closed the audio channel to prevent the prisoners from listening. "The old bastard's determined to hold out. I don't think he believes he's really being killed."

"He's not, is he?"

"Naw. Just getting steadily sicker. He'll be feeling so bad in another hour or two he'll *wish* he was dead."

McGovern walked over and sat stiffly in the chair adjacent to the doctor. "You don't look very good yourself."

Aggeous rubbed his head again, shaking it. "I'll be all right." Changing the subject, he inquired, "Did you bring the boxes?"

McGovern nodded. "What do you want to try?"

"I want to show 'em to the old man, see if he acts like he recognizes 'em, shows any interest in 'em. You know, record his reaction—you're the one wanted to start documenting his behavior."

McGovern nodded toward the case he'd set on the floor. "Let's observe for a while first," he said evenly.

Aggeous looked disappointed, but acquiesced. "What about you? How *you* been feeling?" He watched McGovern carefully for his reaction.

The colonel studied the doctor for a moment before replying, noting the fat researcher really did look ill. "I feel fine—why do you ask?"

"Just concerned about contamination is all. Something is going on out there and it worries me."

"How did Poole do in his physical?"

"He's fine; nothing noteworthy. Could lose some weight," he added, wheezing and grinning at the irony.

They sat there in silence for several more minutes, the doctor obviously trying to keep his eyes off the case. Finally, McGovern asked, "There's something I've been wondering—why has your research been so shoddy?"

Aggeous sat up, defensive. "What do you mean *shoddy*?"

"I mean, at best, minimal, incomplete, lacking breadth and reach, poorly—or not at all—documented, sloppy, waiting decades before you even bothered to try certain things. For the greatest threat ever to face mankind short of some deadly worldwide plague, you seem to have treated it more as a curiosity than anything else."

"Well, first off, it was decades of monitoring before the old man started to reproduce. I never let up keeping track, checking, suspecting—but you have to admit, after all that time, it looked like it *musta* been contained. Once we found them alien threads starting to be passed to animals, I stepped up checking out how they grew and how they were transferred. That's how I discovered it takes *two* hosts."

"*How* did you discover it requires two hosts?"

"Well, um, we lost the first one and I tried it out. It worked is all."

"You had a hunch?"

"No, *it was good scientific experimentation.*"

"I see. Did you try various treatments, medicines, foods, mineral or nutrient supplements—whatever—to see if there was another reason they might be dying before transferring?"

"What're you getting at?" Aggeous shot.

"I want to know why your research has been so shoddy and incomplete."

"Look, I wanted to go balls-out on this thing early on. I *did*. But Higgins held me back. He didn't want me doing too much. I'd need help, assistance, more facility—he was afraid it would attract curiosity, attention. He was mostly worried about just keeping it contained, watching for signs of others that might be out there."

"He was never interested in the possibility of more landings? Of knowing what we would be dealing with if suddenly there were hundreds, maybe thousands or more, out there at large?"

Aggeous shrugged, rubbing his temples again. He was pale, sweating, seemingly in pain. "I asked him once. He was worried there might be just one more—Watterson it turned out—and seemed to think if we controlled what we had, they wouldn't be a problem. He never explained *his* decisions to *me*—that's shithead military for you—so don't be climbing up *my* ass for how *you* guys kept the thumb on me!" Aggeous was getting worked up.

"I just wondered," McGovern said calmly. He was having difficulty trying to figure out how to play the doctor. He'd been miffed at first to think the fat civilian knew more and could decide on his own how much and what information to dole out. Then he'd grown steadily more suspicious that maybe the man was hiding something. *IVG* had been too complacent, too sloppy, had too many gaps in information. McGovern was smart enough to know that meant either incompetence or cover-up. Everything kept pointing to the former, but that uneasy glimmer of suspicion he felt kept the latter always on his mind. The colonel had pushed Aggeous far enough for now. The doctor had taken the dressing-down personally, like he really did want to be thorough but had, for whatever reason, been held back.

McGovern set the briefcase on a low table and opened it, lid toward the glass so the prisoners would not see the contents. Inside, nestled into custom-padded slots, were two black boxes, not much larger than packs of cards, dull with a faint shine, slightly rounded at their edges, to all outward appearances benign. "How would you like to do this?"

"Just show 'em, see how he reacts. We've never let on that we have 'em. Maybe they mean something to that alien in him, maybe not. Higgins wanted to keep the boxes away from him, but I can't see any harm in having 'em *this* side of the glass." Aggeous was breathing hard. The fat doctor sure needed to start taking better care of himself.

McGovern thought it over for a minute. "Proceed," he said quietly.

Aggeous carefully removed one, cupping it in his hands, a puzzled look on his face. He got up, walked to the glass, and held it up where Mr. Hall could see. The old man's eyes remained closed. "Open the channel," Aggeous instructed, nodding for McGovern to activate the comm-buttons. "Billy! Billy Hall!"

The old man opened his eyes, wiping sweat from his brow. He winced, but at the sight of the black box, he just smirked, then closed his eyes again.

Aggeous examined the box once more, then replaced it in its slot before removing the other one. He cradled it in his hands, caressing it for some time before carrying it over to the window and holding it up. "Billy," he said quietly.

The old man looked, his eyes growing wide. He struggled to his feet, still wincing with pain, heaving several times like he might vomit. He pressed his hands against the glass, gazing longingly at the obsidian enigma cradled in the doctor's hands. He swallowed hard several times, then looked up into the doc's eyes, pleadingly, tears forming in his own. "You stinking *son* of a bitch," he whispered. He staggered back and collapsed on his bunk.

"You're *dyin'*, Billy!" Aggeous shouted.

The old man stared at him a moment, then between winces, said, "All you done is made me sick." He closed his eyes and rolled over on his side.

Aggeous shook his head, then whirled and dropped into his seat with a wheeze, still holding the box.

McGovern stood, studying Mr. Hall, then strode to the door and disappeared into the hallway for a minute. When he returned, Aggeous was still sprawled, still holding the box, but his color was back. He wasn't sweating anymore, no longer looked ill. McGovern sat down, calling out, "Mr. Hall!"

Billy opened his eyes, but didn't answer.

"I'd like to introduce you to your new friend, Mr. Dukani." He nodded toward the Haitian; Hall never took his eyes off the colonel. "Now that Mr. Dukani has been here, now that he's seen all this—now that he's been *exposed*, I will be forced to eliminate him—"

"Whut dat mean?" Dukani demanded.

"I am about to have you shot dead."

"He ain't been contaminated by *nothin'*," Hall asserted. He was having trouble breathing, getting the words out.

"Not *yet*. You, Mr. Hall, are about to be killed first—"

A slot opened in the wall below the bookshelf, the barrel of a rifle jutting through ominously.

McGovern held up his hand in a gesture of *wait*. "You will be wounded and allowed to bleed to death. This will give you time to transfer. If you do, that will provide us a reason to keep Mr. Dukani alive. If you die with it still inside you, he will be killed. Now, you have one minute, then you will be wounded. How long it takes your life to drain out in a pool of blood on the floor I cannot be sure."

Aggeous struggled to his feet to watch, still clutching the black box as if it were precious.

"I *don't* wanna die," Dukani pleaded to the men through the glass. "Please don't let me die," he begged Hall.

"It's not worth livin'," Hall gasped. "They'll never let you do what you need—they'll keep you alive and study you, cut your fingers off, drain off your will to live—"

"Do what they say!" Dukani demanded. "Don't want bein' killed *right now!*"

Hall shook his head—

Boom!

The shot echoed in the small space. Hall screamed in pain, clutching desperately at where his leg shattered just above the ankle, already bleeding badly.

Dukani was crying. "Do what he say! *Please* don't let them to shoot me."

Hall gestured for the Haitian to come close, then hugged him tightly, hanging on with uncharacteristic strength. He convulsed several times before suddenly slumping limp, head lolling back, a vacant stare in his eyes. He no longer struggled to breathe.

Mr. Hall's twenty-some-year hell was over.

"Please don't be shooting no more!" Dukani pleaded to the men in the glass, shaking Hall in vain, trying to awaken the old man. "*Please!* He be trying to do it. He *tryin'?*"

"I believe he did it," McGovern said quietly. "You will be allowed to live until such time as we can be sure." Turning to Aggeous, noticing the fat doctor was holding his breath and was clearly shaken by what he'd just witnessed, the colonel asked, "Isn't there something you want to do with the body right away?"

Aggeous shook his head. "No, once he transferred, the core was gone. All the little tendrils are evaporated by now, too. Trace elements are all that's left, and they'd be gone by the time I got him to the lab. I'll check to be sure, but there's no hurry."

McGovern nodded. "I trust you are finished with the black box?"

Aggeous seemed to remember he had it. "Oh! Yes." He replaced it in the briefcase.

"Mr. Hall apparently recognized it as something significant, didn't he?"

"Yes. That's what I wanted to see—if it seemed to be important."

"Why do you think he reacted only to the second one?"

Aggeous looked at the old man lying in a heap where he'd fallen to the floor, a crimson puddle forming underneath and soaking his clothing. He looked at Dukani cowering in the corner, the Haitian still in tears, terrified to get near the body, confused by what he'd seen. "The first one come from Watterson, didn't it?"

McGovern nodded.

Aggeous rubbed his eyes. "I think you recovered a fake."

*   *   *

"It's your call, Eugene," Durbett intoned. "You looked pretty bad there for a while. It'll only cost us a day to swing through Alabama and let the doc give you the go-over."

Eugene seemed to be thinking about it. He was the only passenger in Flynn Durbett's covered pickup as they headed north through Mississippi, approaching Crystal Springs, just minutes away from Jackson. "You said you needed to get back to McEwen."

"We're comin' up to I-20; now's the time if we're goin'. Look, you was sick, hearing noises and ringing sounds and people callin' your name. It could've been nerve gas or maybe you was drugged or something—I don't know what, but *you* was the only one affected. Maybe it *is* something we need to be worried about. Maybe Doc can get samples or run it down before it's all out of your system."

"What if it was the alien?"

Durbett shook his head. "I don't know nothin' about that. What I do know is, government's got all kinds of chemicals and nerve agents—most of 'em tested on they own military troops and captured refugees being held in camps—and I need to know what we's up against."

"I'm all right now. What'd you wanna get back to McEwen for?"

"To search what's left of the Watterson house. Maybe see if I can find that black box you was talkin' about."

"What box?"

"You don't remember?"

Eugene shook his head. "You mean that gun-cleaning box?"

"That's what you called it. But when I made you describe it, it didn't sound like nothin' that had to do with cleaning guns. You said Norm showed it to you—do you remember if he said anything about it?"

"Just to remember it, that I might need it some day. He made sure we all knew where it was in case something ever happened to him. He said protect it."

"Do *what* with it?"

Eugene furrowed his brow, deep in thought. Then he shrugged, shaking his head slowly. "I don't know. Guess he figured I'd know—or maybe he was planning to tell us—" He hesitated, feeling that pang from Russell's death, remembering that *us* was now a *me*. "—Planning to explain after we was trained," he finished quietly.

"Why haven't you brought this up before?"

Eugene shrugged again. "I don't know. I didn't think of it. I guess I just figured everything in the house was burned up."

Durbett considered that a moment, then shook his head. "No. I don't think so. Norman would've kept it in a fire-proof safe or box if it was that vulnerable. What you say makes it sound important to him."

"But the box it was in was just made of wood."

"Well, that's why we left Marshall behind to take care of business—so we can head back. I wanna get you at least closer to Doc and, if you really are better, see if I can find something in that burnt-up house."

"You mean that box might still be there?"

Durbett shrugged, taking his eyes off the road long enough to glance over with raised eyebrows. "Won't know unless I look."

Eugene rode along quietly for several minutes, trying to remember what he'd said during his delirium, why he'd even thought about it.

"One mile to the exit," Durbett prodded. "How do you feel?"

"I'm fine."

"It's your call, Eugene."

"Let's try to find that box."

*   *   *

There were three of them, each pushed by three uniformed men. They looked like oversized coffin vaults with gurney-wheels, all black, festooned with environmental-control monitors and locking mechanisms. The entourage was led by another man in some sort of white lab coat, a mask around his neck.

Down the ramp from the back of the truck, into a nondescript building, met by Colonel McGovern, down to the secured bio-med lab of *Program Invigil*. The colonel ignored the NCOs' attempts to salute and pause at attention. He was losing patience with all that posturing.

"What?! What's this? What's going on?" Dr. Aggeous was caught off guard. He had the nude body of Mr. Billy Hall spread on a stainless-steel rim-top table, preparing to begin autopsy.

McGovern motioned him into the hallway. The man in the white coat entered the lab, waving in the first group of three with their full-body specimen/quarantine transport.

"You've already told me you would find nothing in Mr. Hall's body," McGovern said. "So your examination and oral report are complete." He left the fat doctor leaning against the wall shaking his head and watching as the old man's body was loaded into the carrier.

"What's the other two for?" Aggeous demanded. Peering into the doorway, he found his answer. The remains of both MPs, still in their sealed liquid containers, were being loaded into the other two carriers. "Listen!" Aggeous hissed, trying to motion McGovern down the hall out of earshot of the others.

The colonel, a mask of impatience, relented and followed him a dozen meters. "What?" he asked quietly.

"You don't know what you're doing. You're compromising security here! What—don't you trust—?"

"Listen, *Doctor*, you've already said you cannot learn any more from these specimens. It is my prerogative—though I owe you no explanation—to confirm that independently, and to consider that a researcher of different disposition may approach this problem from a different point of view. I cannot afford to rely solely on *your* pronouncements."

"And you don't think you can trust me!" Aggeous wheezed.

McGovern spread his hands. "You admit you withhold information from me."

"Higgins *wanted* it that way. He was specific about what you could be told and *when*."

"And *when* is it I'm to receive the rest of my briefing?"

Aggeous thought it over a moment. "When you can tell me what happened to those MPs *without* outside help—when *you* can figure it out. Higgins wanted to make sure you could reason this thing out yourself before being trusted completely."

McGovern was unimpressed. "Dr. Aggeous," he started condescendingly, like explaining the art of shoe-tying to a grade-schooler, "I will pursue my own lines of inquiry independently. In the meantime, I suggest you rethink your level of cooperation. My patience grows short—and very soon I anticipate seeking *other* ways to motivate you to divulge what you know about this invasion." He paused to let that sink in. "And do not try to leave this base. See the housing office to learn where your newly assigned billet is. You are not being confined to one of the detention cells—yet—but you will *not* be allowed to leave." McGovern turned on his heel and followed the specimen entourage down the wing toward the elevator.

Aggeous stared after him, wheezing, too mad to know what to say. He caught his breath and punched in his security codes to re-enter the lab—and discovered they no longer worked.

McGovern paused and turned. "By the way, I'm going to want to know more about this so-called nucleotide marker you injected into Lt. Col. Poole—if *I* don't get it figured out sooner *without* you."

They boarded a short cargo-plane flight to Ft. Donelson where McGovern's entourage was met by Major General Ashe and his aide-de-camp.

"It'll be another day before all the detention measures you wanted are in place," the general reported. "Figure about two days before the rest of the lab stuff gets here from Washington. I got a problem with some of the appropriations—"

McGovern cut him off, instructing the team to load up and wait while he went inside to talk with the general.

"You got the forms?"

The general pushed a sheaf across the desk. McGovern wrote in a series of appropriation codes from memory.

Ashe smiled. "That would be that magic wand I needed you to wave. Where's it get its power?"

McGovern certainly wasn't obligated to answer, but Ashe could find out with enough persistence anyway. "It's a DOD budget amendment—" He was referring to the Department of Defense. "—to the '91 fiscal budget through FEMA. The sub-category is publicity-sensitive national emergencies."

"You mean like a plague or something that might cause panic," Ashe tossed out for reaction.

"That would be one example," McGovern replied non-committally. He finished the paperwork, stood and saluted with exaggerated aplomb. "Now if you'll excuse me—"

"One more thing, Colonel. We've had to mobilize a lot of resources. Done a pretty good job keeping it under our hats, but still, you know there's gonna be talk among the troops. I learned a long time ago that, if there's going to be rumors anyway, sometimes it's best to be the person floating 'em. That's usually better than leaving it to their own imaginations."

McGovern paused to think, then betrayed a hint of smile. The paunchy general proved a bit more savvy than he'd thought. "Underground invasion sympathizers," he offered. "The med stuff's just a precaution. Don't let it get too much attention."

General Ashe nodded. He knew how to play that. Still, as he walked the colonel out to the pair of Chinook CH-47s that would carry body boxes and entourage to the old Cumberland Sanitarium grounds, he didn't seem entirely satisfied. He'd cast into the weeds and the colonel had stolen his bait.

Several MPs met the choppers, then led the group toward the old medical building where equipment and supplies were being unloaded from numerous trucks. McGovern allowed himself to be taken on a fast tour of the perimeter, inspecting the newly erected series of electrified fences and razor wire. He looked over the construction going on inside the largest of the resident wards. He noted that plumbing was being fitted just one step ahead of walls going in, creating a series of self-contained sound-proof isolation cells—enough for sixty-four prisoners at one-per.

McGovern was pleased with the office that had been set up for him—with six adjacent smaller ones for senior staff. Lt. Col. Dunkin plus Majors Rawley and Salisbury were already at work. Lt. Col. Poole would arrive from Washington later—he was undergoing a very thorough toxicological physical in a secure lab at Walter Reed.

"Major weapons-supply going through Honduras—fishing boats near the Bay Islands docking at San Pedro Sula—has some kind of connection with U.S. operatives also supplying militias in the Southeast U.S.," Salisbury reported. "CIA is behind it. They're more worried about covering how it's run from *our* end than where the weapons are going. That's all I got that had any kind of militia angle."

McGovern tapped his fingers together, considering this information. "Okay, drop it. Keep monitoring for references, but don't show too much interest in this one."

"Ready for sixty-four detainees by tomorrow," Rawley summarized. "You want to proceed with another forty right away?"

McGovern nodded. "Yes, but hold up after that for now. I don't expect to be rounding them up very quickly—or keeping them around long," he added as an afterthought. "Bio-med set-up's going as fast as possible?"

Rawley bobbed his head. "You wanted it kept low-key. I don't see how I could possibly rush it any more without stirring up too much excitement."

McGovern was satisfied. "Keep apace."

"I got a couple of items of interest," Dunkin reported. "It took me a while to overcome a lot of resistance." He spread his hands in a *what gives?* and shrugged. "You believe that?—from those schmucks at the FBI?" Getting no reaction from McGovern, he continued, "Anyway, I managed to cut through witness protection and—guess what?—Jolene Carter jumped. Your black teenager's nowhere in sight."

McGovern showed more than surprise.

"FBI said it's not their get," Dunkin continued. "If she wants to dump the program and light out on her own, then they're not responsible for protecting her anymore. I definitely detected an attitude from the guy—like she wasn't theirs in the first place, so good riddance."

"What next?"

"I wasn't sure if you'd want to chase—"

"Have them find her—*now!* Put some fear of God in 'em—like they never should've lost her and you can't even *begin* to tell them how high up people are pissed off about it."

"Yes, sir."

McGovern waved off the formality. "What else you got on her? Wasn't her father—no, stepfather—down there in Waverly?"

Dunkin flipped quickly through a file and confirmed it.

"Have him checked out thoroughly—independent of FBI running down leads on her. Come to think of it, don't put FBI on her until tomorrow. Have *him* vanish first—and bring him here. He can break in cell number one while we try to flush her out. What else do you have?"

"Only one more item. An ATF agent chasing militia-tied gun runners in Texas disappeared. Name of Joe Pennington. Ain't *our* problem, but you wanted to hear anything about militia ties."

McGovern thought about that one. "I'd like to know more—but if you nose around any, somebody'll suspect *we* had something to do with him disappearing." He shook his head. "Let it die, but keep your eyes and ears open. I have one more thing for you—highest priority." He buzzed out to his aide-de-camp and had the briefcase brought in, opening it in front of the assembled group to reveal the two black boxes. "One of these is fake—the one Watterson had. He probably had a *real* one, too. We need to run it down. Start by searching his burned-out house in case it was missed by our agents, then search his grounds. If no luck, we need to start rounding up his cohorts and widening the net."

"That could be big-scale," Dunkin cautioned.

McGovern sat back and nodded. "Yeah, it looks like maybe *the war on drugs* with some search-and-seizures may have to be stepped up around Waverly and throughout the south."

"Whatever it takes to recover the box, eh?"

McGovern nodded. "I have a feeling we're not safe until we find it."

The group filed out to get back to work, McGovern watching them go. *Not safe at all . . .*

*   *   *

Licia hurried outside to meet them, running around the passenger side of Flynn's truck to fling open the door. "Hi, Mr. Durbett! *Eugene!* How you doin', Hon? You have a good trip?"

Eugene smiled. "If you don't count being sick half the time and being dragged around all night gettin' no sleep." He climbed out to an enveloping hug and—surprise bonus!—a big ol' kiss on the cheek. He'd been feeling queasy even during the last leg of the long drive—despite the okey-dokey image he'd portrayed for Flynn—but he really was starting to feel pretty good after all.

It was like coming *home* after a long, arduous journey.

Home?

"I bet you guys is hungry!" she announced, turning Eugene enough to walk him up the steps to the big front porch without actually letting go.

Durbett carried some boxes and Eugene's duffel bag inside while Licia started frying bologna sandwiches—lightly toasted bread with too much mayo and thick slices of beefsteak tomato. She grinned when Eugene's eyes lit up—she must have figured it was one of his favorites—as his days-gone appetite rushed back. He'd not eaten more than a few bites since—well, what happened out on the boat.

Durbett pulled up a chair and flashed a knowing smile at the young feller being fussed over by the pretty girl. "Anything important happen while we was gone?"

"Just a letter from Lloyd." She looked grim for a moment while she fetched it from the letter box on the wall by the phone. "He's being court-martialed. Says he'll be lucky if all he gets is a dishonorable."

"Damn!" Durbett examined the envelope. He answered Eugene's questioning look by explaining that Lloyd Stewart was cousin of Marshall and Licia Emery, Army NCO working his way into covert urban-assault operations. Durbett liked having an ally inside—one who could be counted on to turn coat and take a lot of buddies with him if it ever came down to Army troops versus civilians. Two years younger than Marshall, the cousins had similar dispositions, though Lloyd was probably a mite smarter and more reasonable in his outlook.

Licia's attentiveness—offering and bringing, getting him another napkin, refilling his glass, worrying if the bologna was singed enough—reminded Eugene of Mrs. Watterson. This seemed different, though—not like a mom. Licia was like having a . . . *girlfriend?* Yeah, he felt much better.

And he was home.

The sound of crunching gravel signaled the arrival of Jake Coleman. Tracey, the young blond in tight jeans who'd helped Licia the other night, showed up with him.

"Damn!" was Jake's reaction when he read the letter. "He'll be lucky if he don't do some time in the brig or at hard labor."

The women hustled up more sandwiches and put out another bag of chips—Tracey fussing over Jake like Licia over Eugene. Both seemed to know not to intrude when the men got into a serious-thinking mode.

"He wasn't specific," Durbett commented, "about what the charges was—*dancin' with a sixty*—but it sounds like blowing off some steam just *playin'* with one, not *stealing* one."

"Or *more* than one," Jake grinned. "Lloyd never did believe in doing anything small-scale."

Licia turned on the radio—one of the smaller country-music stations carrying a syndicated program out of Nashville. That made both Jake and Flynn check their watches. "Another fifteen minutes or so until the announcement," Jake pronounced.

"We need to put together a night excursion," Flynn told him. "Six guys—maybe seven—night vision, small tools, defense. We need to look for something in the Watterson house."

Eugene knew what they were talking about. The women feigned indifference, settling down to eat their own sandwiches.

Jake got up to start calling people. "I'll get you some of the best."

"Not *you*, though," Flynn added. "Somebody good needs to stay—" He nodded slightly in Eugene's direction.

"You really think—?"

"I *suspect*—and that's enough not to take a chance. Besides, there's no accounting for what somebody *else* might think."

Eugene bristled at the notion of needing to be watched over by bigger, better-trained men—even though he secretly found it reassuring.

Jake made a series of calls; the group would assemble at Emery's at 8:30 that night.

Yessiree, the radio DJ intoned. *They was a sangin' sweet words about takin' a walk in the bee-yootiful Tennessee countryside where it shore is purty this time o' year. Of course, I had to tell the wife's mother to quit walkin' near my neighbor's cow pasture. Three times a calf done got confused who was its mama and followed her home. Then they let the bull out and he took one look at her and knocked down the fence and ain't been seen since! But really, you know I love my mother-in-law. She gets us free veal! This next song's about a feller done found out . . .*

"Mother-in-law three," Jake pronounced before making one last call. "M-I-L-3," he added, apparently referring to some code relayed in the radio announcer's joke.

Though Licia tried to steer him toward a shower and relaxing for a while, Eugene followed Jake and Durbett into the den where Marshall kept a small computer set up inside an old roll-top desk. Jake booted up while the other two watched over his shoulders. The women cleaned up in the kitchen, whispering and giggling. What snatches Eugene could hear suggested Tracey had managed to pout enough the night before to get Jake to use the "L" word, plus she'd figured out Licia was sweet on the fifteen-year-old fugitive and had all kinds of experienced advice to offer.

Jake passed through a series of chat-rooms, then sub-directed into a blind newsline, passwording M-I-L-3 to access a scrollable screen containing a militia newsletter. Across the bottom of the monitor appeared a series of shapes with numbers inside them. Each shape corresponded to a segment of the tic-tac-toe symbol: a box for the center, boxes open on one side for tops and bottoms, two sides for corners. Jake printed the screen so Durbett could translate the code—using the daily cipher grid designated by the DJ's on-air joke—while Jake read the various one- or two-paragraph newsletter articles.

"Couple of weapons arrests—nothing suspicious about 'em. Another property seizure—supposedly taxes. Two property seizures over alleged drug trafficking; couple of local meeting announcements; another cow mutilation and black choppers in Alabama— *Here's* something close to home."

Durbett looked up. "Close to here?"

Eugene watched in fascination, learning and remembering. He kept quiet.

"Yeah, there's reports of activity at and around the old sanitarium up the Cumberland River. There's been airlifts of equipment and supplies, plus covered-truck caravans and movement of personnel from Ft. Donelson and somewhere south. There's perimeter patrols, so nobody's been close enough for a good look. Two guys pretending to fish the river from a bass boat was encouraged to move on downstream. The roads in have been gated."

"Another detention camp?" Durbett mused.

"Sounds like it—but why? And why the rush job?"

Jake pulled a binder from the desk, flipping past clippings and plats and newsletters and computer print-outs until he found what he wanted. It was a series of maps marking the locations of secret detention facilities based on information collected through the militia network, informants, reports from other patriotic or watchdog organizations, and even official government documents obtained through back-door routes—usually in FEMA manuals. "If it's a big one—like thirty- to forty-thousand capacity—that would make at least twenty-four of 'em in the U.S."

The map Eugene could see showed a concentration of stars marking locations in the Midwest, but they stretched nationwide and included Alaska and Hawaii.

Durbett paused from his ciphering to look over Jake's shoulder again. "There's already some close by—especially in Ohio." He rubbed his head in thought. "I doubt they're using them for much right now—certainly can't have 'em full up—"

"What about boat people and what-not?" Jake wondered. "Cubans and Haitians and Asians and even Mexicans—?"

"They've made such a big deal of where they *do* put 'em—like Guantanamo—to draw attention away from the possibility they may have even more inland. I'd be inclined to believe it's *possible*—but people would've noticed more. No, I expect most of what's on your map there is NSA and that whatever's goin' on in Cumberland ain't."

"NSA?" Jake questioned. "Aren't the detention centers controlled by U.S. Army Reserves through the Military Police Prisoner of War Command at Livonia, Michigan?"

"Yes, but NSA gives the marching orders. Army's not supposed to be involved unless the conditions of Title II in that 1950 Internal Security Act are met."

Jake flipped through more until he found photocopies of key pages from Section 102, the detention statute as authorized by Congress. Summarizing aloud, he stated, "Supposed to be if there is an invasion of U.S. territory or possessions—"

"Possessions is a broad term that stretches all the way 'round the world," Durbett mumbled.

"—Or a declaration of war by Congress, or insurrection in the U.S. in aid of a foreign enemy. The attorney general or his designates could detain anyone who *may* conspire—"

"Which is *anybody*," Durbett interjected.

"—Who *may* consipire in espionage or sabotage until the emergency status has been terminated."

"Which is why when *any* kind of domestic violence occurs, they immediately hint at some sort of suspected foreign terrorism or try to hang it on domestic militias so they can push Congress to expand their abilities to spy and wiretap and deport and detain U.S. citizens. There'll be a major foreign terror act on U.S. soil sooner than later, after which peole will let them shred the Constitution out of fear."

Eugene finally spoke up, wondering what they meant by detention camps. "Prisoner of war places right in our country?"

"We have a *history* of that, son," Jake explained while Durbett went back to ciphering. He flipped through more documents for reference, showing Eugene various bits of information. "February 19, 1942. Executive order 9066 under President Roosevelt and ratified by Congress March 21st of that year. It authorized the internment of people of Japanese ancestry. By that August, they had 110,000 of 'em—more than 70,000 legal U.S. citizens—imprisoned in detention camps. Seized their property, shut down their businesses and took their jobs, separated families, some people even think they used 'em for the same kinds of medical and warfare research the Nazis was doing. People convicted of no crime—just being a *suspected* possible threat to the U.S. government."

"We learned about World War II in school, but they didn't talk nothin' about that," Eugene pointed out.

"Ain't no secret—you'll find it in any good history book or college class, but they sure don't like to bring it up." Jake continued, "In 1950, that emergency act Flynn mentioned gave 'em power to set up all kinds of facilities—most of which we probably don't know about— because they's underground. They was so many urban riots back in '67 and '68, that they started using the camps to hold militant colored folks. Once word of that started to spread, they was a big public backlash and Congress wound up repealing the act—when?"

Without looking up, Durbett answered, "1971. But all those facilities are still there—"

"And still being maintained—if not fully used," Jake added. "We *do* know about some underground close by that seem to get a lot of activity: one in the Kennesaw Mountain outside Marietta; under the Green Mountains near Huntsville's Redstone Arsenal; Franklin County, Alabama near Gravel Hill—"

"Jake's people watch *that* one real close," Flynn interjected.

"Because it ain't too far from our own," Jake said mysteriously. "Anyway, they's one near Highway 77 at Elbert County, Georgia, too, that Emery's cousin Lloyd did some training at once."

"How can they keep these places secret?" Eugene wondered.

"They don't. Just most people don't care and don't understand. The camps is mostly in out-of-the way places, always near a large body of fresh water, a railroad line, a major highway, and some kind of airport—all so they's ready for fast massive use."

"Are they still building 'em?" Eugene wondered.

Jake flipped over to a section marked *Operation Rex 84*. "This was authorized under President Reagan. It set up twenty-three of the biggest camps ever—most could hold more than 40,000 people. There was an appropriation to build twenty more in the '90-'91 budget. That's since been canceled, but the camps all still exist. Plus, there's hundreds of small ones, mostly marked *Zoo Annex*, a lot of 'em not much more than open fields with perimeter security. Some, especially in the Allegheny Forest, have towers even though they're marked *Animal Movement Control* and there's one says *International Releafing Project*. Plus, there's a prisoner-transfer terminal outside Oklahoma City, though that's been shut down—moved probably—since the bombing."

"So—what?" Eugene demanded. "They gonna lock up all the citizens?"

Durbett interrupted, "Not likely, Eugene, though some extremists are afraid of that. No, they'll really use 'em if there's a war or invasion, but they can also use 'em to control dissidents and possible uprisings—like local militias defending their rights from government or invaders. Some think they'll use 'em when Congress finally trashes the Second Amendment and outlaws private ownership of guns or if their war on drugs goes the next step, tobacco or even alcohol again."

"Won't be those two," Jake pointed out. "They need the tax money to support the government."

"A lot of people," Durbett explained, "mostly militia members, believe it's part of a conspiracy for foreign invasion of America, like by the U.N. or something under the banner *Peacekeeping Forces*, to establish what has come to be known as The New World Order."

"Which ain't too far-fetched," Jake pointed out.

Eugene sat quietly, thinking it over while Jake carefully put the binder away.

"Damn," Flynn Durbett breathed when he finished his ciphering. "It's about pressure being applied through ATF in Texas and Louisiana over the disappearance of an agent. There are dozens of reports of people being detained and harassed for information. This is unusual for a lone agent disappearing—to make a visible spectacle of it. You'd think they'd investigate quietly."

"Either he was *very* important or there's new pressure on for some reason and he's the excuse to stir up some shit," Jake observed. Watching Durbett for his reaction, he asked, "Who was it?"

Durbett rubbed his head again. "Went under the name Joe Pennington." Looking carefully at Jake, he added, "I expect he's at the bottom of the gulf right about now."

"Clean?"

"Far as I know," Durbett confirmed cryptically.

Eugene watched, eyes wide, but kept quiet.

Jake shook his head, then logged into an e-mail access route and called for an associate in Texas. Using M-I-L-3 to ID the appropriate password, he asked his friend about anything new on the missing-Pennington ruckus. The reply stated that nothing else had happened, assuring Jake that he would be kept informed.

Jake and Flynn both breathed relief at the all-clear. That meant their operation was proceeding apace.

Eugene yawned long and hard, then looked around for a place to sit.

Flynn seemed lost in thought for a moment while Jake logged off. Finally, he said, "Look, I need to go take care of something. I'll be back in about three hours—by 8:30." He checked his watch. "You stay here," he told Jake, nodding toward Eugene to indicate he wanted somebody around who could protect the possible target. "Make him get some rest—he hardly slept on the trip, and was sick to-boot. I think it may be time to move him."

Eugene was barely following the conversation, struggling not to nod off. "Bye, Flynn," he waved as the grim-faced mercenary headed out into the late-afternoon sunshine.

Licia took over, promising she'd see Eugene got some rest, leading him upstairs to one of the bedrooms.

Tracey worked her way into Jake's lap, flirting and nuzzling, then lightly kissing. Shortly, she had him up dancing to some slow country music. They sashayed each other into the back bedroom of the ground floor.

Licia led a suddenly very-sleepy Eugene upstairs and into the bathroom. She set out shampoo and towel, urging him to get a cool shower before settling down. He yawned and scratched his chest, waiting for her to leave, but she teased him about being so tired he'd slip down the drain, then helped him off with his shirt.

He sat on the toilet lid to pull off his shoes and socks, then when he stood, she had his pants unfastened before he realized it. Embarrassed, he pulled away, chuckling to cover his awkwardness. "I'm not *that* sleepy," he protested weakly.

She smiled sweetly, her face very close to his, and whispered, "Hurry now, I'll be right back with some clean drawers for ya." She turned on the shower and slipped out of the bathroom, pulling the door mostly closed behind her.

Eugene dropped his clothes and stepped into the shower, pausing to adjust the water temperature. Concerned she would come back too soon, he washed his hair and rinsed his body as fast as possible, suddenly very much wide awake. He turned off the water and dried himself. He was wrapping the damp towel around his waist when she slipped back in with a pair of his shorts. He took them, then hesitated awkwardly again, so she kissed him on the cheek and eased back out from the bathroom. A few seconds later, towel hung to dry and shampoo put away, he stepped out.

He allowed her to lead him to the bedroom, turn down the sheet, and guide him into bed. He noticed she'd changed into a loose pullover and wondered if she wore anything under it. He found himself quite aware of her scent, her long, silky hair, his own pounding heart.

She sat on the side of the bed and fidgeted with the sheet, straightened his still-damp hair, gently patted his chest. "Are you okay, Eugene?" she whispered.

He shrugged, nervous, alert.

"I get scared sometimes," she said quietly. "These guys is into serious stuff—dangerous stuff. The whole time you was gone I worried about you."

"I can take care of myself," he said defensively—but without conviction. Being cool, acting macho, one of the guys, bigger than you really are—all that public-image-at-school stuff—it didn't seem to matter around her. Especially not right then. She'd seen him cry before, seen him beaten down, seen him scared. And she didn't seem to think any less of him. "I couldn't do it," he said suddenly, surprised at himself.

"They wanted you to do a *hit?*"

Eugene just nodded, turning his eyes away.

"Who was it?"

"Some ATF agent. They dropped him in the ocean."

"Who wanted you to do it? Flynn?"

Eugene shook his head no. "*He's* the one told your brother to leave me alone."

She eased down and propped her head on the side of his pillow, her hand on his arm.

"Flynn's job used to be goin' around the world killin' people for money," he said, shaking his head at the wonder of it. "I think he used to believe it was for America and freedom."

"These guys take that pretty seriously," she said. They were both looking at the ceiling. "I never thought much of it until agents killed my daddy." She shook her head again.

Eugene wanted to learn more about it, but she didn't offer to explain. He could hear her breathing becoming more labored, felt her trembling slightly. He turned his face enough to see tears in her eyes.

"It made Marshall crazy," she sniffed. "He's been tryin' to get even ever since." A tear threaded down the side of her cheek, a wet spot on the pillow.

He put his hand on hers and squeezed. "What about you?"

"They's not a minute since then that I ain't been scared."

He nodded silently. Barely audible, he whispered, "Like since Wattersons was killed." He felt like crying, too, but something held him back.

"Eugene? Do you believe the alien stuff—I mean, being inside you and all?"

He shrugged. "Don't know *what* to believe. Flynn done said don't matter if it's true or not if *other* people think it's so."

"But if you had to say—"

He paused for a long time, then said, "I didn't much at first. Now sometimes I think maybe I do. Is that all right?"

"Sure. Maybe it *is* true. *I* sure don't know."

"What if I do?—have one I mean."

She shrugged, reaching up to wipe a tear from her cheek. "Don't change nothin' about what I *think* of you."

"Good . . . good. Um, what if I'd done that agent?"

"Would you a had to? I mean, did he *have* to die?"

"Marshall thought so, to protect us."

"Do *you* think so?"

"I don't know. I guess if I thought I *had* to for savin' myself . . . or *you*," he whispered, "then maybe I wouldn't have no choice."

"Who killed him?"

The image of what had happened flooded Eugene's mind. He started to tremble a little, too, but he didn't care if she could tell it scared him. His eyes felt wet. He wiped his face, determined not to betray the intensity of his feelings. But then he didn't care about that, either. "Marshall shot him in the head—" His voice cracked, his throat constricted. He choked out, "—in the face."

"Know why you *didn't* do it?"

"Not strong enough." There. He said it.

"*Too* strong. You ain't like that." She was crying openly, squeezing his hand, cuddling closer.

He put his arms around her, holding tightly, her soft hair in his face, her trembling body pressed close. "Then what *am* I like?"

"When the time comes, you'll know."

"*We'll* know."

They cuddled like that for a while, he stroking her hair, she caressing his hand, his arm.

She was watching him breathe softly as he drifted. She put her hand on his chest, settled her face against his shoulder.

Yes, they were both scared. But right then, everything seemed okay.

If only for a little while.

He roused just briefly, only for a few seconds, just long enough to realize she was there, asleep, close. He kissed her hair, softly put his hand in hers.

She didn't wake, but he was pretty sure he felt her squeeze back.

A mosquito buzzed around in the humid, evening heat, a cricket chirping from under the porch, the receding clackety of a freight train heading toward Waverly.

*   *   *

Flynn Durbett made the call from a pay phone at the Dickson exit off the interstate. "Why is ATF nosing public about their man Pennington disappearing?"

"He get in your way?"

"Got in *your* way, too. After four went through Honduras for *you*, number five was *mine*. He was plannin' to bust it. You're supposed to keep these assholes clear of me."

"It's coming from somewhere else. Don't know where or why."

"Get it shut down. Now."

"Count on it."

"Not counting on nothin'. Coulda got me killed. No more's moving until I see it's settled down."

"I can get the investigation quashed—"

"Not enough. I wanna know *where* it's comin' from. Did you find out who done Watterson?"

"Same thing, Flynn. Dead end."

"It's probably same as was tryin' to bust *me*—and it's whoever's going balls-out on an alien hunt right now."

"*Illegal* aliens—?"

"Extra-terrestrial."

The voice on the other end paused, then exhaled. "The *real* deal?"

"Hell, I don't know, but I got stuck protecting one of 'em."

"You keeping it tight?"

"No. And I'm not trying to, either. I'm getting too old for all this bullshit. Used to be, everything was run central and *you* could keep control. Now it's too big, too splintered, too many crazies on both sides of the fence. I owe Watterson—he's the only debt I ain't fully paid. He told me if it come down to this, trust whoever was left. Right now, that's a fifteen year-old kid too scared to pull a trigger. I'm gonna let it play out."

"Could be risky."

Durbett snorted derisively. "What ain't? Listen, you want any more runs, you get me some answers—or else I'll be too busy getting the answers myself to do *you* any good."

*   *   *

Too much moonlight made it dangerous out in the open, so they kept under the tree-line, crossed through scrub wherever they could, and moved into position slowly, pausing every ninety seconds to listen. They wore infrared night goggles with small built-in projectors. Three did the actual search carrying hand-held infrared lights for extra visibility. One man was stationed just off the road east—toward McEwen—while another covered possible intrusion from the creek. Flynn Durbett covered the west end of the road toward Highway 13. They all carried PPDs tuned to the same frequency, keyed for vibration without sound.

The threesome searching the ruins made use of a satchel of tools that had been dropped in nearby brush twenty minutes earlier, usually for prying apart tangles of boards, sometimes for winching up collapsed areas to search underneath.

They rummaged through melted and fused and crushed and mangled items—childrens' toys, kitchenware, tools and household doo-hickeys, burnt and water-logged clothing . . . They found a small fireproof box that proved easily picked open. It contained personal papers, Norman's military medals, some photos of the family. They kept it to examine the papers later, pass along the mementos. Maybe Flynn would want something.

Or maybe Eugene. In the eerie green glow of infrared, they recognized a boy of about seven or eight who must be young Weisman, his arm around another, slightly smaller boy—probably young Watterson. Clad in wet shorts, they were squinting from the bright sun, standing in ankle-deep creek, the path toward home in the background.

They found no mysterious black box. If one were there, it must have been extremely well-hidden, its presence not betrayed by anything like a firebox or safe. Maybe it was buried somewhere nearby, maybe safely deposited somewhere farther away, maybe overlooked in the soot and smoke-stinking ashes and debris.

They were running out of places to search, so three fast and two slow presses on a PPD alerted the sentinels that two were leaving to clean up. Using plastic garbage bags and rubber bands from the satchel, the pair encased their feet and lower legs, then walked quietly down the path to the creek and washed in the ice-cold water. They stepped up onto the bank and rolled up the bags, then headed back up the path. As they approached the road, they felt it—a single PPD vibration.

Intruder. A brief burst of dit-dats told them it came from the west. It must be Durbett sending the warning. They set the bags down, readied their weapons, and took positions about fifty feet apart in the high grass along the road.

The one closest to Highway 13 stood diagonally across from where he knew Durbett would be. After a moment, he saw him raise up just perceptibly, signaling three intruders, to shut off projectors, to wait and let them pass. The plan was to surround them, then determine what kind of support they may have before making a move.

Or withdrawing.

Dressed in black, the intruders also wore infrared gear very similar to the militia's. They were moving along the edge of the road purposefully, if not recklessly. Obviously not expecting any company, they worried mostly about potential road traffic. Two carried bags. All three had PPDs attached to their vests. They were heading straight for the Watterson ruins.

Their infrared projectors worked as beacons to the militia viewers, invisible light shining brightly in the masks of their enemy.

*   *   *

Flynn Durbett watched the intruders from his vantage point crouched in the brush. He couldn't tell who they represented; he saw no markings or insignia of any kind. He figured it a good bet they were after a little black box, too. That meant *they* must not have it, either—but knew it had been there and still wanted it. Maybe even knew *why*.

Flynn wondered just where in blazes it might be hidden.

Or who *else* might have it.

*   *   *

Eugene roused awake first. It looked dark out. The house was quiet except for faint talking downstairs—probably Jake and Tracey. A cacophony of locusts and crickets and all manner of critters sang through the screened window. A faint slash of moonlight cut across the bed, making Licia's hair shine.

She was breathing softly, snuggled against him, one hand lovingly—protectively?—on his chest. Her pullover had hiked up just enough to answer his earlier curiosity. That was *all* she wore.

He was tempted to pull away, but lying so close felt too good. He could feel her warm breath on his neck, her breast pressing against his arm in gentle rhythm. He savored the scent of her hair and of her body in the humid, late-August heat.

He remembered their groggy conversation, sharing their fears and feelings, talking until there was nothing to say, then just lying there together until they'd both faded away.

She'd been the one person who worried about him from the moment she first saw him. She always believed him, and believed *in* him. She tried very hard to show she cared without overwhelming him, somehow sensing the moments he'd needed reassuring, knowing not to smother when he'd needed to flex, to struggle to fit in, to define himself among new people and an unfamiliar world. She seemed always ready with something to eat, a cold drink, a cool shower and clean clothes and place to sleep. A smile meant only for him.

And he understood.

This was not like having Russell for a best friend. It wasn't like the good moments he'd had growing up with Aunt Willow, cuddled in her lap or being tucked in at night. It wasn't like going around with Flynn Durbett and being treated with just as much respect as the older guys who had all the training and experience.

She gradually roused, gently stroking his chest, nuzzling against his neck, breathing harder, her hand moving down.

He turned his face, felt her lips brushing his cheek, against his mouth, kissing in a way that felt *very* personal.

She guided his hands, trembled her approval, helped him with his shorts, with her pullover.

Several years ago this mystery of life had started to reveal itself for the awkward teen. He'd decided back then he wanted to be in love whenever *it* happened. So there, in the faint light of rising moon, the slightest hint of cool breeze floating in across the fields, crickets encouraging him, Tracey down below probably watching Jake sleep and wondering how things were going upstairs, Eugene pondered just for an instant if this really was *it*, if he *loved* Licia Emery with her beautiful hair and sparkling eyes and sweet smile . . .

"I love you, Eugene," she whispered.

He didn't even need to say it.

*   *   *

The intruders moved along too close together to be taken one at a time. The militia men were too spread out to risk rushing them all at once—too much chance of at least one having time to activate his PPD.

Or kill somebody.

Letting them get to the Watterson-house ruins would risk the man still inside. At least in the process of searching, the intruders likely would split up and make noise that could cover the sound of approach—and the debris would provide line-of-sight obstacles not even infrared would penetrate. They needed to move in before the man inside was discovered. All of the militia men had been drilled in covert rescue operations. Except for having a man trapped, they could have faded into the night, nobody the wiser they'd been there.

Launching an assault would give them the element of surprise, but they didn't know who they were up against or how much back-up might be nearby—possibly armored ground defense or air support.

When the others came close enough to see, Flynn Durbett gestured warning about the intruders' vest PPDs. Obviously, the sound of gunshot must be avoided so as not to alert anyone, but snatching the tiny communication pagers would have to be the highest priority in any confrontation.

Behind not getting killed, anyway.

They watched as all three intruders worked their way inside and began to search. One of them carried a small device that looked like a miniature metal-detector, except that some kind of lit monitor displayed on top.

Leaving one man just down the road toward Highway 13 to watch for other intruders, Durbett and the remaining four surrounded the building. They crouched in tall grass or behind piles of debris around the perimeter, then waited.

One of the intruders crawled over a collapsed wall, gently pulling a sheet of corrugated roofing tin, presumably to maximize penetration for the odd-looking detector. He stepped around the partially collapsed brick chimney, then in the same instant got startled by a tug at the PPD on his chest and a hand muffling his mouth and nose.

Before he could react, his throat was slit wide, sliced to the spine. He tried vainly to struggle for a second or two, but proved too weak against the strong arms that held him near-motionless while he bled out.

*   *   *

When Durbett didn't see the intruder come back around either side of the chimney, he knew the man had been killed and carefully lowered to the ground, that it was time to move quickly before the other two noticed the absence. Or smelled the blood.

The man carrying the device proved easier; his attention was focused on the monitor. Exploring what used to be the kitchen area at the back of the house, he didn't notice a shadow moving inside, along the wall. Infrared doesn't help when you don't look. A tug, a grab and fast slice, and his life drained away, his heart pounding furiously in sticky gushes until nothing remained to pump.

Durbett waited outside the master-bedroom window, outside the room where Norm Watterson, his wife, and baby had died. He gestured for another of the men to move to the other side, pointing at his chest to indicate the PPD. Just as the intruder moved adjacent to the window, Durbett tossed something inside, causing the man's head to turn. He grabbed him from behind, holding his mouth closed while the other man snatched the PPD from his vest.

Click.

The intruder became acutely aware of the barrel of a Luger pointing directly into his face. A third man entered the bedroom from inside, assuming a stance some three feet from the captive, leveling an M-16 at his chest. That freed Durbett to use the grip of his Luger to tap the man in a critical spot just behind the temple. He wanted him unconscious, not dead, something he couldn't count on if he'd had to knock him out recklessly at the same time his PPD was grabbed.

Durbett shoved the Luger into his waistband, pulled out his knife, and made a small incision on the back of the man's limp hand. He let the arm dangle, moving it around to make sure a sufficient amount of blood got left in the soot and ashes.

Durbett sent three men, each fireman-carrying an intruder—two dead and one unconscious—to walk the creek toward where the trucks sat parked behind Willow's place. That way there would be no footprints and no chance of leaving a blood trail—as long as they stayed in the shallows as they walked. With one man still watching the road, Durbett operated the detector while the other man moved debris for him.

Still no sign of the box, so after another fifteen minutes, the last three withdrew, their legs bagged to avoid leaving a soot trail, taking the detector and walking the creekbed up to Willow's.

The bodies were already encased in garbage bags and loaded into Durbett's covered cab. The unconscious man was duct-taped like an unwary deerfly caught in a fat spider's web.

Relying on infrared rather than headlights, they drove both trucks toward McEwen, scrupulously avoiding use of telltale brake pedals.

At the gravel-crunching sound of their approach, Jake Coleman greeted them outside, hastily dressed, Tracey watching from the doorway.

"They was three arrived to search as we was finishin'," Durbett explained quietly. "Took two out," he went on, gesturing toward the back of the truck, "and captured the third."

"I can get rid of the two dead ones," Jake said quietly, "but if you need time to work on the prisoner, you better get him out of here. This area could get hot—fast."

"I know. I got their PPDs, which may help us run down where they're from, and a device I figure is programmed to look for the dimensions and density or material of that missing box. We left it lookin' like all three was killed and taken away, but they might come lookin' for bodies or evidence anyway."

"We can look clean as long you keep him out of here. But if they're searching for the boy . . ." Jake spread his hands.

Flynn thought for a moment. "He needs to go with me."

*   *   *

Tracey disappeared into the house and crept up the stairs, listening outside the bedroom door. She tapped lightly, but got no response, so she pushed the door open to find both teens cuddled together, naked and sound asleep. "Wake up," she hissed quietly. "Wake up, you two. Somethin's gone wrong and they wanna move Eugene somewhere else. Don't let Jake find you like this—he'll tell Marshall."

She slipped out while the embarrassed lovers quickly scrambled to dress.

She watched as Jake supervised transferring the bodies to the trunk of a car. He gave instructions on where and how to deliver them to a man who could convert corpses to animal feed in a matter of minutes, no questions asked.

*   *   *

Flynn Durbett came inside to alert Eugene, the bewildered and sleepy teen at the top of the stairs. "Get *everything* you got here—anything that somebody could tell you was livin' here, and pack it up. We gotta move you out *now*. Come down soon as you're ready." He went back outside to discuss his plans with Jake.

Licia helped him gather his newly purchased clothes and a few personal items like toothbrush and combs.

He packed several boxes of ammo into his duffel bag, then loaded his Colt Frontier and laid it on the table at the top of the stairs. He looked at Licia standing there in the moonlight, tears glistening in her eyes, her chin quivering, not sure what to say or do.

"Eugene, I'm scared. I don't wanna lose you *now*."

"I'll be okay—then I'll come back," he whispered, "or bring you wherever I am."

"Promise?"

He nodded, then put his arms around her and kissed her tentatively. "I promise."

He shoved the .22 into the waistband of his jeans and hurried down the stairs. He paused at the bottom and looked up one last time, a lump in his throat, his chest pounding. He could see she tried to look brave, but she was trembling, unable to hold back her tears. He saw her mouth, *I love you*; then he nodded again and gave it his best effort . . .

He smiled more reassurance than he really felt, then rushed outside where Flynn Durbett waited.

Again, it was time to move on.

Chapter 5

Two days making deliveries, checking in at dealerships, signing papers, arranging clandestine follow-ups, compiling coded records, financial transfers, looking over his shoulder every step of the way . . . Marshall Emery was exhausted. A delivery at Decatur, Alabama was his last stop before driving toward the compound northeast of Guntersville.

Heading out of Huntsville, he started down the mountain on Highway 431, disappointed that darkness obscured his view of the spectacular vista. He rubbed his eyes and checked his rear-view mirror. He couldn't see the beige panel truck following approximately a mile behind his nondescript company-fleet coupe. He downshifted on the steep curve as he headed into Marshall County. The engine hummed, new tires gripping efficiently; he took *good* care of all his vehicles. Too bad his left, rear tail-light decided at that very moment to burn itself out.

A state police cruiser targeted its mark—newer car, Texas plates, somebody who'd probably rather pay a fine to enrich the local coffers than bother to follow up with proof of repair. Marshall understood the routine well. Besides, an out-of-state car, middle of the night, not peak hunting or fishing season—the trooper might get lucky, make a bust, earn a feather for his cap.

Marshall acted polite. No, he didn't realize his tail-light had burned out, musta just happened, certainly wanna get that taken care of right away.

The beige panel truck braked at the sign of flashing lights, passing by slowly, cautiously. Marshall shrugged—not quite the *okay* sign because the trooper hadn't yet indicated if he would let him go, write the ticket, or something more . . .

"Live in Tennessee, huh?"

"Yes, sir." *Ain't that what it says on the license?*

"Car's registered in Texas."

Was that a question? "As you can see, it's a company car and that paper stapled to it shows it's for me to use."

"What kinda company?"

None of your goddamn business. You stopped me for a tail-light. "Resale shops."

"You supposed to be usin' your company car all the way out here?"

Are you corporate security? Is it your job to investigate my company business? "It is mine to use," Marshall returned evenly. Polite—avoid unnecessary confrontation.

"What're you doin' in Marshall County?"

"Plannin' to do some fishin'."

"Guntersville Lake?"

"Yes, sir."

"Got your license?"

"Not yet." *Now you're a game warden?*

The trooper shined his flashlight inside the car. The front seat held the remnants of a fast-food meal, obviously eaten on the road. A duffel bag was tossed in the back. No sign of fishing gear or tackle. "Where's your rod and reel?"

Couldn't claim it was at a friend's; the cop would want names. "Lookin' to get a new one," he smiled. "Last one got pulled in the lake when a bass hit after I set it down for a minute."

"Uh huh," the trooper monotoned. He hiked his pants up only to have his gut push them right back down. Blinding Marshall with the flashlight beam in his face, he asked, "Had anything to drink?"

"No, sir."

"Carrying any? Marshall County's dry, you know."

"Don't have any alcohol."

"Stand in front of my car," the trooper instructed, directing him into the beams of headlights and spotlight. He reached inside and pulled out his radio mike, calling in the information from Emery's license and registration. After a minute, a voice confirmed no wants, no warrants.

"Sure you ain't had nothin' to drink?"

"I am sure." Marshall was getting mad, trying not to let it show. This guy must not have anything better to do. He was fishing for a bust or trying to provoke his victim into some sort of confrontation.

"Whatta ya got in the trunk?"

"Spare tire and jack an' all."

"Mind if I look?"

"Yes."

Trooper studied him for a moment. Marshall looked calm, confident. "Yes, I can look?"

"No, yes I *mind*. I don't give permission for you to search my vehicle."

"Why, you got somethin' to hide?"

"I want to go on about my business. You stopped me for a tail-light. Write me the ticket if you want. I don't volunteer to spend my time proving anything."

"What if I look anyway?"

"Do you have a warrant or probable cause?"

"What're you?—a lawyer or something?"

Marshall stood mute, impassive. This wasn't going well. He couldn't—wouldn't—give up his constitutional rights voluntarily, yet he would suffer retaliation if he tried to assert them.

"Turn around and put your hands on the hood of the car," the trooper barked. Authority, he was in charge of the situation, somebody to be reckoned with.

Marshall complied, submitting to a pat-down search. Luckily, he'd slipped his handgun into the secret dashboard compartment while he was being pulled over. The trooper handcuffed him and put him in the back seat of the cruiser, then began searching the interior of Marshall's car. Not finding anything of interest, he took the keys from the ignition and opened the trunk. There wasn't much in there—some tools, full-sized spare tire, jacking mechanism and lug wrench, some survival items like water and rope and such. He found a short-wave radio mounted behind the back seat, wiring leading somewhere inside, probably to the dashboard. He pulled out the carpet and unscrewed the compartment where the mini-tire should be stored, discovering some kind of box built into it. That's where he found it: an Israeli Galil, 5.56-caliber fully automatic with 12, 35, and 50-round boxes capable of 650 rounds per minute.

"Whew! You know this here ain't legal, don't you, boy?" he asked, his pudgy, pock-marked face through the front window, opposite the screen containing the still-cuffed prisoner.

Marshall said nothing.

The deputy glared at him a moment, then used his mike to call it in, requesting back-up. Another car arrived with two more troopers. While one watched for traffic, the other two pulled Marshall from the back seat and demanded to know where he got the weapon, where he was going, what he was planning to do with it. Marshall requested to have an attorney present.

"Don't you be thinkin' about tryin' to run, now," one warned.

"Where'd you get the rifle?" the other demanded. Marshall stood mute.

Suddenly, one spun Marshall around while the other kicked his legs out. Hands cuffed behind, the prisoner couldn't break his fall as he hit the gravel face-first. There was a knee in his back, his head lifted up by the hair.

"Where'd the rifle come from?"

Marshall spit blood and a piece of tooth from his mouth. "I want a lawyer—"

His arm was twisted behind his back, harder and harder . . . He could feel his rotator cuff giving way, his head pulled farther back until he thought his neck would snap.

"We shoot dangerous criminals tryin' to escape," one warned.

"Go ahead," Marshall struggled out. "Your every move is bein' monitored." The troopers started looking around wildly. "Take me in, *now*, or let me go—if you wanna live through the night—if you care about your families," he added ominously. They released his arm, his hair, but stayed on his back there in the gravel, still peering around suspiciously.

A car was coming down the mountain. More than worried about public appearances, the troopers acted very apprehensive about who else might be out there lurking nearby. They jerked him up quickly and hustled him back into the cruiser. The arresting officer called for a tow-truck to pull Marshall's car to the impound lot in Guntersville. He left the other cruiser to wait while he headed toward the county jail with his injured prisoner.

Marshall could imagine the story: poor guy, too bad he'd tried to run, had to be wrestled down and restrained while being cuffed.

*   *   *

Not far away, a scrambled radio transmission relayed on the day's frequency: "They roughed him up, but not too bad. They're headin' toward 79, prob'ly to Guntersville."

"Illegal search?"

"Oh, yeah. No question."

"Let him go. Let's try playin' through the system first."

Hesitation. "You sure? It's just one car, one cop. We can take him easy."

"Nothin' unnecessary. Try the system first."

"All right then. But if that don't work, we'll just hafta get him the *hard* way later."

*   *   *

An older black man, poorly dressed, shuffled down the dark street, stopping in front of the run-down row-house. He knocked quietly. It was the oldest part of Waverly, just outside the area rebuilt after the big train wreck and fiery explosion decades before. It was a good place to buy bootleg whiskey, food-stamps for fifty cents on the dollar, cheap unregistered pistols, maybe a little poontang if you didn't care about it being too clean.

Another gentle knock, then the door opened a crack.

"Leroy Carter!" the man on the street exclaimed, still keeping his voice down. "I got that money I done owed ya, thought maybe you knew where we could get something to celebrate."

Mr. Carter looked confused, not recognizing the man. Surely, he'd remember if somebody owed him money. Before the slight, wiry old white-haired man could reply, the door was pushed open and the stranger wandered inside, friendly, jovial. He closed the door behind himself.

"Anybody else home?"

Carter shook his head. "Don't nobody else live—"

"What about Jolene? How's she doin'?"

Carter eyed the man suspiciously, a hint of fear in his face. "Who'd you say you was—?"

"Leroy—it's me! 'Member? How's Jolene doin' anyway?"

Carter started to inch his way toward the door, then got startled by the visitor's surprisingly strong grip on his arm.

"What's the matter, Leroy? You all right? You don't look too good." A bottle appeared. "Come on, let's sit down and relax with a drink." He let go long enough to open the bottle, waving it under the old man's nose, the pungent odor of strong whiskey permeating the stale air in the run-down hovel.

"Don't drink no more," Carter said quietly. "I'm tired now, wanna get some sleep. Maybe I'll see you—" He was inching toward the door again.

The visitor looked disappointed, reached to put his arm around the old man's shoulders.

Leroy Carter felt a pin-prick in his neck, then saw everything turning blue, purple, black. He could no longer stand. He looked drunk or passed-out as he was led to a car that conveniently pulled in front right then.

*   *   *

The car drove away, leaving the visitor and another man to slip back inside. After what must have been a fast search of the old man's meager belongings, the car pulled up again just as they emerged carrying a small, black satchel, whisking them away.

A very pregnant teenager watched through thin curtains from across and down the street, biting her lip.

Oh, Daddy, what have I done?

*   *   *

Town Creek the little sign on the bridge said. Guntersville State Park, Alabama, had passed only a few miles behind. Eugene had been watching the green hills and small mountains roll by, the patchwork coves and causeways, trying to count black turtles crowding for space on logs jutting from backwash and still waters. Overcast, hot and humid even for early morning, he felt drowsy from the pre-dawn Tennessee departure. He'd tried to sleep while Flynn Durbett drove, but worrying about the mysterious agent they were transporting kept him up. Coming off the Texas road trip, illness, stress, trying to take it all in, the teenager was exhausted. He studied the unflappable Flynn, the balding mercenary at the wheel, and decided the man must never get tired.

In fact, adversity seemed to keep him very alert.

Farther into the woods, climbing over low hills, around and between higher ones, they followed rutted backroads, occasionally crisscrossing their way up what Eugene assumed was still Town Creek. They came upon a rusty old gate in their path, chained and padlocked, an old wooden sign nearby proclaiming: *Camp Lo-ki-star.*

"Wait," Flynn said quietly. He walked over to a hollow tree just off the road, reached up to put something inside the hole, then climbed back into his truck. He backed into a turnaround, honked twice, paused, honked twice more, then slowly drove about a quarter-mile the way they'd come. Then he doubled back. The rusty gate stood open this time, so he drove through, stopped, then got out and relocked it himself. Several hundred more yards and around a bend, he stopped again and stepped out. "Get out and stand still," he told Eugene. "Don't worry."

Eugene had not realized men were all around. Camouflage fatigues, M-16s, a Luger, two men, three, four—they knew Durbett, looked curious about the teen.

"The Weisman boy," Flynn explained.

They peered into the cab, then followed Durbett around to look in the back.

"He sure as hell ain't goin' nowhere on his own," one of the men grinned, peering inside. One was watching up the road while the other three admired the duct-tape and nylon-cord handiwork keeping the prisoner secured.

Two of the armed men disappeared into the woods; the other two followed Flynn's truck into the camp. Eugene found himself quite fascinated by all the activity around the converted Christian children's retreat. With a lot of tree cover, in some places large tarps stretched across the sky, all to conceal from aerial surveillance the various training exercises going on, mostly small groups of white men.

"Flynn! Good to see ya, man. Eugene! Glad to have ya down!"

Eugene recognized him as one of the men who'd escorted him and Flynn to the cemetery the night of the funeral.

"Ray Blounten," Flynn introduced the man. As Eugene shook his hand, Flynn added, "Call him Big Ray."

Eugene had thought of Mr. Watterson as big, but this guy had to be near seven feet tall and big around as a snowball bush. Big Ray's hair looked just like Eugene's—brownish blond, straight and fine, but where the teen's was cut punkish with a longer shock combed over the top, the big feller's was trimmed short and parted perfectly along one side. Eugene's hand got swallowed up in the firm, yet gentle shake.

They were led into the camp director's house, blasted by a wall of air-conditioning, and offered cold drinks.

Eugene opted instead for a trip to bathroom, but paused outside the door when he heard Big Ray tell Flynn, "Deputies picked up Marshall Emery other side of the lake last night. Holdin' him on weapons violations."

"He all right?"

"Roughed him up some, but a chipped tooth is the worst of it."

"Couldn't rescue him?"

"Didn't try. Hoping to get him other ways without bringin' on too much heat."

"No problem with the truck?"

"Went smooth," Big Ray confirmed.

They launched into a discussion about the various weapons in the shipment, so Eugene slipped in to take care of his business. By the time he came out, both men sat at a computer scrolling through various screens.

Flynn looked up, telling the teen, "Make yourself at home." *Don't try to watch what we're doing.*

The place was furnished like any comfortable, southern living room. Eugene wandered into the kitchen, grabbed himself a soda from the fridge, then gazed in fascination at the sweating 250-gallon aquarium along one wall. Gravel-bottomed with weeds likely from Town Creek, it contained fifty or sixty small fish, snails, clams, several turtles, and numerous crawdads. Eugene recognized all the fish. Most were small bream, three or four inches long, including blue-gills and sun perch; the rest included small alligator gar pikes, a pair of very small bass, a half-dozen crappie, plus the requisite suckers and channel cats.

Eugene had already made another bathroom trip, opened his second soda, eaten some cold biscuits with sorghum, and had started naming the fish by the time the lawyer arrived. Flynn and Big Ray were just finishing their work on the computer. They greeted the attorney and assured him he could talk in front of the teen.

"Police report's already online," the legal guy explained, "but arraignment will be held off for three days. By then, the evidence will disappear and the D.A. will have to request dismissal. Marshall knows to chill out. He's mostly mad about his tooth—and losing the Galil."

"That rifle's a pretty gal." Big Ray grinned.

"We'll get him another," Flynn said good-naturedly.

They finally introduced Eugene. The lawyer acted like he already knew about the teen. "Remember, son, you're a minor, out-of-state, without legal guardian, supposed to be startin' school next week. You get wrapped up in the system, it'll be *tough* tryin' to get you back out."

"Yes, sir. I know."

"He'll be stayin' here a while," Flynn told the lawyer.

"Good." They exchanged good-byes and he was gone.

They walked out to one of the other buildings, a plain, cinder-block affair, to check on the status of the prisoner. He'd already been moved into a holding cell, stripped of his soiled clothing, and been hosed down. He sat naked on the wet, concrete floor in the corner, manacled at the wrists and ankles. Eugene started to follow Big Ray up to the bars, but Durbett held his shoulder, keeping him back in the doorway.

"What is your name?" Big Ray asked the prisoner. The man only glared his hatred, thinly disguised fear. "You will be tried for your crimes in a constitutional court of common law. Acquitted, you will be set free. Convicted, you will be sentenced for your crimes. You will be given the opportunity to mitigate your sentence by offering information and assistance."

Eugene noted that Big Ray's friendly demeanor had taken on a hard, serious edge—his eyes intense in a way that made the teen shudder.

"You want we should interrogate him now?" a man guarding the cell asked.

"No. We shall see if he is convicted through due process. Allow him rest and food—nothing to interfere with his ability to defend himself. He will be tried tomorrow at noon."

Eugene noticed that the guard looked disappointed, the prisoner slightly relieved—for a man caught in the jaws of the beast.

Barracks in the compound handled overnighters and extended training sessions—or long-term billeting under battle conditions—but Big Ray wanted Eugene to take one of the upstairs bedrooms in the house for himself. This was after some quiet discussion with Flynn Durbett. After that, both men seemed to be concerned about the teen feeling comfortable with his new digs, wanting him to settle in for a while as if he had space of his own.

Eugene wondered where Durbett lived, if anywhere, and what his life must have been like trotting around the globe, always on the go, always on the run. Then he realized he knew exactly how it felt. Alone in his new room, he stretched out on the big, comfortable bed and gazed around, catching himself longing for the worn-out cot still there in *his* room at Willow's place. He'd thought he would stay with the Emerys for a while, too, and had liked his room there, the feeling of family, the attention and affection of Licia. Another room, another state, no clear concept of the future, a trail of people he'd cared about left behind . . . most dead, the others in danger.

Surrounded by people, he felt lonely.

After a while, Big Ray came in and said Flynn Durbett was doing some weapons training out back with some of the guys, inviting him to join in. Durbett looked pleased when he showed up. With a half-dozen other men, they spent several hours setting up, loading, and breaking down various machine guns, semi-automatics, and small rocket launchers. Nothing actually got fired.

Eugene felt good about his performance. He liked the guys, liked how they all treated him with respect. Though sometimes they seemed to be taking the younger feller under their wings, patient, encouraging, reinforcing, each enjoying the role of teacher and mentor, they also acted as if he was just a regular guy any one of them would be proud to fight alongside.

In no time, Eugene started to feel like he belonged.

The session broke up when most of the guys had to leave for work—everybody had bills to pay and families to support. Big Ray came out and suggested Eugene and Durbett join him for a quick lunch, then a tour of the "refuge," as he called it.

"You *will* be staying at least a day or two, won't you?" he asked Flynn.

"I want to be here for the trial and interrogation—I need to figure out what's going on—plus I want to stay close until Marshall's free. If that situation needs help, I should play a role."

"We couldn't ask for better assistance," Big Ray gushed.

It was becoming obvious to Eugene that wherever Durbett went, he was held in *the* highest possible regard, his knowledge and experience coveted, his words gospel. After some sandwiches and feeding a few crickets to the fish, the trio walked out to the back of the compound. They crossed a small stream and started up a hillside path that led to a long fence with razor wire threading through the woods.

Big Ray explained, "Flynn, I want to show you the new cache areas we've set up. Eugene, you need to know how to get here for refuge, ammunition, or escape in case they's ever a siege."

They paused some fifty feet shy of the fence. Big Ray pointed at an outcropping of rocks, then motioned around the area so Eugene would remember how to identify where he was. Then he climbed up over the rocks and worked his way down along a crevice, Eugene right behind him, Durbett at the rear. The entrance to a cave cut right into the side of the mountain!

Big Ray reached under a small ledge and flipped a switch, scrupulously showing Eugene where it was located. The teen couldn't see any difference, but once they'd crawled under a gap and descended down a half-dozen concrete steps, he could see a long, narrow cavern lit by recessed lights ensconced here and there. A path had been cleared through the rubble and rocks, occasionally bolstered with patchwork concrete. Several places even appeared to have been blasted.

The next series of caverns looked beautiful with mineral formations, stalactites and stalagmites, sparkling crystalline walls, broken geodesic stones scattered around. Dark passageways led several directions, sometimes cracks disappearing upward. They passed a large pool formed by several streams and small waterfalls flowing from somewhere above, reinforced by a concrete retaining wall, then spilling out an overflow to disappear in darkness deep into the earth. The internal lighting was minimal, so they carried flashlights and a lantern picked up near the entrance, the play of beams casting spooky shadows in every direction.

Room after room held stockpiles of supplies, weapons and ammo, foodstuffs, blankets and cots, medical kits, communications equipment, toilet paper, and lots of wooden crates of no-telling-what. Eugene kept expecting to feel claustrophobic, but the constant, cool temperature and fresh air that flowed through various cracks made it feel more open. Still, though, he stayed very close to Durbett.

Eventually, they passed through a long, narrow area with no installed lighting at all, finally emerging into another series of caverns. They could hear voices, the sounds of activity, then saw light up ahead. Several men greeted Big Ray, acted *very* pleased to see Durbett, and introduced themselves to Eugene. The teen hoped there wouldn't be a quiz later; he'd been trying to learn too many names in one day. They were hauling in crates of weapons from the other direction, stacking them in an area along one wall that had recently been cleared of debris.

"We blasted out a clear entrance back of old Carlysle's place," Big Ray explained. "Gives us a second access and better route to bring in major shipments without so much traffic through the main gate."

Flynn looked pleased. He left Big Ray supervising the storage and led Eugene with one of the men to check out the new entranceway. It was likewise concealed from anyone who didn't know exactly where to find it, surrounded by woods, just above an old house. Eugene recognized the beige panel truck parked just below as the one he and Durbett had taken from South Padre Island to Victoria, Texas. They looked around for a minute, then walked back and met Big Ray again.

"Need to get going," the big man explained. "Jackie's got plans for me tonight, and she'll skin me if I'm late."

"You don't live in the compound?" Eugene asked.

"No, son, my wife and boy and me got a place out toward Scottsboro. *Somebody* stays here every night, though, besides you, that is. Tonight it'll be Flynn here," he added as if to reassure.

During the long walk back through the caverns, Eugene asked about the trial to be conducted the next day. "You're gonna take this guy to *court?*"

"We hold our *own* court right here in the compound," Big Ray explained. "A *common-law* court as provided by the Sixth and Seventh Amendments to the U.S. Constitution. You see, the *United States* has become a corporation of the original *United States of America*. That's why in courthouses and government offices you see *two* sets of flags, one with gold fringe. The fringed ones is for the corporation. We've all declared ourselves *free men*, not bound by the laws of the corporation that restrict our common-law rights. We will not be *employees* of the corporation, nor be enslaved by the officers and agents of the corporation. Our property is declared independent, and we are citizens of the United States of America which, now, is a foreign state within the corporate state and subject to sovereign protection."

Eugene's head was spinning at the thought, but they talked it out for a while until he reasonably understood. Flynn interjected only minimally, and then only to help explain something in a way he thought Eugene would understand.

"But is the guy you have on trial subject to *your* laws?"

"Yes," Big Ray said unequivocally. "Norman Watterson had declared his property free and independent—and refused to pay taxes on it. Lucky they was too afraid of him to try and enforce tax collections. But the man that was captured is accused of illegally entering sovereign property for purposes yet to be determined. I suspect his actions will be shown to have been at least espionage, if not invasion, possibly implicating him in the murders of a family that tried to live peacefully in freedom on their own land."

That image of Russell crawling through smoke and flames in a desperate attempt to save his family flooded Eugene's mind again, but he fought down the overwhelming emotion. He replaced it with anger. Who was this man who dared come back and intrude one more time into Russell's home? It was either him or his ilk who'd murdered his best friend.

They walked back to the big house and opened some cold drinks. Eugene was watching the fish when the phone rang.

Big Ray answered it, then talked in hushed tones, agitated. The big man hung up and swore. "Damn!"

"What's wrong?" Durbett demanded.

"That was my contact at the sheriff's department. He says a U.S. Marshal just come with a warrant and picked up Marshall Emery."

"Shit," Durbett breathed.

"Shit," agreed Big Ray. "Look, I'm gonna call Jackie and make her mad so I can stick around here. We need to find out what the hell's goin' on."

"Good," Flynn agreed. "I'll try to check it out, but I can't risk calling from here." He motioned for Eugene to follow him out to his truck for a private talk.

"You're leaving?"

"Got to. I gotta run down Marshall before he gets away from us. I wanna make sure you understand that you're *safe* here. Just stick with Ray and trust him. Do whatever he says. I'll be back later today or tomorrow morning at the latest—" Eugene failed to hide his apprehension. "I promise." He climbed into the truck, then reached through the window and clasped Eugene's shoulder. "Big Ray already likes you. He's a good man with a lot to teach. You just make yourself at home."

Eugene nodded, but something else was bothering him. What was it? What wasn't quite right?

Durbett figured it out just as Eugene was about to ask. "Jake Coleman's already on his way down here, but I'll have somebody head up there and keep an eye on things, keep her informed," he said.

"If Marshall's locked up, Licia's all by herself." His throat hurt, his heart pounding.

"No, Eugene, she's got *all* of us."

He watched the truck drive out toward the main gate, a swirl of dust billowing into the late-afternoon glare of sun. Still, he was worried. He knew she'd be scared, too.

All of us, Licia, especially me.

*   *   *

McGovern looked over the report. Lt. Col. Poole sat across from him in the hastily assembled office in the converted sanitarium along the Cumberland River.

"I'm *fine. They* say I'm fine. There's no sign of anything to worry about. Except for that proteanus in my urine—" Poole gestured toward one of the under-pages in the sheaf McGovern held. "—Which was benign, everything normal. I think he just used a whatcha-call *placebo*, something that wasn't anything just to make me believe whatever he injected would protect me from these so-called aliens that, frankly, *I* ain't yet convinced even exist."

"Hmmm," McGovern said absently, still thumbing through the bio-med and toxicological report. "Do you have any problem carrying out your responsibilities as if there *are* aliens?"

"Oh, no *sir!* In fact, I'm honored to be a part of the team. If there *are* invaders, they'll not succeed for lack of *us* being at the ready."

Okay, Poole had sucked it up enough. Changing the subject, McGovern reported, "Of your two missions, one went well—Mr. Carter is here in custody—and the other was a failure."

"They didn't find the box—?"

"They never reported back for the rendezvous. All three men are missing, as are their equipment and communications devices. Their bicycles were found where they'd been stashed in the brush, but no obvious abduction was witnessed. I sent somebody at dawn dressed like a local for a fast reconnoiter; he's recovered samples of three different blood spots which I've rushed to Washington to have DNA matched. I suspect all three will prove to be from our operatives—and that all three were murdered, their bodies somehow removed."

"Whew!" Poole sat back and removed his hat to scratch his wiry red-haired scalp. "Alien or not, we're up against *somebody*—and they're trained and organized."

"Alien or not, I believe it's local militia. Whether or not *they* know about aliens, or think they're protecting one or more of them, they must suspect that what happened at the Watterson house was no accident. They had to be there searching for *something*, too—or expected *us* to come back and search."

"They must know about the black box."

"And probably *have* it now—at least knew *we* didn't have it and that we still wanted to recover it, or maybe even let *our* people recover it before ambushing them and taking it. Whatever the answer, *we* don't have the box and *they* most likely do."

Poole sat there a moment, pondering the possibilities. "Might the deaths have been faked?"

"Too much blood. Assuming the DNA match, I believe they're dead. They were too highly trained to be captured; they had too much back-up available for anything but an ambush killing to have succeeded."

"So we've been compromised, but not as much as we could have been."

"It could have been worse," McGovern agreed. "Now we'll be casting our net wide and looking for potential threats—and not be so concerned about keeping things neat when we have no choice."

Poole shook his head. "Need to be careful."

"Need to be fast," McGovern added. "Now, it's time to determine the status of Mr. Leroy Carter."

Poole followed obediently, led to the bio-med lab set up in the former infirmary.

The highest ranking of the bio-med team showed them the thoroughly dissected pinkie finger of an elderly black man, along with numerous slides and print-outs of MRI and other scans. "No sign of anything remotely similar to what Aggeous had described or what we found on those slides we recovered from his lab. Unless it's something we can't see or detect through any known mechanisms, the subject is uncontaminated."

"You carefully followed Aggeous's procedures when taking the finger sample?"

"And then some," the doctor bristled.

"Where is he?"

"Back in containment, coming out from under the anesthesia."

"Is he ready to be medicated for questioning?"

The doctor thought it over, then decided, "Probably. Another thirty to sixty minutes would be better."

"I'll call when we're ready."

With that, McGovern led Poole to the containment building where the cells and, so far, only one prisoner could be found. With two armed guards outside the open door, McGovern pulled a chair over to the bunk holding the groggy old-timer. An interrogation expert stood closest to the prisoner's head, Poole off to the side watching.

"Mr. Carter?" the expert started.

"What? What happened?" He kept looking at his bandaged hand, confused, trying to see past the men out the open door, to understand where he was.

"Are you Mr. Leroy Carter?"

"Yes," he said pitifully. "Where am I?" His voice weak, tears stood in his eyes.

"You're the stepfather of Jolene Carter?"

"Am I . . . am I *dead?*"

"No, you're in our custody. Who is Jolene Carter?"

"She's my daughter."

"Stepdaughter?"

The old man nodded, looking confused and studying his bandage. "Does it hurt?"

He nodded again. "What's *wrong* with it? What happened to my hand—?"

"You hurt yourself—your finger. We needed to do surgery on it."

"Will it be all right—?"

"You'll be fine. When did you last see Jolene?"

"Why? Somethin' wrong with her?"

"We need to find her. She may be in danger. You don't want her to get hurt, do you?"

"No! That's why she run."

"When did you last see her?"

"This shore do hurt bad." Mr. Carter winced after gingerly touching where he'd had "surgery."

The doctor had just come in with a bag, so he dug through it, extracting a syringe and small bottle. He swabbed Carter's arm and injected him. "Painkiller," he explained. "The hurt will go away."

"When did you say you saw Jolene?" the interrogator continued.

"Been a coupla months," Carter mumbled. "She only come home twice since she lived with Wattersons."

"After the fire? You saw her after the fire?"

Carter shook his head. "Naw, it was way before the fire."

The expert nodded to the guards outside the door, one of whom nodded to somebody else out of sight. After a moment, a cardboard box was brought in. It contained a hacksaw, many sheets of fine-grade sandpaper—some covered with black dust, some new—and several packets of black chips and dust. Carter had to raise himself up to see clearly.

"What were these used for?"

"Me and Jolene made 'em. Bars of black soap—except they wasn't real soap—just fake for some kinda joke or something. Cut up a old bowling ball."

"For what?"

"She didn't say."

McGovern removed an envelope from his satchel. He extracted a photograph and handed it to the interrogator.

"Did they look like this?"

"Yeah, that's it."

"What happened to them?"

"She took 'em."

"Where is she now?"

Carter shook his head.

Another fifteen minutes divulged no more information. Carter insisted he'd not seen her since, didn't know anything else about the fake black boxes he'd helped create, had no idea where Jolene was and couldn't even hazard a guess. McGovern got frustrated, disappointed, angry. He motioned the doctor and interrogator outside the cell and whispered to proceed with drugged questioning. Noting it would be a good hour before they could make serious progress, he left Poole in charge and walked back to the infirmary building.

"Need at least a few more hours," the team reported. They were working diligently on the body of Billy Hall. "It would probably help a lot to have access to Aggeous—he's got all the experience with this kind of stuff."

The colonel went back to his office and called Huntsville, giving instructions to have Aggeous brought to Ft. Donelson immediately. He called General Ashe's aide and made arrangements for Aggeous to be transported under heavy security to the Cumberland Sanitarium.

How did the MPs die?

That question had been dogging him since Aggeous had made the challenge. It infuriated McGovern to know the man who worked for him was withholding information. Having an interrogation expert with the requisite facilities and capabilities played a significant part in his decision to have the fat, wheezing doctor brought up to Cumberland—that and he wanted to see his reaction to the results of the autopsy and lab work.

You know, record his reaction, Aggeous had said about showing the boxes to Billy Hall.

He called his source at the FBI to check out progress on the Carter investigation. No relatives, no information from neighbors, nobody reporting having seen Jolene for months. He offered good news on the Watterson references, though. They had done extensive computer analysis of their records and matched names with associates—people with whom they could document Watterson having any kind of non-business contact over the years. Cross-referenced with lists of known militia members, they'd come up with more than a dozen names in three states.

He wanted to order them all rounded up and brought to Cumberland immediately, but he knew that would be too far-reaching, moving too fast without knowing the lay. Instead, he ordered that the data be sent to him for review. He needed to formulate a plan, knew he wasn't ready to play his hand.

He needed more information, but the more he got, the less he seemed to know.

He went back to the detention building to watch the Carter interrogation for a while. Still yielding nothing of value, it was starting to look like Mr. Carter would be helpful only to the extent of confirming that Jolene had made several fake boxes—and likely made the switch knowing the one Watterson had was somehow special. McGovern felt like half the people in Tennessee must know what the damned boxes were.

Should he eliminate Leroy Carter? No, he was still trolling for the pregnant, black teen. The old man might make good bait.

Or help encourage cooperation after they captured her.

McGovern made himself relax a few minutes to eat his sack lunch. On an impulse, he picked up his phone and called, of all people, his mother back in Allentown, Pennsylvania. She still lived where the two of them had moved when he was a teen, after his father died in a car accident. The elder McGovern had been an NCO, raising his family on a series of Army bases, frustrated at being left stateside while many of his comrades went to Vietnam. He'd been thrilled with his son's plans to attend the academy and become an officer some day, would've been proud he was now a colonel and project commander soon to become a general.

If all went well.

It turned out, of course, that mom was proud, too. She knew better than to complain about the long gap between phone calls, her military-mother nee military-wife stoicism well-honed, and she understood not to ask questions about the current project that had advanced her boy's career. He didn't mention the pending promotion—no sense getting her hopes up prematurely—but he did promise to see her in the next month or two if all went well. The conversation was brief, leaving him feeling good about making her day but guilty he didn't call more often.

Feeling like he'd killed enough time, he checked back in on Carter to find they'd wrapped up the interrogation still without learning anything else. He talked with the expert in private for a moment, alerting him that when Aggeous arrived he would want him close by to report his impressions on the good doctor.

McGovern walked back to the infirmary. Most of the team was still working either on Hall's body or various samples taken from it. Another man was conducting autopsies on the two dead MPs.

"No foreign presence that we've been able to detect so far—and we've been quite thorough—though there are still a few improbable tests that will take more time," the senior examiner reported. "However, we did find two interesting things."

McGovern suited up. Masked, rubber-gloved, blasted with ionized air, he entered the lab to see some of the collection of samples.

The doctor explained, "First, his blood system—veins and arteries—has barely detectable grooves throughout it."

"Grooves?"

The doctor showed him a series of cross-sectional slides, plus enlarged scans of several lengthwise sections.

"It fits," the doctor explained, "with my hypothesis that silky structures like Aggeous had preserved could have been inside Hall's circulatory system. Attached to the insides of veins and arteries, the grooves would be formed by the build-up of deposits—cholesterol to over-simplify—over a period of time. Then if the thread disappears for whatever reason—dissolves, according to what Aggeous told you—that could very well explain how these grooves would be left behind."

McGovern wasn't surprised. "What's the other thing you found?"

"Well, the grooves extend thoroughly into the brain, so we've been looking for signs of neural changes that might have happened over time. First, we noticed extremely high levels of macrophages present." He watched McGovern to see if he understood the implications.

"I'll need the lay version," the colonel said by way of response.

"Macrophages are the chemicals released in the brain to clear away, shall we say, *debris*. Dead cells, damaged neurons, and so forth. The brain can't rely on things being automatically carried off in the bloodstream, so it has its own little set of maid's helpers. Something made Mr. Hall's brain dump a shitload of macrophages just before or as he was dying. I've never seen anything to this extent. The closest I'm aware of is death caused by massive drug overdose—where the last thing the brain does before succumbing is make a desperate attempt to clean itself out."

McGovern thought for a moment. "So it infiltrated his brain at the last moment, and his macrophages were trying to fight it off?"

"That's possible—but not likely. This thing was spread through every blood passageway—even the capillaries in the extremities—and had been there long enough for the grooves to become obvious. We suspect it had thoroughly infiltrated the brain neurons as part of that process, so we've been looking closely at the neurological structure. For a man as old as he was, it looks like he'd had minimal neuron degradation—in fact, there were high levels of astrocytes in all areas linked to sensory perception and cognitive thought. See, even in brains that have been damaged somehow, the human body has remarkable capability to repair the trauma or by-pass it as needed. That's why there are such astounding accomplishments in rehab of injury or stroke victims. Locuscerleus extends fibers across and around damage, releasing noradrenaline to stimulate astrocytes. The astrocytes release nerve-growth factor to sprout new neurons and reconnect."

"I thought when we lost brain cells, they were gone for good," McGovern pointed out.

"Far as we know, that's true. But we have seemingly unlimited capacity to reconnect or forge new pathways and new connections with the ones we have left. Near as we can understand, that's how we store memories and develop new approaches to thinking."

"And what does this have to do with Hall?"

"Simply put, in *old* coots, we'd expect high degrees of degradation. His brain has an extremely complex network, much of it apparently fairly new. We've quickly isolated dozens of examples of astrocytic neuron growth that were in progress at the time of death. It shouldn't have been so easy to find even one."

"But what about the macrophages? It sounds like you think this thing had invaded *all* of his neurons."

The doctor shrugged. "My best guess is that there was a sudden withdrawal—or dissolution—of the threads, enough to cause massive brain damage. The macrophages dump could've been a desperate reaction like those overdose cases I mentioned."

"Spread throughout the brain," McGovern said by way of thinking out loud.

"*Connected* throughout the brain," the doctor corrected.

"Cause of death?"

"Sudden *dis*connection."

Chapter 6

"Jake! Howdy, guy!"

"Eugene! What's this?" Stepping out of his truck, Jake Coleman touched a finger to the teen's chest.

Eugene batted it away and grinned. He knew better than to look down. "How's Licia?"

Flynn Durbett stepped out of his own truck, having followed Jake in. Big Ray strolled up, hand outstretched.

"I don't know, why don't *you* tell *me*?" Jake teased, poking Eugene in the chest again and wagging his eyebrows. "I hear you know *exactly* how she is." He poked again, continuing the ribbing longer than usual for the normally staid militia leader.

Catching the meaning, Eugene stammered, then blushed visibly. If it had been with just any old girl from school, he would have played it up, would've wanted to review all the delicious details with Russell over and over again. But he felt embarrassed—not just for himself, for Licia. What had happened between them was too special, too private, too personal to talk about with other guys.

Jake sensed this and dropped the teasing. "She's fine," he offered, anticipating Eugene's concern. "I got a couple guys watching the place and Deputy Varne patrolling on a regular basis to make *sure* she's okay. Tracey's stayin' there, too, and they promised to get hold of me if *anything* is wrong."

Eugene nodded, then stepped back for Big Ray Blounten and several other guys who'd wandered up to greet the arrivals. He noticed that Jake, as much as Flynn, was treated like a high-ranker or dignitary.

Big Ray led the small entourage back to the house, so Eugene tagged along with the minnow bucket he'd just filled from the holding cage down in the stream. It was time to feed the aquarium fish, a responsibility he'd taken to heart, something he really enjoyed.

Durbett trailed the group, waiting for Eugene to catch up. "You're not part of the governing council, but you're buddies with the main guys, so I don't think they'll mind you hanging out and listening," he offered quietly.

"Who's in charge?" Eugene whispered back.

"Jake leads the Tennessee Valley Patriots, which includes five militia regiments. Big Ray runs the largest one, the one based here called Sand

Mountain Militia. Marshall runs the smallest, the Humphreys County Militia, out of the farm up there."

Last in the house, Flynn grabbed a seat off to the side while Eugene attended to the huge aquarium and watched the discussion. Having noted that the pair of young bass were usually fastest at grabbing the minnows, he got a kick out of dropping the "bait" behind and as far away from them as possible. Those bass were quick, always first to eat no matter how crafty Eugene was.

"We can't put him on trial," Big Ray was saying.

"Then we can't hold him," Jake countered. "Unless we follow principles of the Constitution, we're no better than that corporate government runnin' this country."

Another man cut in, "But we been compromised. If he's let go, he'll bring back his own and make *us* stand trial for kidnaping and weapons and no-tellin' what-all."

Big Ray ticked points off on his fingers. "We can't let him contact anybody, he'll give us up and set up a rescue. We can't help his defense because that's a conflict—that's no better than these public defenders workin' for the county that poor people get—"

"The ones in the judges' pockets because they gotta kiss their ass to get the jobs," another man cut in, apparently speaking from experience.

"We don't have the time to let him go through all the stages of challenging evidence and stuff," Big Ray continued, "because we gotta work on finding and gettin' Emery back. We can't sentence him to do time, then release him, because we can't hold him *here* for that long and it'll compromise us when we let him go someday—"

"Ain't gonna be a problem *keepin'* him," somebody growled. "When he's found guilty of killin' that family, he'll be sentenced to death."

"We can't presume guilt," Jake said quietly.

"No, but we *did* catch him conducting a raid on *our* sovereign territory," Big Ray argued. His dander was rising. "It's only circumstantial that people dressed just like him killed Norm and his family, but we got him dead to rights for infiltrating."

Jake pondered for a moment, all eyes waiting for his reaction. "If just Norm was killed," he said evenly, "I'd want to consider what-all reasons there mighta been for it. But when his entire family was killed, then was covered up, well . . ." He rubbed his head, lost for a moment.

Flynn Durbett spoke up for the first time, surprising Eugene. The balding mercenary usually stayed out of these kinds of discussions, preferring to fade into the background and observe. "His wife," he said, pausing. "His boy, barely old enough to be a man. Two little girls. A baby in a crib. That's deliberate civilian casualties and an act of war."

Eugene was struck by the quiet passion in Flynn's voice. That feeling welling up inside whenever he thought of Russell mercilessly killed by invaders in the night must be how Durbett felt about Norm Watterson.

"Y'all know I don't belong to your groups," Durbett continued. "But you know I support protecting yerselves and standing up for your rights. *I* got a stake in *this* one. I owe Norm Watterson. He and his family was murdered. I can't say if this man done it, but he's part of it and he knows something. Norm can't take care of his family no more; now it's on me to do what I can."

"Grand jury," Jake muttered, his eyebrows raised at the thought.

"Look," Big Ray cut in, his patience decidedly short. "They's two things on the bottom line. One, we gotta get whatever info we can out of him—fast. Two, we *can't* let him go—never. Don't need no trial to know those is the facts. Let me question him, then we'll do what needs to be done."

Eugene could tell most everyone thought the same. Durbett's expression looked too serene to read.

Jake looked conflicted, like he was about to violate his own principles. Finally, he pronounced, "He ain't no criminal defendant. He's a prisoner of war."

Everybody agreed.

Fifteen minutes and several conversations later, Jake and Big Ray went into the holding block and stood in front of the prisoner's cell, flanked by three men and a woman all dressed in fatigues, each carrying M-16s angled across their chests. A large man, tall as Big Ray but heavier, waited off to the side with a worn suitcase. Durbett and Weisman stood with several other men at the other end, just inside the propped-open door, watching. Bright morning sunlight streamed into the otherwise gloomy interior.

"What is your name?" Big Ray demanded.

The prisoner said nothing. He was sitting on the concrete floor, his back to the wall, dressed in the old sweatpants and shirt that had been tossed to him the night before. A tray with food remnants sat beside him.

"Prisoner with no name," Big Ray continued, "we told you to expect your trial to begin today—"

"Then I want to call my lawyer," the man on the floor said evenly.

"—But your trial has been canceled," Big Ray finished. "Your actions have been declared an act of war by the sovereign state of Tennessee Valley and its citizens, the Tennessee Valley Patriots. You are a prisoner of war."

"So no kangaroo trial, huh?" He acted brazen, agitated.

The prisoner was photographed and, under very heavy cover, had prints taken of his fingers and palms. A lock of his hair was cut and put into a plastic container. Big Ray quietly explained, "These will help in identifying you."

The prisoner tried to look calm, defiant, even confident, but he was obviously worried, composed but inwardly terrified. Eugene knew the feeling.

Big Ray went on. "You are guilty of capital war crimes. We will give you a choice: either cooperate and tell us what we need to know or be executed for your crimes. If you help us, we will hold you as a prisoner until a treaty has been signed or suitable arrangements can be worked out for prisoner exchange."

"And you *may* get rescued," Jake encouraged, good cop to Big Ray's bad.

"If you don't cooperate, you'll be tortured until you yield, then you'll be executed, and one member of your family will be executed for each Watterson who was murdered."

Jake shook his head at the thought. "That's seven, not including you."

"Sev—?!" That was stupid. The prisoner was furious with himself. Of course they knew it was six; Jake had goaded him to react, to give himself away. Everybody realized the slip.

"We'll start by killing your wife, if you have one, then any children or stepchildren you have. Then we'll go after your sisters, then brothers, then mother, then father, then grandparents, aunts, uncles, cousins, whatever it takes until we got six of 'em."

The prisoner said nothing, his face flushed, breathing heavily. A nerve had been struck, but he wouldn't cave easily. He looked like his confidence was wavering, afraid the family threat might not be a bluff. Going off to fight in foreign lands proved very different than war in your own backyard.

"Don't underestimate our sources for information," Big Ray challenged. "We knew you was comin'. We'll know who you are by tomorrow night, whether you's dead or alive. Then we'll find your people." He turned to the huge man with the suitcase. "Let me see them pictures. Come up to the bars," he ordered the prisoner.

The captured agent wouldn't comply, so the bars were unlocked for the big man to step inside, unarmed. Like he *needed* artillery. He reached out, but the prisoner scrambled backward. In one motion, the big guy kicked out surprisingly fast, amazingly nimble. A hard blow to the chest staggered the smaller man into the wall, knocking the wind out of him. He lay there wheezing for a moment until he could breathe again.

The big man bowed graciously, mockingly, and waved his arm toward the bars. "He's invitin' you to look at some pitchers," he said.

The prisoner reluctantly decided to go look at the photos.

Eugene never saw them, but they must have been repulsive. The hard-assed agent had to look away several times.

"This is what happened to your buddies," Big Ray finished as he showed the last four in the stack.

Eugene remembered that the other agents' bodies were to be converted into animal feed. Having grown up in the country, he knew what that involved. He felt queasy trying to imagine what the photos must show. Then he flashed back to other harsh images he'd recently seen. He couldn't shake the vision of Joe Pennington dangling over the dark gulf waters, his face blown away, inky blood flowing heavy, then trickling . . .

What happened next was difficult for Eugene to watch. The big guy had the prisoner against the bars. Somebody was securing his arms from behind. The man still wouldn't cooperate. What was wrong with him?

Eugene recognized the homemade stinger. He cringed from the pathetic screams, retching once from the smell of burning flesh. He wanted to leave, but Durbett was standing strong, alternately watching the grisly proceedings and studying the young guy at his side. Eugene felt like a little kid, like he shouldn't be there, angry that Durbett wouldn't take him outside and protect him from all this, angry at himself for not just leaving.

Then he decided he would be man enough to take it.

Somehow, it seemed Durbett could tell he'd finally reached that point. Eugene's eyes glistened, his breakfast trying to come up, but he steeled himself for the inevitable.

"Cold, hard reality," Durbett whispered.

Eugene nodded slightly, wiping his face, embarrassed about his own lack of composure.

The big guy did some things with a knife, with some kind of yellowish powder, with pliers. When Eugene couldn't stand it, he'd watch the others, wonder what they were thinking.

Several were enjoying this display. The woman looked sad. One of the men looked as sickened by it as Eugene. The guy inflicting such torture seemed to be thriving on it, working himself into a frenzy. Big Ray didn't like it one bit, but seemed to see it as a necessary evil.

Eugene studied Durbett out the corner of his eye. It confounded him that the tall, balding man could watch all this so calmly, with no emotion, like he didn't care. Eugene wondered how much this guy had seen in his life, the atrocities that may have been so much worse, how different it must feel when it's somebody you know, somebody you care about.

The only time Eugene had ever seen Flynn Durbett show any kind of passion was when the mercenary *worried* about somebody, when somebody he cared about had been wronged. Eugene had seen it in his reaction to Norm Watterson's murder. He'd seen it countless times in how Durbett had treated Eugene, worried over him, anticipated his concern for Licia. Durbett was just like Norm Watterson—paying attention, a simple nod, a rare clasp on the shoulder . . . but these guys wouldn't give you the time of day unless they wanted to.

So Durbett watched a man be tortured like it was everyday business, and Eugene watched as much as he could stand, determined to become like Flynn.

Cold, hard reality.

The prisoner wound up talking. He didn't know much about the operation. Knew it was coordinated out of Ft. Donelson, under authority of Major General Ashe, reporting to Lt. Col. Poole, was only following orders. The PPDs were keyed to a mobile station south of Erin; the detector programmed to seek objects the size and density of a solid, black box slightly larger than a pack of cards. The Wattersons didn't suffer during that incursion when the first box was seized, had never seen it coming.

Eugene imagined Russell breathing a short *pffft* in his sleep. He realized that simply torturing the man wouldn't have been enough to make him talk. Fear for his family did him in, the relentless reminders from Big Ray that his wife would be next, his children, his sisters . . . The images in his mind mingling with what he'd seen in the photos had overcome his resistance.

Caring about somebody else.

Who cares about me?

Licia Emery. Maybe a lot of these people. Definitely Flynn Durbett—or so he liked to think.

"You will be executed for your war crimes," Big Ray was telling the crumpled man on the floor. The man didn't look surprised. He showed what?—maybe even relief?

"Because you have cooperated, we will spare your family. You have one hour."

Big Ray walked over to Flynn. "You were Watterson's second," he said. "It is your privilege."

Flynn nodded, then looked at his watch.

One hour.

The prisoner was left alone for his remaining time. Eugene heard part of the discussion outside about how the Ft. Donelson lead would be followed up, whom to contact, who should know. But he was feeling dizzy, queasy, hot. He hurried down to where the stream passed below the cellhouse and sat on the bank. He splashed cold water, wiped his face again, tried to catch his breath.

It was such a nice spot, so much like sitting along Little Richland when he was younger, watching the birds and listening for animals and spying fish in the still pools—but he couldn't find that sense of innocent serenity he used to feel, afraid it had gone forever.

After a while, he heard somebody coming up behind him. He knew Durbett's walk, didn't need to turn around.

"You wanna be alone?"

Eugene shook his head.

Durbett sat down in the grass beside him. "I can't blame you for being mad," he offered quietly.

"That didn't have to happen."

"No, it didn't," the older man agreed. "But it *needed* to."

Eugene shook his head, not convinced, still rattled by what he'd seen.

"He killed your friend."

"Two wrongs don't make a right!" Eugene blurted. Aunt Willow, of all people, used to preach that. He shook his head again. "Weren't right."

"Once our man was compromised at the house, it was kill or be killed."

"Then you shoulda just killed him." Eugene was looking into the water, studying the patterns and ripples of the flowing stream.

"He had information. I agree, torturing a man to confess his own crime ain't right. Bill of Rights say he don't have to. But they got Marshall and we have to get him back. Can't do that without info. They's tryin' to get *you*. Can't protect you without info. If you's the one in danger, then Licia's in danger when you're with her."

Eugene looked up at Durbett, squinting in the bright sunlight. He looked down again.

Durbett continued playing the Licia card. "How do you think she feels about her brother being missing? Being treated no-tellin' how? *Probably* just because they's after *you!*"

Eugene held his breath, then let it out slowly. His heart was pounding again. He thought for a minute. "Maybe he would've talked after a few more days."

"And maybe not. Didn't have time to wait. What he told us is just the start. We still ain't found Marshall or who's after *you*."

Lost in thought, he gazed into the water. He wiped his face. He stared into the water some more. "I didn't expect all this."

"I think Norman was hoping it wouldn't come to this, was planning to look out for you himself. But he *was* trying to get you ready for the worst—just in case."

"He said I had a big responsibility."

"Like a soldier pledging to die for his country. But dying ain't worth it unless you accomplish for your loved ones whatever you was fightin' for. And you gotta be willing to take out whoever's in your way."

"But this is torture and murder."

"And in some cases that's wrong, but this is what you call *situational ethics*. This needed to happen to save Marshall." Then quieter, "And it happened to a man who killed *your* best friend and his dad, *my* best friend. I've seen worse for less reason."

Eugene thought some more, still watching the water, then mumbled, "But two wrongs don't make a right."

"You can't always play fair when you're up against cheaters."

Eugene shook his head again.

Durbett offered, "Look, it don't always seem right to me, neither. But it's the *only* reason *I'm* still alive."

They sat there several more minutes. Durbett checked his watch, then stood up. Eugene exhaled, hanging his head.

Durbett watched him a moment, then turned toward the cell-house. He hesitated and looked back, "Listen, Eugene, I'd like to live the way it *oughta* be. But sometimes, you have to live the way things *is*."

Eugene stood up and faced him. Quietly, calmly, he said, "Cold, hard reality."

Durbett nodded, then walked up to the cinder-block building. He paused outside and checked his pistol.

Eugene stood by the creek and watched him, that confounded trembling coming back, his heart pounding. Then, all at once, he felt calm, serene. The birds stopped singing, the animals stopped scurrying, the sounds of the creek and the wind and the rustling leaves all faded away.

Durbett looked puzzled for a moment, then went inside the building.

Eugene closed his eyes.

Pfoom! Pfoom!

*   *   *

"Died of trauma, that's the prevailing hypothesis," the chief examiner informed.

"Like what?" McGovern demanded. He fingered his face-mask uncomfortably, his eyes averted from the splayed, twenty-years-dead remains of two MPs. He stood stiffly in the precise center of the open area, like the slightest movement would risk contaminating his immaculate uniform with blood and guts and gore—and no-telling *what* more.

The doctor shrugged, picking up a tray of dissected organs, eyeing them curiously. He enjoyed watching McGovern flinch at the sight, shrink away from lurking cooties. "Gunshot, stabbing—hell, a giant worm eating its way out. *I* don't know."

"That's as *specific* as you can be?"

"Just look," the doctor offered, setting the tray down to motion the colonel toward the nearest corpse. McGovern steeled himself, then inched closer. "These guys have been hacked up so bad all I can do is eliminate possibilities. The last autopsy could have obliterated entry wounds here and here, two here, here to the head, and any number here to the abdomen." He was poking around with a long, silver instrument, prying apart tissue, exposing sawed bones and clipped hemostats.

McGovern took a deep breath then, assaulted by the stench, regretted ever breathing at all. "Those weren't caused by the original autopsy?"

"Oh, they were—or at least partly so. Your guy didn't keep very good records—and I don't understand not even photographing each step if this is so forensically important. See, we've eliminated every possible cause known to medicine—even that disconnection phenomenon in the Hall cadaver—"

"*No* sign of alien contamination at all?"

"None. So that leaves us with toxicology—for instance, these mutilations might have obscured poison injection points—but nothing like that is showing up. That leaves physical trauma."

"But that's just a possibility—nothing else to base it on?" McGovern was easing his way back to the center of the floor, his countenance ashen gray.

The doctor sauntered around to the other table, motioning the colonel to follow. "I have no proof, but a couple things make me wonder." He urged the colonel closer.

McGovern wondered if this really was necessary or if some fun was being had at his expense. "Something suspicious?"

"Yeah, like reckless incompetence. If trauma caused blood loss to surrounding tissue, that would show up, even if the wound was damaged, say, in emergency surgery or during a sloppy autopsy. But look, this has been hacked up so bad—" He was peeling away layers of muscle and fat in the man's lower chest cavity. "—That we can't be sure what caused it. There's no record of how *long* after death this was done—which would tell us a lot. There's no record of what condition the surrounding tissue was in, and it was poorly preserved—allowed to deteriorate too much."

"Could it be inexperience, just sloppy work?"

The doctor poked around in the abdominal cavity with a different instrument. "No. Unless he was a complete idiot, it looks intentional. There's no sense in where he chose to make the cuts, which organs were removed and how . . ." A second doctor standing off to the side nodded in agreement. "It looks like these guys were shot or stabbed, then had their autopsies deliberately botched to cover it."

McGovern backed away from the cadavers, tugging at his jacket and straightening his tie. "Keep exploring. If you discover anything else, inform me right away."

By the time the doctor could nod, McGovern was halfway to the exit. Once he'd passed through the quarantine seal, he snatched his face-mask off and, not seeing a trash barrel for it, folded it and put it in his pocket. He marched to the administration building, returning salutes along the way, immersed in private contemplation. Reaching his office, he heard that Dr. Aggeous had arrived and was ready for questioning.

"Have him cuffed and brought in, then leave us alone—but keep a guard posted just outside the door." He'd decided to start with a one-on-one before involving the interrogation expert.

"You'll forgive me for not saluting," Aggeous jabbed, pretending a struggle to get his manacled arm out from behind his back. He wheezed, looked around, and selected the low couch across from the desk to maneuver his frame onto. He wheezed again, then coughed several times, took a deep breath, and finally good-naturedly inquired, "Saved the world yet?"

"No, not yet," McGovern acknowledged dryly. The colonel situated himself at the front of his desk, his butt against the edge, fists on the surface. That put him in the doctor's face—but not within reach—and positioned him higher so he could look down on his captive.

He was startled by a phone buzz. He answered, listened a moment, then directed, "Yes, yes I am. Have him disappear and bring him here. Keep him dark in case he's ever released."

"Just found another alien?" Aggeous taunted, still upbeat. Absent was the rage he'd first expressed at being taken into custody.

"Have you decided to give me more information about the invasion yet?"

"You figured out how them MPs was killed?"

"Major trauma, like shooting or stabbing."

"You don't know which?" Aggeous rolled his eyes, then hocked up a goober. Looking around for a place to spit, he decided to swallow it instead.

"Who killed them?"

"Ain't figured *that* out yet, neither, huh?"

McGovern said nothing, studying the doctor for a moment. They stared each other down.

Finally, Aggeous suggested, "Look, close your eyes and picture the scene."

"I'm not closing my eyes—"

"You want to figure it out or not? I can't stand up right now without help—and you'd sure as hell hear me if I tried. Close your eyes and picture it."

McGovern considered for a moment, then relented.

"Now picture that scene in those photos."

McGovern envisioned the grassy hillock, the ship-damaged patch, several black boxes, a much-younger version of Aggeous, those two MPs looking substantially healthier than in their current assignments. There was a fourth man, presumably General—back then a colonel—Higgins, but McGovern couldn't bring him into focus, couldn't tell where he was.

"You see weapons?"

An M1911A-1 Colt, standard Army issue back then. A .38 in the civilian doctor's hands. The MPs being summoned over to take something . . . then . . . suddenly fired upon! One of them was shot in the chest by Doctor Aggeous!

"*You* killed them. You *shot* them."

Aggeous arched his eyebrows, wry satisfaction on his face. "The *second* one," he corrected. "And I was just following orders. *I* wasn't the one with a big-ass Colt."

McGovern was shaken, struggling for composure. Those images were so vivid . . . "Who shot the other one?"

Aggeous laughed, wheezed to catch his breath, then laughed some more.

"Why, Colonel McGovern, now you could say *you* did."

*   *   *

He thought *he* was just worrying about *her*. Turned out, *she* was also worrying about *him*. Talking with her felt good, but with Flynn Durbett hovering nearby, traffic noise drowning her hollow-tube voice over the pay-phone, stern admonitions not to divulge anything about what had happened . . . it was, at the least, awkward.

But *good*.

She seemed to know better than to ask, to understand that leaving McEwen with a prisoner meant serious business, and had figured that whatever transpired would be a jolt for Eugene.

"Y'all right?"

"Yeah. You?"

"Yeah."

Eugene would be staying a few more days. Had people to visit, stuff to get done, lessons to learn. You know—yeah, everything's all right.

Eugene had to feed change into the slot every few minutes; Durbett didn't want the call billed anywhere. They chattered until the money ran low, not really saying much of anything, but anticipating their reunion in

McEwen a few long days hence.

Eugene strolled into the small grocery and stuffed a listful of sacks while Durbett made several calls. His arms ached from hefting the rations. He'd endured some rigorous drills the last few days—especially early that morning when a lot of the guys were still pumped from the torture and execution. He'd regarded Mr. Watterson as the archetypal proponent of serious training, but most of *this* bunch were outright fanatics. From sessions covering emergency field medicine and constitutional rights, he'd graduated to the fundamentals of building and detonating powerful explosives.

Durbett hustled Eugene back for a drugstore-owner militia-member's seminar on toxic substances.

"It's called ricin," the pharmacist pronounced. He glanced toward the attorney.

"It's illegal if possession is construed to be *intent* for use as a weapon," the lawyer explained. "A smidge to kill raccoons *ought* not to be a problem, but a quantity *could* be—especially carrying it around under any kind of suspicious circumstances. There haven't been but a few popped for it, but the feds have come down *hard* when they have. Some of our brothers up north were convicted for less than a gram."

The pharmacist supported him by wagging a cautionary finger, then explained, "It's extracted from the castor bean plant. It's so poisonous, it ranks behind only plutonium and botulism in toxicity. It first got a lot of attention when Bulgarian secret agents used it to kill a defector back in the seventies."

Eugene noticed that Durbett glanced around for people's reactions before resuming to feign only mild interest.

The pharmacist allowed the audience to pass around a sample of the commonly found plant while he demonstrated grinding the beans, mixing several other ingredients, then boiling it into an ominous, dark paste. He displayed a finished jarful and a dozen vials' worth he'd concocted for storage with the arsenal in the subterranean refuge.

"Damage to the intestines causing severe fluid loss, drop in blood pressure, heart trouble, and an imbalance of electrolytes like sodium and potassium," he listed. "It's also toxic to the liver, the central nervous system, the kidneys, and the adrenal system. It's even been known to cause brain abscess."

The crowd looked impressed. The demonstration with an unwary rabbit proved very moving.

Afterward, Eugene followed Durbett back to the chow hall for the big buffet feast. By this time, more than seventy people were on the grounds, some with families tagging along. Like a big reunion, many gushed over seeing each other for the first time in too long.

Durbett politely greeted the few who spoke first, but he seemed distant, somewhat agitated. Never once did he hint to Eugene that he wanted to be left completely alone. His young protégé was the only person he would allow constant proximity.

Like he *wanted* it . . . or maybe needed it.

Once, when they wandered outdoors with their plastic cups of foamy keg beer, Eugene quietly prodded, "You can't find Marshall yet, can ya?" It was more of a statement than a question.

Durbett looked him over appraisingly, then hinted at a smile. He shook his head no. "Not yet."

Eugene considered a lot of things to say about that, but then decided he couldn't think of anything after all, so he kept quiet.

Every man's got his limit.

It was late afternoon, not so hot anymore, somewhere between the dog days and Indian summer. Somehow, they'd worked their way down to the stream, so Eugene set about filling the minnow bucket.

"Gotta feed them fish," he joked. "If we ever have to hunker down in here for a long time, we may need to *eat* 'em."

Durbett smiled, but he still appeared distracted.

Eugene set the bucket down and eyed the bigger, older man. He tilted his head and stroked his chin, then surprised himself by sagely intoning, "Every man's got his limit."

Durbett snapped from his reverie, studying the teen's face, surprised at the sentiment. "Where'd you hear *that?*"

Eugene shrugged.

"Watterson never said that to you?"

Eugene considered, then shook his head. "Don't *think* so."

Durbett took another drink, draining his cup. He acted like he intended to walk back up toward the buildings, but he lingered.

Eugene looked into the water, watching the minnows dart about in choreographed frenzy. Quietly, he said, "When it's time to climb up and over, you need a plan in case you fall."

Durbett gripped Eugene's shoulder, then whirled him around. "Yes—you—do," he agreed slowly, deliberately.

"That's when Mr. Watterson saved your life—in Argentina, ain't it?"

In contrast to Durbett's perplexity, Eugene betrayed confusion, worry, maybe even fear.

"He never told you about that?"

Eugene shook his head.

"How'd you know?"

Eugene Weisman covered his eyes, then eased his hands away and gaped at them as something unfamiliar. Then he stared into the water again and breathed, "Flynn?"

"I'm right here."

"It's like . . ." There were no words.

Durbett carefully tilted Eugene's face up, searching his eyes. "It's like—?"

"I remember all *kinda* stuff I ain't supposed to know."

*   *   *

Boom! Boom! Boom! Boom! Boom!
Echoing, reverberating.
Boom! Boom! Boom! Boom! Boom!
Relentless, teeth-rattling.
Boom! Boom! Boom! Boom! Boom! Boom!

"*Six* that time," McGovern gasped, exasperation on his sleeve.

"He's on his way up," the interrogation expert bemused, not as shaken by Marshall Emery's conniption. "He rides 'em up a while, tires himself out, backs off until he remembers his situation again, then off he goes."

Boom! Boom! Boom! Boom! Boom! Boom!

McGovern assessed the integrity of the steel cell-door. "We should have confiscated his boots—maybe *that* would discourage him from that *damned* kicking."

"He would've just broke his foot by now—and even then it might not stop him." He chuckled.

Boom! Boom! Boom!
Boom! Boom! Boom!

"He's out of control," McGovern pronounced. The colonel's world divided between those who respect authority and those who don't; this guy seemed to be so far out there that he shattered the paradigm.

Boom! Boom!

Boom! Boom!

Boom! Boom! Boom! Boom! Boom!

"Ahh . . ." the interrogator mused, "he's *not* out of control. He's asserting what little control he *does* have over a situation that is upsetting him *terribly*."

"But what's he accomplishing?"

"He's got *you* worked up, too, doesn't he? Maybe forcing you into reacting prematurely."

Boom! Boom! Boom! Boom! Boom! Boom!

"Maybe get me to shoot the son of a bitch," the colonel growled.

Laughing now—at the colonel? "Give me time to get out of the way before you open that door! Heh heh—he'll be climbing *right* up your ass quicker than you can get a bead."

Boom! Boom! Boom!

McGovern tried to pace off his exasperation. "He is absolutely berserk."

"Not at all. He's varying his pattern to avoid boring himself. Show me the same pattern for two straight days—until he doesn't know whether he's even doing it or not—and I'll show you berserk."

Boom! Boom-boom! Boom-boom-boom!

"Heh heh heh heh."

"I'm glad *you're* enjoying this." McGovern stopped pacing, suddenly self-conscious about being studied by the expert. "How do *you* handle these types?"

He shrugged. *Boom! Boom!* "Normally you wait until they pass out and go in with a three-man team and restraints—or open the door and shoot him with a dart. But you can't risk either of those if he might be able to alien-contaminate with *any* physical contact. Even dead asleep, he could all-of-a-sudden come up at you."

Boom! Boom! Boom! Boom-boom! Boom!

"He wasn't like this in county custody down in Alabama—"

Boom!

"There, he understood what game he was playing," the expert pointed out. "You already *know* he's militia. He's a gun-toting paranoid government-conspiracist obsessed with his rights. He's the clean freak who knows he's fallen in the septic tank—" *Boom! Boom! Boom!* The examiner glanced at the steel vault, not quite as amused as before. "—And he doesn't see the way out."

"I need to interrogate him. How do I proceed?"

Boom! Boom!

"I say flush the water out of his toilet, then tap in with a potent mixture of goodies. That way, the water in the bowl and what comes out of the faucet will both be drugged. Sedate him."

Boom! Boom! Boom!

"How long will *that* take?"

"He'll suspect you—may try to hold out until he just *has* to drink." He shrugged. "Couple of days, fade him out, then still hit him with a dart when you open the door just in case—and go in with armored quarantine suits to make extra sure."

"Two days?!"

Boom! Boom! Boom!

"*If* he gives in and drinks. He may dehydrate himself to death if he remains *this* stubborn."

"But I *must* see what information he has. He's my best lead at this point."

Boom! Boom! Boom! Boom!

"Then let's just wait and see. I'll tell you one thing, though. Rushing to minimize awareness and impact with this guy don't matter. Whether you get your info or not, he's going to wind up dead either way."

Boom-Boom!

McGovern looked puzzled, the interrogator matter-of-fact. "Why?"

Boom! Boom! Boom! Boom! Boom! Boom! Boom! Boom!

"He's too dangerous to get back to his people. You can't *ever* let him go."

Chapter 7

He sighted down the barrel of his new Browning, a .380 semi-automatic with 7-shot clip. Then he paused. He'd lost his view of the target, was waiting for movement to betray its presence. The intended was a master of camouflage, equally adept in the trees and on the ground. Eugene's only advantage was that it didn't know a predator lurked nearby.

Except for pausing occasionally to scan the area, all it cared about was foraging for new-fallen acorns. It moved again, a flick of its bushy tail.

Eugene aimed, pretended to pull the trigger.

"Quit worryin' about that ol' squirrel and pay attention," Big Ray admonished.

Eugene followed him and another man farther into the woods, trying to appear interested. Truth was, except for the kick he was getting out of carrying his first pistol with big balls—and having a new Glock 19, 9mm semi-automatic back at the house—he couldn't keep his mind off Licia.

What was she doing right then? Did she miss him? Was she thinking about him? What did she have for breakfast? How many strokes to brush her long, beautiful hair? Sure, sometimes he imagined her in the moonlight in her pullover, holding him in her arms . . . but he found himself thinking more often about moments like her frying up fat bologna sandwiches for him, showing him her album of family photos, her eyes glistening when she talked about her daddy, a lifetime of shots of the pretty little girl who'd grown up to be a beautiful young woman. One who loved Eugene as much as he loved her.

"Eugene! Come here. *You* do this one."

He shoved the Browning into the back of his waistband, noticing how tight his jeans were getting, how fast he was growing. He hustled over to assist the man, watching as they used a small, metal tool to create a foot-deep slit in the ground, semi-circling a giant oak they'd identified from a hand-drawn map. Eugene unrolled more of the tubing-housed flash-burning primer cord and inserted it in the ground. He used a hand-tool to nick the outer layer and insert a small thread, pulling it through so it looped the cord. He selected a small odd-length of already-cut tubing and stripped back an inch or so. He inserted it into another trench leading directly to the tree, leaving several extra feet at the other end, and used the thread to pull the cord through the notch he'd cut. He tied it off, then gooped the connection before wrapping it in plastic tape. He carefully pressed it into the ground and covered up all of his work except the exposed end by the tree. Big Ray and his cohort watched intently, satisfied. Eugene studied the trunk of the tree carefully.

"Good. If you can't find it when you know it's there, we done a good job," Big Ray boasted. He reached down along a decades-old fungus crack and carefully peeled up a flap of old, mossy bark near the base. A long, hollow notch had been chain-sawed into the wood, then packed with plastic explosive wrapped eight times around with primer cord.

"This one's supposed to be a *trip*, too," the other man pointed out, studying the plat.

Big Ray nodded, then stepped back to watch the lad work.

Eugene removed a tiny, spark-inducing popper from his backpack and carefully tacked it near the bottom where the bark flap would obscure it, its detonator ring downward. Next, he tamped a small eye-ring into the wood about a half-inch above the ground, aligned it visually and, satisfied, asked, "From where?"

"Whatta you recommend?" Big Ray quizzed.

Eugene studied the area, considered probable routes of infiltration, the direction of the road and where the camp was located. He selected a pine some ten feet away. Big Ray nodded approval.

He tamped an eye-ring into the second tree, positioned out of sight from intruders who might be working their way toward the compound, then tied the end of a roll of fine trip wire to it. He ran the wire across the ground toward the explosive tree and cut it, leaving an extra foot or so. He threaded it through the first eye-ring, measured it carefully, then tied a small hook onto the end aligned with the popper ring and snipped off the excess.

"Where's it set?" Big Ray asked, but Eugene was already turning the setting on the popper to maximum tension. He understood they couldn't risk an animal setting it off. It would take something as big as a person to snag the wire before enough pressure would be created to make it blow.

Eugene carefully placed the hook through the ring, then lowered the bark and gently pressed it into place. He walked back along the wire and obscured it with sticks, rotting leaves, a few rocks, whatever he could find.

Everybody was satisfied. Eugene felt silly wondering if Licia would be proud.

They moved on, still inserting primer cord into the ground. Eugene followed along, hefting and aiming his Browning, trying to get used to the feel, hoping his exuberance looked more macho than childlike. They paused to splice the next roll.

Big Ray mused, "I still don't see why Norm left you with nothin' better than that pussy .22." He'd made the same remark when he and Durbett presented the new pistols to their teenage protégé.

Eugene tucked the Browning back into his pants, then inspected his own hands as if they were somehow, suddenly unfamiliar. "Handling a weapon is the last stage of becomin' a soldier," he offered quietly. "You need to develop your instinct, your senses, your ability to improvise, whatever it takes to get the edge. You learn to depend on your weapon too much and you won't fully use what-all else you got. There's more to surviving than good aim."

They studied him for a moment. Past his reverie, Eugene looked sheepish. They continued the trenching.

"Can't never argue with Watterson," was all Big Ray had to say about it.

Back at the big house in the compound, Eugene found Jake Coleman at the computer, Flynn Durbett watching over his shoulder. Both appeared stymied, frustrated.

"I thought if anybody could track him down, you could," Jake remarked, logging off, closing out with M-C-M-12, *My Cousin Marty tried at least a dozen times* . . .

Durbett shook his head. "It's being worked on, but that carries risk all its own. I *need* what's set up for me—can't afford to compromise it askin' too much."

Jake stood, carefully donning his blue-jay fedora, then rubbed his eyes. "You can't ask, *You seen my pig?* without admitting your pig got loose."

"And that you *have* a pig," Eugene rejoined, dead serious.

"Or *had* one," Big Ray countered. "You guys got *nothin'* so far?"

Jake looked toward Durbett, shaking his head. "Lotsa reports of activity, mostly places we knowed about for some time. Whatever's goin' on at that Cumberland Sanitarium has been since Wattersons' murder, but I can't get a handle on it. Don't know if it's false scent or the big one, but we got nobody inside we can trust. Got one guy says an older black fella was taken there, no doubt as a prisoner, though he didn't seem dangerous.

Don't seem to be one of ours—we don't get many blacks and I can count the older ones on my fingers—but if citizens is bein' detained there for whatever reason, it might be where Marshall was taken."

Big Ray wondered, "How many *reasons* can you think of he mighta been grabbed by feds?"

"Weapons or alien hunt," Jake tallied. He seemed to run out after two items, so he repeated them. "Weapons or aliens."

"And I've just about eliminated weapons investigation," Durbett added.

"They've connected him to me," Eugene said quietly.

"Ain't nothin' said they even *know* about you," Jake argued. "We know they was on to Watterson—had him killed even—so they probably connected Marshall to *him*."

"Then it's only a matter of time until they know about me," Eugene said matter-of-factly. "From Marshall or if they got Jolene or if somebody else knew."

"Nothin' on *her?*" Big Ray wondered.

Durbett shook his head. "She got beyond the control of the FBI. If she's back, it's in the hands of these people I can't crack—*my* people can't crack. Odds are, unless she's just recently been picked up, she's still out there somewhere."

"Or dead," Eugene pointed out.

"Or dead," Jake agreed.

"Maybe we need to find her," Durbett tossed out. "If she knows about Eugene, she's a security risk. And maybe she knows something about the black box everybody's after."

They all looked at each other for a moment before Jake logged back on the computer again. M-C-M-12 got him through a final screening process to access daily militia communications. He consulted a worn notebook from his satchel numerous times, working feverishly. Big Ray called to check in with his wife as he set about making sandwiches, so Eugene went out to the cricket box and used the worn toilet-paper roller in the bottom to scoop up several dozen of the little chirpers and pour them into a small, round basket. He fed nearly a dozen to the pair of bass before those denizens of the aquarium slowed enough for the others to get their share.

Finally, Jake stood up, satisfied with his progress. "I need to make two calls and confirm," he said.

"I need to make a few myself," Durbett returned, not offering to explain.

"And I need to call Licia," Eugene interjected, quick to get in his bid to tag along. He knew the phone calls would happen from out-of-the-way places in the surrounding area, understanding how easy it was to wiretap phones, legal or not.

During their drive to the city of Boaz, factory-outlet capital of the U.S., Jake explained he'd need to wire some money and arrange a pick-up in Waverly in order to follow up on one lead, plus he needed ideas on how to handle another. "He's not one of ours—none of 'em are—but I got a guy that ID'd one who's right inside doing MP at that new set-up in Cumberland. Says can't trust tryin' to get to him direct, but he knows the feller's got leave time coming in three days and ain't planning to go nowhere. Just wants to get away from the base and get laid and piss beer for a while."

"I'll handle it," Durbett said cryptically.

"Good, I'll get the details when I call."

They stopped at various places with pay phones, making one or two calls at each before moving on. Before dialing one, Durbett asked, "How big a line do I give this guy?"

"He's straight up," Jake assured. "I'd make it wide open. He'll only do what needs to be done."

"Will he do *enough*, though?"

Jake only smiled.

Eugene was fascinated by all the billboards and outlet stores as they got into the commercial district of Boaz. Durbett motioned Jake to pull into one of the biggest, one specializing in jeans and casual wear.

"Time to get you some clothes that fit," Durbett said evenly.

Eugene was surprised and pleased. He owned next to nothing, and what he did have had been outgrown months before. Mrs. Watterson always had a way of shopping for Russell that included accidentally coming home with too many pairs of everything, some too big for her own son. Though he was feeling a bit too financially dependent on Durbett's charity, Eugene was grateful for the chance to stock up. He wanted to look nice on his next trip to see Licia.

Jake was grabbing a few items for himself and some on-sale jeans for Tracey while Durbett hovered around and kept an eye on Eugene. He slipped the teen a sheaf of bills, watched him pay the cashier, then walked him out to the truck. During the drive back, Eugene politely thanked his benefactor.

"Now you owe me," Durbett said, more serious than good-natured.

Eugene looked out the window, avoiding eye contact. Finally, he murmured, "You want me to try again, don't you?"

Durbett and Jake Coleman looked at each other.

"All I've told Jake is that you think you're getting memories from Watterson, that the alien inside you is doing it," Durbett clarified. "He's safe to talk in front of, or we can do it later without him, but you did promise to try to sort it out for me."

Eugene gazed out the window, saying nothing.

"Look, Eugene," Jake explained. "It don't matter if the alien stuff is true or not. Me, I don't believe it. Flynn here says probably not, but he ain't closed the book on the possibility. *You* believe it and Norm Watterson believed it—that's pretty good credentials backing it up in my book. Somebody in the government believes it enough to kill Wattersons over it. They think there's a black box has something to do with it, maybe they got it, maybe they don't. Whether it's true or not don't even matter as much as where it's got *us*. So don't think you have to convince *me* or anyone else. Killed over a lie or killed over the truth, you're just as dead both ways."

Still looking out the window, Eugene said, "Mr. Watterson helped pay for your mama to be in that nursin' home, and you and him was the only ones knowed about it."

Jake was taken aback. "Did he *tell* you—?"

Eugene whirled and stared at him defiantly. "He didn't tell me *nothin'*—and I didn't know who you was back then."

"What say we set a spell?" Jake asked rhetorically, pulling into the lot of a big discount store and parking back near the employees' vehicles with a clear view every direction. "Nobody knew that," he declared. He looked to Durbett, but the balding mercenary didn't appear surprised.

"All Mr. Watterson told me was he had a alien inside him that was here to help us and that there was another one, too, but he didn't know what happened to it. He figured government got it and killed it or had it in captured-it-ivity," he stumbled.

"In captivity," Durbett supplied.

"He said not to worry about nothin', but that if anything ever went wrong and we needed help, the black box would do it. He said he thought everything was okay until a couple years ago, then he expected we really *was* in danger, so he wanted to give us each a part of the alien in case some-thing ever happened. Then we could do it without him. He butchered them cows and said we each had a new alien in us and we'd know what needed to be done if the time ever come. He used to teach us how to hunt and stuff—me and Russell, I mean—but after that he was teachin' us how to fight enemies and not get captured. He never said nothin' about Flynn or you or nobody else."

"Why you think he done that?" Durbett wondered. "Why you think he wanted to train you, but wouldn't tell you nothin' about it?"

Eugene closed his eyes and considered, an aura of serenity smoothing his face. "He hoped it wouldn't ever matter."

"How you know about my mom?" Jake cut in.

"It's the alien," Eugene said reverently.

"Cut the crap," Jake admonished. He was growing impatient.

"I'm learnin' how to talk to him," Eugene said.

Durbett's interest was piqued. "That's why these memories are coming slowly?—you have to wait for him to *tell* 'em to you?"

Eugene's eyes remained closed. He thought, then slowly shook his head from side to side. "No, he lets me remember whatever I want. It's just too much to sort out, like a bunch of people screaming all at once. I remember everything that happened to me since I got the alien, but I can also see it from a different . . . um, *attitude*." He wasn't satisfied with his limited vocabulary.

"Like—?" Durbett prompted.

"Like it was worried I wouldn't be *serious* enough, or *quick* enough if I needed to do something."

"Do *what*?"

He shook his head. "Don't know yet."

"What about remembering about Watterson?"

"I keep gettin' these flashes remembering things in his life, even before Russell was born. It's like havin' lots of years of his life all wrote down, but I don't know about 'em unless I read the pages or something reminds me to see what they says."

"Like about him saving my ass in Argentina," Durbett prompted.

Eugene nodded, his eyes still squeezed shut.

Jake listened, alternately watching them both and scanning the area for attackers. He'd been shaken by the revelation about his mother, forced to confront for the first time the possibility that Eugene might truly be con-joined.

"How far back does it go?" Durbett prodded.

"All the way."

Durbett waited. No explanation followed. "All the way?"

Eugene nodded. "Ain't nothin' like anything I ever knowed. I tried to look close but got too scared—"

"Like last night," Durbett supplied.

Eugene nodded again. He suspected Durbett had heard him cry out in the night, figured that was why the muscular, balding man had peeked in a few minutes later.

"You're gonna need some time with it," Durbett observed.

Eugene nodded.

"I'd like more proof," he suggested.

"Me knowin' stuff only Watterson knowed?"

"That would do it."

Eugene opened his eyes and studied Durbett's face, then broke into a wry smile. "Stop me when you hear enough," he began, an impish twinkle in his eye. "Banqué de Venezuela, charter through Dominion Guaranty, Republic of Cayman Islands, blind account number 8674-B-2397—"

"That's enough," Durbett said quietly.

Eugene took a deep breath and looked at Coleman. "Watterson paid off your mortgage, Jake, same time as Flynn paid off Emery's."

"Why?"

"Because you promised to help people protect themselves from what he was afraid was coming."

Jake was rattled. He'd never had that conversation with Durbett or Marshall or anybody. He doubted Watterson would have related it to a mere boy—especially about a man the lad had never met.

"Eugene?" Durbett interrupted. "What's the first things Watterson wanted you to know?"

Eugene closed his eyes and thought. After a few minutes, his breathing grew labored. He sniffled a few times, wiped his eyes. Sadly, just realizing the implications, he whispered toward Durbett, "Both you and him is—was—rich." He wiped his eyes again. "Mr. Watterson had college ac-counts set up for each of his kids . . . and—" He stammered. "There's one for me, too."

Jake was surprised, but Durbett wasn't.

Eugene's face showed amazement as he recalled more, almost blurting each time he thought of assets to add to the list. "He owns that property where the compound is, and thirty-some other properties, and he's got accounts, and he's got funds set up to pay those lawyers and that doctor and to support all those militias and to have lots of money for his family and . . . even for me . . ."

"You remember where it all is?" Durbett wondered. Past the point of doubt or surprise, he was earnest in his questions.

Eugene nodded. "I'd have to write it all down. It's all in that letter the lawyer's got—"

Durbett explained for Jake that directions for overseeing the disposition of his and Watterson's assets had been left with a lawyer in Nashville, occasionally updated by one or the other privately. Knowing his friend's intent had been foremost to look out for his now-dead family, Durbett hadn't focused much on how to handle the estate after the murders.

"The letter says to divide it up between whoever survives," Eugene said quietly. Then he stammered, choking back a sudden wave of grief. "And I'm the only one on the list that's still alive," he whispered.

"Let's get back," Durbett instructed Jake.

After a few miles, Eugene casually remarked, "Mr. Watterson wanted to settle down; *you* were the businessman." He regarded Durbett with a sidelong glance. "The gun shops and the factories and apartment buildings and all kinds of stuff—even that place where Big Ray works—you're makin' all kinds of money and you just keep moving it out of the country so you can run off and hide someday."

"Don't say *hide*," Durbett warned. He'd been rankled; that must have poked an old wound.

"Mr. Watterson was mad at you, wasn't he?"

Durbett nodded. "You know why?"

"Because *you* took the job and killed those guys in Colombia."

"South America?" Jake asked.

Eugene shrugged. "He quit but *you* took it. By then, he'd decided the government he was workin' for was bad—was gonna turn against its own citizens. What you did helped 'em. He said you didn't care no more because you was gonna take your money and retire in some other country. But *he* had his family here and he needed to fix whatever he could about what he'd done. That's why *you* take *your* money away and *he* supported all these militias so citizens could protect themselves."

"The idealist," Durbett mumbled, turning his face away to watch cars going the other direction. "He thought the battle could be won. I didn't."

"And then the aliens come along."

"And I never believed in 'em."

"You shoulda." Eugene grimaced. "You shoulda."

"But it made no sense!" Durbett was defending himself from the absurd. "It made no sense. He said he had an alien in him and he was in charge of watching for other aliens and if they come, he had to get help and save us all from 'em. It sounded like so much hooey."

"He didn't understand it back then, either, and then you guys never talked about it after that. It took *him* years to figure it out."

"Do *you* know?"

Eugene didn't answer for some time. Jake was holding his breath. Durbett was looking down at the top of the teen's bowed head, watching for the slightest clue. Finally, Eugene just shrugged.

"Yeah, I just gotta figure out how to explain it."

*   *   *

"You're *bull*shitting, man. Ain't nobody *that* stupid—or *that* drunk." Babyboy Moller was stacking sacks of hard-corn from a pallet, his last task before knocking off for the night. He was passing the hours at New Johnsonville's biggest feed distributorship the usual way, arguing with his co-worker, the other stocker. Two young black men, muscular, sweat-veed t-shirts, dusty in the dry September heat. Don't call Babyboy by the name his grandmother had given him unless you're good friends, and then only good-naturedly.

"He was dead serious, man," Co-worker asserted, "like he done seen it hisself."

"Well, how would *he* know? Did he even *know* them people who burned up out there?"

"Said he knocked up his girl and she moved in with 'em to eat better and so a doctor would look out for her baby."

"Then the police come in and killed 'em because they was aliens," Babyboy mocked. "What kinda *bull*shit is that?"

Co-worker grinned and backhand-wiped the sweat from his brow. "Some people believe all *kinda* shit. I just thought it was funny. I'm tellin' ya, he was *dead* serious."

"Well, what happened to his girl?"

"She's hidin' somewhere in Waverly, I guess. Said he be needin' to get a little pussy when she ain't mad at him or worryin' about it hurtin' the baby."

"She's plannin' on havin' it, then?"

"I guess."

"He gonna be drinkin' at Mac's again tonight?"

"If he can bum some money."

"I'll tell you what," Babyboy offered, hefting the empty skid and carrying it to a stack by the open bay door, "You get him and bring him down there and get us a table in the back so don't nobody else be comin' around stirrin' up some shit and *I'll* buy all the beer he can drink, but if he can convince me they's aliens out there, I'll buy shots, too."

"For *me*, too?"

"*If* you can get him to talk to me."

While Co-worker rushed off to find his source of evening's entertainment, Babyboy Moller jumped into his rusty LeBaron, cranked up the thumping speakers he'd mounted in the back window, and drove straight to the bank in Waverly.

It was after hours, but he walked up and rapped on the window until he had the attention of a woman inside. She motioned him around to the drive-thru. He signed the back of the money order, watched the tube vacuum-suck its way into the building, then grinned when it came back stuffed with two envelopes full of cash.

He nodded his thanks and drove on. He picked up carry-out burgers, then ate them during his cruise to Erin. He stopped at three people's houses, staying only a few minutes at each, then drove back past Waverly to his apartment not far from Hurricane Mills and the Loretta Lynn Ranch.

He showered quickly and changed into the kind of bar clothes he'd want a good-lookin' babe to see him in—*if* one ever walked into the godforsaken place he was going. He pulled on boots, then carefully loaded his Browning .380 and tucked it down next to his right ankle.

It was a place off Highway 13, south of Waverly, just outside jurisdiction. A weeknight, not too late yet, there weren't many patrons. Everybody was black. Even on busy nights, white exceptions were few, and then only in the company of a group.

Babyboy waited about thirty minutes before Co-worker arrived. The man with him was a young buck, probably not yet twenty-one but with false ID, carrying himself like he was *bad*. Probably believed it, too.

Babyboy didn't talk so much like the local brothers any more. He was about to start his fourth year on the GI Bill at Middle Tennessee State University over in Murfreesboro. He'd seen several corners of the world and was working hard to make something of himself, so he felt contempt for those he'd grown up around who were satisfied just to fester. "Wuss up? Name's Moller," he introduced himself, submitting to the current fashionable hand-clasp-jab-bonk that passed for the rural version of an urban handshake.

Two hours later, the jukebox blaring tribute to Babyboy's roll of quarters, Young Buck slurred, "Jus' a ho-ass bitch. Ain't nothin' but a ho-ass bee-itch. She owe me *big*. Wattersons was givin' her money and she wouldn't come up off'n none o' that shit. Then she gets all scared about aliens and shit—bitch walks away from a hook-up where they was payin' her bills *and* givin' her cash." He shook his head, took another swig of his beer, eyed the empty shot glass, talked about taking a leak, then decided to wait.

Babyboy scoffed. "Bitch ain't thinkin' right, talkin' some shit about aliens. What—they ain't gonna get her if she's up north?" He was talking the talk to fit in.

Young Buck shook his head, half-laughing, half-snarling his disapproval. "She had an apartment up in Ohio all paid-for, then when those people was burned, she left *that* and come back and started hidin' out *here*."

"Why back here?"

"Ain't *no*body got no sense," Co-worker asserted, *his* words slurred, too, "who be comin' back to *this* shithole."

"Why back here?" Babyboy prodded. Only he and the bartender knew that the last four dark-beer bottles he'd drunk really had cola in them.

"Said she hadda be close—case something happens."

"In case what?" Babyboy urged.

"*I* don't know what she be talkin' about. Don't wanna tell me." He drained his beer and glared at Babyboy. "Tired of thinkin' about it. Just makes me mad."

"Yeah, but at least you still get to see her."

"Not fer a few more days. Bitch moved again yesterday, told me don't come around yet."

"And this new place is the one . . . you know, over by, um . . . ."

"By Trace Creek."

"Yeah, that's right."

Young Buck looked suspicious. "How *you* know where she at?"

"*I* don't know. You the one knows. You said you wrote it down, right?"

He looked puzzled for a moment, his hand reaching back for his wallet. He remembered, "No, *she* wrote it down for me, said don't come around for a couple more days." He glared into his empty bottle, swaying slightly, having trouble focusing. "Ho-ass bitch!" he bellowed. "Tell *me* don't come around yet."

Babyboy didn't like the attention they were attracting. The place was getting busier, too many patrons sitting within earshot. He leaned forward, almost whispering in Young Buck's ear. "Do a little 'caine?"

Young Buck looked around, had to make sure no one could hear. "You got some?"

"Back at *my* place."

Co-worker looked surprised, intrigued, expectant.

"Well, let's get on outta here, then."

"Remember, you gotta piss first."

"Yeah!"

Babyboy nodded to Co-worker, indicating he'd like him to go to the restroom, too, to keep an eye on the man. "I'll be out at the car."

After the twosome swaggered off to the men's room, Babyboy Moller paused at the pay phone and made a very fast call. Then he met them in the parking lot, urging Young Buck into the back seat. He pulled out going the wrong direction, then seemed to have second thoughts. "Listen, I'm holdin' a *lot* for someone—big uncut rocks. He ain't gonna like somebody knowin' where it is. I know *you're* used to stayin' down so you don't see where, but *he* ain't gonna wanna do that. Maybe we should just drop him—"

"*I* can stay down. I understand keepin' confi-den-shul."

"Well, if ya think so—"

Both passengers crouched in their respective floorboards, heads down, out of sight and unable to see where they were going. Babyboy doubled back and drove to his apartment. He pulled up as close as he could to the three-step stoop that led into his unit, announced their arrival, and told the others to keep their eyes closed when they stepped out. Co-worker knew better, instead helping Babyboy lead the vulnerable, half-drunk braggart, a well-placed hand blocking his view even if he did peek.

Babyboy poured some shots of tequila and set out some beers, stalling about the cocaine, trying to get Young Buck to talk more about his pregnant girlfriend and her outlandish tale. It wasn't working; the man was getting edgy about the promised goodies, breathing heavily, his face flushed, sweat on his brow.

Babyboy went to the other room, then returned carrying a small mirror with a half-dozen rows of sparkle-white powder, a single-edge razor blade along the side. He set it down, then produced a plastic fast-food straw and announced, "This is just what I had out. Let's blow this so I can clean the mirror. Think you can do that much all at once?" he challenged Young Buck, amused at the man's wide eyes.

It was a valiant effort, but the braggart only managed to snort four lines up his nose before he ran out of breath. He gasped, accidentally blowing a small cloud with the rest, then looked around like he was very confused, studied the floor for a moment, and slumped down with his butt on the tile. He vomited once, then lay down beside the puddle and started to snore.

Babyboy shook his head, wrinkling his nose at the mess.

"Shit ain't no 'caine," Co-worker observed.

Babyboy produced a hundred-dollar bill, stuffing it into Co-worker's shirt pocket. 'Nuff said.

The slip of paper was in Young Buck's wallet. Address for Creekview Manor—those places over along Trace Creek, all right. No phone number, just a name: Jolene.

Babyboy made a call, reading the address and name. Then he and Co-worker walked/carried their drunken friend out to the car and took him back to the dive he called home, not far from the railroad tracks, close to the Highway 13 bridge. They drove back to the bar so Co-worker could pick up his car.

"See ya."

"Yeah, thanks."

"What was—?"

"Don't ask."

Co-worker patted his shirt pocket and grinned. "See ya."

*   *   *

Babyboy Moller was back home cleaning up the puke when two men, dressed all in black, stepped across the near-dry chert-bed stream that ran along behind Creekview Manor.

They listened outside a window, motioned into the trees, waited for another man to move up closer. The third man was dressed in street clothes. He stepped into the lighted entranceway and knocked lightly on a door. The sound of movement was barely audible before somebody peered out the peephole. At the same time, the other two men entered the window in back. The man in street clothes looked up at the number, seemed surprised, and wandered off.

A moment later, a car crossed the Trace Creek bridge, then the smaller culvert, and pulled over to the side of the road. A door opened and closed quickly. The car drove away at a leisurely pace, a man in civvies at the wheel, two men all in black crouched in the back.

Between them, unconscious, sat a very pregnant black teenage girl.

*   *   *

Two plain, metal coffins were wheeled out and loaded into the back of the unmarked transport truck. It drove out of the Cumberland Sanitarium compound, pausing at the sallyport to allow four nondescript escort vehicles to pass through, each manned by heavily armed MPs in civilian clothing.

Colonel McGovern watched from his office window as the entourage disappeared into the woods on its way to a private crematorium in Paducah, Kentucky. He paced his office, anxious to go over to the infirmary before the chopper arrived, hoping the call would come in soon.

The phone rang. He straightened his jacket and tie as if the caller would be able to see him, then opened the line and activated the decoder. A voice asked him to stand by. After another minute, he was talking with Four-star of the Joint Chiefs.

"You're finally up to speed now?" Four-star asked.

"No, but I'm to the point where I believe I can figure it out myself. I don't need the bogus sham of *research* to answer my questions."

"Good. How much are you going to keep?"

"A basic set-up in Huntsville, duplicated here."

"Yeah, we may need to back up our claims in a crisis, but the more you got, the more risk there is—especially of one getting away."

"I'm concerned about talk and rumors. Had to have one man thrown in the brig and isolated at Donelson for running his mouth to his buddies about how this must be about aliens or something. It was just talk after several of them had watched some kind of alien-conspiracy tabloid show on television, but he's cooling off to learn a lesson in thinking out loud."

"Yes. Conjecture can be even more dangerous than facts."

"Whatever *those* are," McGovern quipped uncharacteristically.

"You need to keep Aggeous close because he still might be able to help you more than you think—especially if you do locate more contaminants," Four-star advised. "But loosen a bit. There's a few things he needs to take care of for us and I don't want to have to bring in and brief somebody new."

"Yes, sir." McGovern didn't like it, still resented that the fat doctor knew more than he and was apparently involved in other projects, too.

"I take it you still haven't ID'd anybody else?"

"No, but we have some promising prospects. We can't risk physical contact by moving too fast."

"Do what you must. Just don't ever let anybody *leave* once they have a clue what's going on."

"Yes, sir."

"Colonel, you understand why you were briefed in—oh, let's call it *stages*?"

"Yes."

"We couldn't risk you panicking and doing the wrong thing. Had to get you used to the idea of how this operation works, wanted you to have time to get your bearings."

"Yes, sir. I understand. And I believe in what has to be done."

"Good. Good, then. By the way, you're on the list."

"I *am?*" McGovern was instantly angry at himself for betraying his excitement.

"When you get back from Huntsville, check in with Major Keegan and he'll help you plan a ceremony that fits your schedule—and gives you time to get your mom down for it."

"Thank you, sir."

"I'm thinking just do it right there at Ft. Donelson if you want, or maybe up at Belvoir."

"I'll work that out with the major."

"Good. Now, take care of Huntsville and keep me apprised."

Colonel McGovern would have plenty of time to walk to the infirmary before the chopper arrived, so he watched Marshall Emery through the small window in the steel door for several minutes. He was pleased the pounding had stopped, figured lack of food and water had made the prisoner weak, hopefully ready to break down and drink the drugged water soon. He considered having the door opened, a dart fired in before the emaciated man across the floor could jump, but he decided against taking the chance. A few hours or a day wouldn't matter that much at this point.

Dr. Aggeous traveled with Colonel McGovern back to Huntsville. The fat doctor had again resumed the role of bio-med projects specialist, but he let it be known that the ignominy of his brief stint as prisoner still stung. There was no affection lost between these two alien-hunters.

First, they inspected the holding cell where Billy Hall had been killed, his alien transferred to Haitian refugee Kemo Dukani. It had been cleaned up, the books and tapes and equipment removed, everything else sterilized.

Then they moved to the lab area. Aggeous had to step back so McGovern could key in access and open the sealed door. The fat doctor wheezed and coughed, but said nothing.

They spent three hours packing boxes for incineration, McGovern mostly watching and directing. By the time they were through, two plastic Dumpsters had been taken out under guard, rolled into the back of a small truck to be taken directly to the disposal facility at the other end of the compound. One large box was left in the cabinet, marked *IVG* and *Classified*. They exited the lab, each carrying oversized, handled cases. McGovern still had his personal briefcase, setting it down long enough to seal the room.

They boarded a golf-cart, McGovern driving. Aggeous was surprised to see they were heading toward the underground specimen and testing facility. Once inside, McGovern completed some paperwork and informed the staff that care for the quarantined animals would be terminated.

Aggeous tried to argue against disposing of his aliens, but McGovern removed the service revolver from his briefcase, inserted the barrel into an opened slot, and dispatched them quickly. The rabbit lay on its back and twitched for a half-minute, but after watching all three animals for nearly ten minutes, McGovern was satisfied they were dead, the aliens they hosted destroyed. He informed the staff that the specimens were to be security incinerated, that there was no threat of contamination.

The shock absorbers squeaked under the weight of the doctor, the golf-cart riding slightly lopsided. They headed toward one of the chopper pads to catch a bird back to Cumberland. The doctor hadn't said a word since his animals were killed. Finally, he could stand it no more.

"They might've had some benefit you know."

"How?"

"Don't know—that's just the thing—" He wheezed and held tightly to the roll-bar, trying to keep his balance as they rounded a curve.

"Can't risk it." McGovern didn't need to explain himself to this civilian, but he was developing a habit of at least humoring him, hoping he'd reveal something interesting, maybe even something important.

"We could've studied them more and learned from 'em."

"There's nothing else to learn."

"Maybe a better way to detect might be developed someday—"

"We don't have a someday. We need to contain this thing now—something we're very close to achieving. Having unnecessary specimens somewhere so a lapse might lead to recontamination isn't worth the risk."

They passed several more buildings, gusts of wind tugging at the colonel's hat, threatening the neatly combed hair concealed underneath. The doctor wondered, "What are you going to do about getting that missing box?"

McGovern considered his answer a moment, then responded, "If I contain the alien, the other box will never matter."

"So you got one Haitian under control plus no-telling who-all Watterson might've infected. Think you can round 'em up?"

"Yes I do. And I think it'll be very soon."

*   *   *

"The difference is, *I* use working *for* them to my advantage. *He* decided that *not* working for them was to his *own* advantage," Flynn Durbett argued. Accompanying the balding mercenary on his frequent trips out of the compound to make phone calls or meet a man at a truck stop was becoming routine for Eugene.

"Mr. Watterson had decided to start doing only what was *right*," Eugene argued heatedly.

"Listen, guy, we *both* crossed that line at the same time. Only difference was, I decided case by case, Norm decided on no more—period."

"Because he decided *nothing* that helps our government get more powerful can be good."

"I know, I know. He thought the United States—the corporate governmental body of this country—had become the *real* evil empire, not to be trusted, bad and dangerous top to bottom. I'll tell you, it *is* dangerous, and it's got a lot of evil, but it's got just as much good about it and good people in it who do what they believe is right."

"Don't make it so simple," Eugene shot back. "He knew that; he knew most government employees is honest people just doin' a job, supportin' what they believe is right, but he thought this big experiment in democracy was a failure. It failed because it's controlled by people and voters who want to make everybody live and believe what *they* want—that the tyranny of the majority had won. He thought the people in power *bought* their control by buying votes, by creating a welfare state so everybody would vote for what got 'em the most money back—and not just poor people, but old people, too, and minorities, and big companies that take our natural resources and even old-fashioned farmers—just about everybody."

"And he was going to do something to stop that?"

"Refuse to be a part."

"Listen, Eugene. Government is an institution just like any other. It gets so big that it keeps increasing what it does until it takes on a life of its own. Part of that is protecting itself, its survival instinct just like any dog loose in the woods has, and it's the people in it who have the most to lose if it dies. My job, *our* jobs, was to get paid real good to help it survive. I never did understand why a man with a family living in some godforsaken holler in Tennessee when he could afford to live anywhere in the world—why he would want the government to collapse."

"Not collapse, be cut back to what it was supposed to be, for the common good, to help communities do for themselves and let a man and his family live in peace."

"These is awful big thoughts for a fifteen-year-old," Durbett teased, shrugging off his own ire. Eugene suspected that nobody but Watterson had ever been able to raise Durbett's hackles like that.

Eugene looked at his lap, slightly embarrassed. "Flynn, I gotta think about my *own* future. You was gonna run off somewhere someday and get away. Mr. Watterson and his family was gonna stay and find a way to make it work." He looked out the window, watching trees go by. "I don't know what Russell was gonna do; we wasn't ready to think about that yet except to say we both wanted to go to college. We both done good in school, used to talk about gettin' out of Waverly someday and seein' other places . . ."

"And now?" Durbett prodded quietly.

"I got Licia to think about." Simple as that, taking responsibility for somebody else. "I need to get emancipated or something and get back in school—finish high school. Then when I get old enough, I can claim what Mr. Watterson left me and afford to pay for college for both me and Licia and then start a business or get good jobs or whatever we both decide we wanna do."

"Live on the Emery farm?"

"Maybe. And maybe get an apartment by wherever we go to college. I don't know, whatever we decide together."

"You two have talked about this?"

"Well, yeah. She don't know I'm gonna have money, though, but it don't matter to her. We just wanna be left alone, no government telling us how to live and taking our money and stopping us from our rights. She's just as scared of militias as she is of government."

Durbett turned into the gravel road leading up to the compound, quiet for a moment. Finally, he asked, "What about that alien in you?"

"I just wanna do my part and be done with it."

"You think that'll be easy?"

Eugene regarded the bigger man and shrugged. "Piece o' cake."

"What's stoppin' you?"

"I need to find that black box."

*   *   *

Flynn Durbett and Eugene Weisman returned after the big meeting had already started. Jake Coleman was guest-speaking.

Over the past few years, Jake had become increasingly popular at various militia- and patriot-organization gatherings. He was a good speaker who could put forth ideas eloquently, yet was mild-mannered enough to eschew some of the fanatical zealot aura that surrounded many of the other leaders.

Though Eugene had heard much of it before, he watched from the back of the assembly hall in the compound. He was fascinated by the reactions of the crowd, a phalanx of everyday citizens with strong beliefs, a passion for liberty, and an unusually high dose of paranoia. It was an outlook he once found both amusing and scary, but one circumstances had forced him to embrace.

"This country was *founded* by patriots just like you and me—people who rose up and said *enough! Enough* of living under the rule of a tyrannical government! *Enough* of paying an unreasonable burden of taxes—*not* for the common good, but to support a bureaucracy! *Enough* of religion controlled by the state! *Enough* of liberties denied! Patriots who demanded to speak and write without censorship! To assemble peaceably! For the sovereignty of every citizen's private property! For freedom from unwarranted searches! For freedom from unlawful seizures! For due process under a just law! To bear arms and protect our homes and our families and our neighbors!"

Much of the crowd was on its feet, hooting and hollering, clapping, sometimes echoing Coleman's words. They were mostly men, mostly white, a few exceptions. They ranged from ex-military to laborers to professionals, some very outspoken, others quiet. Eugene was surprised at the number of young people, especially teens around his age.

"What did we do?!" Jake shouted.

"We rose up!"

"What did we do?!"

"Drove the bastards back to their *own* country!"

Some laughter, a smile from Jake.

"Our militias laid claim to this land for *our* citizens. We defended our homes and our property and our people; then we paved the way for a *new* nation! The greatest nation on earth! A bold, new experiment! A constitutional democracy founded on the concept of freedom and liberty! Free from the tyranny of big government! From the tyranny of the majority! To live our lives as we see fit! With the freedoms God gave us! To respect the rights of our neighbors and be left alone!"

"Ain't like *that* no more!" an older man shouted.

"What happened?!" Jake challenged.

"Government got too big—too much power!" a man shouted.

"Federal income tax!" from another.

"Slavery!" from one of the black men. He didn't get quite the noisy support from the crowd as the others. With so many militias founded by separatists, minorities had to be careful which groups they tried to join. Or they started their own.

"Women's rights denied!" called out one of the wives. That brought a few chuckles but no overt derision. Several other women shouted for solidarity.

"Sing it, sister," one exhorted. More chuckles, all good-natured. Aunt Doris was well-known around these parts. Everybody had heard at least one or two of her opinions, interested or not.

Jake grabbed the attention again. "What do we have *today?*"

"Taxes and deficit!"

"Yes! Eighty percent of every dollar you earn! A huge chunk in corporate taxes and fees and levies and regulations taken from business. Then a quarter or more right off the top before you get a paycheck! Services you pay for doubled in price so *they* can shoulder their tax burden! Then what you have left is used to pay property taxes—*rent* paid to the government for land *you* own which can be *taken* from you for not paying! Then you pay *sales* taxes, *gas* taxes, licenses and fees, hidden surcharges, registrations, expenses like background searches on *you* and to prove your car runs good—!"

Jake paused to catch his breath. The crowd took over shouting out examples of taxes and fees and hidden government-supporting expenses.

"And the IRS is fascist, doing whatever they want, presuming people guilty and exacting penalty without due process or just cause. You deal with the IRS, and you're guilty unless you can afford to prove yourself innocent—and *then* they still don't have to follow the law!"

"Don't get me started on IRS!" shouted a man. "I lost my auto-parts business to IRS seizure over how my accountant had done filings!"

"Now government is running us and our children and their children into debt," Jake started again, quieter. "Sixteen percent of our Gross National Product pays interest on that debt. In five years, nearly eight-five percent of our income will be needed *just to pay this debt!* Why are we running into debt? Because government growth is out of control! And the politicians in power use *your* money to buy votes from special interests! And they use *your* money to invade your lives and your privacy and police you until you stay down under their thumb!"

"It's a police state!" a burly steel-worker thundered. "My brother's in prison, framed by corrupt cops!"

"The king's men used to search the homes and seize the property of our forefathers until militias rose up and stopped them. Now, every year, the due process of search and seizure is eroded. They can search your car without a warrant, without probable cause. Homes no longer need a search warrant, just so-called good-faith. It's fishing, where they can just take their chances or even plant false evidence. They suffer no penalty for being wrong, so why not try? In other countries, if police enter your home illegally, you have the right to protect yourself *and* they can be charged with a crime. Here, their only penalty is the risk that maybe evidence will be ruled inadmissable, and even that is changing."

The audience fell quiet. Eugene had not thought about many of these issues before. He could finally feel the passion Mr. Watterson had honed over the years. Durbett looked bored.

"There are more than two-hundred seizure laws now—so-called *takings* laws. Government can declare your land an environmental zone and prevent you from using it. Government can *rezone* your land, make you give up part of it to get permits—all without constitutionally required just compensation. Now they have drug laws and RICO laws where property is seized unless and until the citizen can *prove* he legally earned the money to buy it. They bring civil cases *against property*—like property can commit a crime. Million-dollar boats taken because a crewman—not the owner—had a joint or some pills in his locker—like the *boat* is guilty and deserves to be forfeited!"

"Happened to my uncle!" one of the quieter women called out. She stood up, not much taller than five feet, a hundred pounds soaking wet. She fingered her long, auburn hair nervously. Jake's gesture encouraged her to tell her story.

"Uncle Bob owned a couple of hundred acres up in Michigan, nice place, big house and stuff. He don't get around good no more, mostly stays in or sits on the porch. A couple of kids or someone plants some pot out by the woods along the freeway. Their *Operation Hemp*—spendin' hundreds of millions of *our* tax dollars worryin' about people growin' herbs—they spotted 'em from a helicopter.

"Then they seized *every*thing!" She paused for emphasis. "Everything my uncle owned—his land and house and cars and *everything!* Said was illegal profits! He tried to tell 'em didn't know nothin' about no plants—if they was there, far as *he* knowed, *police* planted 'em so they could do this! They just laughed at him.

"He had *seven* days to post ten percent *bond* on the value—which *they* said was four-million dollars even though weren't half that—that's $400,000 he had to post just to *reserve* the right to try to *prove* he was innocent. We couldn't get that kinda money. Couldn't get a loan—had nothin' to put up! Had to spend all his savings on a lawyer who said even if he wins, they can charge him for the expense of them doing it! Lawyer had to cut a deal to *give* 'em most all of the land so Uncle Bob could keep his house and belongings. Then had to sell his truck to finish payin' the lawyer."

Her voice was cracking with rage. "That land was supposed to be left to me and my brother—been in the family over a hundred years." She misted up and got tears in her eyes. "Ain't so much that as what it done to Uncle Bob. He's in bad health now. Broke his heart. Saw his picture in the paper callin' him some kinda drug kingpin . . ." She wiped her face, was hugged by the woman next to her, several men close by.

Jake just shook his head. Her powerful story spoke for itself.

"Now they got new wiretap laws," Jake said quietly. "And they do a whole lot more of it than the law allows. It's like Iran or the KGB. They can wiretap, detain, even deport! They can deport people and claim it's national security so they don't even have to produce any evidence!"

"That's not constitutional!" the burly man growled. "That ain't facin' your accuser, confronting your evidence—don't even know who they is."

"Couple hundred years ago the militias rose up and took back our land from the tyrants." Jake looked around at the attentive faces. "Now government's taking our guns so we can't do it again."

"Just let 'em *try* to take *mine*!" one of the ex-military locals dared. Others echoed his sentiment, many chuckled.

"They can't do it all at once, so it's a piece at a time. Outlaw some kinds, then others, then add fees, then waiting periods, keep chippin' away. Now, with registration, they got lists of who's got what so when the time comes, they can round 'em all up. And those that resist will be killed or put in concentration camps they already built all over this land."

"That's part of The New World Order, the police state being created by the United Nations," announced a teenager in the front row. He didn't appear much older than Eugene. A slight, studious-looking lad, passion and rage—maybe even fear—played across his face. He sat with an even younger boy who listened intently.

"A soldier was just discharged not long ago for refusing to wear the UN Peacekeeper symbol on his uniform," Jake said quietly.

"What about these space aliens invading? I heard that's why Watterson and his family was killed."

Jake looked surprised, at a loss for words. Durbett looked alert, Eugene wide-eyed.

"Be straight with us, Jake," the burly guy exhorted. "No *mis*information from our *own* leaders now."

Jake weighed his words carefully. "Yes, Norm Watterson believed we was bein' invaded by aliens. We think it's why his family was killed. We don't understand much more, but we're investigating. If we come to understand it, I'll be the one to tell you. We won't let outsiders take our freedom and our way of life, be it foreigners, our own government, The New World Order, or God-knows-what from outer space."

Several people snorted derisively at the idea of extra-terrestrial invaders, but most took the potential threat very seriously.

"What about the boy?" a man in the back asked, turning half-way to look directly at a startled Eugene. Durbett tensed. "He on *our* side?"

"Yes." Eugene surprised himself by speaking up so quickly. "Yes." He said it again, then offered nothing more.

"We've said too much," Jake said evenly. "We have common values and common goals."

Jake tried to get back to his proselytizing, but the crowd seemed uneasy, dwelling on the bombshell rumor finally in the open and all but confirmed. He ended with a rousing declaration of unity and sent everybody off to the chow hall for sandwiches and fixin's.

Flynn Durbett and Big Ray both stayed close to Eugene. The teen felt very self-conscious, the center of attention, object of whispers and curiosity. But everybody acted friendly, none willing to broach the subject too directly. At one point, the burly man sauntered over, urging Eugene and his protective entourage to wander outside with him.

Walking down toward the stream, keeping his voice low, he asked, "I understand you was friends with Wattersons—grew up with their oldest, looked out for by Norm and Ethyl?"

"Yes, sir," Eugene confirmed, glancing toward Durbett.

Burly Man nodded, seemed to think that over. "If Norman trusted ya, I can."

Eugene just nodded; Flynn and Big Ray waited.

"Don't understand this malarkey about no aliens or nothin', but can't take no chances." He reached up and ran his hand through his scraggly hair, then tugged at his ear.

"I think it's true," Eugene said quietly.

"Well, don't much matter what's the truth," Burly Man said, clasping Eugene's shoulder, nodding to Big Ray and Durbett before starting to leave.

He half-turned to finish his thought, tugging at his ear again. "And don't always matter what you *believe*, neither. Whoever's got the gun barrel in your face?—right then it's what *he* believes that matters."

*   *   *

They stood in a restaurant parking lot just off Highway 79 in Scottsboro. Flynn Durbett hung up the phone, clearly frustrated.

Then Jake Coleman made a call that was obviously going much better. He and Flynn wound up involved in a three-way animated discussion. Jake motioned for Eugene to climb out of the truck and come over. The teen walked up in time to hear him assure the caller that he'd arrange some expense money to cover the next few days.

Then Jake offered Eugene the phone. "Somebody needs reassurance and *we* need to confirm identification."

Eugene accepted the phone, puzzled. "Hello?"

"Hello—Eugene? Eugene?!"

"Jolene! Well, how are ya?"

Chapter 8

McGovern looked up to see Lt. Col. Dunkin poking his head into the office. Still on the phone with his mother, the colonel motioned his domestic-information specialist into a chair.

"You're *sure* missing the luncheon won't be a problem? Good then. Well, your tickets will be at the check-in. You'll have a plane change in Memphis for a commuter flight to Paducah. I'll arrange to have you picked up there by one of Ft. Donelson's transportation officers. There'll be several other civilians coming in for the promotions of family members at the same time. You'll all be at the same hotel." McGovern paused. "Yes, Mother. You, too."

"They've taken a finger," Dunkin reported, stepping woodenly into the room.

"Safer than how they did Carter's?"

Dunkin shrugged. "Chief was satisfied. Aggeous and Rawley went round and round about it. The doc was more worried about preserving the sample than protecting personnel; Rawley was more worried about contamination. Won't surprise me if he comes in with elaborate plans to set up a better quarantine system, something with more safeguards."

McGovern nodded. He sat back, straightened his jacket and the knot of his tie. "That's his job."

"Anyway, they're working on the finger now, but chief already says it looks clean. Once he decided that, he took it out of the preservative and started dissecting it out in the open air."

McGovern scowled. He didn't know if he should be glad there was no alien or disappointed he'd not rounded up another. "When will questioning begin?"

"'Gator said another hour," Dunkin answered, referring to the interrogator's assessment of when Marshall Emery would be conscious but still so out of it his resistance would be low. Besides, the prisoner had to wake up before a potent combination of "talkies" could be administered to facilitate questioning.

McGovern and Dunkin spent some of that time reviewing a stack of FBI reports detailing militia activities during the past seven days. Not much appeared different from any other week: a big meeting in Guntersville, but those happened every month; lots of field training, Tennessee and Arkansas in particular, same old stuff; a list of members of the Humphreys County Militia. McGovern pulled it out for scrutiny. Though Norm Watterson hadn't officially been in the HCM, he was linked to it many ways. And of course, Marshall Emery served as its leader.

With nothing else of interest in the pile, McGovern left Dunkin making some follow-up contacts and walked over to the infirmary.

"Nothing," the examiner reported, waving the colonel off so he could continue his work without distraction. He mumbled something about Major Rawley already pestering him about precautions.

McGovern and the major talked while they watched through the protective glass screen that separated them from the autopsy theatre. Aggeous hovered around until satisfied Emery's finger was normal, he decided to seek the comfort of his office couch. Having been benched, he preferred heading to the showers over watching the new quarterback from the sidelines.

"Major, if *you're* not satisfied, *I'm* not satisfied," McGovern agreed. "Draw up a proposal for tightening the quarantine system. Plan for us to bring through as many as a dozen at a time, but most likely one or two every few days. Can't get *too* carried away."

"What kind of non-contact threat might there be?" the gaunt, spectacled major wondered, probably rattled by this whole concept of aliens whose nature he didn't comprehend.

"None. Of this I am positive. Focus just on preventing any physical contact."

Rawley didn't look satisfied, but he capitulated. "Yes, sir."

"*My* highest priority is to be able to question them right away. None of this wrapping them in plastic, then tossing them in a cell and having to wait for them to drink drugged water. This botch with Emery cost us some valuable days."

"I have several good systems in mind. In fact, I have an emergency quarantine manual devised by the CDC in Atlanta. I'll have preliminary proposals on your desk by tonight."

"Good. Good, then." McGovern shuddered at the sight of a finger-length vein being extracted from the splayed, dismembered digit. "Dunkin's got a narrowed-down list of militia members who are in with Emery—the group Watterson was most associated with. Keep the LEIN alert—" he instructed, referring to the Law Enforcement Information Network, a database set up to help police investigate criminals, growing every year with new kinds of information about more and more Americans from all walks of life, "—but work something so anybody from this list can get pulled in faster. Emery took us too long to get after he was picked up—there's too much of an arrest and detention record out there."

"We did manage to make the federal warrant disappear, but at the county level, it shows he was picked up by a U.S. Marshal. We couldn't change those records to reflect release because too many locals saw him processed through."

"That's what I mean. Try to work it so we find out as soon as one of these hits the system. Then arrange to have him released with minimal processing so FBI or whoever can be waiting just outside the door to make him disappear."

"If you want to start screening these guys, why not just round 'em up?"

"Can't attract *that* much attention—or risk stirring up retribution. Let's just hold for now to those who have a *prima facie* legit reason for arrest—most likely a weapons violation or drugs or something—so if we decide right away they're not going to be useful to us, we just release them none-the-wiser and they'll be happy they got off—or turn them over to locals for state prosecution on whatever they did."

"Or were *suspected* of doing," Rawley rejoined.

McGovern snorted. "Every one of these guys is guilty of something."

Rawley snorted back. "Laws are getting to where *every* American is guilty of *something*."

"You a front man for the ACLU?" McGovern asked half-jokingly. Still, he was studying his minion carefully for his reaction.

Rawley snorted again. "*I'm* not complaining. Long as I'm one of the *good* guys, just makes *my* job easier."

McGovern flashed on the image of his mother's face. There was a woman who wouldn't roll through a stop sign even if she was on her way to the hospital having a heart attack. "Not *every* American," he retorted defensively.

Rawley chuckled. "So maybe a *few* need a little help, but they can all be made guilty of *something*."

Normally, McGovern might have smiled and agreed, but the image of his mother was still there and the thought of somebody setting her up, framing her, doing something at least immoral if not illegal, well, it just bothered him. Just for a second.

An MP informed the colonel that the interrogator was ready to begin.

Marshall Emery was strapped to the bunk in his tiny cell, ankles, knees, thighs, abdomen and chest, arms and wrists, loosely around the neck. His left hand was bandaged where it had been immersed in a tub of preservative, its smallest finger removed and sealed from outside air.

McGovern studied his prisoner: young, muscular, trim, wavy brown hair, and vivid blue eyes, now dull and unfocused. Lips were chapped, skin dry. He looked slightly emaciated, dehydrated, probably from his ordeal and going without food and water so long. He looked weak and helpless, but McGovern didn't doubt the captive would summon some unseen reserve of strength and still be very dangerous if those straps were loosed.

*   *   *

"What happened to my hand?" Marshall Emery asked.

The colonel deferred to Interrogator.

"You've had a finger removed."

Emery started jerking his arm against the straps, but he was too weak to persist for long, wound up panting from the exertion.

"We're here to help you," Interrogator said soothingly. "We need you to help us, too."

"Ain't helpin' you *shit*," Marshall mumbled. He tugged again at the straps, winced with pain. The local anesthetic was wearing off.

"I'll give you something for the pain," Interrogator offered.

Emery watched as a doctor stepped forward with a hypodermic. He looked past him at the colonel standing authoritatively, though awkwardly, in the corner. Another man stood in the doorway with a pad, taking notes.

"Don't want your shot."

The needle was inserted into a vein in the crook of his arm, slowly emptied of its contents. Emery felt very warm, thirsty, heavy . . . tired. He no longer cared that he was strapped, imprisoned, surrounded by strangers. He wasn't afraid, had forgotten his outrage.

Just thirsty and tired. Very tired.

And didn't care anymore.

Marshall Emery wouldn't remember much about the questioning. He was wondering if they'd ask about the huge weapons caches on his and several nearby farms, but they didn't. Didn't seem to be interested in weapons at all. Just people mostly. And something about a black box, but Emery didn't know about that. No matter how many times they brought it up, he had no idea what they were talking about.

That black thing they showed him didn't look like a box anyway, more like a black bar of soap. Put some buttons on it, run a wire to the cigarette lighter and you've got a radar detector, a cop buzzer.

They wouldn't tell him what the box really was—wanted *him* to tell *them*, but still he had no idea, never seen one before.

Never heard of Jolene Carter, either. Didn't know many black folks, certainly not no teenage girls.

Yeah, Watterson. Good man.

Oh, she was that girl stayed with Wattersons a while? Didn't know her, only saw her once.

What black box?

Weisman? Yeah, Eugene. Licia's sweet on him. Stayin' at the farm. Nice kid. Lived by the Wattersons.

Found him in the woods—had run away. Thinks whoever killed Wattersons is after *him*, too.

Because he thinks he's got to protect some alien that Norman Watterson put inside him.

Says he's the only one left.

*   *   *

"I was instructed to report directly to you, Mr. Dunkin," the agent began. "I checked with one of our informants about the Weisman kid. You want me to play the tape?"

Lt. Col. Dunkin wanted to hear all of it. Slightly distorted over the phone, it was a conversation between the agent and some local feller.

"Yeah, it's me," the good-ole-boy confirmed. "Hey, I still ain't been paid for last month."

"Should be any day now."

"I sure hope so. Lotta risk talkin' to you."

"You haven't been compromised, have you?"

"Aw, no. Nobody."

"Have you detected any activity in the hate groups?"

"Well, the Aryans was all pissed off over some nigra boy showin' up at the school dance with a white girl."

"The incident where the principal got involved?"

"Yeah. Sure don't take much to make the news no more. Anyway, they got all worked up about it at first, but looks like they's gonna let it die down and not do nothin'. Just bitching, using it to stir up a little shit. Don't think nothin'll come of it."

"And the other group you monitor?"

"Well, it's gettin' real weird. Their leader, that Emery feller, he's been missing. They's convinced he's being held illegal prisoner of some secret government operation. Now they're all kinda talkin' about some outer-space alien invasion or some shit, but they's takin' it *real* serious-like. Lot of 'em don't rightly believe it, but they *do* think government's after 'em over it. Some's talking like it's time for something big to happen. They's gettin' ready, except I don't think they know who to go after."

"Do they have any targets? Any terrorism plans?"

There was a pause on the tape. "Can't rightly say. Ain't nothin' I done heard, but ain't hardly nobody around the area right now."

"What about Jake Coleman—he involved?"

"Seems to be, but *he's* gone somewheres, too."

"You don't know where these people are?"

"Naw. That's why it looks like something may be happenin'. It's all secret-like. Even ones who like to shoot the shit ain't talkin' right now. I don't wanna look *too* curious."

"Do *you* have any ideas what might've happened to Emery?"

"All I heard was he was arrested in Alabama. I checked and found out he was picked up on suspicion of illegal firearms, but released to U.S. Marshals before he was charged with anything. Ain't no record of him after that."

"Who's at his house?"

"Just his sister, Licia Emery, and Coleman's gal Tracey's been stayin' there when she's not working. The boys been taking turns keepin' an eye on things there—at least one, sometimes two at a time."

"Does the name Eugene Weisman mean anything to you?"

"Sure. *He's* the one started with all that alien stuff. Said he saw Watter-sons was killed by secret agents or something. He's that teenager who run away and was found in the woods down there by the creek."

"Where is he now?"

There was a short pause. "Can't think of nobody sayin'. He was only there a couple of days—been gone ever since."

"Is there any more information about him?"

"Well, he's the kid lived up the road from Wattersons. Stayed with his aunt. She was a drunk—went on a bender when he left. Fell and hit her head. Another woman found her dead."

"Anything else?"

"Naw, not really. What're you after?"

"Just curious. If it's Weisman's story that's got a hate group riled up, we need to understand what it's about—try to anticipate any problems."

"Sounds like some super*stitious* shit to me."

The agent could be heard chuckling. "Were there any gatherings or meetings or anything?"

"Just the day of the funeral."

While Good-ole-boy related information about the small pre-funeral rally, stumbling for a while trying to list who was there and who attended the services, Dunkin watched Rawley typing information into a computer database. Running a cross-check on Licia Emery, he found no entries other than as sibling of Marshall. A cross-check with classified data fields matched her with the name of her father, but access to the elder Emery's file was blocked, a security lock-out code flashed mockingly on the screen.

Rawley covered the mouthpiece and whispered, "You want to stir up something with her?"

"No. Let's just watch for anything about the Weisman youth."

Rawley set about tracking down the source of the security lock-out to see how he might crack the elder Emery's file.

Dunkin listened patiently to the rest of the tape. It was ending with a wrap-up.

"Thank you for your help," the agent said. "Contact me next week or right away if there is any new information either about Weisman or activities that might interest me."

"You got it—just get me paid."

"Let's close the report for the tape."

Good-ole-boy stated the date and claimed all information was eye-witness.

"And your name, deputy?"

"Marty—Martin Varne."

*   *   *

It was a glorious day! All posturing and pomp, ceremony and tradition. Of course, McGovern would have preferred Ft. Belvoir where more of his old rivals could attend. And he'd rather Four-star had come in to make the presentation, too, but Major General Ashe it turns out knew how to throw a good party and Ft. Donelson proved a fine place to have it.

McGovern looked snappy in his dress greens, starched and pressed, campaign ribbons proudly displayed, epaulets straight and ready, soon to be festooned with the single star of a brigadier general. Brigadier General Chester McGovern.

He liked the sound of it, but it also brought a wave of melancholy. Even more than settling for a smaller, out-of-the-way base; even more than being pinned by some old southern major general he hardly knew and didn't like; even more than the frustration of having *the* most important assignment in CID but not being able to win accolades for his work—he wished his father could be there to share the moment.

The old man had been strict but loving when Chester was a boy. A lowly NCO who believed in his country and was dedicated to his job, he exemplified pride and honor, discipline and tradition, always encouraging his son to achieve the kind of stature denied a father with little education and humble beginnings. McGovern had learned to play the military game his father's way. Then when the old man died suddenly, he became the man of the house, throwing himself into his studies, shouldering all the responsibility Mother would allow, striving very hard to live up to the ideals laid out for him.

Brigadier General. Still in his thirties. His *thirties!* Sgt. McGovern would have been proud.

Mother McGovern greeted her son, inviting him into her hotel suite. They hugged briefly, somewhat awkwardly. He inspected the accommodations he'd reserved for her, allowing as how it was all very nice. She pointed out that it was much more luxurious than necessary, but she was gracious and grateful. She understood—a brigadier general doesn't put his mother up in a cheap motel off some highway exit-ramp.

She thought the corsage looked just gorgeous, a simple statement of three miniature roses—red, white, and blue—nestled in a spray of clipped fern and baby's breath. She reached out and gingerly touched his campaign ribbons, admiring them while he carefully pinned the flowers to her muted, sky-blue chiffon dress accessorized by a paisley-turquoise silk scarf and opal brooch. Her outfit was light for a hot, southern September, dressy for an elegant affair, understated so as not to compete with her son's dress-green uniform.

During the drive to the base, he briefed her on what to expect at the evening's festivities. Both tried to act dignified, reserved, even nonchalant about the whole thing, but Mother's excitement proved so infectious that they found themselves grinning a lot.

"I knew from the time you were little you'd be an important man."

And important was how he felt, walking his mother across the base, saluted at every turn, all that deferential posturing serving an important role after all.

The assembly hall was decked out in patriotic colors with bunting and streamers and centerpieces and beautiful place-settings. It was crowded, full of smartly dressed officers, wives and guests, NCOs circulating with hors d'oeuvres and sparkling champagne, the lively tempo of light jazz from a nine-piece orchestra on the dais by the dance floor.

Chester McGovern's ranked highest of the evening's promotions, so he and his mother were the center of attention as they circulated through the crowd, meeting and greeting, sharing anecdotes, sipping champagne, distinguished and proud. Mom got introduced to General and Mrs. Ashe, Lt. Col. Dunkin and Major Rawley. She laughed at Lt. Col. Poole's tales of southern shenanigans and was instant friends with his delightful, young fiancée, Vivian, a brassy southern gal obviously in love with her career-Army hometown boy. The only member of the *IVG* team who'd been assigned to Ft. Donelson long enough to become a part of the community, Poole delighted in welcoming everybody to "the land between the lakes *and* the states, the heart of Kentucky and Tennessee." Everybody agreed with the sentiment.

The crowd parted for a contingent of MP honor guards marching smartly through the hall in full dress uniform. Then everybody quieted and moved to their seats. The band played something spirited and patriotic followed by a short speech from Ashe—sidetracked several times by funny stories, the major general thoroughly enjoying one of his favorite jobs as base commander. More than a dozen advancements were awarded, culminating in a formal presentation to Poole in recognition of his field promotion several weeks earlier. Any mention that it had coincided with assignment to something called *Program Invigil* was scrupulously avoided.

A delicious dinner followed. The band played, people danced, more champagne flowed, and dusk turned to night, a cool breeze wafting through high windows. A drum roll, officers snapping to attention, it was time for the final presentation.

Brigadier General Chester McGovern acted positively regal, precise and articulate, but not too stiff—respectful affirmation of his commitment to God and country. He would do right by the United States Army, the best man for the job. He felt bigger than life, the whole world in his pocket . . . and there sat Mother McGovern, head high, eyes glistening.

He would defer credit to the fine men and women with whom he had the privilege to serve. Then, snappy salutes, hale and hearty handshakes, a slap on the back, cigars handed around, hugs from the ladies, a proud mother in tears.

Mother McGovern would allow as how there was never a nobler calling than protecting American families, safety and security and freedom, a sentiment shared by all.

On the way back to the hotel, she made it clear that she understood Chester had new responsibilities, was busy with something very important, would have time only to see her in the morning before sending her off to her volunteer work and sewing and friends back home.

She said good night, giving him one final hug and whispering, "You know your dad and I are *both* proud of you, son."

"I know," he said quietly.

She pulled back just a bit, dabbed her eyes, then straightened the knot in her son's tie and brushed away some imaginary lint, lingering to admire the single gold star gracing each of his epaulets. She smiled, almost laughed. "You know he's up there handing out cigars and bragging on you to all the angels, don't you? He's saying, *That's my boy!*"

"Then he's adding, 'And that beautiful young woman with him is my wife, yessiree!'" He smiled, touching her cheek lovingly before she could dab again.

*   *   *

They shared breakfast the next morning in the hotel coffee shop. He in dress uniform, she in a smart pantsuit for the drive to Paducah and flights home, they lingered over croissants and compote with coffee. The McGoverns had indulged their feelings the night before; next mornings were always for getting down to business. He had a secret project to run, a world crisis to avert, a mystery to solve. Mother was finally more direct wondering about his job.

"Assignments at small bases in the middle of nowhere don't usually generals make," she observed.

"I need to be close, and Donelson is the nearest resource. I've established my *own* theatre of operations someplace nearby," he explained dutifully. He could trust his mother never to talk about something that might be even remotely confidential and he didn't want her to think his role was unimportant. "I have another operation in Alabama, plus I'm commander of the program at Ft. Belvoir."

Mother was impressed. He was in charge of a far-flung, multi-state, obviously secret project. She knew her son was CID, wouldn't be tinkering with something unless it was very important. "Your Aunt Sylvia says now that we beat the communists, the biggest threat we got is terrorists and hate groups right here in our own country—that all these bombings are just the tip of the iceberg." She was equally adept at measuring her comments to fish for information as to make her opinion known.

"There's a lot of truth in that," Chester remarked casually. Though most people on a first-name basis called him Chet, to Mother he'd always been Chester—or *Chester Davison McGovern!* if he was about to be called on the carpet.

"I don't put much stock in all those magazines at the grocery store—" She grinned mischievously, remembering how her teenage son had always teased her about buying them—*why do you read that nonsense?* "But I've been seeing it more and more on TV lately—even on *The Discovery Channel*—" She paused to emphasize the credibility that conferred. "—That there are all kinds of secret military operations about extra-terrestrials, with captured space ships and alien autopsies and new weapons and so forth . . ."

"Mother, you know better than to follow that kind of stuff." He wanted to scoff but not sound patronizing.

She smiled, then stirred her coffee pensively. "Still, though . . ."

"You *know* if there was *anything* that might be dangerous, we'd be on top of it. We also wouldn't be giving information to tabloids and causing unnecessary panic."

To Mother McGovern, that comment meant confirmation. She didn't know what to say for a moment, surprised so wild a shot had hit target. It was a subject she normally wouldn't have broached, wouldn't even have seriously considered, except that her sister Sylvia, the sci-fi fanatic and tabloid maven, had been voicing elaborate conspiracy theories for so long. "At least with the communists, we understood who our enemy was—" She leaned closer to whisper, Chester flinching reflexively from years of trying to avoid her wiping his face with her hankie. "If it's aliens, how can we be sure?"

"Never underestimate the U.S. military," he said reassuringly, still trying to put a smiley face on the whole topic. "We can handle any kind of enemy."

She took a sip, he several bites. She mused, "Sylvia says odds are even or better that alien visitors would be here for good reasons as bad."

Chester chuckled. "I think if they come in the spirit of peace, they'll do it the right way—send an emissary to hold audience with the president or congress and wait to see if they're invited."

"Unless they don't know our ways—"

"Then they should ask," he pronounced, caught up in the conjecture, amused at the topic.

"Unless they don't know if *we* can be trusted or not."

Chester waved off the idea, concluding, "If aliens were invading the United States, we would have to stop them. Nothing could be good about *any* kind of invasion."

They would finish their breakfast with her reminding him how proud she was, how proud his father would have been, a hint or two about calling more often, maybe that it was time to think about settling into an area for a while and finding a nice young lady who wanted children . . .

There was one thought she couldn't shake, though—something Sylvia had said. She decided to leave it unspoken. If her son really was in charge of some kind of alien defense program, he would know what to do, would do the *right* thing. After all, he'd been *raised* right. He was a McGovern.

But Sylvia did have a good point.

Maybe some aliens are good and some are bad. Just like people.

*   *   *

"Well, *Lloyd Stewart!*" Licia squealed. "Get in here and let me hug your neck!"

Her cousin Lloyd burst through the screen door, tossed his duffel on the floor, and grabbed his young cousin, lifting and twirling her around. Tracey watched from the kitchen doorway, a militia member standing beside her and munching a sandwich.

"You always was a pretty little thing, but you's gettin' to be quite a young *woman*," Lloyd pronounced, holding her at arm's length for inspection. "You sure are gonna be breakin' some hearts—and *soon*, I'm a-guessin'!"

His arm around her, holding her close, he finally turned to acknowledge the others.

"Lloyd, this is Tracey—she and Jake Coleman's sweet on each other—though she ain't tied him down yet," she added with a conspiratorial grin. "But she's *almost* got him to where he ain't gonna know what hit him!"

"Pleased to meet you, ma'am," Lloyd acknowledged, tipping his imaginary hat. What a charmer; growing up he was quite the hell-raiser, but he always fooled the elders into thinking he was just the *sweetest* lad.

"And Chuck's from Waverly. He's part of the militia, using his day off from work today just helping keep an eye on things."

Lloyd and Chuck shook hands, quickly sizing each other up in a friendly way. Lloyd looked like a younger, more muscled version of Marshall but with a flat-top haircut. Chuck was tall and gangly with thick brown hair and thick brown-frame glasses. Licia smiled, figuring each had decided he could take the other in hand-to-hand if it came down to it.

"Done got yourself kicked out, didn't ya?" she tut-tutted.

"A full *dis*honorable," he boasted, wearing it like an accomplishment. "Couple of us took a M-60 dancing where we wasn't supposed to, and we did just a little bit *too* much damage." He rolled his eyes and spread his hands like *Hey, these things happen!* "C.O. couldn't talk it away. It got out of hand, *almost* got us court-martialed."

"*Court*-martialed!" Tracey blurted. Licia was surprised, too; she'd heard her share of military high jinks, but never any that turned into serious charges.

"Yeah, coulda had me breakin' rocks with a toothbrush for five years and putting 'em back together for another five. Cut a deal, though. You know, to avoid the *embarrassment.*"

"Theirs more than yours, I bet," Chuck harrumphed.

"Army first, people last," Lloyd agreed.

They moved into the kitchen for sandwiches and iced tea. Lloyd chattered with Chuck about guy stuff, flirted shamelessly with Tracey, reminding her several times how lucky Jake was, and if that feather-hatted fool ever lost sight of that fact, old Lloyd would be ready to come in from the bench.

"What about you, sweet gal?" he teased Licia. "How many of these farm boys up and down the road you got bringin' you flowers and tryin' to get you to run off to Mississippi to get married?"

Licia blushed, but with an unmistakable twinkle in her eye. "My boy-friend's name is Eugene," she reported shyly. "He's fifteen. He used to live by Wattersons but now he's stayin' here and—" She hesitated, finishing, "—And traveling around some."

"Eugene . . . Eugene . . . I don't think Marshall ever mentioned him. What's his last name?"

"Weisman."

"Hmmm . . . Never heard of no Weismans around here."

"He's a *very* nice young man," Tracey vouched, "and he just *adores* Li-cia."

Lloyd grinned. "Well, good for you!" He hugged her again.

Changing the subject lest her cheeks turn beet red, Licia asked hope-fully, "You don't got no place to stay, yet, do ya?"

"Naw. They fined me pretty good, so I need to get a job fast."

"Well, you can stay here as long as you need."

"Sure was hopin' you and Marshall would say that. I'd like to save some cash and head to Florida in time for the holidays—got some good oppor-tunities down there along the gulf coast."

"Well, we sure could use some extra help around here," she started. She cast her eyes down, looking sad for the first time since her favorite cousin had walked up the gravel drive. "Especially until we figure out how to get Marshall back."

"Get him back? Where is he?"

Licia and Tracey took turns laying out the story. They held back on things they'd been cautioned were confidential, like Durbett's involve-ment, the compound near Guntersville, Eugene's belief that *he* was the one carrying the rumored alien, a tale that was starting to spread out of control.

Lloyd could hardly contain himself. He stomped around, getting mad-der by the minute, ready to bust out and do something rash. Chuck, nor-mally quiet, was getting caught up in the spirit of outrage, too. They aimed imaginary weapons at phantom captors, declaring something must be done and done fast—

Tracey kept trying to calm them down. Licia felt scared, at one point reduced to tears, only to be hugged and assured by Lloyd that something would be done, don't you worry.

"Well, if Jake's in charge—and has plans already worked out, then you couldn't ask for none better," he reassured. "Whatever he decides, I'm ready to help any way I can."

They wound up sitting out on the porch, watching blue jays and sparrows light at the feeders, a pair of hummingbirds sipping colored water, chipmunks scouring the ground, a gray squirrel shaking his tail at everything that invaded his turf. Their frustration was put aside temporarily, but it still simmered just below the surface.

Lloyd wondered, "You believe all this stuff about some kinda alien invasion?"

Licia looked off toward the woods along the creek and thought for a moment.

"Yeah," she whispered. "I guess I do."

*   *   *

Big Ray Blounten and Flynn Durbett came into the main house at the Guntersville compound. They headed to the refrigerator for cold beers, nearly tripping over Little Ray, Blounten's oldest, a rambunctious nine-year-old who looked like a miniature copy of his dad except for longer hair and the explosion of freckles spilling across his nose and cheeks. The lad peered into the freezer, checking on some secret project, then tried to scamper away.

"Ho! Hold it, son!" Big Ray snagged the boy with his beefy hand, catching him mid-stride. "What's goin' on in the fridge?" He opened the door of the side-by-side and scanned the shelves. There, near the bottom, were two ice-cube trays with a crayon-lettered index card warning, *Don't use! For Eugene & Ray.* He pulled them out and saw they were not quite frozen solid. In one of the trays, each cube had something inside of it—what it was, he couldn't tell—plus two short lengths of pipe cleaner sticking out. "What're these for?"

"For our project."

"Your big battle simulation you guys been workin' on every day up in Eugene's room?"

"It's his *his*tory," Little Ray corrected.

"Ain't doing nothin' dangerous are you?"

"No, sir. Just alien history."

Big Ray and Durbett looked at each other. The mercenary asked, "You guys don't mind if we come have a look at your project, do ya?"

Little Ray shrugged. "Eugene said he wanted you to see it when it's ready anyway." He darted up the stairs in a flash.

"Is this why he's been bringing boxes of toys every time he comes here?" Durbett wondered.

"Must be. They's his toys *and* stuff from around the house. Today he brought the rest of his plastic soldiers and animals, a sewing kit, his globe, most of his balls, some toy cars, a paint set, and a roll of tape," he ticked off, trying to recall what he'd seen, "plus no-tellin' what-all else was down in there."

They went upstairs and found Eugene arranging items on a plastic tarp spread over his bed. These included a lit lamp without its shade, the world globe, what appeared to be fertilizer sprinkled around, a pile of sand, a doll house, two toy pickup trucks, plastic barnyard animals, and various kinds of food. Eugene appeared to be deep in thought, barely acknowledging the two men surveying the scene from the doorway.

"Ice is almost ready, Eugene," Little Ray reported.

"You keep vigil, soldier," Eugene replied, arranging the truck and farm-animal toys. He looked up at Big Ray and Durbett, matter-of-factly stating, "We still ain't doing it right, but at least we're getting closer."

Big Ray started to demand explanation, but Durbett put his hand on the big guy's shoulder, getting him to hush.

Durbett quietly asked, "Okay we stay a while and watch?"

"Ain't ready yet, but sure," Eugene acknowledged, engrossed in his arrangements.

Little Ray was moving around the room tweaking other elaborate displays—toys arranged around baseballs or basketballs, odd scenes set up on tables and the dresser and a footlocker dragged in from another room, plastic garbage bags spread around. Big Ray looked puzzled, his son acting like it all made perfect sense to him.

Durbett stepped out of the room for a moment, then returned with two folding chairs he set up just inside the door. "Here okay?"

Eugene nodded.

"You ready for the ice, Eugene?"

Eugene shook his head.

The older men sat quietly and waited.

Eugene looked tentative, then chargrined. He admitted, "Look, I feel kinda stupid doin' this—"

"We're havin' fun!" Little Ray exclaimed.

Eugene smiled, clasping the boy's shoulder. "It's just, well, kinda like the only way I can figure this out."

Durbett nodded. "It sounds like you're doing just fine."

"Do I get to do the space ships and stuff?" Little Ray asked.

"Sure! We're depending on you. Just like we *been* doin'."

"Yes, sir!" he enthused. Then he looked pensive for a moment. "Don't know what to do with the ice, though."

"I think they's instead of chocolate," Eugene guessed. "We'll just make it up as we go along."

Eugene stood there for another moment, Little Ray perfectly still. Big Ray had never seen the little one stay in one place for so long.

Then Eugene walked over to where he had dozens of threads, hundreds of knots tied in each, hanging from a toy soldier on the corner of the dresser. He tied one more, then closed his eyes and ran his fingers up and down each strand. By the time he opened his eyes again, he looked queasy and was breathing heavily.

Durbett whispered to Ray that he recognized that look from their trip to Texas, that he was fighting a strange urge to protect the teen from unseen boogeymen, to stop him before he could get worse.

But then Eugene seemed to be okay again. He put the thread-draped soldier carefully on the bed and moved over to the footlocker where Little Ray already waited in anticipation. The youngster apparently had the routine down pat.

"It's how they remember," Eugene explained for the audience, referring to the threads he'd been stroking.

On the footlocker sat a baseball arrayed next to a string of Christmas lights, plugged in but with only two bulbs lit, yellow and orange. Clumps of tied-together thread were arrayed around the scene, as were marshmallows and jelly beans.

"Time for the ice," Eugene said quietly.

Little Ray dashed from the room and returned with the trays moments later. "This time can I be the smart marshmallows?" he requested.

Eugene nodded.

Little Ray dropped to his knees beside the footlocker and grabbed a fluffy treat in each hand. He jiggled them up and down like little characters, sing-songing in a high-pitched cartoon voice, "Oh! Look at us! We're the marshmallow people and we're really smart but we don't got no hands!"

Eugene looked sheepish as he cracked several plain ice cubes from one of the trays. Holding them near Little Ray's 'mallows, he jiggled them around, but his sing-songing was unintelligible, nasal and muffled from closed mouth, sounding like somebody who is gagged. Next, he picked up one of the tangles of thread, scissored off short snippets, and used a tooth-pick to poke them into jelly beans. Then he *mooed* several times. "Moo-ooo!"

Little Ray giggled. Still cartoon-voiced, he made his 'mallow creatures talk to the jelly beans. "You get big and strong and I'll get melty critters ready for you!" He walked his 'mallows over and escorted Eugene's ice cubes to the beans.

Big Ray snorted and started to speak. Durbett cut him off before the first word was out. The balding mercenary was watching intently. Big Ray studied him curiously for a second. Apparently the big guy was missing something, so he decided to remain quiet and watch.

"You want the other ones now?" Little Ray whispered.

Eugene nodded again, so his young assistant cracked two of the pipe-cleaner cubes from the other tray while Eugene sing-songed, "Time to go in the melty critters now." He pulled the threads from the jelly beans and laid them on the melting ice cubes. He picked up the jelly beans, shrugged, then popped one in his mouth. Little Ray opened his mouth and caught the other in mid-air, giggling at his own prowess.

"Ready for 'em?"

Eugene put the cubes he'd been using back into the tray. Little Ray set the pipe-cleaner cubes on the wet spots, pronouncing, "Now the threads is growin' in the melty critters that grows arms and stuff for whatever you need."

"Yep," Eugene confirmed. "Now, how does that help the marshmal-lows?"

"They can build things and they's stronger and can do all kinda stuff the 'mallows can't do. And with those threads in 'em, they's smart now, too, except the 'mallows is *real* real smart and they done figgered out how to build *space*ships and stuff."

Little Ray retrieved several toy spaceships from the shelf and brought them to the footlocker. Together, they pretended to have the melties with arms build the ships while the 'mallows instructed and watched. Then they put one of each kind of creature on top of a ship.

"Your creature's gonna have to fly because *mine* don't got no arms! Ahhh! No arms! No arms!" Little Ray was jiggling the 'mallow and giggling. "I get to fly, right?" he whispered to Eugene.

"Don't crash 'em," the teen warned good-naturedly.

"Four . . . three . . . two . . . one . . . blast-off!" He made guttural rumbling sounds, carefully holding the creatures in place while he flew it over and landed on the table where sugar cubes and popsicle sticks surrounded a lamp and basketball.

"That planet only has *one* sun?" Durbett asked quietly. Eugene nodded wordlessly.

Big Ray was catching on; he leaned forward to study the contents of the table, intrigued. "Natural resources," he mouthed almost breathlessly. Durbett nodded slowly like it had been his guess, too.

By this time, Little Ray was loading sticks and sugar into a little box. Eugene was flying one of each creature on a second ship over to the same planet.

Little Ray landed his ship on the footlocker and disgorged his cargo. "Yay! Now we can build all kinda stuff! Yay!"

Eugene's ship carried a similar load back to the footlocker planet, his marshmallow suggesting, "Hey! Let's go to some more planets!"

The creature pairs flew to the other low table, making several trips back and forth with BBs and nickel brads.

"Ore," Durbett whispered, smiling.

"Now we can build even more stuff!" the creatures exclaimed.

Big Ray whispered to Durbett, "Why don't the threads live inside the marshmallows?"

"Why? It wouldn't make the marshmallow smarter and the threads wouldn't be able to grow arms or whatever they need."

Big Ray's expression indicated he agreed with the logic.

One of the spaceships was flying to the night stand. As soon as it landed, the cube squealed like the wicked witch in Oz. "Ahhh! Help me! I'm mel . . . ting . . . !"

"We forgot the water," Eugene pronounced, sounding frustrated at the interruption to their little drama.

Little Ray dashed off to the bathroom and returned with a cup of water. Eugene splashed a small puddle onto the plastic, then laid a tangle of threads in it. "Help! I need to go inside you before I melt!" He poked the thread into the 'mallow with a toothpick.

"What happened—why did my changely creature melt?" he asked, jiggling the protruding thread with the toothpick.

The marshmallow looked around, then studied the fertilizer for a moment. "Nitrogen," it replied, bouncing up and down in agitation. "And you can't come out of me *here* because *you* was gonna melt next."

"Now we can't leave! *You* can't grow arms to fly the ship! And if they try to rescue us, *they'll* get trapped, too!"

Eugene quietly told Little Ray, "Now they're sad." Little Ray nodded agreement.

Eugene left them stranded on the fertilizer planet and went back to the footlocker. He removed another cube with arms and put it by the second one, pushing another 'mallow over to form a group in spirited discussion.

"Our ship didn't come back. We have to see what went wrong."

"What if *we* get trapped, too?"

"We have to make a way to talk through space."

"Yeah!"

Little Ray set an assortment of gizmoes out one at a time. One or another of the creatures kept pronouncing, "That don't work."

"That don't work."

Then Ray put out a transistor radio.

"Hey! That works. But it's too big for a space ship."

"I know, lets keep the big radio here and make little ones that work off it."

"Yeah!"

Little Ray fished something out of his pocket. It was two small erasers like they used in school, except they'd been painted black.

"I'll be damned," Durbett breathed.

"It's them black boxes, ain't they?" Big Ray whispered.

"The threads is the only ones can use 'em. And they's not real good because you can only say a little and then only by answering questions. But at least we can use 'em to find out what happened."

Another spaceship with a pair of creatures and black eraser flew to the fertilizer planet and landed.

"Oh no! I'm melting!"

They repeated the process of turning the cube into a puddle and inserting the wad of thread into the 'mallow. Then one of the 'mallows climbed up on the black-box eraser. Eugene carefully arranged the threads so two of them touched it. Little Ray was already waiting at the radio.

"What happened, you guys?"

"Nitrogen. Don't come here because the threads will die unless they go in the marshmallows, but then you can't fly away." He had the creatures look around at the collection of BBs and paper clips and sugar cubes and salt, a plastic ring with rhinestone, plus popsicle sticks and peanuts and more. "Too bad, too. This planet has the most stuff!"

Little Ray asked earnestly, "They died, didn't they, Eugene?"

Eugene nodded sadly. Reverently, he put the threaded 'mallows into the trash and, as an afterthought, covered them with a tissue.

They produced several more spaceships, one a rather crude mock-up from clay. This time, two teams flew to a planet populated by toy monsters.

"Hi! We're the thread people and the marshmallow people."

"Hi! We're the wooga-wooga people."

"Do you have stuff we can take back home?"

"No. We just barely have enough for us."

"Okay, then. Bye!"

The ships flew back to the footlocker.

"Hey, if we put threads inside those wooga-woogas, then nitrogen wouldn't melt us and we could fly to fertilizer planet to get all that good stuff."

"Well, we have to ask 'em if that's okay."

Little Ray was taking great delight in piloting ships back and forth and providing all the sound effects. "Come on, Eugene! Your ship ain't making the sound."

Eugene glanced surreptitiously toward the men, a bit embarrassed, but he joined in anyway and voiced the *zoom-zooms* with not quite as much exuberance as the youngster.

"Can we put threads inside you?"

"No."

"But then you can fly places with us!"

"No!"

"Okay then. Bye!"

Back at the footlocker, one of the cubes argued, "We could still do it anyway."

"No!" They all joined in. "No! You can't *never* do something to someone after he done said no."

The spaceships resumed their galactic exploration, stopping at various planets, peering under the bed and dresser, once even leaving the room—Durbett had to move out of its way—before returning with a cup of sand. Finally, two ships landed on the bed next to the globe and unshaded lamp. There were all kinds of objects scattered around, including dolls and plastic soldiers and fertilizer.

"Oh no! Niter-gin!" Little Ray had trouble with the pronunciation. "Ahhh! I'm melting!"

The threads went inside the 'mallows, leaving only puddles where their cubes had been. Suddenly, soldiers captured the threaded 'mallows, herding them to a baby-doll crib and locking them behind bars.

One 'mallow said, "Now I've had enough time to learn how they talk. Let's ask."

"Okay."

"Hey! Can we put thread inside you?"

"Not inside *us*, but we'll bring you a prisoner."

A man was marched in, then a thread wad removed from one of the 'mallows and hung around his neck.

"Oh no! I'm dying!" the 'mallow cried. "You can't take all the thread out because it kills me!" The 'mallow who'd lost his thread died, consigned to a box covered with sand. "Now he's under the desert," Eugene explained.

"And I think I know where," Durbett said evenly.

"We can do it with just part of the thread and make a baby so I don't die," said the other 'mallow.

Another prisoner was brought in, this time receiving only a snippet of thread. Then the prisoner said, "I don't want no thread in me," and apparently committed suicide by hanging himself with a bedsheet.

"You killed him with your thread!"

"No I didn't. Thread wanted to live, too. The man just didn't want it in him. It should never be in a man if he don't want it."

"Then you will have to stay in that cage until you die. Are more of you coming?"

"They are calling to see what happened. If you let me hold that black box, I will tell them don't come here because the cubes melt and the people don't want the threads inside them. They won't come because we got no way to leave. Even our spaceships melt here."

"Well, okay then. Here's the black box."

Eugene explained for the men, "He musta died after a few more years because he was a old one." He consigned the 'mallow to the trash, hidden underneath the tissue.

The spaceships continued exploring other worlds. Then a conversation took place back on the footlocker between two ice cubes while no 'mallows were nearby.

"Hey! If we go back to that place, we can go inside them people and won't have to worry about melting no more. Then we go can make new ships and take all their stuff and go anywhere and we won't need those 'mallows no more."

"Yeah, let's do it!"

They flew to the bed with the globe, the first time a ship ventured out with two thread-wadded, pipe-cleaner-limbed cubes and no 'mallow. Eugene then set the ship and creatures on the floor and splashed a puddle where it had landed.

"What's that mean?" Durbett asked.

Eugene snapped to attention as if his trance had been broken. He thought for a moment, then decided, "Don't know what happened to 'em—can't even be sure it was Earth where they landed." He looked impatient with the interruption and walked to the footlocker.

"Hey, they stole a ship to go to the people planet! They're gonna go inside people even though they said no."

"Oh no! We have to stop 'em!"

A ship with two threaded cubes, a 'mallow, and three black erasers left for Earth.

Little Ray confirmed, "Two cubes so they can kill or capture the bad ones and a 'mallow so he can tell the radio what happened in case they melt too fast, right, Eugene?"

"You gotta good space memory there, feller," Eugene praised with a grin. Little Ray beamed.

That's when it hit Big Ray. After being little more than amused at the whole idea, and just a bit uneasy about his son being exposed to Eugene's crazy tales, all of a sudden he started to believe. What appeared to be a silly, childish play-game was actually telling a plausible, though outlandish, story. He felt like a witness to history, and was oddly glad his son was there not just to see it, but to be a part. He felt goofy, but drawn in.

The ship landed on the bed.

"Oh no! Just puddles. They musta died!"

"Maybe they went in people."

"There's not many people around here."

"But we can't be sure."

"If we stay, we'll melt—and the 'mallow will get captured so he won't be able to find out."

At that point, Little Ray retrieved two toy pickup trucks, giving one to

Eugene. He *vroom-vroomed* his to the landing site.

"We think bad ones might be here livin' inside people," one of the cubes explained to a plastic Old MacDonald, the farmer with the E-I-E-I-O. "We came to find out and help get rid of 'em. But we're gonna melt and the marshmallow might get captured. What should we do?"

"How can *you* help if we been invaded?"

"If we find out they're here, we can use these boxes to tell our planet and they'll send stuff that will kill all the threads. But we don't want to unless you're sure because we don't know if it will hurt some of the other creatures on your planet."

Eugene explained, "They're melting fast."

"Hurry!" the 'mallow said. "One of you come in me."

"Won't hurt will it?" asked Old MacDonald.

"No!"

"Okay then."

Eugene arranged a small puddle, then loaded the marshmallow and three erasers into the back of the pickup. Ray drove it over to a doll house at the same time Eugene's truck pulled up. Ray made the sound effects, scowling at Eugene for being reluctant to add to the realism.

"Norm!" said Old MacDonald. "Aliens mighta invaded Earth. Three more come to get rid of 'em before they spread. They live in people's bodies like parasites. I got one of the good thread ones in me; the other's in him."

"CID's on the way here. They'll capture him or kill him."

"Then let me put the thread in you," 'mallow proposed. "I'll die, but nobody'll know *you* got threads in you. Then if you find out the bad ones is here, you can tell the black boxes next time the radio calls."

"But you'll die," Old MacDonald argued.

"I'm gonna die anyway. This way it will be for a good reason."

"Okay," Norman-doll agreed.

Eugene put the threads on Norman-doll, pronouncing the marshmallow dead.

"I should leave before they get here. I'll get rid of this," Norman-doll said, putting the dead 'mallow and one of the black erasers in the back of his truck.

Eugene carried the truck over to the trash basket, putting the 'mallow under the tissue, explaining, "Animal feed."

Eugene stood there looking at the tissue, transfixed. Little Ray tugged at his sleeve. "You gonna finish this time, Eugene?"

He nodded, then closed his eyes for a moment. When he opened them, he started calling out instructions. By the time he and Little Ray were finished, the Norman-doll was at a farm house surrounded by a half-dozen dolls. He named them off, pausing at the last two.

"Russell . . . and Eugene."

The Norman-doll talked to somebody on the phone. "They *are* here. And they're spreading." He hung up and made another call. "Flynn. I'm gonna make more good aliens. Will you? No? I sure wish you said yes. Then it's gonna be my family and the Weisman boy if he agrees. I'm gonna change my records to include him—name's Eugene. If something happens to me, you look out for 'em. Bye."

Eugene took the wad of threads from the Norman-doll and cut off snippets, putting one piece with each plastic farm animal. Then he pretended to kill the animals, moving each thread to a toy doll.

Eugene suddenly looked agitated, distraught. He clenched and unclenched his fists, then sat on the floor and pulled his knees up, wrapping his arms around his legs. "Don't wanna do the next part where they got killed," he breathed, profound sadness in his face.

The men watched him. Little Ray fidgeted awkwardly at the bed. Durbett asked, "What about Jolene Carter? Did she ever get an alien?"

Eugene crinkled his face. "Don't remember Mr. Watterson's part after threads got put in the cows. It's only *my* memories after that."

Durbett nodded. He rubbed his hand across his head several times, also agitated. Finally, he asked, "Why didn't Norman explain all this when he called me with these tales of aliens? Maybe I would've believed him if he'd just explained . . ."

Eugene looked up at the mercenary, his expression both accusatory and hurt. He shook his head no.

Durbett looked down as if he was embarrassed—or ashamed. He quietly admitted, "You're right. I thought he was losin' it—post-trauma reaction or whatever from the things we'd done."

"He *counted* on you—and you let him down." Looking away, he added, "He died thinkin' you let him down."

"No, Eugene. I just didn't believe him right *then*. I made a mistake, but I haven't let him down." He looked right at the teen still huddled in the middle of the floor. "I'm here *now*, doin' what he thought needed to be done. And most all of it's been on faith."

Eugene's face softened, but he was breathing hard, his heart pounding. He gazed at the floor in front of himself, his eyes brimming with tears. He sniffled once or twice and wiped his face. "I guess it really *is* on me to save the world," he whispered, like finally accepting of the idea.

Nobody spoke, an awkward silence in the air.

Little Ray picked up a wad of thread and the plastic soldier that had represented Eugene. He gathered up three more soldiers, then sat on the floor next to the older boy.

Apparently sensing that the teen's breathing was relaxing again, that he was regaining his composure, the youngster held out the three soldiers and quietly pronounced, "Here's Mr. Durbett and my daddy and me. Then he offered Eugene the last soldier with its wad of thread, holding it out until Eugene took it.

The teen looked in the boy's eyes, the slightest hint of smile on his face.

Little Ray grinned impishly. "We're gonna help ya finish the story."

$*$ $*$ $*$

He hitchhiked out to Dickson, then walked to a pay phone at the beverage store and called the number he'd memorized.

"Hello, Dunkin? Yeah, it's Lloyd Stewart. I'm in. Still ain't found out where the Weisman boy is, but I know he'll be back at Emery's tomorrow.

"Yeah, I'll be ready."

Chapter 9

"It's not always smart to work alone," Jake Coleman argued.

"Listen to what he's sayin'," Big Ray Blounten agreed.

Flynn Durbett shook his head. "No, often as not, alone is better than a crowd."

"I'm tryin' not to take that too personal," Jake shot back wryly.

"You guys got too much goin' on down here." To Ray: "With that last truck comin' in, I don't trust nobody but you to handle things here." Then to Jake: "It *ain't* personal, Jake. Ain't nobody I'd more trust to op with. But all these people this week is here to see *you* and to go through all the stuff you set up. You can't leave now—"

"But if it gets hairy, you may need—"

"If it gets hairy, I may need you and *all* your troops," he returned with a touché. "Take care of your militias. I'll make the run."

The men reluctantly agreed. Eugene, standing off to the side, had kept quiet. He waited until Durbett headed indoors for his duffel, following him to talk in private.

"I'm goin' with you," he said evenly. No debate, no discussion. Actually, he held his breath like he was *hoping* there would be no debate, no discussion.

"No."

"You're stopping at Emery's, too."

"Yes, so?" He knew what the *so* was.

"Then I need to go."

Durbett took a deep breath. His duffel ready, he donned his suede vest and started to arrange his holster. "Ain't smart, Eugene." Yeah, like that would convince a love-struck fifteen-year-old.

"She's scared to death, you know. Her brother's missing—maybe dead. I'm gone. Ain't had Jake around to help her feel safe. She needs this." So there!—it was completely altruistic. He needed to go for Licia's sake.

Durbett tried to suppress a grin. Give the lad credit; he intended to go and he'd put a lot of thought into how best to make that happen. "She'll feel better knowin' you're down *here* safe." Thrust and parry.

"Come on, Flynn, you know women. She won't feel better unless she can really *see* me."

"No. Just be harder on her when you have to leave again right away." He was cleaning his pistol, trying to avoid eye contact with the earnest teen.

"Now I understand things more, I can talk private with her and she'll— Then she'll be able to— She—"

Durbett looked up. His opponent had lost his stride, was open for the kill. Eugene was practically shaking, his face creased with the intensity of his emotions. He wanted desperately to go, but was seeing his chances crumble.

"You're *not* bein' fair to her—" Eugene insisted.

"I don't have to be fair to nobody," Durbett shot back. He turned away and packed up the ammo case he'd been working from.

What? No response. Eugene said nothing more. Surely he wasn't out of ideas *that* fast.

Durbett wasn't sure exactly when he'd decided Eugene could go along, could stop and spend some time with Licia, but he *would* have felt bad if he'd just walked out and left him there.

"Flynn?" the teen said quietly.

Durbett turned.

There stood Eugene, his eyes cast down, a bead or two of sweat on his brow. He looked up, desperation in his eyes. He wiped his face and took a deep breath. He had only one word, heartfelt . . . "Please?"

Durbett's shoulders dropped, a long exhale. Quietly, "I assume you're packed?"

A nod.

Durbett headed out of the room, armed and ready, duffel slung over his shoulder. "I'll tell Big Ray you're going with me."

*   *   *

Once he'd cleared the doorway, Eugene turned away and grinned. "Ha!" He punched the air with a victory jab.

Piece o' cake. Parry and thrust, point and match.

*   *   *

Brigadier General McGovern carried it into his office, followed by Dr. Aggeous. While McGovern set the case on his desk and opened it, the fat doctor maneuvered his frame onto the low couch, wheezed and coughed from the exertion. He produced a hankie and wiped sweat from his brow, then motioned for the case to be brought over to him.

McGovern was staring in disbelief. Something looked different about the real black box. The fake one still looked like a bar of polished black soap.

"Gets obvious which one's real when you know what you're looking for, don't it?" Aggeous loosened his collar and belched.

McGovern wanted to touch the real box, but he held back. He would've been hard-pressed to describe the change. It felt like the air around it was charged with some kind of halo effect, like wavy lines above a hot barbecue grill, the corona around an eclipse, the afterimage of a camera flash in your eyes, the blurry edges of fast vibration, the color of an oil slick constantly refracting and undulating.

Again Aggeous motioned for him to bring it over. He was growing impatient, looking rather ill. It was very hot in there—even the general was breaking a sweat, breathing hard.

McGovern tried to focus on the box again, but it hurt his eyes, gave him a headache, made him feel sick to his stomach. He reached out gingerly to touch it, then pulled back. Finally, he carried the entire case over to the low table adjacent to Aggeous.

The doctor reached out and picked up the genuine box, cradling it in his hands. It lasted ten seconds, maybe fifteen, then it was over. The box again looked like the fake one, nothing special, inert. The doctor looked relieved, his breathing slowed again. He continued to cradle it, though, like a drunk clinging to his bottle.

"Billy Hall was getting the call that time you showed him the fake box," Aggeous explained. "That's why he could see it wasn't the real thing."

McGovern removed his cap to run his fingers through his short hair. Hot and sweaty, he felt more disheveled than he normally would allow. "How often do, um, do *they* call?"

Aggeous shrugged. "Ain't consistent. Every now and then."

"And you have to actually touch it?"

"Just hold it and think."

"Hold it and think." McGovern seemed lost in thought. *Hold it and think.*

That's all it takes to keep more aliens from invading.

*   *   *

"You feel better now?" Durbett asked. He had pulled over to the side of the road.

Eugene rinsed his mouth and spit again, leaning out the passenger side. He sat up, closed the door, and wiped his face with a hand towel. "Yeah. It's gone now."

"That one didn't last as long."

"Somebody musta got right on it."

"Yeah, but who?"

*   *   *

Passing through Dickson, only minutes from McEwen, Eugene could hardly contain his excitement. Durbett had been quiet most of the drive, lost in his thoughts, every now and then asking a question or two. He asked why it had taken so long for the teen to "get in touch" with the alien inside him. They decided it was a matter of learning human physiology, of knowing where and how to connect, of lengthening that thread of memory knots with each new experience.

Every new experience.

Even the events of everyday life, the routines, what we take for granted—it all started with a first time . . .

"Something you need to think about, Eugene—"

"Yeah?" The teen was watching out the window, fidgeting, playing with the radio, inspecting his clothes and nails and hair in the mirror, that infernal zit staking claim to territory beside his nose.

"She's a sweet girl and pretty as can be," Durbett started.

"And smart and honorable and has a big heart," Eugene added, quickly wanting to elevate what he knew deep inside was true love and not youthful lust.

"Still, though, you need to remember she's only sixteen—"

"Almost seventeen," he exaggerated.

"And you're just fifteen—"

"We're not gonna get married until we're older."

"Well, now, that can be a *good* thing," he allowed. "That's a good path in life, becoming a family man, maybe raising up a little Weisman or four and teaching 'em right from wrong. That's the way Watterson decided he wanted to play it . . ." Durbett had a faraway look in his eye.

"But *you* never wanted that kind of life," Eugene tested.

"We're not talkin' about *me*. We're lecturing *you* right now."

Eugene tried to suppress a smile, but wound up chuckling. So did Durbett, just a little.

"But really, if you're in love, well, that's probably a good thing. And she's as good a gal as any man could ever want and she comes from a good family and she's got a good head on her shoulders. So *don't* ruin it."

"*Ruin* it? How?"

"Pushing her too far too fast, expecting things to be like you're both older than you are, getting into stuff you two's not mature enough yet to handle, givin' her expectations you can't promise yet to fulfill—" He paused. "Getting her *pregnant*."

Eugene was ready to argue all the points until the last one. He felt embarrassed, not so much that Durbett might think the teens would be that intimate, but that they *had* and hadn't been smart about it. Hadn't taken *precautions*. He'd not cared enough about her to be sure she wasn't put into a complicated position as a result of their passion. No, it wasn't not having cared enough, it was not being . . . Damn, that word Durbett used was all he could think of: *mature* enough.

Durbett was watching the inner debate play out in Eugene's face. He quietly offered, "Norman once told me he loved Ethyl so much that he put protecting her above everything else, no matter how he felt at the time. Then when he decided to retire and go marry her, he said now they was ready and gonna do things the right way."

Eugene stared out the window for a minute. Finally, he said, "I understand."

"I figured you would."

They rode on in silence, Eugene fidgeting, checking the mirror, worrying over that zit. By the time they pulled into the long gravel drive, he was poised to leap from his seat.

Everybody hurried out onto the big, wide porch—cousin Lloyd, Tracey, militia-man Chuck, another woman and Licia running out to jerk open the truck door as Durbett was rolling to a stop.

The teens hugged and kissed and hugged some more, both grinning like waifs with big candy.

*   *   *

Tipping his imaginary hat, Durbett greeted the gang on the porch. "Tracey, Chuck—Lloyd! Lloyd Stewart! Booted yer ass out, eh?"

"Yeah," Lloyd responded sheepishly.

Turning to the new woman, he looked her over good-naturedly, then said chivalrously, "Welcome to McEwen, Miss Lena. Thank you for coming."

"Y'all owe me *big*, Flynn. It's a good thing I *like* your scurvy hide."

"And that *I* like your *soft* one."

Inside, everybody had a cold soda while Lloyd related the grisly details of his discharge. Then Durbett explained he and Lena had some business to take care of and that they'd be gone until late, if not most of the night. It was agreed that Eugene wouldn't leave the Emery farm and that at least Chuck or Lloyd would be there for protection at all times.

Durbett hugged Tracey and Licia—quite friendly for the normally stand-offish man—shook the guys' hands, then looked puzzled and reached toward Eugene's chest. Caught off guard, the teen didn't stop himself in time to keep from looking down. Finally, with a wink for the protégé, Flynn and Lena were out of there.

Durbett was pleased she'd already rented a second car, this one with Tennessee rather than Texas plates. They lingered for a moment. "We got three hours before we meet him and have to get set up. I was hoping to take that time and brief you," he explained with a suggestive smile.

"Why, Flynn Durbett!" she mocked. "And here I was hoping we'd have time so I could *de*brief *you!*"

"Only if you'll still respect me later."

"Why should I start *now?*"

He followed her in his truck, pulling into the motel just outside Waverly where she had a room. Inside she'd left a cooler full of his favorite beer, some flavored sparkling water for herself. She wouldn't drink alcohol hours before such an important, potentially dangerous job.

Durbett wanted to explain all the details and contingencies first, so she rushed him through the briefing, impatient at how worrisome he could be. Durbett always took even the smallest operation *very* seriously.

Finally, after quizzing her too many times, he was satisfied. She opened another beer for him; he cautioned it would need to be the last since he was acting as her back-up later, too. She pressed "PLAY" on a portable cassette player and asked him did he want to dance.

He must have, because he held out his hand for her, then pulled her closer, hands on her waist, her arms around his neck. They swayed back and forth to the lilting strains of soft, country instrumental, sometimes looking into each other's eyes, sometimes with his hand caressing her neck and down her back, her cheek against his chest.

She unbuttoned his vest and made a rude noise about the holstered pistol. He removed it for her, laying it on the table. Her blouse fell open. Still dancing, he stroked her cheek with his hand, then kissed it, nuzzling tentatively before kissing her full on the mouth. A practiced, deft maneuver with her hand loosed the bra, allowing it to slide up and out of the way.

She steered him slowly toward the bed, gradually removing his clothes, helping him with her own. Horizontal, they continued to sway with the music, back and forth, she on top, then he, then side-by-side.

She used all of her tricks, touching carefully, carrying him to each plateau, lingering tentatively, taking him just a little higher, slowly playing out all that she knew he liked, adding the unexpected, varying and experimenting. She was a professional, a skilled artisan, and this rare opportunity she had with her favorite guy, she obviously strived very hard to make it the best, for this day to be the ultimate.

Durbett was having a good time, have no doubt, but he was holding back, maybe not fully willing to let himself go. Sometimes he diverted her moves, countered with some of his own, catching her by surprise. Whenever she breathed harder, made cooing sounds, signaled her pleasure, he would quickly change. What was to be her magnum opus was confounded every step of the way by this man who refused to let the artist work.

At one point, slightly exasperated, she whispered, "Flynn honey, what would you like—?"

"I'm no john, Lena. Don't wanna be."

She nuzzled his neck, tears starting to brim in her eyes. "Flynn, ain't nobody in the world I'd rather—"

"Then punch out, darlin'—get off the clock." He looked in her eyes and smiled, then wagged his eyebrows.

She smiled, too, letting him gently wipe away her tears with the backs of his fingers.

Once or twice he caught her trying to perform, but that melted away soon enough. She'd been climbing up the cliff so long, maybe she'd never realized how it could feel just to float away on the wind.

He felt self-conscious once or twice, too, reminded how uncomfortable he'd always been with the idea that she serviced him as if a high-paying client.

But she gave in, so he did, too. They trusted each other enough to go for the ride, wherever it might take them.

For once, he wasn't a mercenary on guard and she wasn't the pro.
Some might've called it amateur hour, except that it lasted nearly two.

*   *   *

The hottest part of the day, dark stormheads threatened from the west,
air thick and humid. Eugene and Licia cuddled in a lounger on the big
screen porch, a small fan oscillating on the table nearby. Lloyd and Tracey
were inside enjoying the air conditioner, Chuck over on the lawn with a
garden hose washing dust and bugs from his Cherokee, occasionally scanning the area, keeping one eye on the teens.

"I sure did miss you," she said quietly for the third or seventh time.

"I don't like being away—and not just because I miss you, neither." He
squeezed his arm around her shoulders. "But I don't like not being able to
protect you when I'm somewhere else."

"I'll be okay."

He fell quiet for a minute, then explained, "Used to be all I worried
about was doing good in school, hangin' around with Russell, and lookin'
out for Willow." He took a deep breath. "Russell was killed without me
being able to help. Then Willow died—maybe she was killed, too—when I
shoulda been there."

"Eugene, you can't be responsible for everybody—"

"Maybe *not*." He was angry. "But I can be responsible for *you*—I mean,
help take care of—" He stammered, trying to express commitment rather
than dependence or protection. "*Together* I mean, lookin' out for each
other."

"I'd like that," she agreed. Still, though, she seemed sad, not as excited
as he'd hoped. He was trying to say something important here!

He just didn't know how.

"I was thinking," he started. It was a good bet they'd *both* been thinking. "We could live wherever you want, here or whatever. I'm gonna have
a lot of money Mr. Watterson left me—and property and businesses and
stuff. We could buy another place if you want. We could finish school and
I could pay for college." He looked down again, embarrassed. "We could
get engaged or something and then get married when we're older."

Now she was crying. What *is* it with her?

"Why, *Eugene*, are you *proposing* to me?"

Shock. He'd not thought of it in those terms. Stupid stupid stupid. He
should have a ring or something, be kneeling down. "I'm sorry. I didn't do

it right."

"You did it just fine," she smiled. "I'd like that, too—only . . . Eugene, I been afraid. You're my one true love—I know it in my heart. Daddy used to tell me I'd know when it happened and he was right. But things ain't like you's picturing 'em."

He raised up and looked at her, used his fingers to wipe the tears from her tan cheeks.

"You got that alien thing to take care of and all these problems—"

"But I done figured out most of that," he blurted urgently. "We just gotta get one of those boxes and answer the next call—"

"And my brother—"

"We're gonna get him, Licia, no matter what it takes. We're probably gonna know where he is by tomorrow."

"And there's something else." It was her turn to look down, avoid his gaze.

"What, Licia?" he whispered, suddenly conscious of Chuck not too far away. "Don't matter what it is. Tell me."

She was crying again. "Oh, Eugene. You really wanna stay with me, no matter what?"

"I *said* that, didn't I?" Dammit, his word was golden.

She nodded. "Yes you did. That's why I'm cryin'—because I believe you."

"Then what is it? What's wrong?"

"You remember what happened up in my room that night?"

He was embarrassed again. "That's okay, Licia. We can wait until we's married or whatever you want. Ain't nothin' wrong long as we love each—"

"I believe you, Eugene. I do. And I love you with all my heart."

He was quiet, waiting.

"But it can't be exactly like you said."

"However you want, whatever it takes." He'd made his pledge. And he meant it.

She took a deep breath. "After what happened upstairs . . . well, I missed my period—"

"We're gonna have a *baby?!*"

She looked up and saw that he was smiling, then burst into a wide grin of her own, tears flowing down her cheeks. Maybe it would be okay after all.

"Well—when?"

"If he comes when he's supposed to . . . same day *you* turn sixteen."

*   *   *

Back to the fort to get changed, stuff a duffel, pick up his cash, make a call confirming his buddy had already left to come pick him up, the MP was ready to go. He studied himself in the mirror, ran a comb through his thick, black mane, cut short so only one of its waves rippled through. He added a bit more aftershave, checked his teeth, wished for the umpteenth time that he was taller and a few pounds lighter, then closed his locker and walked out toward the gate.

His buddy was a communications specialist at the fort, had suggested that MP use the first two of his three days of leave to party in Nashville. It seemed Buddy's fiancée had a girlfriend who'd just broken up and was ready to step out for a little fun. After two straight weeks at Cumberland Sanitarium, MP was ready to get drunk, get laid, then get laid again. Buddy had suggested all three were high probabilities.

He climbed in and off they went, 49 toward Erin, ready to tear it up, but first the bad news. The girlfriend had patched things up with her guy. No cause for concern, though, Fiancée said come on by and she'd start making some calls.

Not more than a mile or two down the road, there she was, over to the side, her car broke down. Thirtyish, great body, shoulder-length brunette with highlights in a chic, waved-under cut, brief halter-top cut-off jeans short short *short!* And sandals. Sultry in the heat, vulnerable, in need of assistance.

Turns out she was just out of gas, so they rode together down to Erin to fill her can. MP was going to hit on her, but she saved him the trouble. The way she sat up against him, tentatively mouthed the cool, wet bottle of beer they'd offered her, licking her lips and breathing heavily—she was making her interest known. MP had to shift in his seat several times to give room to his own interest expressing itself.

Her name was Linda. She had been visiting an elderly aunt near Kentucky Lake, had done modeling on and off but was between jobs, had her own place out Duck River south of Waverly not far from the freeway.

Heading back to the car with gas, Buddy asked MP where he wanted to be dropped. A slick ploy. "If you can find a date and wanna go out with me and my fiancée later, give us a call."

"Don't have no plans yet," MP shrugged, "and three days to fill."

Hint hint hint. Linda looked very intrigued. "I must have a leak or something to lose all that gas." She pouted. "Sure would feel better havin' somebody like you to ride with me back to my place—you know, in case I need help again."

MP grinned. Buddy grinned. Linda licked her lips seductively and cuddled closer, her warm breath and the hot air mingling with the musky scent of their bodies.

They poured the gasoline into the tank, Buddy lingering long enough to make sure her car would start. MP couldn't believe his luck!

*   *   *

Another vehicle with a young black man slowed and checked to make sure they were all right, satisfied when Buddy signaled an okay, then moved along. The driver got just out of sight, then called on his radio. "Babyboy say all okay."

Babyboy Moller was washing his windshield at the gas station when Linda and the MP stopped to fill her tank before heading south.

"Babyboy say two on the way."

Over the next twenty minutes:

"Hank say two over the bridge."

"Van say two past the mill."

"TJ sees two past the motel."

Flynn Durbett was monitoring it all in his pickup, using a listener planted in the car and a mobile radio. He followed, staying no more than a mile or so behind them all the way. He'd had misgivings at the last minute about using Lena as "Linda." It was like the last few times he'd done "wet work" with Norman Watterson. You always have to look out for your team, but you can't afford to care about them—it's a distraction, a potential hesitation, the wrong thing to consider when making decisions on the fly. He used to wonder if he was getting soft; now he was all-too sure.

He didn't like having Lena play the lead in this one.

During the drive to her place, Linda/Lena got the MP to brag about his important, macho work. The more he talked, the more turned-on she got. She liked important, powerful men in uniform, men who handled guns, got involved in secret operations, could kick some real ass.

MP talked just a bit too much, but stopped short of revealing what was going on out there at Cumberland Sanitarium.

Durbett passed the house and parked in a gravel cul-de-sac, then plugged into a wire jack that was run through the woods. He listened to what was happening inside, maintaining radio contact with Hank, Van, and TJ, all parked close by.

Inside, Lena started by serving up a cold beer—with two dissolved Rohypnols. The "roofies," insomnia tablets recently banned in the USA, mixed with the alcohol to induce a drunken, sleepy state after which MP would never remember what happened.

Lena was a master at questioning. She kept him talking, allowing him to move forward sexually, but only in incremental stages. The more he bragged, the more he furnished juicy details, the hotter she got. When he held back, she acted disappointed, aloof, not quite as aroused.

She pretended to know people who worked at Cumberland, knew all about the project, that there were prisoners—but didn't believe *he* was important enough to be *inside*.

He tried to convince her he was.

When it reached the point where he would divulge no more information and was so aroused as to be frustrated, impatient, even resentful that maybe he was being dick-teased, Durbett decided it was time to go in.

*   *   *

MP was surprised to find himself suddenly surrounded by four heavily armed men. Groggy, he tried to get up, but his body was too heavy, his arms and legs wouldn't work quite right. He wondered where Linda was going, what she was doing with the tarp, why spreading it out, why the towels.

Okay, okay, he'd lie on the tarp, but he didn't like it. What were they going to do to him, anyway?

"We're gonna trade secrets," Durbett explained. "The tarp's in case you don't wanna play." Durbett pointed his Browning at the MP's face. "You don't play, I blow your head apart. Towels keep blood and brains from running off onto the rug. We wrap up what's left in the tarp, tie it real good, drop you in a hole in the woods, won't be in *this* century your bones turn up."

MP wet his shorts—didn't want to, but couldn't stop it.

"*What* secrets?"

"Well then, I'll tell you mine first. I'm gonna take the sanitarium. Your part is to answer questions that'll help me do it."

"And then you'll kill me." MP grew furious, but all that energy just made him tired. Scared he could still muster. Wasn't any way to escape. Didn't look good.

"Don't need to if we swap secrets. You won't remember enough about this conversation to ID any of us—don't even know who we are. You spend your three-day leave drinking and laying a local hooker who can testify you was with her the whole time an' *my* part'll be over by the time you report back for duty. If you *don't* swap secrets, then I have to find somebody else who'll play. Slows me down. Means keeping you alive becomes a security risk for me. Can't *never* let you report back then."

It made sense. Wasn't any other way out alive. Why should *he* care what happens as long as he can make sure it's before he gets back.

The militia seemed to know enough about Cumberland to test the veracity of his information. He tried to pretend he didn't know where the fence electrification transformers were located, but they'd observed him on perimeter patrol at least twice.

"He's done. Lies don't help us." Durbett turned his back and nodded toward Van. The heavyset, white-haired man stepped forward and leveled an M-16 at the MP's face.

MP remembered what he'd forgotten, begging desperately to be friends, spilling his guts to prove he wanted to swap secrets.

Several names seemed of interest. General McGovern. Doc Aggeous. Some old black guy name of Carter—Lee or Leroy or something. Emery—Marshall Emery.

Nothing about aliens, though. Some kind of medical thing, some doctors and a quarantine lab, nothing that could spread to the MPs or staff.

Sure wasn't a whole lot of defensive capability in place; couldn't be that big a deal. More security would've involved more people, equipment and supplies. McGovern seemed to want to keep it low key, was more worried about secrecy than fortification.

They spread out a plat culled from old county records. MP answered all kinds of questions, pointed out locations, could specify exactly where Carter and Emery were being held, positions of sentries, the lab, McGovern's office, where McGovern's desk and chair were situated.

The questions eased up. So did MP's consciousness. Only fight-or-flight adrenaline was keeping him awake.

"You're gonna kill me anyway, ain't you?"

Durbett knelt down and looked him square in the eyes, penetrating . . . cold, hard reality.

"No. A deal's a deal."

MP started shivering, felt cold.

"Now what?"

"We're gonna hold you until your leave is almost over. By then we'll know if anything you told us was a lie. One lie, you're dead, body never found. All truth, you go back with a hangover and fuzzy memory, surprised at what happened while you were gone."

MP nodded, struggling to sit up. "It's all truth."

The blocked-off area in Van's cellar wasn't comfortable, but would be okay for a few days. All he'd be given to drink was beer and whiskey—and "roofies"—so it wouldn't be hard to claim he spent his time drunk.

And he *had* been in the arms of a beautiful woman, at least for a little while.

*   *   *

Babyboy waited outside. Durbett walked Lena to her rental.

"Straight back to Texas," he said quietly.

"Ain't got no plans, Flynn. Let me stay fer a while—"

He shook his head. "I'm working."

She knew better than to argue. She studied his face, her lip quivering. How could he just pay her off, send her away, not think of her until the next job?

"This was the last one, Lena," he said. He looked off into the trees, the placid green water of Duck River visible through the branches.

She searched his face, not sure of the implications, a sinking feeling deep inside.

"I mean it, Lena. No more work for you. *I've* got some obligations every now and then, but . . . well . . . Listen, I got fantastic places on three islands, need a better one somewhere here in the U.S. If you want, you figure out what and where and we'll buy it or build it. Then I'll take you to every island and let you pick the curtains or rebuild from scratch. But you don't work no more. You enjoy the rest of your life . . . and . . ."

She was holding him tenderly. "And what, Flynn honey?"

"And *I'll* try, too."

"It's not hard to learn, you know." She was giddy with what he'd said, had never seen him so vulnerable, wanted to be sensitive in how she handled him.

"May need to keep the kid and Licia around for a while," he cautioned her, "especially if we don't get Marshall back safe."

"Why Flynn Jonas Durbett, you *care* about them young'ns, don't you?"

"It's an obligation to—" he hastily tried to explain.

She put her finger to his lips, hushing him up. "Admit it," she teased. He smiled.

"Admit it!" she insisted, smiling back.

"Okay, dammit, I admit it."

"Then I accept your offer," she announced, "but I can't teach you somethin' you already know."

"What makes you think—?"

"Hush, silly. You just *admitted* it."

*   *   *

"Mr. Watterson used your name," Jolene Carter confirmed. "Said you was the only man to trust 'sides his family and Eugene."

"Good then. I hope you've not felt you were being held here against your will," Durbett assured.

"Well, I *was* kidnapped!—but Moller said I could go. I was waitin' for *you*, though. I wanna see Eugene." The pregnant black teenager shifted uncomfortably in her seat.

"He's lookin' forward to seeing you, too." Durbett smiled, trying to seem friendly, encourage her to relax. Four weeks shy of her due date, whisked away by strangers in the night, no-telling what else she'd been through before that—he felt sorry for her, wanted her to believe she was with people she could count on. "I sure have a lot of questions—"

She shook her head, determination in her face. "I'll talk to Eugene," she insisted.

"I understand. Something I need to know right away, though—we've learned of an older gentleman being held at a military facility, wonder if you know who he is—"

She sat forward, eyes wide with hope and expectation.

"Name's Carter, either Lee or Leroy—"

"Is he all right?!"

"Don't think he's hurt, but he's being held in quarantine." Durbett decided not to bring up aliens; she wanted to talk to Eugene.

"He's my daddy. My stepfather. They was looking for *me*."

Durbett studied the young woman. She had to be sixteen, seventeen maybe. She was pretty, thin except for the pregnancy, with high cheek-bones and a regal air that reminded him of an Egyptian princess. Her hair was braided in rows, her maternity frock and sandals shabby. Her large obsidian eyes glistened with a hint of tears.

She sniffled several times and took a deep breath. "I was afraid they'd hurt him or . . ." Looking up suddenly, she asked, "Can you help him?"

Durbett nodded. "We'll do our best."

She cast her eyes down, then used one hand to caress her abdomen gently, shifting her weight uncomfortably again. Babyboy Moller asked if she needed something to drink.

"Lord, I pee every five minutes *now*," she offered by way of declining. News that Leroy had been located, that Durbett would try to help, her spirits seemed better than since she'd been abducted.

"The other thing," Durbett started, "is that it's not safe to keep staying here at Moller's. I want to take you to see Eugene, then put you up at a safe compound where he's staying in Alabama."

"He'll be there, too?"

"Right in the same house."

She wanted some time to freshen up, plus neither she nor Babyboy had eaten, so Durbett left for McEwen first.

Babyboy would drive Jolene, stopping for fast food in Waverly.

*   *   *

It was dark as they pulled out of the burger joint, the storm clouds having turned to rain, a cool wind, flashes of lightning followed by thunderclaps. Babyboy headed out Highway 70 toward the Emery place monitoring CB channel 11 when he recognized the mercenary's urgent voice.

"Babyboy pass by! Go straight there! Acknowledge."

"Got it! What's—?!"

"That's *all!*"

Babyboy quickly turned around and headed back to Waverly to pick up Highway 13 south.

Something was wrong, better to get Jolene straight to Guntersville.

*   *   *

Durbett had driven past the Emery house, ditching his truck in a pull-off by the woods. He jumped out, scanned and listened through the patter of soft rain on trees, then reached under the cab and pulled a lever. A drawer swung out on a swivel, revealing a cache. He slipped into an ammo vest, then quickly assembled and loaded his M-16A1 with M-203 grenade launcher. He strapped on his infrared mask, swung the drawer closed, and disappeared into the dark, muddy woods.

Coming up from the rear, he scanned the area around the house, then worked his way along until he could see the front.

There, what had alarmed him, was Chuck lying face down a dozen yards out from the porch, perfectly still. He wasn't breathing. Durbett could see he'd taken at least one shot to the head, had another exit wound in his back.

The house was quiet, only one light inside.

Toward the back again, quickly crossing the open space, pausing below the rail at the back porch. Look through the window, kitchen and dining clear, nothing disturbed. Utility room, pantry, storage . . .

Over the rail, outside the door. No sound but rain.

Quickly inside, crouching, moving toward the front. Living area undisturbed, door standing open.

Headlights coming down the road, pulling into the gravel drive. It was one of Jake's cars. Skidded to a stop, then backed away.

Lloyd Stewart jumped out, M1911A-1 drawn. He ran along a row of snowball bushes, rolling into a crouch out of Durbett's sight. There were two windows along that side of the house, the first in the living room.

Durbett eased over to it, listened, heard the slightest rustle, then had his M-16 barrel aimed before Stewart could rise up to peer in.

"Freeze," he whispered. "I'm Flynn."

"What happened here?" Lloyd whispered back.

"Where were you?"

"Out for groceries. Chuck's been shot."

Durbett pulled him through the window in one deft motion. They crouched there, both wet, Flynn muddy, a puddle forming on the rug.

One each side of the stairs. Anybody above would know people were in the house, no need for silence.

"Who's up there?" Durbett called out.

Movement. A .45 pointed down. It was Tracey.

"Flynn?" her voice trembled.

"Me and Lloyd. It's okay."

He crept up the stairs. The gun wavered in her hands. She was crying. He reached out and gently took it.

"Who else?" he asked, moving past her.

He found Licia crouched in the corner of her bedroom, back against the dresser, her rifle on her lap. She appeared terrified, unable to move.

"Licia!"

She looked up, recognized him, and started sobbing.

He set the rifle aside, then lifted her into his arms, holding her tight.

"You're okay, Licia. It's all right. Where's Eugene?"

"Oh Flynn, they *took* him."

Chapter 10

"You all right?"

Jolene Carter stared intently out the car window. She was breathing heavily, clenching and unclenching her fists, pressed up against the door, practically cringing from Babyboy Moller.

"Look, Jo—Miss Carter, either you're going into labor or you're scared. We're almost there; I wish you'd relax."

Almost there didn't calm her, but rather had the opposite effect. "Where's Eugene?" She'd asked it before.

"I told you he's probably on his way down here, but I don't know what went wrong. We'll see what we can find out when we get there."

There had been explained to her as a private club in an old country camp. "Take me back to Waverly," she said evenly, still staring out the window.

"Come on, Jolene, you need to give me some *play* here. Think about it. We *rescued* you. You stayed at my place a coupla days, able to leave if you really wanted. You talked to Eugene—"

"He didn't mention *you*."

"We're *all* members—lookin' out fer each other," he explained to the back of her head.

"Members of what?"

"It's a patriot organization—rich folks *and* workin' people, plus there's several militias that belong."

"And Eugene?"

"I *guess* he's a member now. I ain't never met him. But we's protecting him because one of the founders woulda wanted us to—same reason as you. I'm talkin' about Watterson."

"What're *you* doin' with 'em? Militias is racist skinheads and all."

"Naw, only some of them organizations is racist. The ones with the *most* members is quiet—patriots and libertarians, business people and bankers and doctors and them, everyday citizens wanting less corrupt government and taxes. Look, I got a brother in prison doing forty years for drugs, an honest business transaction between consenting adults exercising their right to free commerce and control over their own bodies. I was ridin' the bus to see him on a visit and I got to talking to some other visitors who belonged. I wound up joining. Ain't never belonged to nothin' before," he added.

She fell quiet for a minute, not quite as scrunched against the door, no longer asking to be taken back to Tennessee. "Mr. Watterson told me about their ideas a coupla times—sure didn't see nothin' *wrong* with believing that way."

Babyboy wanted to keep her talking, focusing on the familiar until he could get her inside. It was gnawing at him, wondering what went wrong in McEwen, hoping no major surprises awaited at the compound, afraid something would spook Jolene even worse. Durbett had said it was important to protect her and get her to Eugene Weisman so they could talk. "You knew the Weisman boy pretty good?"

She took a deep breath, then turned away from the window, staring forward, still not looking directly toward Babyboy. "Not until I moved to Wattersons'. Him and them was all good people. Russell was kinda the little old bad-ass, Eugene the sweeter one. Sometimes Russell'd be doing chores and I'd find Eugene waitin' on the bluff by the creek, just watching the water like something was gonna happen. He'd always run off and find a flower to pick for me so I could put it in what-he-called my *curly-doo hair that holds flowers so good.* He was always wondering about the baby—" She stroked her abdomen lovingly. "He couldn't understand how I could, you know, get *close* like that with a man I didn't wanna stay with—and it twisted him all up that a daddy could run off and not stay around to help take care of his own child. Once he told me that's what *his* daddy done, and *he* weren't never gonna be like that."

"Neither would I," Babyboy said quietly.

She looked at him for the first time since they had passed from Tennessee into Alabama. "Mr. Watterson sure did try to do right by his family."

"I never knew the Wattersons." Babyboy hesitated, then added, "Word is, he was an *alien*—that they was *all* aliens."

She stared at her lap, then back out the window.

"That Weisman boy's saying he's an alien, too—or got one in him or something—and that he's the last one left."

*   *   *

You will be captured or killed.
Jolene started to speak, but decided against it.

People who know a lot are either the ones to trust or the most dangerous.

The routine to get past the compound gate reminded Jolene she was scared, unsure of where she was going or why. Of course, it wasn't like she had anyplace else she could run.

"You're the one lived with Wattersons," Big Ray said by way of confirmation when they'd been introduced.

"Is Eugene—?"

Big Ray shook his head, leading Jolene and Babyboy into the house. "Jake, Van, TJ, and Hank." Big Ray waved. They knew who she was. The group huddled around the dining-room table, note pads, weapons, a blueprint of some kind spread out.

"They took Eugene," Big Ray pronounced.

"Damn!" Babyboy looked mad. "Durbett?"

"He got there too late. They killed Chuck, though."

You will be captured or killed.

Jolene noticed a boy of nine or ten watching from near the top of the stairs, worried but resolute, a little tough-guy who looked like maybe he'd been crying a little.

A woman came in from the back. She'd heard the introductions. "Lordie, girl, let's get you a seat. You're making *me* tired watching you stand." She pulled a comfortable chair in from the family room. "Let me get you something to eat. How about you—?" she asked Babyboy, apparently not sure of his name.

Not waiting for an answer, she set about pouring ice tea for everybody and warming some biscuits, then setting out jams and margarine.

"Durbett's workin' a plan," Big Ray explained to Babyboy. "Wants us up there right away. We're leaving soon as a few more get here who can protect the place."

Babyboy nodded. No hesitation. Jolene noticed the little boy was nodding, too, wanting something done about Eugene's abduction.

Not much was said about the plan; nobody knew what it would be. "Durbett's on it," seemed to sum it up.

There were a few polite questions of Jolene—was she okay, when was she due, had she liked the Wattersons, how long since she'd been seen by a doctor. Jackie was appalled to learn it hadn't been since Mr. Watterson had driven her for regular exams. She immediately called a physician-member and asked him to come by after his office closed that evening, Jolene protesting politely, but gracious and grateful—relieved actually.

When a big, burly guy came in, the men started gathering their things in preparation to leave. Jackie helped Jolene upstairs, introducing Little Ray, and showed her to a vacant bedroom, telling her to make herself comfortable and don't you worry you can stay here as long as you need. She promised to bring her a change-of-clothes soon, even to take her shopping "when things settle down." Jolene noted the woman was trying to be friendly, but seemed distracted, even nervous, by what the men were planning.

With Jackie gone back downstairs, Jolene went to the bathroom. When she came out, Little Ray had set a tray with more ice tea and some cookies on her night stand.

"Thank you, Raymond."

"Mama calls me that, but everybody else says Little Ray."

She sat on the side of the bed, patting next to her for him to sit down, too, then sipped her tea and ate several of the cookies, sharing them with her little buddy.

Babyboy Moller stuck his head in, coming over to squeeze her hand and let her know he had to leave, promising he *would* be back. "You'll be all right here."

She watched from the window as they loaded into vehicles, Big Ray lingering for a moment to hold Jackie, assuring her he would be careful, all would be okay. She walked around the room, examining the dresser and table, the hope chest and upright clothing cabinet, the beat-up roll-top desk.

"You wanna see Eugene's room?" Little Ray offered.

She was surprised by the strange array of plastic sheets and toys and stale food scattered around.

"This is Eugene's alien history," the lad explained matter-of-factly. He jiggled one of the marshmallows, high-pitch sing-songing, "Hi, Jolene! We're the marshmallow people. We's smart but we ain't got no arms!"

Jolene chuckled, but she was surveying the whole panorama, somehow struck by it, as if it meant something significant.

"You wanna play alien history?" Ray prodded. "I know the whole thing—Eugene's been teachin' me."

Yes, this really was where Eugene Weisman had been staying, was someplace he'd decided was safe, with people he trusted, where his secret had been accepted.

"Sure. What do I do?"

Little Ray looked pleased. "You wanna be the 'mallow people or the melty creatures that grow arms?"

Jolene laughed. Sure, why not. It looked like she just might be here a while.

Take a chance. Trust your instincts. Sometimes they're all you got.

*   *   *

Cinderblock walls, steel door, stainless steel toilet/sink, military-style cot, shackles on his wrists. Not dressed for a surprise abduction, clad only in undershirt, boxers, and socks, a fifteen-year-old military prisoner.

You will be captured or killed.

Never being discovered was no longer an option.

Eugene Weisman was distraught, but he couldn't help think that maybe, after all, it really would *not* be better to die.

Even carted away and caged, as long as he lived, there was hope. A chance. Possibility.

Especially when you have people out there you can rely on. And somebody you're in love with.

And a little one on the way, one who'll need a dad.

And a goal . . . *freedom*. Freedom from alien enslavement, from government oppression, from strangers' selfish notions of right and wrong.

Persevere, no matter what, and wait for your chance.

There were aliens on Earth, beings who coveted our dexterity and would stop at nothing to control it. If Eugene was the last hope, then there had to be a way. It couldn't end like this, not here, not now, not with so much at stake.

It's not over 'til you're dead.

Whoever had been sending the all-clear with the black box had the most to lose if Eugene could call for help. That's who would need to neutralize the only good alien left. That's who would capture—or kill—Eugene.

He must be close—close to finding out who and where the bad aliens were, to finding the other black boxes Mr. Watterson had spoken of.

Make the most of your chance Eugene.

If you wind up in a swarm of bees, might as well snatch the honey while you're there.

*   *   *

"I'm going to *kill* him. What else would you have me do?" McGovern straightened his tie, then shifted his weight back onto the front of his desk, resting his knuckles on the surface.

"Use him to find that other box," Aggeous argued, pausing to wheeze, then cough up phlegm.

"But it must be lost or *hidden* somewhere; nobody's been using it. Once these last two aliens are dead, won't anybody but us ever know what the boxes are anyway. Then we just keep sending the all-clear and we'll be safe from invasion."

"But with another box, *either* of us could signal; we could keep 'em in different locations in case something happens to one." Aggeous shook his head. "You're shithead military; surely you understand the strategy of *that*."

McGovern did, but didn't want to dwell on the fat doctor's more-calculated reasoning. McGovern was surprised at himself, wondering why he let emotion creep so much into his decisions. "But keeping the boy alive for a while, trying to question, it just increases the risk of contamination."

"He can't contaminate you or anybody else. Ain't old enough to be one of the original carriers like Billy Hall was. Watterson had the only other one and it wasn't *his* that got into the boy or he would've died. Watterson was still alive when *your* guys got him. That means the boy's got one of the alien's offspring and had to get it just in the last two or three years ever since Watterson's was able to spread."

"Then it will be at least a decade before the one in the boy can procreate—"

"Nearly *two* decades."

"So now Dukani's is the only one that can spread," McGovern concluded. "What about this *disconnection*? Couldn't the boy's leave him and go into another host?"

"Yeah, but a militia boy isn't going to let his alien into the very man trying to eliminate them. We're the enemy."

"What about it leaving him against the boy's wishes?"

"They aren't like that." Cough cough. He struggled to sit forward. "Besides, it knows whatever the boy knows—knows we're the enemy. Nope, we're safe—and we need to find out what happened to that box before you kill 'em all off."

"Okay, first we find out about the box."

"Then?"

"Then we kill them."

*   *   *

"I'm General McGovern." He stepped into Eugene's cell, a silver case in one hand, a .45 holstered at his waist. "Dr. Aggeous," he added, gesturing to the fat man in the doorway.

Aggeous wheezed greeting. McGovern motioned the doc farther in.

"You're Eugene Weisman," McGovern continued. The teen just looked at him, playing it cool. "You've got an alien in you, one put there by Watterson."

Eugene tried to look bored. Why didn't he feel scared? Where was that pounding heart? Had he been around Durbett long enough to learn calm during maximum adversity?

It's okay to get scared—later, after it's all over.

McGovern drew his sidearm, leveling it at the teen's head. "Follow me, got some people for you to meet." He led the manacled teen to another cell. Aggeous found a wall to lean against so he could watch.

"You know this man?" Eugene peered inside. An older black fellow, gray hair, panic in his eyes, sitting despondently on his bunk, nothing to do, no place to go, there alone with his speculation and fear.

"No."

"How about you? Know who this is?"

Carter looked closer, trying to be sure. He shook his head. "Don't know him."

"This is Leroy Carter."

"Jolene's stepfather?"

Carter was alert, rising to his feet, obeying McGovern's gesture with the Colt not to come any closer. "You seen Jolene?"

"Not since she lived with Wattersons." Technically, that was true. He'd only talked to her on the phone.

"Don't know nothin' about what happen to her?" Carter pleaded.

"No." Technically, that was a lie. He felt bad, could see the pain in the old man's face, his slumped shoulders, watched him drop dejectedly onto the cot. Eugene wished he could tell him she was okay with Flynn Durbett, the one person who could be most trusted to look out for her.

McGovern opened another cell. Marshall Emery was clearly thrilled to see Eugene alive and apparently okay—for the first second or two. Then he grew furious. Neither hid the fact that they knew each other.

"Eugene, I was the one give you up." Marshall pulled against the ankle chain bolted to the wall, Eugene noting his bloody and raw skin. "They drugged me, got it out of me," he snarled.

Eugene tried to project calm, assurance. "No you didn't. Not if it was taken against your will."

"I resisted, son. With all I had." His rage ebbed, leaving dejection, a beaten man.

"They killed Chuck," Eugene explained, telegraphing a message to the chained man. "He was the only one hurt. Everybody's fine." He could see the sigh of relief. He knew Licia would've been the next question, but didn't want her named, no more attention on her, nothing to suggest she could be an effective pawn for eliciting cooperation.

As McGovern was closing the steel door, Emery mouthed, "I'm sorry."

"It ain't over yet."

McGovern seemed amused by his captive's brashness.

As they entered the next cell, another black man pulled his legs up and backed into the corner, cowering in fear. Eugene admitted he didn't know him.

"He's got the other alien, the one that was in that old man from Camden."

Billy Hall. So he was captured after all.

"You two are the last ones left—Mr. Dukani here with one of the originals, and you with the last of Watterson's offspring. Isn't that right, Kemo? Haven't you got the alien in you?"

"Don't t'be know nothin' on no alien." He was studying Eugene curiously, apparently clueless why this mad military man thought these two had something in common.

To Dukani, "You gave Watterson one of the boxes, didn't you?"

He spread his arms to show he was confused.

McGovern gestured Eugene onto the bed, the thin black man recoiling from the teen.

"Where's the other box?"

Eugene was reluctant to converse, but McGovern dramatically aiming his pistol toward the Haitian's face urged him to play along. "I thought *you* had it. Didn't you take it?"

"The one we got from Watterson was a fake."

Eugene looked surprised, which McGovern might suspect was an act, but, well . . .

McGovern opened the case, allowing Eugene to see both boxes. "Which one's the fake?"

"How should *I* know?" He was studying them carefully, but they looked similar. There were minor differences, but what was to say which had the correct look?

"You can't tell?"

He shrugged, shook his head.

"Why not?"

"You know why. It's not time."

"You mean because there's no call coming right now."

Eugene raised his eyebrows and cocked his head in veiled assent.

"You've never used a box to answer a call?"

"Never even *had* a box to use."

"How did you know it would look different during a call?"

"Whatta *you* think?"

"Watterson told you?"

That shrugged assent again. "How do you know one of 'em's fake?"

"I've seen them during a call. Only one has that fuzzy glow that's supposed to happen—"

Aggeous spoke up hastily, "Don't *matter* what it looks like. Where's the other one?" he demanded.

"He's seen it glow, too?" He was looking straight at McGovern, but talking to the fat doctor.

Wheez. "Look, kid—"

McGovern cut him off. "Yeah—so?"

"Then *he* was the doctor there after the first landing." Eugene couldn't help but to let both recognition and alarm play across his face. "But *you* weren't there."

McGovern watched Eugene like he wasn't sure what to say. He was growing agitated, glancing over toward Aggeous several times, apparently waiting for somebody to speak.

Eugene snorted. "The other man who was there, you were with him when he died, weren't you?"

McGovern's expression answered.

Eugene inched farther back on the cot, a symbolic-more-than-pragmatic gesture. "Only people with aliens inside them can see the glow during a call."

McGovern whirled to glare at Aggeous.

Eugene drove his point home. "The more connected you are to your alien, the more the calls make you feel sick."

He wondered if McGovern had seen the doctor get ill during a call—or if he'd even felt the nausea himself yet. McGovern's face suggested he had.

"*You* two are the bad aliens mine came to find—the ones trying to make slaves of people!" Eugene accused.

McGovern was breaking a sweat, breathing hard, panicky. He leveled his .45 at Aggeous's face.

"No! What're you doing?"

Eugene pressed on. "Whoever had the alien was *touchin'* you when he died, *wasn't he?* That's when he put it *in* you. That's why he died *sudden.*"

McGovern swung the pistol around and aimed at Eugene, then at Aggeous again, then back to Eugene. He grew frantic, surrounded by aliens.

"Has to be an *alien* that answers the call. Regular people can't. Only aliens. Who's been answerin'? If it wasn't you, then was it him?"

Turn your enemies against each other.

"You didn't *know* he was inside you?" Eugene was jabbing harder. "Don't he talk to you? Or is he keepin' himself secret until he has *total* connection and can take you over and *control* you? That's the kind of alien you got, you know!" Eugene was getting louder, stabbing his points.

McGovern shot at Aggeous, "Well?"

The doctor stammered, wheezing and trying to catch his breath. He looked very pale.

Eugene hammered, "Tell him he's in the wrong country. This is America. You and fatso ain't *enough*, not where they's free citizens, where government don't have total control. Not now that the people know you're aliens!"

"Shut up! That's bullshit. There's no alien inside me. *You've* got the invaders! Where's the box? I said *where's the box!?*" He took a bead on the teen's face.

"You'll never find it," Eugene growled. "And there's *too many* of us to get us all."

"You *lie!* You've been telling people you're the last one left."

"It's what I *wanted* 'em to think—to protect the others. I don't even *know* who-all they are."

"That's not true! Where's the box?!"

Eugene shook his head, calm in spite of the weapon trained on his face.

"Talk to me!"

Eugene looked resolute. He said nothing.

Boom! Boom!

Dukani's head exploded onto the cinderblock wall, a large splotch starting to trickle down in grotesque rivulets, blood splattered all over Eugene and the bunk. The victim twitched a few times, what was left of his head lolling, his only intact eye staring in disbelief.

"Only one alien left," McGovern said quietly, nearly panting from his rage and panic.

Eugene swallowed hard.

It's not over 'til you're dead.

"Where's the box? Your friend Emery'll be next, then that black girl's father.

 Where's the box?"

"I don't know. If I did, why tell you?"

"To save your friends."

"Ain't no guarantees."

Persevere, no matter what, and wait for your chance.

"If *I* got the box, *you* can't answer the call. Ain't no reason not to let you go. Hell, you can start your own cult of freaks and alien conspiracists. Won't anybody who matters take you seriously. Just *give up the box!*"

Eugene shook his head.

"Then my alien problem ends here and now."

Eugene looked down the barrel, closed his eyes, one last thought for Licia.

I love you—

*   *   *

After dark the command center at Cumberland fell relatively quiet. Two men monitored the sensor array: audibles, photo-electric perimeter cells, oscillating thermal imaging display from vantages at the front entrance and in the rear along the river, plus six unit cams, alternating onscreen in ten-second intervals.

That mountain-tour operator they'd been monitoring was still working on his chopper—a late-model Jet Ranger—at the pole-barn garage on his property between Dover and Erin. Three days he'd been firing it up only to have it stall unexpectedly. Didn't seem to know what he was doing. Wind up crashing a bunch of camera-faced Jap tourists into the side of a mountain one of these days.

Couple of local fellers shinin' for deer along some of the access roads.

MPs had run 'em off the night before, so they weren't getting as close tonight. Gonna need to call in the game warden if they don't lay off. Heard shots earlier, figured they bagged something.

Big tits on the vid-screen. Size: VHS. Woodrow had brought it. McGovern didn't like it much but wasn't going to interfere with keeping up morale. You want your guys awake, and that's what big tits'll do.

More local fellers were fishing the shoreline, moving in and out of each cove every ten or fifteen minutes, lantern over the water, some nice large-mouth, a few surprise crappie, couple of shad. Doing all right, sounded like about a beer per fish. Woodrow monitored occasionally, could hear them clearly enough to know that one was bragging his was eight pounds easy—a trophy bass, if you're a tourist.

Two shots from the converted residence hall, the secure-cell detention section. Radio confirmed all okay. General was either scaring up some co-operation or blowing somebody away.

He got to have *all* the fun.

Big tits on the TV.

Fishermen stumbling up on shore to pee, comparisons to race horses, argument about passing one of the coolers over to the other boat.

Deer shiners coming too close again. Gonna have to give 'em some religion—

*   *   *

1 second.

FM jam on all UHF bands, three-mile radius. All radios go static.

Audibles detect Jet Ranger lifting off.

2 seconds.

Three explosions! "Whiz-bang" concussion grenades from M-16-mounted M-203 launchers, direct hits on telephone junction and both rear power couplers.

McGovern aiming at Eugene's head.

Lights out.

"Wha—? Shit!"

Boom! Thermal panel out, cameras off.

Silence.

3 seconds.

Roar of two motorcycles from back of the deer-shiners' truck.

Three HE (high-explosive) rounds from truck-mounted Carl Gustav launcher, sallyport and front area wide open.

Two "whiz-bangs" riverside, double fence out.

Three more HEs into the command center, obliterated.

5 seconds.

Emergency generators on.

McGovern slams door, Eugene locked in with Dukani's corpse.

Men in the bunkhouse scrambling. Motorcycle-one straight in, shooting one M-203 "Willie Peter" at the entrance, its spray of white phosphorus burning concrete and window frames. Cycle-one continuing around, another "Willie Peter" at the rear, two dead men caught coming out the door, building sealed.

Cycle-two spraying M-203 fragmentation grenades, several more MP sentries down.

Boat men fanning across grounds, drop and scattershot, three routes to the residence wing, no resistance.

14 seconds.

"Whiz-bangs" hit the generators, dark again.

Intruders using infrared, defenders caught blind. Both motorcycles ditched where lone Black Hawk chopper sits on pad. Big Ray "Vietman Qui-nhon" Blounten powering up—gimme four minutes, thank you very much—Van manning defensive gunnery. Only one MP trying to move in, one taken out.

34 seconds.

Jet Ranger overhead, pinpoint strafing.

Administration building hit with two "Whiz-bangs," one "Willie Peter," ruins aflame.

Flynn Durbett and Lloyd Stewart moving in. Lloyd laying M-16 fire every direction, Flynn carrying two M-16s, one with the mounted 203, plus bolt cutters.

71 seconds.

Infirmary hit. Bunkhouse strafed to discourage survivors. Durbett snatching keys from dead MP—too easy. First door, second door, moving inside.

Jet Ranger circling the perimeter, scanning access routes, one "whiz-bang" to crater the road—and just for laughs. Mighta got a deer after all.

87 seconds.

"Eugene!"

Boom! Boom! Boom!

Infrared face in the window. Key in the lock.

Boom! Boom!

Door open.

"That's Marshall bangin'!"

Boom! Boom!

Bolt-cutting manacles, Eugene hefting his own Browning—the surprise appearing from Durbett's belt.

"*Took* you long enough, Flynn."

"Had to teach you a lesson."

96 seconds.

Route to the boats secured, alternate route through the former sally-port secured, Jet Ranger still patrolling by infrared only.

Emery's door open.

Durbett: "How many more?"

Eugene: "Jolene's dad—two doors down." Too dark for Eugene to see, hand hooked in Flynn's belt, Browning ready.

109 seconds.

Chains off Emery, armed with Flynn's basic M-16.

"Don't know if there's any more!"

Lloyd Stewart checking other cells. Carter freed, scared and confused, can't see in the dark.

Keys to Stewart. Emery and Durbett laying down cover fire to lead the teen and old man outside.

All clear to TJ, Babyboy. Moving parallel to the center of the compound. Jet Ranger circling back.

Stewart checking cells, second from the end, four eyes glowing infrared, fat man panting like a heart attack, McGovern aiming .45. Stewart unlocking the door, handing off slip of paper, turning to run out.

Hank waiting, cover clear, flanking Stewart toward the Black Hawk.

173 seconds.

Fanning out to encircle the landing pad.

Two "whiz-bangs" hit near bunkhouse, one near the detention wing. Keeping them low in case more prisoners inside. Jet Ranger coming around. Black Hawk roaring to life. Durbett barking instructions to Eugene, Marshall, Leroy Carter.

Hank zagging toward one of the powerboats.

207 seconds.

Black Hawk rotors turning, Jet Ranger coming in. Van standing clear.

Ranger landing, Van first aboard, then Eugene and Carter.

Black Hawk lifting off, banking toward lake chasing Hank in the boat. Emery on board Ranger. Stewart up and in. Durbett lobbing concussion grenades three directions before boarding.

281 seconds.

Ranger up and hovering, infrared brightening the lake.

Black Hawk lowering to fifteen feet over the water, spray drenching Hank and the boat some thirty yards away. Big Ray taking Hawk even lower, stepping to door while holding stick, pushing it rightward as he falls in. Hawk away thirty, forty, fifty, sixty yards before rotor catches the water. Flips and starts sinking.

Ray climbing aboard boat, turning and full-throttle.

Five minutes.

Boat running up through the marsh, skidding onto solid ground.

Jet Ranger coming in to set down. Everybody down low.

Hank and Big Ray scrambling aboard. Lifting off and heading south, blacked out, infrared, below the fifty-foot ceiling, fast as hell.

Boom! Explosion from deep in the lake, wake swamping the shores.

Carter looking sick, Eugene queasy from the motion.

"That's Dibbie!" Durbett shouting, pointing toward the pilot. The long-hair half-turning, waving with a grin, having a good time.

Very crowded, people whooping, Big Ray dripping all over everybody, Eugene still bloody from the murder of Dukani. TJ and Babyboy on guns.

"Jolene's okay!" Eugene shouted to Mr. Carter. Grateful, satisfied.

"We're takin' you to her now," Durbett yelled.

Eugene shook Flynn's hand, a spontaneous bear hug.

Hank scanning infrared rear. Up and over the next ridge. South by southeast.

"How's—?"

"Licia's fine—just' worryin' about you, is all!" Shouting over the engine noise.

"Flynn, I felt bad about tricking you into takin' me to McEwen!"

"Didn't bother me a bit making you do your song and dance."

"Thanks for comin' after me!"

"Had to—you'd forgot to take your new .45!"

Chapter 11

By dawn, the Cumberland casualty count was confirmed at twenty-four. Though Dr. Aggeous had been sent to Ft. Donelson as soon as troops moved in, McGovern stayed long enough to learn that Dunkin, Rawley, and Salisbury had perished. Lt. Col. Poole survived because he had spent the night at his fiancée's, leaving him the only other remaining member of the *Invigil* core team.

General Ashe made an appearance just before McGovern departed. Calmly performing his duties, securing the area and conducting a preliminary investigation into what had happened, he seethed under the surface, his contempt for the younger general obvious. Ashe liked to see soldiers grow old and retire. Sometimes dying in the line of duty couldn't be helped, but at least it should be for a higher cause. Ashe didn't believe these deaths were unavoidable, wasn't convinced they'd died for something worthwhile. He didn't even know what that was.

Worse, it was the kind of military screw-up that attracted civilian attention. Too many in their nice homes scattered around the lake had seen or heard the explosions, the gunfire, the copters and bright lights, could still train binoculars across the water to see smoldering ruins. That somebody had successfully attacked the U.S. Army where no installation should be—where something secret must have been happening—it was a story rife with speculation that must be recast quickly.

Ashe's priority was to make all this look routine, like the rescue had been war games or assault training. It was a tough row to hoe; people build fabulous homes along the lake portion of Cumberland River for the scenery, the good fishing, to watch eagles and herons and geese and sunsets—not to be jarred from their tranquillity by apocalypse in their neighborhood. There would be hell to pay.

Ashe looked at where the "Willie Peter" had burned right through the bunkhouse, shaking his head, mumbling, "I *knew* there was some dirty shit going down."

Whatever secret malarkey McGovern was into, at least maybe this debacle would get it moved out of General Ashe's backyard.

*   *   *

General McGovern didn't see any Appalachian scenery during his Eagle flight to Ft. Belvoir that night. He landed without fanfare, then was immediately whisked by car to the Pentagon, arriving before dawn.

Four-star was not pleased.

Surprisingly, he wasn't as upset about the casualties and destruction of Cumberland as he was about losing Weisman.

"We underestimated them," summed up the superior officer. "You did such a good job getting so close so fast, we just didn't expect that punk kid to be so plugged in—to have militia behind him. We should have moved him somewhere decidedly less conspicuous."

"We were close to having the threat eliminated—maybe even learning the location of the last box. The alien in the Haitian had been dispatched, so Weisman was likely the only one left."

Four-star shook his head. "I thought you had an informant operative to prevent this."

"We still do—the cousin Lloyd Stewart—but he didn't find out until it was too late to contact us. He did manage to save *my* life *and* the doctor's by diverting attention from us and delaying long enough to save the building where—" he stumbled, not wanting to use the word *hiding*, "—which we were *defending*. He passed us this." McGovern slid the rumpled sheet across. "Now we have names and know not only where the Carter girl is, but that Weisman was to be taken there, too—where he is right now."

Four-star finally looked pleased about something. "So it doesn't matter which one took Watterson's box—"

"—Where they're both hiding, that's where we'll find it," McGovern concluded.

Four-star sat back and rubbed his chin. "We need to move you closer. Will you require more staff right away?"

"No, let's keep it simple. I don't need the layers; I'm closing in."

Four-star nodded, then took a deep breath. "Guess I'll have to send a public-relations team down to handle the locals around Cumberland, plus any media if it gets that far out of hand." He was lost in thought a moment, shaking his head. All this happy-facing must make him weary. Doing a job sure wasn't what it used to be. "So where are they?"

"It's an old Christian children's camp near Guntersville Lake. Bunch of podunks set it up so they'd have a weekend retreat to hunt and play soldier. Shouldn't take much to get in and out with what we need."

"Hmmm . . . Okay, let's run through your strategy. It's time to wrap this thing up."

*   *   *

Bright lights, commotion, people yelling, running—Jolene jumped from bed and ran to the window. She'd only been dozing, lost in scary dreams, overwhelmed by all that happened and unsure of what would come next.

She could see fully armed people taking positions around the open, flat area in the center of the night-lit compound.

Jackie's head in the door. "Jolene, honey? You up? We need to get downstairs. It's probably just the men back."

Little Ray rushed downstairs ready to lead the women to safety—*without* his pistol since Mom's notion of appropriate age was much higher than Dad's. They hurried over to the rear of the bunkhouse, the shelter closest to the secret cave entrance, just in time to hear the choppper coming in from behind the ridge to land.

Big Ray debarked first, to Jackie's obvious relief. Then Eugene, making Jolene feel much better. Little Ray stopped the women from approaching, reminding them that until an all-clear signal, the situation was still dangerous. After all, they might've been followed or be eluding a chase.

Watching the others climb out, Jolene was surprised and elated. They were helping an older black fellow down—her stepfather.

Finally, the little sentry let the women go, a rush of greetings, Jolene hugging Eugene first, both grinning as he gently felt her swollen abdomen. Then she looked tentatively at Leroy, depth in his eyes and creased face, the awkward embarrassment that happens when love has been compromised by harsh words and stubborn ideas. Holding each other, none of that mattered anymore.

Little Ray shook Eugene's hand, punching him lightly in the chest, razzing him about traveling in his drawers but sobering when he noticed they were splattered with blood. Then he got swept up onto his father's shoulders as they all marched to the house.

Though several of the victors acted jubilant, others seemed subdued. Durbett sobered the group by reminding them a lot of good, innocent men had died for nothing more than their loyalty and duty.

That's when Jolene noticed Eugene was covered with blood . . . and she wondered who would die next.

*   *   *

Everybody who hadn't been to Cumberland was sent away before the debriefing. Big Ray explained that the details needed to be kept secret to protect people. Jolene took her stepfather upstairs to work on patching their rift. Jackie practically had to drag Little Ray. The boy wanted to be a part of what was going on until a very stern look from his father reminded him that leaving would be for his own good—in more ways than one.

"It was General McGovern and Dr. Aggeous," Eugene began.

"No doubt," Emery concurred. "Never heard the general's first name, but the doc was Calem. The guy doing interrogations seemed important, too—"

"McGovern and Aggeous are hosting the two original aliens," Eugene continued. You could hear a pin drop.

"How sure are you?" Durbett finally asked.

"They admitted it—but I could tell anyway. They was the two runnin' things, knew all about the black boxes, knowed what they was for. They was more worried about finding the *last* box and cuttin' off our communication than about how many of the *good* aliens there might be. But McGovern didn't know he had the alien in him until he admitted he'd seen the box look different during a call and I told him that's what it meant. Doc was tryin' to keep him from finding out. Turns out doc was at the landing site, and the other guy who was there touched McGovern when he died."

Everybody was breathing hard, adrenaline pumping strong, weighing the implications of this new information.

"The dead man in your cell?" Durbett asked.

"Some foreign guy—"

"That's what the shots were? They killed him?" Emery interjected, furious at the thought.

"He had the other good alien, the one from Billy Hall."

Van and TJ looked skeptical. Durbett realized this was the first time they'd heard the rumor first-hand, saw it being discussed as fact. Accustomed to seeing conspiracies everywhere, Hank was drawn right in. He didn't know Babyboy, but the man had seen what this belief had done to Jolene, had seen it mobilize an entire underground militia network. To be pragmatic, assuming it *could* be true made the most sense.

"Was McGovern and Aggeous at Cumberland when we come in?" Durbett asked.

"They was in the cell with *me* when the power went off."

"Nobody come out of that building," TJ supplied.

"And there was only three casualties inside," Durbett thought out loud. "How was they dressed?"

"The general was in full uniform. The doctor was a big, fat guy wearin' some kinda blue doctor thing."

Durbett looked to Lloyd, both shaking their heads.

"I couldn't see nothin' else after the emergency power went out," Eugene apologized.

"None of the casualties fit those descriptions."

"I checked all the cells," Lloyd Stewart asserted.

"Couldn't have been thorough, though, not in infrared and with no time." Durbett was perplexed.

"Unless they had an escape route or hidin' place—or was scrunched back under a couple of bunks," Stewart hypothesized. "I wasn't lookin' for hiders, just a quick-see for more prisoners."

Durbett waved off the apologies. Stewart was right; he wasn't charged with search and destroy. It was a simple rescue operation. Truth be told, he'd hoped McGovern and any important minions had been neutralized when the administration and bunkhouse buildings were destroyed. He didn't expect the key players to be *with* Eugene so late in the day.

"They didn't get outta there," TJ asserted, "unless it was a tunnel or something."

Durbett shook his head. "Likely they was still inside, close. It's a classic strategy. Usually the safest place for captors to be during a rescue is close to the prisoners. It's the one place ain't likely to get blowed up." Having ventured into speculation, Durbett shifted back to the practical. "So both original invader aliens is likely still alive." Looking to Eugene for confirmation, he added, "That means they could be spreading—probably already *have* spread."

Eugene nodded. "McGovern can't right now, though. Since he didn't know he had it in him—or wasn't sure, anyway—he's probably only had it less than a year and it ain't connected enough to completely control him yet."

"But the doctor still having an original makes *him* a possible spreader," Big Ray clarified for himself.

"And whoever had McGovern's before him could've had a couple years of spreading before he passed it on," Durbett added. To Eugene, "How many?"

Eugene was lost in thought a minute, then shook his head. "Can't be sure. Mr. Watterson wasn't sure—just knew he coulda done a lot more people except he didn't wanna be spreading more than we needed. *Our* alien—the one in *me* that remembers what its parent in Mr. Watterson knew—he's still learning about humans. Remember, it takes another animal first, best if it's a cow."

Durbett explained for the others who didn't know, "When Norm passed along protector aliens to his family and Eugene here, he had to use cattle to, um, *incubate* 'em first. Then after so many months, he slaughtered 'em and, from what Eugene described, seems to have got the main part of 'em out directly from vital organs, like probably the heart or something."

"You mean cattle mutilation is a step in spreading aliens?" Van looked aghast. "Hell, they's been reports of that for decades *all over* the U.S.!"

"They couldn't have been doing it *that* far back—least I don't think," Eugene pointed out, thinking deeply, rubbing his eyes. He looked a grisly site, still clad in undershirt and boxers, spattered with blood, hair matted and dirty.

"Unless they figured something out," Big Ray guessed.

"Or was experimenting," Durbett allowed.

"There's aliens *everywhere!*" Hank announced. He'd said that more than once over the years, but this was the first time a group took the statement seriously.

Everybody fell quiet, waiting for Durbett to consider his next question. "Eugene, what if there's a call and nobody answers?"

He thought it over, then shook his head. "They'll think we're dead."

"And?"

"Just keep callin' in case they get an answer."

"They wouldn't send more?"

Eugene screwed his face up in thought. "No. It's been too long that they been getting all-clears."

"Then we got three priorities: get *any* of the black boxes for answering the call, protect Eugene so he can *use* the box, and take out McGovern and Aggeous in the meantime to keep invaders from spreading even more. If we bust up McGovern's ring, that'll force a shake-up in the military and probably give me better access to information—this one's been real tough to crack. Worst case, if we can't get a box—or lose Eugene," he added quietly, "at least having Aggeous out of there will slow down the spread. If we track 'em down but let 'em have time to pass the aliens on, it'll just slow 'em by a few years. But if we can wipe 'em out, we got a decade or more to hunt down and eradicate every one of their offspring."

"A daunting task," Van mumbled, running his hands through his silky white hair. "Wish this'd happened when I was younger."

"Let's make sure it don't come down to that," Durbett pronounced.

"Flynn?" Eugene started.

The mercenary anticipated the teen's question. "We're gonna go get 'em tonight—bring 'em here. We need either Ray or Dibbie to fly—"

"I know the area where we're goin' better," Ray offered.

Durbett nodded. "And Lloyd has legit reason to go there in case it's being watched. So it's Ray, Lloyd and me, up to McEwen tonight. We'll leave the bird at Van's, then you two go by car to get 'em, then back to Van's and fly straight here. While you're driving, I'll start making contacts and see what our little excitement tonight stirred up. Maybe I can learn something that'll help us take out McGovern and the doctor."

"Need to move soon, then," Jake pointed out.

"We'll race daylight, but shouldn't be a problem."

"Who we getting?" Ray asked.

"My sister," Emery announced.

"And Tracey," Jake added.

"Rest of you need to stay here at least a day or two to protect our friendly alien," Durbett instructed. Everybody agreed.

Eugene studied Durbett for a moment.

"Don't even think about it," the older man warned, cracking his first smile in days.

"But—"

"But nothing. You're stayin' right here where you're safe. We can't do *anything* that risks losing you. Hell, *you're* the goddamn *savior*."

Marshall Emery wanted to go, too, but Durbett dismissed the notion quickly. "Just like Eugene, *you* are a fugitive right now. You know too much; you're a target. Besides," he added assuringly, "we need you here. I got your sister covered."

"Eugene's gonna be getting a lot of questions in the morning," Big Ray pointed out. "The alien story's starting to spread."

Durbett thought it over. Then to Eugene, "Tell the truth. People you're gonna depend on deserve to know what they's fightin' for. I think it's time."

Eugene nodded, wondering how he would explain it all. Somehow, the little marshmallow skit didn't seem up to the task.

"We need fuel," Big Ray announced, getting up to rummage the fridge.

"You need to clean up, son," Durbett told Eugene, remembering he'd promised never to call him that. "Don't worry about the women. We'll have 'em here *safe* soon enough."

Eugene wasn't hungry, so he started toward the stairs for a shower and change of clothes. He hesitated on the third step, then motioned Durbett over to tell him something. They were eye to eye when Eugene leaned over and whispered, "I got her pregnant."

Durbett didn't look surprised. "Does that spread aliens?" was his first response.

Eugene shook his head. "No, Mr. Watterson done figured that much out."

"You plannin' to do right by her?" he asked, knowing full well the answer.

Eugene didn't dignify it with a verbal response. He stood there resolute, projecting all the determination he could muster. Durbett expected nothing less.

Durbett studied the teen's face, his own features softening. "You always do right, don't you, son?"

"Near as I can figure what it is."

The mercenary understood that, respected it, admired it. He even envied it, just a little.

They looked at each other before Durbett broke the tension. "*Flynn's* a good name for a kid, y'know."

Eugene rolled his eyes and trotted up the stairs.

*   *   *

Up in the hallway, Jackie looked Eugene over, shaking her head at the awful mess. He could tell she was fighting down the urge to be sick as her mind raced ahead with speculation about what horrors this mere boy, not half a dozen years older than her own son, had seen in the past few days.

"You ain't got no clothes here. Can't go out shoppin' for you until late tomorrow. You get in the shower and I'll find a robe or something that'll get you through the night."

Eugene was drifting off into the land of marshmallow people, hot water massaging his aching shoulders and cascading over his body, enveloped in steam, when he heard Jackie slip in to leave him something to wear.

His mind drifted again, looking forward to seeing Licia, holding her in his arms, someday not having to worry about aliens or government or anything. He was grateful Flynn always seemed to understand this, had been anticipating the teen's concerns about her, making sure she was fine, getting ready to get her and bring her here—the one man he could trust to take care of her.

Eugene remembered cringing on that cot, the Haitian's blood wet and sticky, the gun aimed at his face, ready to die . . . Then those lights went out and he knew—he *knew* it was Flynn Durbett, come to take him home. Having somebody he could count on . . . *loyalty*, it sure made all the difference. He understood what Norman Watterson and Flynn Durbett had once shared, how it amounted to more than just a friendship.

Eugene felt sad, remembering he'd once had that with Russell, too—had looked forward to it lasting a lifetime. *It did last a lifetime—Russell's.* Eugene had lost his best friend; so had Flynn Durbett. Both in the same night.

Eugene felt awkward, like he wanted to tell the older man thanks again for the rescue and everything else. No, that wasn't enough. Maybe it was a promise—a guarantee that as long as he lived, Eugene would find ways to pay him back for what he'd done.

And not because it was owed.

Because he wanted to.

He shut off the water and hastily dried himself, chagrined that all Jackie had come up with was a feminine-looking chartreuse pullover, terry-cloth robe, and a pair of her wading sandals.

Whatever . . .

He hurried downstairs to talk to Flynn, maybe grab something to eat, relax a minute before his older friend flew into the night to save the young messiah's lady.

He was met by the sound of a chopper fading into the star-sparkled sky, Jackie and Little Ray watching, worry in their faces.

Rats! Missed him. Oh well, he'd tell him in the morning.

There would be *plenty* of chances to have that talk.

He hoped.

Then he felt overwhelmed by an ominous sense that just maybe not all would go well, stark remembrance that this was dangerous work and anything could go wrong.

He shook it off, convinced he had to have faith.

All we can do is our best.

He eased up behind Jackie and her son, putting his arms around them both, feeling them squeeze back, hands locked, afraid but confident, together.

They watched the sky until the sound disappeared, replaced by a cacophony of insects and slithers and the gurgling stream.

And still they watched . . . just a little while longer.

*   *   *

Jolene carefully inserted the stem of wild daisy under and through one of her tightly braided rows of hair, arranging the flower just so.

Eugene watched from his seat on the side of her bed, carefully smoothing his robe, self-conscious about wearing nothing under it except a woman's blouse. It was late, stepfather Leroy already packed off to sleep, but the teen wanted to have a little time to talk in private before the morning's commotion. He looked up at her image in the mirror and was surprised to see tears. "You okay, Jolie?"

She took a deep breath and shook her head. "No, Genie."

Normally, he would have bristled at the moniker she used to reserve for teasing—and sometimes to show affection. But not tonight. "What is it?"

She turned, standing there looking helpless, a glistening line down each cheek. "I'm the reason they's dead."

"The Wattersons?"

She nodded.

"How?"

"I'm the one give 'em up. I was a spy, was the only reason I was there."

Eugene took his own deep breath, then patted the bed for her to sit beside him. "Tell me about it."

She buried her face in his chest for a minute, he holding her tightly. "I was tricked," she sobbed. "Didn't think nobody would get hurt. Was just supposed to be about that damn old box."

After several more minutes, she regained some of her composure, wiping her face, placing her hand on Eugene's cheek and managing a wan smile. "Always knew you was such a sweet boy."

He hesitated, then urged her on. "You need to tell me."

She nodded agreement, then took another big breath before telling her story. "That night me and Daddy was arguing again and he slapped me, so I packed up some clothes and left. I was hitchin' a ride to Nashville, but this Army feller picked me up and took me to a place outside of Dickson instead and tried to get it on me. He was all drunk, so I just sorta let him, but he was hurtin' me, so I hit him with a lamp and knocked him sleepy, just a little blood on his head. I run outside but this deputy was drivin' by and he grabbed me and took me back in and saw what I done. Feller was up by then, said I was breakin' into his house. Deputy said I was goin' to prison and they'd take away my baby and—and—"

She was fighting back tears, so Eugene hugged her again and waited patiently.

"When they found out my story, Army guy said needed somebody who knowed the area to do a job. Deputy said he'd let me off if I'd go with the soldier. He took me to Ft. Donelson and some men come and said I should show up at Wattersons and say I needed help and try to move in to help with their new baby. Said if I helped find the black box, they'd gimme money and a new place to live and doctorin' for my baby and everything. You understand, don't you, Eugene?"

"If you didn't think nobody would get hurt and was doin' it for your baby, course I do."

She smiled through her tears, touched his cheek again, and continued. "Wattersons was so wonderful I didn't wanna leave. I was callin' in ever' week and sayin' no sign of the box yet. Five months I was there, course *you* know. Then the Army guy got all mean and said I was lyin' and they wasn't gonna gimme the money and apartment and all if I didn't find the box. I knew where it was and that it was important because Mr. Watterson done told me, so I called baby's father one day and he picked me up on 13 and we went to Daddy's and made a fake one so I could give it to 'em and get the money and all."

"Why did Mr. Watterson tell you about the box?" He was surprised and confused.

"He done told me about the alien and saving the peoples and all and he put one in the other cow and a few months later he butchered it and put it in me."

"There's a Watterson alien in *you?*"

"*Please* don't tell nobody, Eugene. *Please!* You's the only one I told and that's 'cause I can trust you and you's the only other one's got an alien, too."

Eugene was reeling. He'd wondered, speculated, even decided the odds were good that Jolene was a carrier, too, but this was great news—especially since nobody else knew. Eugene's story had already gone public, both drawing attention to the danger he was in while increasing that very threat. But Jolene . . .

"*Nobody* else knows?"

She shook her head. "Mr. Watterson done said if people found out I could get captured or even my baby and me both killed."

"Giving you the alien didn't matter that you was havin' a baby?"

"He said alien knowed not to get in the baby, just in the rest of me. He already learned that alien can connect real fast in kids and animals but should wait until they's a little older and can understand. Said he learned that with his own baby and wished he'd a-waited until she was at least four or five."

"Did he explain about the box and calls?"

She shrugged. "All he said was I'd know when it was time, that the box was for tellin' 'em if we found out bad aliens was here. Then they'd come and had a way to kill all the aliens and that ours'd been in humans long enough so they could tell 'em how to so it wouldn't hurt the people they was in. He said don't call unless I was sure 'cause it would kill the good ones in us and the good ones that was comin' to help us, too, plus it might hurt some of our tiny animals here. They was willlin' to die, but didn't want to unless it was to save people from the bad ones."

"What'd you do with the fake box?"

"Well, I was gonna give it to 'em, but I started thinkin' if they knew about it and wanted it so bad, maybe they was the bad aliens Mr. Watterson was worryin' about. I was afraid they'd know the box was fake and hurt me. I told Mr. Watterson some men was axin' about him and all but that I didn't know who they was. He said he was gonna gimme a story to tell if they talked to me again."

She took a deep breath and caressed her abdomen. "That night, I was scared, so I switched the boxes and put the fake one in the gun-cleaning case and I hid the real one. The next morning I was walkin' down to Willow's to tell you about it when a car stopped and made me get in. They took me back to Army base and said they was gonna *abort* my baby right then and there if I didn't tell 'em where the box was, so I told 'em in the gun-cleaning case so they'd only get the fake one. Then they kept me locked up and took me up north a coupla weeks later and put me in an apartment and gimme money just like they said. Soon as they was gone, I called Daddy and he said Wattersons was all killed and you'd run off. I been hidin' ever since, except I seen my baby's daddy coupla times because he was suppose to be helping me find *you*."

Eugene squeezed her hand, trying to keep the urgency out of his voice. "The real box is still hidden?"

She nodded.

"Where?!"

*   *   *

"Eugene?"

"Mrzugglivoo."

"Eugene!" Little Ray was poking sleepy-head in the shoulder.

"Gerbalushlah."

"Eugene, here's your stuff. Mama washed it."

"What's that?" Eugene mumbled, touching the boy's chest.

Little Ray wasn't falling for that.

"Mama says lotta people here already, wanna talk to you. Everybody talkin' about Cumberland being on the news."

Eugene slipped into the still-warm boxers and undershirt, scratching here and there, clearing his throat and rubbing his eyes. The first light of dawn was filtering through the window. With nothing else to wear, the chartreuse pullover, lime-green robe, his socks, and Jackie's sandals completed the ensemble. "Let me drain the snake first. Got a toothbrush?" He trundled off to the bathroom, Ray promising to scrounge up his request.

His hair must have been still damp when he'd crashed the night before, several minutes of concerted effort failed to tame it. Getting bushy, need a cut.

Embarrassed at his goofy appearance, he wandered down to see what was going on.

"There he is!"

"It's him!"

"That's Eugene Weisman!"

They ushered him into the meeting hall and pressed him to the front where Jake was explaining how things had come to this point. Several dozen more crowded in, some Eugene recognized, hand-held video camera at the rear, the black man who'd been at the Cumberland rescue leading in sleepy-faced Jolene and her stepfather, Jackie at the door, Little Ray right up front nodding encouragement. Marshall Emery came in last, still half asleep, looking distracted, sometimes shaking his head for no apparent reason.

People were shouting out questions, Jake telling them to signal and wait to be called on. Eugene felt like the president at one of those televised press conferences Mr. Watterson always insisted the boys sit and watch. Of course, the commander-in-chief usually didn't dress in colorful women's blouse and robe, sandals, hair every-which-way.

"Where's Big Ray and Jake—and what's goin' on with these aliens and so on?"

Eugene took a deep breath, nervous, speaking quietly at first, louder as his confidence grew. "Army's covering up an invasion that happened more than twenty years ago near Camden, Tennessee. It was aliens come from a place where they was smart ones with no arms and hands and other ones not as smart that had to live inside something else because they was like threads. They used to live in these creatures that had no brains but could grow arms and legs and stuff if they was told to. They started building spaceships together and goin' places. They found out the soft ones melted here on Earth because we got nitrogen in the air and that people here didn't want no threads livin' inside 'em. But a coupla bad threads come here anyway and took over some government people—a doctor and a soldier. Another ship come here to see where the bad ones went and got permission to live in Billy Hall and Mr. Watterson."

"Norm? Norman Watterson?"

At Eugene's nod, there was a buzz of recognition, finally understanding some of their former benefactor's veiled references, why he'd been preparing more for confrontation with government factions than foreign or United Nations invaders. Several glanced at Emery, their primary source for illegal weapons, and at Jake, the man who'd been their leader for so long. Jake always used to argue that known enemies are dangerous, but the unknown is most dangerous of all.

"Their job was to keep vigil," Eugene continued, "to see if the bad threads was here, and to call for help that would come kill *all* the aliens—good ones *and* bad ones. The bad government ones caught Billy Hall and kept him prisoner, but they didn't know about Watterson 'til they found out and killed him and his whole family."

More buzz. This was explaining a lot.

"What about you? You got Watterson's alien in *you* now?"

Eugene hesitated. His secret *was* already out. Like Durbett had said, these people, if they were to stand by him, deserved the truth. "*One* of 'em—one of the young'ns."

"You're sure he's a *good* one?"

Eugene nodded.

"Got any proof," a woman shouted, "of *any* of this?"

Eugene considered for a moment. Anything he could offer would give away too much. "No. Government people's got all the evidence and they's trying to get me so nobody's left."

"What happened up the Cumberland River?"

"I was being held in a secret headquarters. They killed the guy that had the alien that used to be in Billy Hall and they was also gonna kill me."

Some looked stunned, others mad, most worked into a near-frenzy, vowing to throw in and help protect him, to fight this invasion with whatever it took. Jake waved them down, trying to restore calm. Several more called out, all asking the same thing.

"Now that you know the bad aliens *is* here, did you call for help? Are they comin' to wipe 'em all out?"

Eugene couldn't admit he didn't have the box yet, couldn't take a chance that word would leak before he could answer the next call. Not when he was this close, not when he finally knew where Jolene had hidden that last box.

"Have you called for help?" somebody else repeated.

"Yes," he lied. "They's on the way."

*   *   *

Several needed to leave for a while; more were coming in. The men running security at the main gate were keeping identification and clearance procedures tight. Jake left long enough to make several calls in town, returning with news that Durbett had sent a message saying Licia and Tracey were retrieved without incident, temporarily holed up at Van's place by Duck River. Not wanting to split up the group, they were all waiting for Durbett to receive some calls with critical information. Having failed to beat daylight, they needed to wait for dark before flying south to the compound.

The man who had shot the video of Eugene's speech wanted to go get his wife, to bring her back to the compound so she would be safe while he helped protect the teenager—at least until Big Ray had things under control again. He wanted permission to take the video out, to put it in a safe place in case something went wrong and the story needed to be told. Not sure what Durbett would say, Eugene reluctantly agreed.

Jolene avoided the group, spending her time with her stepfather and Babyboy Moller. She seemed distracted, uneasy, downright worried. At one point, Babyboy followed her upstairs for a private talk. Afterward, explaining to Jackie that he had to make a phone call from outside the compound, he asked for a vehicle he could use. She offered her car, a late-model Grand Am, giving him the keys.

In all the commotion, nobody noticed that Jolene slipped into the front seat just before he headed down the road to the gate. Since the men guarding the entrance had no reason to detain anybody, they were let out.

Eugene felt panic when he discovered she was gone, but by then it was too late . . .

*   *   *

"You're sure you don't wanna wait?" Babyboy asked again.

She shook her head. "Eugene wanted to wait for that Flynn, but I got a bad feelin'. I want us to have that box soon as can be."

"Then we'll get it and get right back fast as we can. Here, you know how to use this?" He produced a .22 from his boot, satisfied that the .357 holstered under his arm would be enough for himself.

"Looks like the one Eugene used to use—"

Just before the gravel access road joined the black-top that wound up through the hills, their route was blocked by a blue panel truck. Then Babyboy noticed several men on either side of the road, ATF flak-jackets, semi-automatics not aimed but ready.

He gunned the engine and swerved through the high grass on the shoulder, skidding round the van, only to find a caravan of vehicles easing down the road, agents on foot, one unloading men who were disappearing into the woods.

He kept going, struggling to keep control of the car, hoping to get past before they could stop him. He needed to get a warning out.

He needed to get Jolene away.

Getting past the vehicles, shots were fired, shrapnel puncturing but not blowing a tire, causing him to spin out and spray gravel. Backing onto the roadway again, he saw one agent running toward him, rifle up.

Only this one man was between them and getting away.

Babyboy spun the wheel with one hand, took aim with the other.

Jolene screamed.

The car was riddled with M-16 fire from three directions, men under cover of trees, advancing carefully toward the vehicle.

The horn was blaring, Babyboy slumped over the wheel, blood trickling down his face, from his nostrils, clotting in his hair.

Both car doors were yanked open simultaneously, two tiers of weapons trained on the interior.

Babyboy didn't move, never would again.

*   *   *

Jolene fell to the gravel, clutching her swollen abdomen, blood oozing between her fingers, rifles pointed at her face and chest.

"Secure," one man reported into his radio.

"Shit!" was the response. "No time now. Go to Delta-two."

"Delta-two!" the man shouted to the others, most falling out and heading up the road.

Time to move, no time to spare.

Jolene was sobbing and panting, trying to catch her breath, holding her belly, wincing from the pain. "My baby—my—my baby—oh, God, Eugene you was—you was right—my baby—"

She was rolled over, face down in the gravel, arms pulled behind and wrists cuffed. She was squirming in the dust, trying to turn back over, to keep from crushing her unborn child.

Bleeding heavier.

"Please help—my baby—"

Dirt and grime in her face, caking on her lips.

Panting, can't catch her breath.

"Oh, God, please, my—"

Sobbing, choking.

Two men stood over her, weapons trained.

"Please—"

Panting.

Blood.

"Plea—"

Chapter 12

Good aliens, bad aliens. Far as McGovern was concerned, *all* aliens were bad, had no business here on Earth, whatever their intentions. And they had no business living inside humans.

And if he had one inside himself, he would find a way to get rid of it. There had to be a way.

In the meantime, he had a job to do, and infected or not, it was time for McGovern to get it done.

He stepped down from the chopper, holding his hat against rotor wash, tie flapping wildly in spite of itself, then trotted to a waiting shuttle-car, his RTO and equipment in tow. During the short ride to the admin-istration building at the front of Huntsville's Redstone Arsenal, temporary controlling office for *Program Invigil*, the radio buzzed. RTO checked and handed the phone to McGovern. The general wasn't pleased with what he heard.

"Both dead, unavoidable. Her ID said Jolena Keila Carter; it's likely her. Pregnancy matches the profile."

"How long at Delta-one?"

"Eleven minutes now. They'll be ready in about five more."

"Public knowledge?"

"None we know. Remember, I agreed to run ATF for you on this just for the weapons bust—"

"*And* for the glory of breaking a militia—"

The voice cut back, its tension plain, "And I can weather these two because they made a break and fired on agents. But if CID is taking bod-ies—*and* prisoners—direct from the site, my ass is *way* out there covering up for you—"

"Then *don't screw it up* and get everybody up to the attorney general nosing around," McGovern shot back. Zing! Calming, he added, "Look, you lost the one—the Carter girl. Now get the Weisman kid out fast and quiet, then secure the place and find that box while everybody's patting themselves on the back."

"My team'll run tight—unless you got surprises they're not prepared for . . ." The voice hesitated so the general could offer more information.

Getting no response, he continued, "This is still too much artillery and too many people you got shadowing us. I just hope they don't trip on their schlongs—but *we'll* keep it tight."

"Don't interfere with your back-up," McGovern warned, "because they're all that's between any holes your people leave and the downfall of our nation."

"And this punk kid and a black bar of soap is going do us all in—" the voice restated, dripping with derision. McGovern knew he'd just as soon take a pass on all this horse shit, but he couldn't afford to let FBI or some other agency score the direct hit on a militia. Not after the beatings *his* agency had been taking the last few years. Not since Waco. He needed a score.

"You got a reading yet on how many are in there?"

"No. Now that shots have been fired, we're still securing the perimeter before we scramble, then— Ah, show him in," he said to somebody off-phone. "Your Lt. Col. Poole has arrived. I will keep him informed, then he can report at your discretion." He seemed pleased finally to have a layer between himself and McGovern.

The shuttle stopped in front of the administration building. McGovern thanked his driver, asking his RTO to come in long enough to check the communications set-up in whatever ramshackle office they'd scared up for him.

It turned out to be fairly nice, sterile and plain, facing the front where he could see the main gate from the window. RTO was satisfied with the full array, including teleconf and encode/decode systems.

McGovern immediately called the Pentagon, getting through to Four-star fairly quickly for a change. He reported how the simple operation at Guntersville had already resulted in casualties, one being the person most likely to know the whereabouts of the missing box. Four-star seemed frustrated but satisfied that plans were still proceeding apace.

"One more thing," Four-star interjected, "I understand you have the doctor in custody at Donelson."

"Yes, sir." Deferential. "Some things were said that gave me suspicion of security risk. I just wanted to keep control of the situation until I can finish collecting information—"

"Look, there's no reason to consider him a risk," Four-star admonished.

McGovern found that odd. The old man hadn't asked why he thought the doctor could be a problem. "I'm having him brought directly here so he can assist me once the boy is captured—or in case surprises occur."

"Good. You keep him close. He might be more valuable than you think."

"Yes, sir."

McGovern contacted Ft. Donelson and arranged to have the doctor transported immediately—as a prisoner. He'd never trusted the fat researcher, now suspected him of being an alien collaborator, even a contaminant.

He sat there staring out the window, uneasy, but confident all would go well. Aggeous was on the way, Poole in Birmingham at ATF headquarters monitoring the raid, the teenager and likely the missing box pinned down in Guntersville.

But just maybe there was one more loose alien *inside* McGovern.

Get the situation under control, secure *both* remaining boxes, then find a way to determine if he was infected or not. That was the plan.

This might work out yet. He just wished he could shake that feeling of uneasiness.

Maybe he had time to call his mother and try to cheer her up a little.

*   *   *

NO TRESPASSING

SOVEREIGN STATE

Violators Subject to Arrest

Will Use Deadly Force!

Though only a cyclone fence, warning signs were posted prominently. It circled a buffer zone around the inner compound fence, an area ranging two-hundred feet to three-hundred yards wide. Locals knew it was patrolled regularly, had been warned about detection devices and explosives, had heard that rumor about a fisherman seeing pieces of antler rain into Guntersville Lake after a wayward buck had tripped a mine.

Yet the U.S. Army back-ups assisting ATF crossed the cyclone. Sure, agents had questioned several area residents, had even heard a tale or two, but everybody admitted they were just nonsense stories. *Ain't nothin' goin' on over there except a bunch of good-ole-boys bitchin' about taxes and doin' target practice.*

More than a hundred soldiers deloyed, four-teamed with a radio-man, two- or three-hundred feet apart, not very far in. Most carried M-16A1s, several with 203s, a few M-60s. They didn't want to alert anybody in the compound that it was being ringed.

Two Black Hawks with registration numbers but no insignia sat at the small airport on 431 across and down the lake, attracting curious attention from flyer's-club members. The choppers were powered up and loaded, ready to deploy.

It was time to take the compound . . . and capture the boy.

*   *   *

Shots in the distance from the direction of the road! Big Ray away, Jake Coleman in command. A quick blast on the horn, people scrambling center.

One man zipping up on motor-scooter to report: "Road is blocked. Couldn't see, but musta traded shots with that black feller and the pregnant girl!" He was panting, pumped up.

Eugene rushed up, Little Ray on his heels, just in time to hear.

Jake: "Marshall! You and you! Take weapons from the bunker and seal the gate. You six, hit the cave and break 'em out for full defense, rest of you on the path until you're armed. What are the drillls?"

More people running up and announcing their contingency assignments, then heading toward the cave to be passed additional weaponry.

"Anti-aircraft," from several.

"Monitoring!" one announced, heading to the command bunker below the block house after a nod from Jake.

"Perimeter!"

"*Inside* the big fence," Jake instructed. "Button it up. Nothing except as I mark—unless you *have* to. Eugene! Van! Women and children into the refuge, round 'em up and protect 'em—"

"*I'm* not gonna run and hide," the tall woman argued.

"You're *not*. You're defending the other cave entrance. With you and you," he added designating two more men. "You two, bunker defense. Rest of you—"

"We know our place," one shouted, a group following him to the cave with its frenzy of activity.

Van positioned himself to direct people underground, Eugene running around the compound to round up others, Little Ray shouting into the main house and bunkhouse, then checking the meeting hall in case somebody hadn't heard. Six, eight, nine children; eight women, several armed; Leroy Carter looking for Jolene, confused and scared; Ole-man Jenkins, his teenage daughter helping him walk.

Jake and the monitoring and communications men positioned themselves in front of the massive electronics console down in the bunker, linked by wired phone/mouthpiece to outposts around the perimeter and inside the cave. No radio communications, all frequencies could be subject to eavesdropping.

"Wow!" Monitor exclaimed. "Movement inside the fence, all the way around. Must be hundreds. None on cam yet."

"Movement inside the fence, all sides," Communicator repeated into the phone. All three watched a series of screens, dozens of blips registering from several kinds of scanners.

Monitor strained to listen through headphones. "No aircraft," he reported, confirmed by a peakless jiggly line on all four audio-scopes. "Grounders are holding."

Jake and Communicator both donned their headphones. Reports were coming in from the outposts, everybody armed and ready, people in position awaiting status updates or orders.

"They're coming down the road," Emery reported, a growl in his voice.

Jake instantly regretted letting Emery be a front man. This was too soon after his captivity. Already strung tight, the man was too risky, too volatile. He should have been put inside the cave in some sort of defensive role. Not that he would have accepted that.

The gate camera picked up movement coming around the bend in the road. Communicator increased the volume.

It was a column of six men, ATF flak-jackets, flanked by an armored blue panel truck, more men behind the truck. They were all armed, most with M-16A1s—but slung at their sides, hands out to appear less threatening.

They passed the sign on the road warning they were in sovereign territory and would be treated as trespassers. Still they walked slowly forward.

"Post three, four, five—one man from each to back up the main gate, move now," Jake all but whispered into his mouthpiece. "It's time."

*   *   *

Everybody in the cave was listening to a speaker. They had moved to the rear chamber where most subsistence supplies were stored and communications equipment was set up. Jackie sat on a low cot, picking at her hair, nearly in tears, worried and scared. Eugene sat beside her, his Browning on his lap, a gentle hand on her arm.

"Let him be," he whispered. She was trying to get Little Ray to sit, to come away from his vantage near the chamber entrance, to put the rifle away. "He's protecting you."

"But—"

"But you don't ask a man to sit and behave when his family's in danger. Let him be."

Tears spilled down her cheeks, but she remained quiet, watching, not sure if she felt angry or proud. Scared, that she was sure of . . .

*   *   *

"Come no closer!" Emery warned the approaching column. "You are on sovereign land. Leave immediately or you will be arrested!"

The approaching group stopped but gave no indication they would leave. "Bureau of Alcohol, Tobacco, and Firearms! We have warrants!" the lead man called out, holding up some papers.

"Your warrants don't count here!"

"We have a federal search warrant and arrest warrants for four people."

"Who?"

"And who are you, sir?"

"I'm a free citizen—" Emery growled. He was getting madder, but still curious. "I've delayed arresting you long enough to let you tell me who your warrants are for. Answer or leave!"

*   *   *

Jake heard a report from one of the outposts: "We can see more moving in on both flanks. If something starts, they's at least twenty can open fire on the gate."

"Concussions and scatters ready," another voice reassured. They may take out the men at the gate, but ATF wasn't going to come through—not alive.

Jake noted the position of the tree signs, estimating that the intruders' truck sat directly over road-buried explosives, the agents serving warrants approximately thirty feet in front of the foremost charge. Location ideal.

"They're for Raymond Blounten, Sr.; Jacob Coleman; Marshall Emery; and Eugene Weisman. Are you Emery?"

"Don't answer," Jake instructed, adjusting his mouthpiece.

Gate man on the phone gestured a throat slash to Emery.

"Time is up. You need to leave now. You're trespassing."

"I'm afraid I can't do that, sir."

*   *   *

"Damn," the site commander in the ATF truck huffed.

"I said *leave!*" the militia man ordered, fire in his eyes.

"Bring the birds to the edge, but not a fly-over," Commander ordered, an RTO barking into his radio in the back. "Get me thermals to see how many and where they are."

The front agents stood their ground. The men at the gate raised their rifles ominously.

"Part—let 'em see the truck," Commander told the front agents' earpieces. "Back off a few feet. Don't provoke. Birds are coming. Next truck, slow up behind."

The front group carefully eased back a few feet and parted to give the armored truck a clear route, though the vehicle didn't offer to move. Soldiers flanking both sides in the woods came closer, sighting individual targets.

The blind bravado of these militia yokels proved both amusing and nerve-wracking.

*   *   *

"Sound of choppers—lakeside," Monitor announced.

"Shit!" from Jake. "Grails! Take 'em down if they cross perimeter airspace—but *not* before. Everybody else, that's when it'll hit. Gate, the instant the birds are fired on, drop or scatter. It may touch 'em off, but we'll blow the road first. Don't get hit before we take 'em out."

*   *   *

Gateman on the phone rushed over and warned Marshall and the others the road would be blown seconds after the choppers were fired on—to clear out. Marshall didn't like it. He wanted a piece of the SOB staring him down. But he knew the strategy. He'd play it straight.

Make your plan, prepare contingencies, execute.

Son of a bitch was so damned smug.

Ready your weapons; plan your escape.

The sound of choppers, gatemen looking up, agents straight ahead. Knew they were coming.

Ready to drop into culvert either side of the road the instant of rocket fire, wait and secure the road, take out any survivors.

Bastards were warned. They had their chance.

Choppers closer.

Two men on the right flank moving up closer—!

Tripwire—*Boom!*

Soldiers firing, gatemen caught cold, one squeezing as he fell, taking out two agents up front.

Man with the warrants down squirming in the gravel.

Soviet Grail SA-7 Rocket-Propelled Grenade Launchers (RPGLs) firing, shells piercing the sky, first chopper exploding, second banking away.

Boom! Boom! Boom! Boom! Road blowing in sequence, one truck obliterated, second aflame.

Second chopper's rotor hit, spinning and smoking, banking toward the lake, losing altitude, taking out two boathouses on impact.

Boom!

*   *   *

"Coming through the woods—both sides!" Monitor shouted.

Jake's fingers on the keyboard, blowing trees twenty-six and twenty-eight, not the closest to the road, but just in front of the advancers. Wait four seconds, blow twenty-five and twenty-nine. Grounders in retreat.

Smoke and dust settling on road, camera still working, tilted off-side, Monitor trying to toggle it around, partial view mostly downward.

All gatemen down and still.

Marshall Emery's body riddled and bleeding. One to the temple.

Jake wanted to let the rest of the out-perimeter grounders retreat, but Emery's bloody body filled the screen in front of his face. Tripwire cost dearly, cost him his friend.

Fingers on keys, blowing eighteen, fifteen, forty, forty-four, eight, fifty-two. Running soldiers trip-wire blowing number fifty-three.

"Scattershot through the trees," Jake ordered. He was breathing hard, a bead of sweat snaking around his eyebrow. "Can't you get that camera up?" He didn't need to look at Emery's body.

"They're all dead," announced Monitor, jiggling the camera around enough to see all four at the gate, some of the front agents lying in the road. "They're *all* dead."

*   *   *

Down in the cave, women and children huddled close, a gasp, some sobbing. Tears on Jackie's face, but no sound from her.

Eugene and Little Ray, armed and ready.

Waiting.

*   *   *

"They're withdrawing to the main road," Monitor announced.

"Bunker detail to clean up, secure gate. Outposts—any casualties?"

"All clear."

"None."

"Clear." Other voices echoing.

"Back six, one man each to cover the front—back up clean-up."

Voices, commotion.

Camera shots on the skewed camera, militia moving in to secure the blown gate.

"Move that damn camera so I can see down the road," Jake growled. He took a deep breath and sat back. Shit. This was only a break.

But for how long?

*   *   *

Eugene comforting Jackie, calming the children, assuring the others.

Little Ray crouched behind the rock, weapon trained, muscles taut, unmoving.

Nobody was gonna get past him and kill *his* mom.

*   *   *

"We interrupt programming for this special report from Chattanooga WCHT TV-60 News-team."

Paint graphic: *Seige at Guntersville*, ADO over-the-shoulder.

Super lower-third: *Norse Worthy, News 60.*

"We have a breaking story at this hour. A war-like battle has broken out at a militia compound just outside Guntersville, Alabama. Agents from the Bureau of Alcohol, Tobacco, and Firearms serving arrest warrants were fired upon, resulting in what appears to be heavy casualties."

Full screen: map of Northeast Alabama, Huntsville, Birmingham, Guntersville marked with a small swastika. ADO over-the-shoulder.

"Eye-witnesses report considerable gunfire, explosions, and at least two helicopters shot down. The WCHT TV-60 Traffic Copter will be on the scene in a moment."

Glancing off-screen, shuffling notes on desk.

"The compound is reported to be headquarters of the Sand Mountain Patriots, an underground militia group of self-styled citizen vigilantes. Many area residents report having been recruited by members of this extremist hate group, headed by Scottsboro-resident Ray 'Big Ray' Blounten to overthrow the government and establish a New World Order under their own leadership. A spokesman for ATF has declined comment at this time, promising there will be a press conference possibly later today."

Looking off-screen again, paper handed into view.

"One eye-witness who wishes to remain anonymous claims direct knowledge that these militia extremists also were involved in yesterday's incident at the closed-down Cumberland Sanitarium just north of Erin, Tennessee. Originally thought to be some kind of military training exercise, sources say it was a secret Army facility where militia members were being held prisoner until yesterday's rescue."

Crude full-screen, middle-Tennessee map, Nashville, Waverly, Cumberland Sanitarium marked with star.

"Reports are coming in of a helicopter crashing nearby—"

Cut to traffic-copter footage scanning the shoreline.

"—And possibly a separate explosion."

Tilting head, listening.

"I understand Hiram Lukesy has a report."

Cut to wavering aerial footage, super lower-third: *Hiram Lukesy, TV-60 Traffic Copter.*

Voice-over, background engine noise: "This is Hiram Lukesy near Guntersville Lake. Air-control is preventing us from getting any closer, some kind of emergency declared. But the area where you see smoke is reported to be the location of the compound—"

Cameraman trying to split difference between zooming enough to show detail and keeping the shot steady.

"If we can get a shot—yes, there it is. As you can see, what appears to

be a helicopter has crashed and destroyed two boathouses along the southeast shore of Guntersville Lake. The area has been sealed off by either
National Guard or Army units. Commercial boat traffic is being held back
near the Guntersville Dam locks, local boats are being kept out of the area.
There seems to be a lot of activity—"

Camera jiggling around, zooming in and out, focusing on two all-black
boats with frogmen in a small cove off the main channel of the Tennessee
River.

Norse Worthy, back on-cam: "Hiram! Can you get another shot of the
compound?" Worthy head-shot ADO to small box in upper left corner.

Camera focusing on area of woods stretching up low ridge, three trails
of smoke wisping into the sky.

("Network is picking us up for national feed.")

Worthy: "We're now going to take you to New York with SBC Anchor
Tom Fleury . . ."

Fleury repeating what had been covered locally, slicker graphics, corrected information. Potentially slanderous statements now couched with
phrases like "alleged," "thought by some," "known in local circles as," and
"likened to"—particularly in reference to the militia being a "hate group"
or "extremists." Labels like "neo-Nazis," "skinheads," and "Aryans"
would be avoided until affiliation clarified—allegedly, anyway.

"We have just confirmed that warrants were issued for Raymond
Blounten, thought to be the leader of the Sand Mountain Patriots; Marshall
Emery, a weapons dealer and alleged head of a militia group in Tennessee;
Jacob Coleman, known to groups throughout the country as a staunch
anti-government spokesman; and Eugene Weisman, a fifteen-year-old fugitive wanted on weapons charges who may be linked to the arson murder
of a family in Waverly, Tennessee."

("Feeding in five, four, three . . .")

"We now join Norse Worthy with our affiliate at WCHT TV-60 in
Chattanooga. Norse, I understand the TV-60 traffic copter is on the
scene?"

Split screen, new "siege" framed graphic including torso of man in
camouflage fatigues wielding a generic machine gun.

"That's right, Tom. Air-control is preventing us from getting closer—"

Full-screen copter footage, smoke wisping from the woods. Repeating
about the boathouse destruction, boats working crash-site in the lake, still-

store freezes of earlier footage with clearer shots. Camera focusing on caravans of military and ATF vehicles moving in and out of the area around the compound.

("Ask Hiram what he's been observing.")

Lukesy: "—Looks like quite a few bodies have been removed. They're bringing in flatbed trucks to pick up debris, covering it with tarps for transport out. Some vehicles are coming in from the direction of Birmingham on 79, but most appear to be from Redstone Arsenal just outside of Huntsville. Those leaving the compound area are all coming around the lake to take 431 toward the city."

Fleury: "And what about the activity in the lake?"

Background noise, limiter turned up, bass boosted. "So far at least one body appears to have been recovered from the lake crash—"

Stills of body being lifted into boat and covered.

Fleury: "If you've just joined us . . ."

Repeating and beefing up, more emphasis on obvious death toll, driver's-license shot of Big Ray added.

Cutting in shots from remote crew out of Huntsville, microwave feed, Army trucks rounding curve at the "Y" and heading up the mountain toward Huntsville. Next shot, truck crossing the Guntersville Bridge, swinging around to focus on smoke curling into the sky from down-lake.

Repeating information, better selection of stills.

Fleury: "We are receiving reports from affiliates all across the country that local militias are gearing up for confrontation. There are no reports of violence yet, but organizations are calling in their members and arming themselves. We have Lori Barbadol from our Grand Rapids, Michigan, affiliate at the scene where members of the Kalamazoo Regiment are mobilizing. Lori?"

"Thanks, Tom."

Outdoor shot, man in aviator shades and military fatigues standing along gravel road, white farmhouse in the background, pickups and 4x4s, a few dozen men standing around looking tough.

"I'm here with Phil Jarvi—" referring to notepad, "commander of the Kalamazoo Regiment, a local militia here on Stubbs Road west of the city. Mr. Jarvi, what's going on here today?"

Deliberate, chopped words, camera-awkward, "We're mobilizin'. Ready for the showdown. The attack on free people in Alabama is just one more example. Ruby Ridge; Waco, Texas; Jordan, Montana; Decker, right here in Michigan. We're startin' at the local level and gonna take our country back before the UN so-called Peacekeepers run us over—"

"Do you have anything specific planned?"

"We're just gettin' ready, watchin' to see what happens, ready to offer assistance. We're *tired* of payin' taxes and givin' up our constitutional rights, and we ain't gonna take it no more—"

"So would you call yourselves *tax* protestors?"

"This country was taken over by the Jews, just so they can pillage our great land and take our money. They's the ones started our downfall by bringin' in all them nigras to—"

Cut back to Tom Fleury. "Excuse me, Lori. Have you seen any evidence that violence is planned?"

Close-up of Barbadol. "One man who drove up just moments ago *was* seen taking a shotgun from the trunk of his car."

"Thank you. That was Lori—"

"—Will break into regular programming—"

"—Tonight a special report: *Hate Groups in America*—"

"—Live on the scene—"

"—Sizable number of casualties—"

"—Unconfirmed reports—"

"—Siege at Guntersville—"

*   *   *

Flynn Durbett left a dust-cloud trail behind his truck, rushing down the back roads along Duck River to Van's place. Jerking on the emergency brake, he jumped out, simultaneously signaling the all-clear. Big Ray and Lloyd Stewart confirmed it was him and lowered their weapons, relaxing, if only a little.

Durbett rushed inside, turning on the television. Tracey and Licia gathered round, the other men just behind.

"They hit the compound," he explained, remote-flipping through channels looking for news coverage. Licia and Tracey gasped.

"Damn!" from Big Ray.

"—Siege started earlier today when agents from the Bureau of Alcohol, Tobacco, & Firearms tried to serve warrants—"

They showed new footage, the same information. The fires had gone out, so earlier shots with visible smoke were used to show the location of the encampment.

"—Heavy casualties—"

Licia put her head down, crying quietly. Tracey put an arm around her, fighting back her own tears.

Durbett continued scanning channels, gleaning information, looking for clues, studying the shots.

There was Eugene! Speaking! "—Job was to keep vigil, to see if the bad threads was here, and to call for help that would come kill *all* the aliens—good ones *and* bad—" The lower-third super identified him as *UFO Cult Leader.* He looked like some kind of guru, robe and sandals, purple and green, hair swept up into quasi-horns. "—Got all the evidence and they's tryin' to get me so nobody's left—"

"He's still okay," Licia choked.

"There's Jake!" Tracey blurted.

"And Marshall!" Big Ray added. The camera moved several times, revealing some of the people up front.

"—Video taken just hours before the siege—"

Maybe they *weren't* all right.

The announcer was naming all four listed in the warrants, license photos, school-yearbook shot for Eugene. "—Still thought to be inside the compound. The fourth, Marshall Emery, believed to be killed when the shooting broke out—"

Big Ray thundered his rage, kicking a hole in the wall. He figured his wife and son were safe inside the cave, but still . . .

Licia couldn't look at the screen, just staring at her lap, still crying quietly.

"—Unusual in that this group believes aliens have invaded our country and infiltrated government, and that Weisman is the messiah who will bring more aliens from space to save us—"

Shots of Eugene again, robed and sandaled. "Yes," he was nodding. "They's on the way." He looked like some cult guru in that get-up.

"—Attorney general is stepping in to—"

Licia looked up at Durbett. The mercenary was furious, but still calm, quiet. She stood up, searching his eyes, standing there alone and trembling. His face softened, his throat caught. He reached out, wrapping his arms around her and letting her cry.

"You can rescue 'em, can't you?"

He didn't answer, couldn't be sure of speaking truth. So he just held her tight, running through scenarios in his mind.

Big Ray kept flipping the channels, scanning the coverage, Stewart standing numbly off to the side.

"What'd you learn?"

Durbett answered, "McGovern has set up new headquarters somewhere down there, probably at Redstone. When I check again in an hour, I should know for sure exactly where he is."

"What about a rescue?"

He shook his head, avoiding Licia's pleading eyes. "Not yet, not now—not half-cocked. They's safe for a while. It's too political now, too much like Waco, too many people involved. They ain't gonna make a move until they sort it out."

From Big Ray, "What about—?"

"We got a higher priority," Durbett interrupted, "Takin' out McGovern and the doctor. We have to assume feds'll probably get our guys out, but Eugene and Jackie and the boy ain't done nothin'. Jake maybe weapons charges." He hoped, anyway. "But if McGovern is still calling shots—or if he's been replaced and the doctor is advising, then we have to worry about Eugene being turned over to 'em. Can't be many people—if any—know truth about the alien part. Another hour I can confirm where they's at. We need to plan some wet-work."

Assassination.

"They's just the three of us," Stewart pointed out.

"And we got women to protect," Big Ray added.

Beep! Sensor alarm. A car was coming down the gravel road.

Women down in the cellar, men armed and in position.

It was a late-model coupe, barreling along at a high rate of speed, up the drive, stopping short of the porch.

Weapons trained, fingers tensed.

A woman stepped out.

"Lena! Get in here!"

Coming in the door, "Is that how you greet your one true love?" she jabbed, wrapping her arms around Durbett. He hugged her back, nodding to Stewart that Licia and Tracey could come back up. "What're you doin' here? You're *supposed* to be in Texas," he admonished.

She pulled back just enough to flash a teasing smile. "Figured ya might be needin' some help, so I stayed close. Been watchin' the news. Took me all afternoon to figure out where you was."

"It's not a good situation, Lena."

The women came into the room now, not recognizing Lena but obviously an ally by the way Durbett held on to her—and she to him.

"No, and I figured you guys was gonna have to get out and get dirty—or *wet*."

"You're not goin' with us," he cautioned.

She mock-pouted, but apparently not surprised. "Maybe not, but looks like you could use some help protecting the women-folk while you boys go out and play."

He snorted.

She wagged her eyebrows. "So are ya gonna send me away or can I stay a while?"

He snorted again. "Like I have a choice—"

*   *   *

"He was right," Lt. Col. Poole reported. "Probably shouldn't have used military to surround 'em—just incites 'em."

"Look," McGovern barked into the phone. "I don't need second-guessing now. You saw the kind of firepower they had. Without the perimeter ring, they would've walked right out of there. Then we'd have lost Weisman and probably the box, too. It's only a matter of time; they can't resist forever. Now I'm gonna be up to my ass in alligators and politics. Keep up with ATF and FBI as they run down every lead—there's people out there who know the set-up, how much and where their artillery is, who-all we're dealing with. So it wasn't pretty—at least it's contained."

A buzz. McGovern was informed of Dr. Aggeous landing. He ordered for his prisoner to be taken to the sealed *IVG* holding cell. Next, he called the Pentagon.

"You jacked us off," Four-star started. "I got the president climbing up my ass now. Attorney General's going to be here in fifteen minutes for a briefing. The alien angle was supposed to be suppressed, but now I have to dance."

"Are there any changes in the command structure that—?"

"*Hell* yes. It's gonna be a goddamn committee now. But you know, that's not *our* problem. That's why *IVG* is buried in CID while ATF and FBI have been out front—just in case something like this happened. So here's how I'm playing it. Watterson stole some classified foreign technology we were studying—a black box, possible new kind of communication. The Weisman kid stole it from him for rogue members of the militia, then started the fire. Now he's holed up with the box in the compound. We don't care who or what or how they want to take control of the situation as long as the kid comes our way and we get to sweep for the box."

"That'll fly at the Justice Department?"

"I can make it work that way—especially since the president's behind us. But he *does* have to worry how the public side of it plays, the politics. I think the militia already solved that problem for him, showing off that they got the illegal firepower to make a third-world country jealous. They're not just kooks, but *dangerous* kooks. Waco smeared ATF because when the smoke cleared, it turned out to be just a bunch of freaks that weren't much of a threat to themselves, let alone anybody else."

"So I should pull back our people a little, let ATF get all the face time," McGovern confirmed, "but not enough to let there be any holes. Just be ready to move in, get the kid out, and find that box before the media and public get too good a look-see at what's going on."

"That's it. Is your guy still in Birmingham?"

"Yes."

"Keep him all over it. I don't want those yahoos forgetting we have priority at the scene. Meantime, get everybody briefed. Nothing's going to happen for at least thirty-six, maybe forty-eight or more. It's going to take me that long to write a new song and learn to sing it."

After Four-star rang-off, McGovern stared at the phone for a full minute. Good, there had been no mention of a role for Aggeous. Get the kid; get the box. McGovern could get his arms around that.

It was time to go see the fat doctor.

But first . . .

"Hello, mother?"

"Why Chester! Is everything all right?"

"Yeah."

"I've been watching the news all day."

"Yeah. It's something, ain't it?"

They talked a full fifteen minutes, leaving more unspoken than said. She ended by reminding him how his father had always tried to teach him we all have responsibilities greater than to ourselves.

"Do what you know is right, whatever the consequences to yourself."

Moms . . . oftentimes so naïve to the world.

McGovern carried a briefcase as he shuttled to the far end of Redstone, working his way underground along the ridge in the hills. The fat doctor lay sprawled on the cot where Billy Hall had spent the last years of his life. Separated by thick glass, they regarded each other without speaking. Finally, McGovern made sure the two-way audio was activated, then pulled his chair over and sat in front of the glass.

"Good aliens . . . and bad aliens," the general said. He removed his hat, setting it on the table, loosened his tie. It was hot in there, stale air.

Aggeous scratched his paunch, cleared his throat. "That's how *I* see it."

McGovern looked weary, running fingers through his hair. "What's the difference?"

No hesitation, "I figure trying to live free, colonize new worlds and a new life—that's good. Trying to kill somebody off just to control 'em, to hold 'em down—that ain't."

"It's that simple, huh?"

Aggeous shrugged.

"So the alien in you is just after freedom, and the one in the Weisman kid is here to kill him for no good reason."

"You got it." He wheezed, hacking up a lugie.

"So who am I talking to? Alien or Calem Aggeous?"

The doctor snorted and shook his head. "I'm the same person I was born." He spread his arms with a *what-you-see-is-what-I-am*. "I'm just more now." His expression hardened some, looking intently at the general. "I'm a *lot* more now . . . on my way to becoming more than you can imagine." Then he smiled slightly, shrugging again. "Everybody wins!"

"And what about me?"

"You win, too. You lucked out, spun the big wheel and came up with the only other number one."

"So you admit there's an alien inside me."

"If *you're* ready to admit it."

"Why doesn't he reveal himself to me?"

"Ah, but he has. Seems like it's only been when necessary, though. Like helping you picture how them MPs was killed."

McGovern had no argument. Seeing and knowing—more accurately, remembering. Still, though . . .

"Far as him not *talkin'* to you," Aggeous was continuing, "I don't know. I guess probably two reasons. Maybe he ain't connected enough yet. We figure the younger the person, the faster it can connect—that's why you're so young for a general, for a commander—about as young as can get away with in the U.S. Army without attracting *too* much attention. You were being *groomed* for this. I'm starting to think maybe there's another reason he ain't talking—like maybe he doesn't *trust* you yet." He wheezed again, adding under his breath, "I know *I* sure don't."

"So how is it right just to kill these other aliens—and the people they're in—like the one in the Weisman kid? Justifiable self-preservation?"

"Actually," the doctor said evenly. "*You're* the one who's been doing that. Higgins was satisfied to let old Billy Hall live out his life, long as we kept him contained. Our experiments with him spreading were all animals. *You* killed Hall, got the alien to transfer to that Haitian, then killed *him*. Higgins was dying anyway when *his* alien jumped to you."

"What about Wattersons?"

Aggeous snorted derisively. "That come from higher up—took advantage of Higgins being down sick. Aliens can't be no better than the humans they're in."

"Why did you and Higgins kill those MPs? Did the aliens take control of you that fast?"

"Naw, not that fast. I was just doing what he told me. His orders were to eliminate *all* witnesses if it really turned out to be an alien landing."

"Something I've been wondering—if you haven't been able to identify who has an alien without amputating and preserving a specimen free of nitrogen contamination—"

How do I know about nitrogen?

He hesitated, then continued, "How did you know from those samples that the Wattersons were contaminated?"

"If you mean how'd I know they had aliens in 'em, I didn't."

"Then—" McGovern was at a loss.

"Then *nothing*. Finding the black box was confirmation enough—why else would he have it? Had to stick with that story because it was back before you knew as much as you do now—"

"Back when you were holding out on me, waiting until I was *ready* to understand?"

"Yeah, sure, something like that."

"And you held out—why?"

"Was told to by Four-star. Couldn't risk you running off doing something stupid before it had a chance to start connecting inside you." Aggeous smiled mischievously. "That and had to be able to tell if the transfer worked—unless you wanted to donate a finger to the cause. Course your new guy claims to have some way to confirm without amputating." He looked skeptical.

"When were you sure?—about mine, I mean."

"When you figured out the MPs."

McGovern got up and wandered over to the electronics console, his back to the doctor, thinking. Without turning, he asked, "You've been spreading them. That was your other project."

No response, good as confirmation.

"Four-star?"

Affirmative silence.

"How many?"

"Several hundred."

He walked to the glass. "People given the choice—asked did they want these aliens inside them?"

"Well, no, but ain't had any complaints once they see the advantages."

"Who?"

"Can't say—don't even know for sure. Wasn't in charge of deciding. Pretty much military, though, from what I can tell, and executive branch. Took three tries to get the president, I hear."

"The man with all the power . . ."

"Ha! For now. It's you and me who got the originals. In a couple more years ours'll be mature enough—you ain't even *tasted* power until then. We're gonna be *running* the joint."

"And what kinda power is this?"

"Don't even know—just know it's coming. Takes about thirty Earth years for the next phase to kick in, and ours is in their upper twenties by now. We're decades ahead of all the others—"

"Even the one in Weisman—"

"His is just a second generation, too. A couple more years—long as we can keep him from answering the call until then, won't have to know where his is—or the box for that matter. We can wipe him out before he's mature enough to reproduce. Just a couple more years, is all."

"So that's it, then—nothing else you can tell me."

"The rest is in your head." Wheeze. "Just give him some time—then let him talk."

"What if he says he doesn't want to *share* the power with you? What if he wants *me* to be the only one?"

Aggeous stood up, walking to the glass directly in front of the general.

"What're you saying?"

"I'm asking—what if he wants me to eliminate you so *I'm* the only one to have all that power?"

"*He* wouldn't. That would be *you* doing that."

"How am I to know? I've *already* done things Chester McGovern wouldn't do—so he must have *some* control over me. I may have the other mature alien, but he's not been in my body as long as yours. What if mine's keeping quiet until he knows he has full control. What if you're already being controlled—no say left in what you do? Tell me, Doctor, what if?"

Aggeous stammered, not sure what to say.

"Good-*bye*, Doctor. I can't see as how I need you anymore."

With that, he picked up his briefcsase and strolled from the room, the door locking behind him. The doctor stood there staring vacantly.

After a moment, the slot in the wall slid open, the muzzle of the general's M1911A-1 jutting through.

The doctor had trouble catching his breath, backing away, trying to speak. He wheezed, then started to choke.

"But—!"

Chapter 13

"You're really stretching my capabilities, Flynn. I'm running a goddamn inter-agency covert operation to feed you info. What you've been asking is outside my normal channels."

"So we owe each other. You're just getting a notch up is all," Durbett told the pay phone wryly.

"A notch, *hell!* This noise you been making about retiring—"

"It's not just noise—"

"Well, it's going to have to be. For what you're asking, I'm going to need another two years—"

"Look, if I take out my target and you're the one set me on him, I'll *go* another year, but you gotta—"

"Flynn, Flynn—" placatingly, "we can work that out later. I'm getting close. Problem is, the Guntersville crisis has moved some of my people. I just managed to get a man into the federal building in Birmingham, access to a Lt. Col. Poole, Army CID, who's reporting directly to McGovern. But he's keeping his superior close to the vest, so everybody there is dealing directly with Poole."

"Communications?"

"Secured—and I don't have a way to crack that—least not for the next day or two. So my guy's watching for clues, hints, casual conversation, any changes—*anything* that'll indicate *where* McGovern is working from."

"Anybody else who might know?"

"They're all too high up. With this turning into a media circus, I can't afford to get caught with my sniffer too close to anybody's butt."

"I can't afford it, neither," Durbett returned.

"Look, I'm on it."

"How often should I check in? Still every two hours?"

"Spread 'em out more—not more than twice a day for now. Just listen to the radio. If he makes a joke about getting a call from anybody, you'll know to get back to me."

Durbett hesitated a moment. "You be careful."

"You're the one who's risking his life and all he's worked for."

Durbett couldn't think of anything else to ask, so before signing off, he added, "I *do* owe you big, and I mean it when I say I'll look at giving you another year—"

"And *I* mean it when I say we're talking at least two."

*   *   *

"Siege at Guntersville: Day Two—an SBC News Special Report, with your host, David . . . and former FBI Director . . . Leader of Panhandle Militia . . . founder of the Alien Preservation Society . . . here in the studio . . . commentator and cult expert . . ."

". . . Could've been prevented if law enforcement wasn't so restricted from gathering advance information with wiretaps and . . ."

". . . Expected large numbers of militia members and government protesters to flock to Guntersville, but instead the town has been flooded with UFO watchers, alien conspiracists, Trekkies and X-Filers and other fanatics . . . holding a rally this afternoon at Guntersville State Park . . ."

". . . Press conference this morning stressed it has nothing to do with what he called this new *crackpot* alien angle, that this is simply a cult amassing a cache of illegal weapons and possibly involved in some murders and other crimes still under investigation . . ."

". . . News has learned that self-styled alien spokesman fifteen-year-old Eugene Weisman of Waverly, Tennessee, is being investigated for murder in the arson deaths of the Wattersons, a family who lived near the home he shared with his aunt, Willow Weisman. Norman Watterson, a retired U.S. Army special operative, has been linked several ways with underground militias and is known to have provided weapons training for some of the local groups. It is suspected that Weisman was stealing guns to defend himself from what he believed to be alien assassins and burned the home to cover his crime. After that, his aunt was found dead from a blow to the head. Interviews with classmates where Weisman was a freshman at Humphreys County High School last year . . ."

". . . He was always takin' his gun and goin' out in the woods with some boy went to the middle school—but they wasn't huntin', they was practicing defendin' theyselves. He once told me he had to be ready in case something happened someday, but he wouldn't say what . . ."

". . . We got more than two-hundred members in three states prepared to defend theyselves from foreign invaders or government . . ."

"Yes, aliens, too. Ain't never seen none m'self—" A chuckle. "But dammit if this ain't America and they's got the right to believe anything they want—just like freedom of religion guaranteed in our Constitution . . ."

"That's right, David, studies have shown that more than half of adults in this country believe in some sort of alien theory . . ."

"But it *is* like religion. There doesn't have to be proof of existence for people to embrace the belief that there are beings out there of greater . . ."

"Sure it's on the increase, especially what with all this science fiction and TV shows and all. As far as explaining why so many people believe it, I think it *is* like religion, and my philosophy professor back in college summed it up nicely. We'd spent a month debating whether or not the existence of a god could be proved and had to conclude it neither could nor couldn't. Then a young woman in the back stood up and said there simply *must* be a god or why would so many people believe it. He just smiled and said 'Because so many *other* people do.'" A chuckle from the panel.

". . . Unable to negotiate with anybody inside so far. Obviously, the highest priority is to see if the women and children being held hostage can be released without harm . . ."

". . . Local therapist and expert on sexual molestation says drawings made by one of the little girls who had been inside the compound on several occasions indicate that she has, indeed, been the victim . . ."

". . . Like at Jonestown, one of the biggest dangers of these fanatic cults is mass suicide or a murder-suicide pact. There are estimated to be as many as fifty innocent children . . ."

"Confirmed from one man who had attended . . . now in custody on weapons charges . . . training in the manufacture of ricin, one of the deadliest . . . concerned about possible acts of mass terrorism, especially from other members not inside the compound . . . infecting the area's water supply, or . . ."

"To recap, the siege at Guntersville is now in its second day . . ."

*   *   *

"It's a security issue," Jake pronounced.

"It's a *safety* issue," Jackie argued.

"But I thought it was a *rights* issue," Eugene pointed out.

The children were being kept in the cave for safety. Some of the women had opted to stay underground, too, but Jackie and Eugene were in the bunker discussing strategy with Jake Coleman. The militia leader looked weary—unshaven, unshowered—but alert. Eugene wore coveralls that had been in the cave, gathered in and hastily sewn by one of the mothers.

"Anybody who walks out of here now," Jake started, "before we can negotiate some kind of sovereignty and safety for us—that's a security risk. They'll be whisked away and grilled about every detail, numbers and location, weaponry—they'll find out about the refuge and that there's a back entrance."

"People can be trusted not to—"

"Jackie, I trust everybody here, but you're underestimating their tactics, the pressure they can put on you. They got *Marshall* to talk." Jake felt a stab of grief at the mention of Marshall Emery.

"But we got kids and scared women and even a few of the men—though they won't admit it. They can walk on out of here with their hands in the air and know they won't get hurt. If they stay in here—if my *son* stays here—then agents come in with all kinda firepower, people are gonna get hurt." She was pacing, but stopped to fix Jake in her gaze. "People are gonna get *killed*—and it doesn't need to be innocent children."

Nobody spoke for a moment. Eugene, sitting in a spare chair adjacent to the communications console, quietly explained, "Either way, it's still all about rights. People oughta be free to come and go as they please. If somebody wants to leave—or if their parents wanna send 'em out—then to say no is violating their rights same as you say government is trying to do. If you say somebody can't leave, then you've turned 'em into a prisoner."

Jake shook his head, then rubbed his eyes. He couldn't argue with the teen's logic, already knew it as truth, didn't want to accept it.

Finally, without looking up, he spoke softly. "Preserving people's right to decide their own fate—that's what we've been fightin' for. The right to be safe, to look out for your children, that's got to be one of 'em. I just hope people who decide to walk out understand what they're gonna go through when they get out there. It's not goin' home and watching TV and takin' it easy. It's into custody—becoming a prisoner though I can't say for how long—and being forced to help the enemy against the rest of us who've stayed."

"Then come out with us," Jackie breathed. "We all walk out and worse that'll happen is weapons charges against some of the people. It's the best you can hope for no matter how this works out."

Jake shook his head, finally looking up at Eugene. "You ready to walk out?"

"You will be captured or killed," Eugene muttered. Then he clenched his mouth, shaking his head resolutely. "It's all over if I do. I gotta figure out how to help the alien survive until I can get that box, until the next call."

A buzz sounded on the short-wave radio. Communicator answered, then squelched and turned to Jake. "It's them again. They're asking about releasing the women and children."

Jake looked at Jackie again, then back down at his lap. "Tell 'em anybody wants to leave is free to do so. We'll let 'em know how many's comin' out in an hour." Then to Jackie, "Let's talk to everybody together. That way, they'll hear both opinions and make informed choices."

"It's the right thing, Jake," Jackie said softly, a hand on the leader's arm.

Jake nodded. He knew she was right. To Communicator and Monitor, "You can hold it down. Nothin'll happen when they think people are coming out soon."

Jake stood up, put on his blue-jay feathered hat, tugged his sleeves down, and prepared to watch his group shrink—if not walk out completely.

"Let's start here," Jackie said, sympathy and compassion in her voice. "How about you two?"

For Communicator and Monitor, there was no question. They were in for the long haul. "We're facing charges either way. Sometimes you have to be willing to pay the price to stand up for what you believe in."

Jackie nodded. "What about you, Eugene? Why don't you take your chances—walk on out? You got the whole country's attention now. Can't do *too* much to you."

Eugene rubbed his eyes, ran his fingers through his hair, then shook his head. "My only hope is some kind of escape—but right now I don't see how—"

"Then give it up—"

Shaking his head more firmly. "No. Mr. Watterson asked us was we willin' to take the responsibility. We did, and *they* all died for it. If I'm the last one left, then I got no choice. Can't give up the whole world fooling myself into thinking it'll be okay for *me*."

Jake started, "Maybe it's not—"

Eugene held up his hand. "We all know how it is. Unless I can escape, ain't no way I'm getting out of here alive."

*   *   *

"It's not safe to call *anybody* in that area," Flynn Durbett argued. "Let's see what I can find out before you tip off wire-tappers."

Big Ray was eaten up with worry over his wife and son, wondering if they had come out earlier when seven "hostages" had been "released" from the compound. Deferring to the mercenary's judgment, he waited in the car, head low, glancing every direction. Ray's face had been all over the news; it was too risky even to walk to the pay phone, let alone call cohorts around Guntersville and Scottsboro.

Durbett heard a beep, so he hung up immediately. Perplexed, he dialed another number and punched in a series of codes, waiting each time for confirmation. He connected with some woman at the Social Security Administration office in the Birmingham Federal Building.

"Oh! Hi, Flynn! I just wanted to let you know I *can* have dinner with you after work. Wanna meet half-way? Say, Florence? At the Surly Sirloin right in town?"

"Okay if I bring my brother along?"

"Been wanting to meet him. See you at six-sharp."

They decided there wasn't enough time to drive back up Duck River and let the others know, so they headed south.

She was an older woman, silver hair, a severe cigarette habit. She'd been waiting just inside the restaurant, coming out to get in Durbett's truck the second time he cruised past. They went for a ride, backroads and farmland. Durbett's guess proved right; his contact was too embroiled in something, under too much scrutiny to take unappointed calls. Marlene worked for him.

"They're on no-move status at least another thirty-six hours. They're debriefing the women and kids who come out to see what they know, then they have to run the info up and down through the channels."

"*Who* come out?" Ray wanted to know

"Two women, five kids. All with last names Binderson or Sharham."

"No Blountens?"

She shook her head sympathetically.

"She done let Little Ray get his way," he mumbled mostly to himself.

They turned around and headed back the way they'd been driving, much of the dust cloud they'd stirred up hanging in the still, evening air.

"Where?" from Durbett.

"Medical quarantine somewheres below Redstone Arsenal. Medical examiner who was researching at Cumberland's headin' down from Washington with some new way to test for contamination. They're treating it as a secret medical emergency. Something that killed the other doctor, that Aggeous feller, and had 'em cremate his remains to keep from spreading."

Durbett and Ray looked at each other. "McGovern still in charge?"

"Of the secret and medical aspect, plus the weapon, that black box, and the fugitive Weisman. He's not calling the shots, though. Just gets to step in when they recover what they're after."

"Then McGovern killed Aggeous," he said more for his own benefit, surprised, trying to reconcile it with his notions. "What do they know from the women and kids?"

"All I could get was a copy of the prelim. There's a small cave with food and water and medicine and stuff, but no more weapons far as they know. Thinkin' is: they done shot most of what they had." Durbett didn't offer to contradict the assumption, so she continued, "Confirmed Weisman is in there, movin' around. Far as the other indictments, Emery's dead, Coleman's inside, but they think Blounten's not." She looked at Big Ray knowingly. "Only other thing I got is the location you wanted. He said you're out of the loop for a while after this. It's just too hot to feed any more information."

Durbett nodded, checking for cross-traffic before pulling onto the main road to head back to town. "Where is he?"

"At the Arsenal, administration building out by the main gate, fifth-floor front, second set of windows east side." She dug in her purse for a document, offering it to Ray since Durbett was driving. "Turns out this was fairly easy to get. He thought you might want it."

Hey! Durbett was very pleased. It was a listing of all civilian-company supply deliveries to Redstone Arsenal for the next week.

They thanked her, left her at her car, then went in search of an out-of-the-way pay phone. Durbett wanted to call the radio station in Nashville before somebody left for the day. Back on the road north, they considered their options. After pulling off for Durbett to make another call, he reported that two of the panel trucks registered under Marshall's name were available. "Dead man leaves a cold trail," he explained.

They drove until they found a pull-up pay phone out at the far end of a truck-stop lot so Ray could make several calls without leaving the vehicle.

"Farmhouse outside of Tuscaloosa, southwest of Birmingham. You get a truck there by mornin', they can have it loaded by lunchtime." Back on the road north, he added, "They's both offerin' to help."

Durbett shook his head. "No, we'll just pick up the truck. You, me, and Lloyd's enough to get this done. I just hope the truck'll be enough."

Big Ray grinned. "I've seen that administration building; one truck'll be *more* than enough to level that sucker."

*   *   *

"Probably bomb-sniffers," Jake Coleman guessed. They watched two large dogs being unloaded from a truck. The shot looked grainy, zoomed in from quite a distance, blurry branches and leaves in the foreground.

"Taking 'em up the trail," Monitor guessed. "We need to stop 'em fast. Don't want agents learning how it's all rigged."

"You just stay on the beams and sensors," Jake instructed. Communicator paused from scanning short- and long-wave frequencies.

"Cutting inside, right at nineteen," Monitor announced, but Jake was already watching, punching up a diagram of various configurations for detonating explosives.

"Shit. They's two trip wires through there, each set to blow three trees. Don't wanna shoot that much off, leave a hole they can punch through."

"You got one underground first. Dogs ain't gonna pick that one up. Blow it just as they's—"

"No. Gotta put the fear of God in 'em. If I blow the ground when they's approaching, they'll think *they* set it off. If I let 'em get far enough to find the first trip—and they know they's trips out there anyway—then I can blow behind 'em to prove they can't sweep 'em all."

"And warn 'em we got control from inside, too," Monitor agreed. "That'll slow 'em *way* down from tryin' anything else."

Another sensor confirmed a small group moving in slowly. Even without cameras, Jake knew there would be two front men, each with a dog, probably twenty to thirty feet apart, moving a foot or two at a time, studying the dogs' reactions. There would be at least one double team behind each man, probably thirty to forty feet, everybody heavily armored. Two dogs, four to eight men, one explosion.

"Will it take out the closest rigged trees?" Communicator wondered.

Jake shook his head. "Not if they's charged right. It's straight plastic concussion—no metal for detectors to pick up, buried two feet down in turned-up concrete sewer pipe. That'll direct most of the force cone-wise up."

"How's it triggered? Primer cord?" He was probably just making talk to break the tension. Everybody watched for the next sensor to signal.

Beep! Directly over it.

"That'll be the dogs and handlers," Jake guessed, his fingers poised over the keyboard.

Waiting.

Waiting.

Beep!

"They's up to the first wire now, probably studying it," Monitor whispered. "Don't give 'em *too* long."

"They's not in a hurry," Jake whispered back. Then, half-under his breath, "Studying, calling back to inform 'em, tracing the wire . . ."

Jake's fingers tensed. Holding his breath.

"Give 'em time . . ."

Tap.

They could hear the explosion in the distance, saw new activity on the screen, agents rushing about, the bloody remains of a man being fireman-carried out of the woods.

"Ah-hoo!" shouted Communicator, he and Monitor pounding each other's backs.

"Dead doggies!" whooped Monitor.

Jake sat there quietly, still watching the screen, the sensor array, his computer.

"Wonder how many we got," gushed Monitor, still half-shouting.

"Back on your job," Jake said evenly, "and count 'em as they bring 'em out."

Reined in, he pulled his headphones back on and sat down in front of the displays.

Communicator was still up, punching the air with his fist. "We done made them sniffer-dogs' *fur* fly!"

Eugene stood in the doorway, watching, profound sadness in his eyes. "Them dogs never done nothin' wrong to you."

"Them dogs was helpin' the enemy," Communicator argued. "They *had* to be taken out."

"Ain't never said they didn't," Eugene countered, turning to leave.

"Geez, what's with him?" Monitor asked rhetorically. "We done it to protect *him.*"

Jake looked up, the same sad expression as Eugene. "He believes in doing what you gotta do—" He took a deep breath. "But that's different than enjoying it."

*   *   *

". . . Standoff continues. Of the four members indicted, it is confirmed that Marshall Emery *was* killed in the confrontation that resulted in nine deaths and sixteen injuries of ATF agents and back-up personnel. It is believed that, in addition to Emery, three other cult members perished. Three more agents killed in today's explosion bring the estimated death toll to sixteen. A spokesman for the Justice Department has expressed concern that the women and children still being held hostage inside the compound may be sacrificed in some sort of suicide-murder pact . . ."

"Licia, Hon," Lena soothed, "Tracey, you two don't need to be watching this. I gotta keep track of new developments for Flynn and the boys, but—"

Lloyd Stewart paced in and out of the kitchen, nervously sipping a beer. Lena shot him a look; she'd been trying to talk him out of drinking the last three.

Yearbook shot of Eugene, ninth grade, hair wet and combed, hint of a smile somewhere between wanting to look handsome and being too self-conscious. ". . . Just announced that Weisman has been indicted on six counts of felony murder and arson in Tennessee for the deaths of the Watterson family . . ."

Licia had been sitting numbly on the couch, Tracey beside her, holding hands. She closed her eyes and started crying again, tears spilling onto her cheeks.

Lena took charge, hustling both women up and into a back room, insisting they stretch out and rest while she made them something to eat, waving off claims they weren't hungry. "Girl, you don't take care of yourself and you're gonna lose that baby. You got people who love ya working on the situation out there."

Tracey was echoing her sentiments, but both still worried why Durbett and Big Ray had been gone so long.

"They're doing whatever needs to be done," she assured them. "Look, I don't know Ray, but ain't nobody gettin' over on Flynn, believe you me." Tracey agreed, Licia lying back and taking a deep breath, so she left them and went to make sandwiches.

Stewart opened another beer and leaned up against the counter to watch Lena work. "Licia ain't gonna make it—can't take the pressure," he announced.

Slicing from a block of cheese, Lena tried to ignore him.

"Girl that age ain't got no business carryin' no child from no fifteen-year-old daddy, neither."

She snatched the beer from his mouth, a splash on his shirt, and poured it into the sink, pointing the knife toward him with the other hand. "You shut up, Lloyd Stewart. Don't nobody need your smart mouth. What's done is done. Now she's just a scared girl with no mama, daddy killed, brother killed, and no living relatives left but a sorry shit like you! Her boyfriend's wanted—*might* not get out of there alive—and other people who she mighta counted on like Jake is going to prison if *they* don't get killed, too. *You're* the only one not got a warrant out for you. When this is over, *you're* gonna be the only one she's got to help look after her and that young'n. Not that a woman *needs* a man these days," she growled, "but she's just a girl."

Stewart stammered for a moment, rinsing the front of his shirt in the sink and wringing it out. "I'm not planning to stick around after this is over," he said quietly. "Ain't gonna be no peace around here. I'm gettin' the hell out of this country and make my fortune the way Flynn did. Besides, he ain't wanted, neither. What about him? Why can't *he* look out for her—for *both* of 'em? You watch, he's gonna disappear so fast you won't know he's gone."

She shook her head vehemently, but remained quiet a moment, slicing meat. "Fine, you run off then. Flynn'll take care of things."

Stewart tugged at the damp shirt and snorted, pressing his point harder. "Hell, *you* ain't been able to pin him nowheres. What makes you think he'll play nursemaid to these other two and a baby from some mad-dog punk kid alien-boy?"

"Ain't like that no more. He used to be like you, no commitments, didn't trust no one, nobody to care about . . ." Why was she explaining this to him? Maybe it was to herself. "Norm Watterson was the only person he ever counted on. I once asked how they came to be friends and all, and he didn't wanna call it friends. He just said ain't many people you can count on to get things done—and even less you can trust. Watterson was the only man he ever knowed was both."

"So Watterson's dead. Why don't he cut and run? He don't owe the kid nothin'." He reached into the fridge, but Lena brandished the knife to make her point, so he came out with a can of soda.

She stopped working and looked off into the distance of her mind. "I think Watterson gettin' killed hit him. Even more, the whole family gettin' killed—the one thing Watterson loved more than anything else, the one thing Flynn never had and maybe never understood . . ."

She stared a few seconds, then snapped from her reverie and started assembling the sandwiches. "Eugene's the legacy of what Flynn would do for Watterson. Least that's how it started. Turns out, I think he *likes* the kid—and it matters to him what Eugene thinks of him. Here's a teenager been trained not to trust nobody and no thing, yet he sized up Flynn and decided he could stake his whole life depending on him."

She smiled slightly, her eyes sparkling.

"Don't think Flynn never had *that* happen before," she chuckled. "Helping Eugene ain't just for Watterson no more. Everybody needs someone, but not everyone gets to be the one somebody needs."

Stewart reached around her to snag one of the finished sandwiches, pulling a chair to sit at the table.

Her back still to him, she said quietly, "Sure would be good for you to let your cousin know you'll look out for her if her baby's daddy gets captured or killed."

*   *   *

Beep! Traffic down the private drive. The sound of crunching gravel.

Stewart and Lena were both armed and at their vantage points within seconds. It was Flynn's truck, a red glint in the moonlight.

Ray lumbered in and started on a sandwich. Flynn briefly embraced Lena, a quick awkward kiss, assuring her all was okay and that they had some serious planning to do. "The other two resting?" he asked, his voice low.

Lena tilted her head toward the upper back room. "They's worryin' themselves to death. Licia heard 'em announce Eugene was indicted fer murder. Ain't eat all day. I'm worryin' about that baby."

He nodded, then to Ray, "Why don't you get 'em caught up? I'll be down in a minute."

"Flynn!" Licia rushed into his arms, her face buried in his chest. Tracey rushed over, then stood awkwardly a few feet away. Apparent that Licia wasn't about to relinquish her spot, he reached out and pulled Tracey in for a triple hug that lasted a full minute.

"Everything's moving on," he assured them. "I gotta work on the plan now, but it's safer for everybody if you two don't know about it, so you stay here and rest a while."

"Women," Stewart chortled when Durbett came back to the kitchen. *Smack!*

"You watch yer mouth," Lena warned him, a red handprint appearing on his cheek. He hadn't even seen it coming. Durbett chuckled; Big Ray guffawed.

"Ain't because they's *women*," she corrected. "I know a few women'll kick *your* ass while you're sitting down."

"I see there's three companies from the Decatur area making Arsenal deliveries tomorrow afternoon," Durbett interrupted, scanning the list Marlene had given him. "We'll stake-out 72A and commandeer one of those trucks. We'll have ours waiting somewhere off the main road, then either transfer the explosives to theirs or use their paperwork to get ours through the gate. Lloyd, since you're not a known fugitive, you drive it to Redstone while Ray rides in the back. I'll shadow from a distance with Lena in her rental car in case I need to move in and get you two out. Once you get through the gate and parked by the building, signal Ray to start the five-minute timer. Let him out, then both of you walk clear, however seems least suspicious at the time. I'll be somewhere just outside with a scope and enough firepower to clear you both a path if something goes wrong. If you're not out when it blows, run like you're in a panic—you won't be the only ones. If your exit's blocked, I'll blow a hole wherever you need one. Lena will be cruising and pick us all three up soon as it's clear."

"Late afternoon?" Big Ray asked.

"However it times out. Even if it's after five, McGovern'll still be there. He's not punching no time clock these days."

"Where we gettin' this truck?" Stewart wondered.

"Tuscaloosa," Ray answered. "It'll be loaded and ready by noon."

Durbett explained, "We'll drive down there and scout our ambush locations first; then me and Lena'll wait while you guys go get the truck. Take 20 up to the Birmingham bypass, then 65 north until you cross over the Tennessee River and pick up 72 east to wherever we're waiting."

"What kind of ambush you thinkin'?" Big Ray wondered. "Silencer? Blow out a tire so he has to stop?"

"Unless you got a better one."

Big Ray shrugged. "Works for *me*."

"You sure you can trust these guys riggin' the truck?" Lena asked.

Big Ray grinned. "They been practicing for years."

"I mean can you *trust* 'em?"

"They don't know nothin' about the plan," Durbett interrupted before Ray had time to be indignant. "Soon as we drive away, we'll stop and sweep for bugs and homeys, too, just in case."

Licia had rushed to the bathroom to throw up.

"There's nothin' here to give her," Lena said helplessly. "She oughta have something for nausea and to help her sleep. Is there anyplace I can—?"

Stewart spoke up. "This late'll be hard to find someplace." He got up and stretched. "I know the area better than you three. I'll go see if anybody'll open for me. You guys is the strategizers—work out all your details and fill me in when I get back." Durbett had to give him some money, Lena her car keys.

*   *   *

Lloyd Stewart drove straight to a pay phone at the plaza in Waverly, dialing a number of times before he reached whom he wanted. He talked for more than thirty minutes, then hung up, looked at his watch and headed back, all apologies that he could find no place to sell him medicine.

Feeling better, Licia had gone to sleep; Lena was grateful he'd at least tried.

Everybody went to bed.

*   *   *

Lena cuddled up to Durbett, a slash of pole-light cutting across his hairy chest. He lay on his back, wide awake, alert, lost in thought.

"Get some rest, Hon," she whispered.

"Not yet," he whispered back. "This night ain't over."

*   *   *

At that moment, two men, dressed entirely in black and carrying small bags, were working their way along Duck River—pause and listen, infrared scan, pause and listen—

They were heading toward the house.

Chapter 14

It felt good to be back in the cat's seat. McGovern could see the runway lights of Birmingham's international airport, the lighted helicopter landing pads at the adjacent military-vehicle depot. Chopper landed, he was whisked to the federal building where makeshift anti-terrorist operations had been set up. ATF, FBI, the watchful but non-interfering eyes of another half-dozen agencies—all were waiting for Brigadier General Chester McGovern to take charge.

Actually, to milk his information and run things their own way.

"Trackers'll be there on time?" was how he greeted the assembled investigative and enforcement hierarchy.

"Field agent will be at the Waverly Plaza *by* seven o'clock. He'll have a pair of twist-activated trackers, one for back-up. He just needs to know what info you want delivered. Will he know how to use 'em?"

He noted that Poole wore the only other military uniform. He took his cap off and carefully placed it on a shelf, shook hands with nearly a dozen men, lots of shirtsleeves, beard stubble, loose or missing ties, coffee cups and snack containers and ashtrays. Sloppy work areas always suggested sloppy thinkers to him. At least Poole had exercised enough decorum to button down before the arrival of his superior.

"He's used 'em before. He's the one suggested twisters, anticipating they might sweep before taking the truck on the road. Your man got his photo and contact—"

He was waved off by the tall, skinny guy, the only non-military in the room still wearing a jacket. "Just what more info to pass him," he prodded.

"Tell my guy it won't happen until they're well north of Birmingham, past the populated areas, so he can wait until he crosses outside the city line to activate if necessary—but not much longer than that. You guys'll want a big margin to confirm, even if he's being sighted."

"Oh, he'll be sighted," another man boasted. "Nothing bigger than a breadbox coming from anywhere *near* Tuscaloosa into the city will get by us."

McGovern had been humbled enough in the past week to have little tolerance for smug self-assurance. "Also, give him a direct, local-dial number to reach me here—and make sure he knows the location of this building. These guys are slick, sometimes not keeping him apprised of last-minute developments. We need a way he can call or show up here fast to alert us if anything changes."

"You anticipate any kind of role for him when it goes down?"

McGovern shrugged. "He'll figure out his smartest play. He knows we won't hit him, also to act surprised and mock defend, but he'll be ready to stop 'em if anybody looks like they might get a shot at us or detonate the bomb."

"You're *sure* it'll just be him and Blounten?"

McGovern spread his hands. "I'm only sure that's the *current* plan. Stewart driving, Blounten in the back out of sight. I told him we'd arrange a flat tire or some reason for him to stop so we can separate Blounten from the explosive, but he couldn't promise somebody else might not be involved at the last minute. We may learn something new when your guy meets him at eight, maybe get a call later—who knows?"

"I don't like it," Tall & Skinny announced, "not when there's buildings and countless lives at stake, not something this shaky."

"Look," McGovern explained testily, "You can't make a war neat. You devise your best strategy based on available information, and you prepare to improvise. There's no way that truck is getting around us *and* all the way to Huntsville *and* inside the Arsenal. But I do think we'll close down the administration building, evacuate the area, no explanations needed. That's why I moved out of there and came down here to coordinate."

"But won't evacuating risk tipping 'em off?" Poole asked awkwardly. McGovern wanted to be solidly in charge, Poole number two on the scene. He shouldn't be questioning his commander in the presence of others.

"Last minute is what I mean." It hadn't been, but it suddenly made sense. "After we've confirmed the location of the truck, go ahead and empty the building just in case your guys have the wrong one or some other surprise comes around." Tall & Skinny bristled. "At least if they have a mole in the Arsenal, he won't be able to communicate that it's *target non grata* because we sounded the fire alarm too early. Colonel, you coordinate that evacuation. Use your judgment as to the best time."

Tall & Skinny couldn't argue with McGovern's jurisdiction over the evacuation of a military facility. He obviously resented the general having any role at all other than to accept custody of the Weisman kid and the damnable foreign communication device that was so coveted. But it *was* McGovern's operative who had uncovered the bombing plan, was inside at ground zero, their source of info and assistance on the spot, a position no FBI or ATF agent had a chance of achieving on such short notice.

Or long notice for that matter.

"Now," McGovern continued, pulling over a chair to make himself comfortable. "My people around the compound are to provide back-up only; you guys call the shots and handle the politics so you can keep me out of it—" Admitting exactly how much turf the others held, he wanted to be sure they thought it was because he wanted it that way. "But you might consider taking the compound just *before* news of the bomb abortion hits the media. Striking fear in the hearts of the public will skyrocket public opinion in favor of taking the compound at *any* cost, even if it's just been botched—they'll be a lot more forgiving if you have a bomb truck to point to and hint that dozens more would have gone out if you'd not moved in right away. Besides, if they know about this inside, they'll be sitting tight waiting for news, not quite as ready for you to march in."

"What if something goes wrong with the bomb truck?" Tall & Skinny asked.

"Then you've got a *major* excuse for moving fast. Either way, no matter what, you need to take control of that compound tomorrow afternoon."

*   *   *

Flynn Durbett lay silently, eyes open, alert. Lena was drousing, cuddled close, not quite asleep.

Durbett gently laid her arm aside, then slipped out from under the sheet and quietly pulled his pants on. She roused and started to ask, but he touched her mouth, signaled her to hush. He held up a finger, indicating she should wait. He pulled on his shirt and vest, hiking boots and infrared mask, holstered his .45, and checked the clip on his M-16.

Sliding the screen up, he turned and touched his lips, held up his hand, then slipped outside and activated his mask. He disappeared into the darkness, working his way to the river, moving west through several narrow paths, pausing to listen at sporadic intervals.

He saw them before they could spot him. Moving off to the side, he found a good vantage point, watched, and waited. When they were close enough to toss a stick at, he whispered their names.

They froze, looked around, guessed the direction of his voice. One mouthed, "Durbett."

They approached each other, eschewing pleasantries, Durbett and one of the men whispering while the third scanned all directions and then some.

"Five calls, the last one more than a half-hour long, never went nowhere else."

Durbett thought for a second, then nodded. "What'd you pick up?"

"Couldn't get direct on the long-range mike until later in the conversation—even then, it's spotty, but he confirmed several times that somebody would be meetin' him there at eight with something—didn't say what. Last thing he did say was, 'Big Ray is supposed to be the only other one in the truck. Make sure I don't get hurt and that you got a way for me out,' was what he said."

"No mention of me or Lena or a car?"

Durbett saw him shake his head in the eerie green infrared. "Nope. He said no one'd be trailing, so put a body in the truck and identify it as Stewart."

"But—" Then Durbett realized the implication.

"And with Big Ray killed, he can't never say different."

*   *   *

"Look, I can't sleep, neither," Lloyd Stewart whispered. "I'm gonna run up and get Licia some medicine before we hit the road."

Flynn Durbett nodded, waving off more coffee from Lena. Big Ray stood in the doorway scratching his belly. The driveway light shining through the window blinked out in deference to rising dawn.

At the crunch of gravel signaling Stewart's departure, Durbett and Ray snapped to, donning vests and armament, slipping outside to crank up Van's old Ford Ranger. They followed a minute or two behind Stewart during the drive to Waverly.

The Ranger pulled into a burger place near the plaza, meeting some fellers pulling a boat full of fishing gear. Ray stayed in the vehicle, head buried in a map. The others milled around, blocking the view of passersby so Durbett could admire a new depth-finder, actually watching Stewart on a small monitor, pointing a directional mike to hear what was being said.

The rendezvous man was giving Stewart a very small satchel. "Two homing devices, twist to activate. Both the same, second one is just for back-up. Don't turn 'em on until you're leaving the city limit. We'll have visual by then and be all over you. Everything still go?"

Stewart grunted. He was glancing every direction, nervous. "Just make damn sure you got a way to slip me out."

The man nodded. "General wants you to know his location is changed. He's at the federal building in Birmingham just off—"

"I know where it is. Is there a direct phone?"

He repeated the number twice and the man was gone. Stewart slid the case under the car seat, then walked down to the just-opening drugstore at the other end of the plaza.

Durbett scratched a message and phone number on a slip of paper and left it with the fishermen. By the time Stewart emerged with a small sack of medicaments, the Ford Ranger was gone.

"We got a problem, don't we?" asked Big Ray.

Durbett snorted. "Let's just call it a change of plans."

*   *   *

"That *lazy drunk brother* of mine, now he wants me to invest in a *two-tailed cow* . . ." The country-station DJ went on to make fun of his brother before sobering and saying, "I guess I oughta shut up—looks like he's comin' over this afternoon and he's still a whole lot bigger than me."

Eugene's eyes were wide, Jake Coleman rubbing his own.

"He's doin' the morning program for a change because we needed that message," Eugene decided.

Jake nodded. "You two take turns havin' a break while I check the computer. Looks like nothin'll happen this morning, but it *will* hit later today."

Eugene followed him to the house, watched him log on, go through a series of blind scrambles, then key in LDB-2 (lazy drunk brother, two-tailed cow) to access the underground militia information network. The message was tagged confidential, so Jake used his personal codes, not surprised to see that it was for him.

They learned about the cave from Ferguson, are massed outside back entrance.

Entry planned for mid-afternoon today. Expect McDog dead by then, which may delay or change their plan.

One more for EW.

Eugene reached over and typed in the short private code Jake and Flynn had assigned him, noticing that Little Ray was watching from behind. His personal message was revealed.

FD vows she will always be OK.

Eugene cast his face down, eyes squeezed shut. Even Little Ray seemed to understand the implication that Eugene might not survive the day, that Flynn had made him the Watterson promise knowing it would help Eugene do whatever needed to be done, that he would always look out for Licia, no matter what.

"Little Ray," Jake said quietly, "Go to the cave and tell them I said ATF knows about the other entrance, to move everybody to the middle and start bringing major weapons and more provisions out to the bunkhouse."

"Yes, sir." He hesitated, looking back and forth, then scurried away to mobilize the troops.

Jake logged in receipt verification, then looked at Eugene, the teen's head still down. "You *can* count on him, y'know."

Eugene looked up. He knew. "Jake . . . You can't keep the United States government from getting in here, you know that. And you can't stay in here forever—"

"I was hoping we could negotiate—"

Eugene shook his head. "You done heard the news. They keep talkin' about how we's refusing to, but the public don't know they ain't never even tried. They don't wanna talk because they know I'm not gonna give myself up, no matter what. They wanna look like the good guys, comin' in here rescuing all these so-called hostages, then capturing or killing me. I don't want nobody else gettin' killed when can't no good come of it."

"There's chance of a *rescue*, or—"

Eugene shook his head again. "That's why I waited *this* long. But it's gonna end today. It's *me* they's after; *you* can survive."

"What about putting the alien in *me*?"

"They'd find it out. Everybody coming out of here alive is gonna be checked for aliens in 'em. No, you have to destroy all the evidence, so they don't never know if the black box was in here or not."

Jake clearly didn't like the implications, but he played along. "You done told the whole world that aliens has already been called to come rescue humans."

Eugene looked hopeful. "That's the best chance. I don't know how long in Earth time it takes 'em to get here, and I don't think the bad ones does, neither. If they's afraid of eventually being killed, maybe by five or ten years they'll get a way to leave this planet and never come back. We gotta make 'em run."

Jake was considering the idea. Eugene could tell he was impressed with the teen's strategic savvy. "Destroy all evidence . . . but—"

"Blow the house up. Blow it and burn it so bad ain't nothin' left, no way to know if the box was in there, no way to be sure if there was an alien in me or not—"

"Burn *you* up? No way—"

Eugene grabbed Jake's arm, holding tight. He stared purposefully into his face. "I can't let 'em take me alive or this plan won't work."

"But I can't *kill* you—!"

"You won't have to. I'm just saying, if I'm dead, you blow it up and make sure it burns all the way down, then you and everybody else give up."

"Surrender—?"

"No! Survive! That's the *only* way we're gonna win."

*   *   *

Rising sun filtering through the curtains, medicine on the nightstand, Licia Emery on the side of the bed, cousin Lloyd Stewart sitting beside her . . . she was fingering the dogtags hanging around her neck—her father's from Korea.

"How come you to wear them, Licia?"

She shrugged. "Daddy said they was lucky, got him through a lot of stuff. But he wasn't wearing 'em the day they killed him. After that, Marshall used to wear 'em ever now and then when he went on missions. He shoulda had 'em—shoulda had 'em when . . ." She kept fingering them, finally looking up at her cousin, big brown eyes glistening.

Stewart pulled her into an embrace, felt her trembling.

"Please be careful," she whispered. "I don't know what I'd do . . ."

"We'll be all right—you will, too." He held her tight, knowing this would be the last time.

*   *   *

Downstairs, Flynn Durbett and Ray Blounten were prepping and packing ammo. Durbett nodded to Lena, confirming that the two inactive homing devices she'd selected matched the ones from the small bag in Stewart's ammo case. She quickly made the switch, Durbett packing the real ones in his own case.

Tracey was making sandwiches, pausing to bring coffee for everyone. Licia and Stewart came down, she heading into the kitchen, he checking his own weapons.

Just about ready to leave.

Licia and Tracey came out with four small sacks of sandwiches, four sodas in foam cozies. The men looked puzzled, but Lena quickly spoke up.

"Why *thank* you! What a good idea." Shooting a look toward the men, "Everybody's doing their part, contributing. Getting hungry or thirsty would slow us down." The men were suitably grateful, packing sandwich bags in their cases, putting cold drinks in their respective vehicles.

The man with the boat arrived so he could look out for Tracey and Licia. They swapped quick hugs all around, Durbett hurrying them before it got too maudlin.

Flynn drove his own truck, Stewart aboard, Lena in her rental with a hunched-down Big Ray. Finding a suitable ambush site proved easy, a service road along the highway leading off into a hilly area of woods, a perfect tractor turnaround with no way out. Stewart took over Lena's rental to drive himself and Ray to Tuscaloosa.

"We'll cruise this stretch and scope delivery trucks. If the right one hits before you're back," Durbett explained, "we may just take it and have it back in there ready."

They waited several minutes after the rental drove out of sight, then pulled onto the highway and followed its trail.

*   *   *

Lt. Col. Poole was surprised to see McGovern spending so much time by himself in the office next door rather than staying to oversee the strategy briefings. New topographic charts of the region had just arrived, underground-sonar overlays hastily added.

A man was explaining, "The only one who admits knowing of the cave is the old man whose property backs it up. Claims he's never been in there very far, used to be where they run a still and stored moonshine back in the forties and fifties."

A geologic expert was examining the new overlays. "That whole ridge appears to be a series of cracks. Most would extend down into what would be water now, ever since TVA flooded the river valley when Guntersville Dam was built." He indicated two long ridges extending toward the militia compound. "This area's high enough; there could be a series of caverns connecting all the way through."

"You can't tell?" Poole was trying to decipher the series of colored, squiggly plotter-lines.

"Rock's too thick over it. These are *satellite*. Can't get any closer right now."

Poole turned to the ranking FBI honcho. "Any chance they've been moving people in and out—or supplies?"

He shook his head. "Whole area's been sealed off. We didn't know there was a passage through there, but it's been so tight—your men included," he added, dripping derision, "the most anybody could've done is stick his head out for a breath of air. Your superiors got any problem with us moving into the cave and securing that end first?"

"General's deferring to you—that's as high as we need to go. Get us the kid alive, then we all sweep for the box," he repeated dutifully. It had become a mantra. "We'll lay low long as you keep it contained. Anybody busts through and we take the gloves off."

FBI nodded, apparently satisfied, his Pyrrhic victory akin to winning the lottery over who got to hold the leash of a rabid Pit Bull.

Poole walked next door and reported to McGovern. The general seemed satisfied, if not oddly distracted. The colonel studied him for a moment, then left him alone.

The general was sitting at his desk, the black box in front of him, regarding it curiously.

He was obviously thinking about *something*.

*   *   *

For once, Big Ray didn't have to remain hunched down, his face hidden. Poking his head out the car window, recognized by allies, allowed them safe passage down the gravel road through plowed-under fields to the old farmhouse surrounded by barns, a silo, and numerous outbuildings. Whitewashed and red-painted, the old structures looked clean and meticulously cared for. Six men, most in fatigues, several dressed farmerly, an older woman—it was old-home week. Big Ray was respected and liked, admired and supported. Lloyd Stewart was treated cordially, everybody getting down to business.

Marshall's beige truck sat next to a maintenance blockhouse. Stewart was directed to drive the rental around, leaving it parked behind. Ray inspected the homemade bomb in the back, a series of barrels, kerosene, fertilizer, small charges of plastic explosive, all wired. He was satisfied, even impressed, his approval meaning a lot to the group.

Everything ready on the truck, he and Stewart walked back and retrieved their ammo bags from the rental. Ray removed an electronic bug and homey-sweeper, then made great show of checking for electronic devices on or around the truck, the people, himself and his own bag, Stewart and his. Twice around, everything looked clean.

Short on time, Big Ray loaded into the back and sealed in. Stewart climbed behind the wheel and started the engine, sitting there a few minutes talking to one of the men through the window, confirming it was fully gassed, fluids and systems checked, tires and air, the route back to the highway . . . just long enough for Big Ray to slip out through a trap door. The big man disappeared into the maintenance building while Stewart was too distracted to notice in the side-view mirror. Luck and Godspeed, Stewart drove away, a trail of dust whipped up in the midday breeze.

By the time Marshall's second beige panel truck rolled out of the maintenance shed, Flynn Durbett's pickup appeared from a side road. Ray introduced everybody round, Flynn's reputation preceding him, Lena readily accepted. Two arguments started, Durbett having the last word on both.

"Radio detonator for each of us—*no* timer, *no* dead-man's trigger."

"But they's only two of us. If we both go down—"

"Then it's all over for now."

Big Ray grumbled.

"Take three barrels out," Durbett also declared. "A very small blast, enough for distraction, not mass destruction. Too many innocent people; don't want to bring down the whole building."

"But McGovern—"

"We just need to get him out of the building—or to clear the crowd before we go in after him."

"You ain't never before worried about civilians—"

"It's always depended on who I was working for. This one's for Eugene. Next time I see him, first thing he's gonna ask is did anybody else get hurt."

Big Ray snorted, then broke into a wide grin. "And Little Ray'll be standin' beside him waitin' for the answer."

*   *   *

They removed most of the barrels and the timer, then rewired the makeshift bomb with less detonator plastics and shorter primer cord. While empty containers were packed in to limit load shift, Durbett set about altering his pickup. He changed license plates, added fake-wood side panels, packed ammo into both secret compartments he'd built into the undercarriage, then changed the plates on Lena's rental.

Durbett didn't like emotional scenes before missions. A few moments' back-pounding, some hearty handshakes, it was time to leave.

He did have to hold Lena for a full minute, whispering some encouragement to her. Such a hardened lady, so many jobs in her past, getting soft with the burden of new priorities and passions unleashed. Or maybe dreams about to be realized . . .

Lena led the caravan in her rental, Flynn driving the panel truck, Ray bringing up the rear in the red wood-panel pickup.

Destination: federal building, Birmingham.

McGovern.

*   *   *

"Chester! What a surprise. I wasn't expecting a call from *you* today."

"Just had a minute, thought I'd see how you're doing."

She hesitated. This was very unusual for her son. She was used to being told when his next call would come, of him having several specific things he wanted to discuss before the chit-chat phase of their conversations, brisk and business-like in a friendly sort of way. This time he sounded distracted, worried even. She knew better than to push . . . "I'm doing fine, son. I hope everything is okay with you."

"Oh sure. Fine. You having a busy day?"

"I'm going shopping with Allison—you remember her—later this afternoon. I just had some lunch, was watching the Noontime News." Her words were tentative, her answers short.

"Anything interesting?"

"A lot of new stuff about that hate group holed up in Alabama. Police are releasing all kinds of bad information about those people. They're not talking about the alien part anymore, though. But I know a lot of people like your Aunt Sylvia who think it could be true."

"We'll probably never know." Pause.

"I guess not. TV keeps saying all those bad things, but this bunch doesn't seem to be crackpots so much like some of those other groups. I don't believe everything in the media. It's getting to where you don't know *who* to trust."

"It's not always just good guys versus bad guys anymore. So many people believe so many different things, who's to say what's right . . ." His words trailed off as if lost in thought.

Mother McGovern didn't speak for a moment. When her son offered nothing else, she quietly said, "I trust *you*. Sometimes I wish *you* were in charge of everything. *You* know right from wrong."

*   *   *

General McGovern chatted with his mother several more minutes, finally starting to feel better. Every time she pressed the moral high ground, he couldn't help but chuckle. *Mother.* From guilt trips to ethics lessons, she had her own style. "When I run for president, I'll need you to get all your friends to vote for me!"

She laughed, too. "And you'll be wanting contributions, I'm sure!"

He asked about where she would be shopping, what kind of plans she had. "I need to make an important call at 12:30, so I better run."

"Love you, son."

"I'll call you tomorrow, Mother."

His phone appointment was for 12:30 exactly, but of course he would have to wait. Four-star would be available to talk in just a few more minutes. Sure, what the hell. There's all the time in the world.

McGovern's patience was growing thin.

*   *   *

Lloyd Stewart couldn't recall ever being more nervous—yet he didn't know why.

Piece of cake. Activate the homeys, drive along, get waylayed somewhere down the road, disappear into some waiting vehicle to be casually driven away. Money, passport, hearty thanks, don't even stick around long enough to watch the news. Travel light and fast, don't look back.

He sure hoped Licia would be fine. She would lose Eugene, that was a sure bet, but Flynn Durbett would look out for her. He'd been careful to leave the mercenary's involvement out of it, had never mentioned him even once to McGovern. Sure, he and Lena would be somewhere in the area, maybe following, maybe waiting, but they wouldn't try to get involved once the bust went down. There would be no point, nothing they could accomplish.

Licia would be fine. She probably wouldn't understand, but that was *her* problem. Old Man Emery was long gone, could no longer fix his nephew in that steely gaze that demanded he explain himself. Marshall was dead, would never know what his cousin had done. Licia was too young to understand, too much a girl.

Let Durbett set her up. She had the farm, her family's assets, Marshall's businesses. She'd be doing a helluva lot better than a million other young, single moms.

And he'd never see her again, so what was to explain?

Slowed by downtown lunch-hour traffic, he worked his way north toward the city line. He pulled his ammo case out from under the seat and opened it. He removed the small satchel holding the homeys, took them out and set them on the seat. The cozie soda had sweated some, a damp spot on the canvas sack that held his 9mm clips. He opened it and took a long drink, propping it next to the shifter. A bite or two of sandwich sounded good, so he fished inside the paper sack.

First he heard them jingle, then he felt them. They were Mr. Emery's dogtags. Licia had sent them with her cousin for good luck.

He still couldn't recall ever being more nervous.

Damn that girl.

And whatever made him think he could trust those military people anyway? He knew too much. His knowledge was as much a threat to them as Eugene's. What's to stop them from killing him, too?

Only a few more miles and the ambush could happen anywhere. He pulled up an exit ramp to the right, trying to calculate which direction to the federal building. He put the chain around his neck, dropping the tags down his shirt front, slid the unactivated homeys under the seat, pushed the sandwiches off to the side, and removed his fully-automatic HK MP-5, leaving it covered with a towel.

There would be no way to alert Durbett, not while driving a truck that would be watched, if it wasn't already.

Big Ray was still in the back, everything still rigged to blow an entire building.

Lloyd Stewart just needed to come up with a plan.

And he was out of time.

*   *   *

They circled the federal building twice, then drove a half-dozen blocks farther and stopped in a loading alley to switch vehicles.

"That place I pointed to is where you'll leave the truck," Durbett explained. "Lena, you pull around Ray just as he parks so he can step right into your car, then drop him across from the left rear of the building. Ray, when I activate the homeys, McGovern'll probably see the truck out the window, most likely run out the back way, so be sure you cover the corner exit. Get behind the trash bins where you won't get crushed in case the truck has to be blown."

"How long?"

"Figure twenty seconds for 'em to pinpoint the location."

"Hit every military uniform?"

Durbett shook his head. "Officers only. Don't spook 'em. They may send foot soldiers out first. But it's a sure bet McGovern won't be far behind."

"If they *don't* see the truck, they might come out the front."

"I'll cover that and the fire doors along the right."

"Where you gonna be?"

"Parked across the street alongside that orange-brick building. I can get up and over the blocks to drive straight outta there if necessary. Lena, you keep circling close to Ray so he can get out the back way if things is too hot. Each pass, try to keep visual of my location in case I have to abandon the pickup and move out on foot. I may need to climb in from either side, so keep all your doors unlocked."

"Rendezvous Tuscaloosa if we split?"

Durbett nodded.

Lena looked slightly nervous, but she took a deep breath and steeled her resolve.

Flynn and Ray thumped each other in the chest.

Time for some wet work.

*　　*　　*

"Everything's clear to take the compound in another hour?"

"Yes, no problems," McGovern reported. "And so far all's smooth on the bomb-truck interception—"

"I don't care about that. Just make sure the—"

"I'm *making* sure," McGovern snapped.

There was a slight pause, then Four-star continued, "And just what the *hell* were you thinking by killing Aggeous? I just found out—"

"You're the one who wanted all the loose ends tied up. Isn't that why we're going in after the Weisman—?"

"So why the *doctor?*"

"Didn't trust him. He was holding out on something."

"Hell, he was *supposed* to until you got your bearings—"

"Yeah, well, I've got them now. I don't need him anymore."

Hesitation. "What're you talking about?"

"I'm fully *connected* now."

A long pause. "You're sure?"

"Clear as day."

"*Talking* to you?"

"A goddamn chatterbox. I know everything."

"Good then, but I'm still gonna kick your ass over the doctor later. Just make sure you shut down the kid and bring me that last box for a bonus."

"That's the plan."

"Everything's all set?"

"Yes, *sir.*" Deferential—ha! "I know *exactly* what I need to do."

*   *   *

Lloyd Stewart was being followed, that much was obvious. He'd lost one car, but not the other.

And there was no telling how many more might be out there.

Proceed calmly. This will work.

Nothing to be alarmed about.

*   *   *

You lie! I've never spoken to you.

McGovern started mouthing replies without sound. "Oh, so *now* you finally have a reason to talk."

You told him you know everything. Liar! You know nothing.

"I know enough." McGovern was rearranging his briefcase.

Calmly, even condescending, *But there's so much more to learn.*

"After *you* have full control. But you don't have that yet, do you?"

A pause. *I have enough.*

The briefcase was suddenly flung to the floor. McGovern picked it up, started arranging it again, sweat on his brow.

"This is not what *I* want."

Yes it is. You just don't understand yet.

McGovern removed the black box from its carrier, putting it carefully into his briefcase.

It's too late.

"Not as long as I have the box."

It'll be weeks before the next call. By then, I'll have full control. Don't make me take over completely.

"I won't need to wait that long."

What can you—?

"Poole!" he shouted into the phone. "Pull a chopper here—now! I'm going out to the compound." McGovern straightened his tie, carefully donned his cap.

Poole burst in. "They had one comin' in—rerouting it here. Be on the roof any minute. What—?"

"Just following up on something. Be prepared to call off the compound incursion on my signal."

"I'll send word—"

"No! No hints. Wait for my signal."

McGovern hurried past the befuddled colonel, heading toward the stairs, up to the roof.

You're making a big mistake.

"No, I *made* one. Now you're gonna have to watch me fix it."

*   *   *

Ray parked adjacent to the handicap spaces close to the front lobby, then stepped out and into Lena's car. Nobody paid attention. In less than a minute, she had dropped him off by the alley, his duffel concealing an M-16 with RPGL. As she pulled away, she could see Durbett's pickup pulling into position.

McGovern stepped out onto the roof, briefcase in hand, breeze tugging at his tie. He scanned for signs of the chopper.

Lloyd was stopped in traffic two blocks away. Damned red light was a long one. Too many pedestrians.

Lena signaled Durbett that Ray was in position.

Durbett twisted the homey, fully activating it. He pulled a flap of masking tape over it, padding it in a heavy, baseball-sized wad. He shotput it across the parking lot and street, causing it to roll under the panel truck.

"Homing device is on!" the tech upstairs shouted. Agents crowded around, Poole watching from the side. The tech's fingers were flying across a keyboard, maps on the monitor breaking into grids and enlarging, closer, closer, closer . . .

McGovern could see a speck coming from the direction of the airport, but couldn't yet hear the chopper over the sounds of city.

"Downtown! He's downtown!" Closer, closer. "Shit! It's on *this* block! It's *here!*"

One man was already at the window. "It's parked right below us. Everybody out the back—now!"

"Wait!" Tall & Skinny shouted, breathing heavy, whirling on Poole. "He's *your* man. Is he here to tell us something or do we need to get out?"

Poole stammered. This was unexpected . . .

Durbett could hear the chopper same time as McGovern. He whirled and spotted it, then squinted to see up on the roof. There stood a man in dress greens.

McGovern!

Squealing tires, the crunch of side-swiped car. It was Marshall's other truck, Stewart at the wheel! Through the intersection, straight across the lot, clipping and turning the other panel truck, bouncing up two steps and crashing into the glass lobby!

Stewart jumping out with MP-5 blazing security guards, struggling to open the back of the truck. Durbett couldn't hear him shouting for Ray.

Door open, Stewart trying to scramble inside.

Chopper directly overhead.

Shit, Durbett can't help Stewart now. Kicking open a pickup-truck compartment, SA-7 in hand, loading and locking.

The chopper landing, McGovern and briefcase aboard, taking off.

Big Ray pressing the remote, but the second truck won't blow. Stewart's crash must've knocked the detonator loose.

Durbett rolling flat with the 7, sees Stewart dropping from a hail of gunfire, desperately trying to blow up a truck full of just water and grease.

Chopper banking away.

One shot, a thin trail, direct hit.

Boom! Echoing through the canyons of downtown, a fireball in the sky, debris raining everywhere, large burning chunk hitting the car lot.

Durbett running along the building to shield himself. No way to get his pickup out.

Turning to aim— *Boom!* His own pickup a fireball.

Aiming . . . *Boom!* Nothing left of the large chunk of chopper.

People screaming, running every direction.
Durbett out to the street, over to the other side.
Lena driving up, Ray in the back, fast stop.
"Looking for a ride?"

Chapter 15

Little Ray hustled inside the house weighted down by two more five-gallon gas cans. "Jake had to tell 'em to let me be," he explained, breathing hard. "Wanted me to stay in the cave."

Eugene was just ahead of him carrying several buckets from the nearby shed. Little Ray could see where the teen had already gathered every available jug and pitcher and jar—any containers he could find in the house. They were piled in the front room alongside eight more cans of gasoline and several sticks of dynamite.

"Did you get the ricin?"

"Yeah." Ray fished a small plastic tube out of his jeans pocket, offering it to Eugene. "Mama tried real hard to stop me from takin' it. I had to promise no more trips, that I'd finish helpin' you and come back in the cave where it's safer."

"We're almost done." Eugene was pouring gas into various containers, Little Ray watching curiously, careful to leave a good bit in each of the large cans.

"Why you gonna burn the house down?"

"*You* are."

Eugene was carrying containers upstairs, motioning Ray to follow with several more. He placed them in various rooms, close to interior walls or under curtained windows.

"What do you mean *I* am? I'll get in trouble—"

"Jake said do whatever I told ya," Eugene reminded him.

Back downstairs, filling more containers. "One of us has to blow it up. If I don't get it done first, then *you* have to promise to do it yourself—*no hesitation.*"

"I promise."

"Good. You're my buddy I *always* know I can count on."

Little Ray was proud, but still unsettled. He didn't understand why they were doing this. "You can tell *me*," he prodded.

All the containers were distributed, the large cans arranged at interior doorways. Eugene carefully placed the sticks of dynamite adjacent to load-supporting walls.

"*C'mon*, Eugene."

"Can I trust you to keep a secret for a long time, to do something for me?"

Little Ray nodded earnestly, smirking indignance. After all, who did he think he was talking to?

Eugene was looking at the giant fish tank. Activity was visible through the window, men carrying supplies and weaponry to the bunkhouse and control bunker.

"Gotta get rid of all this water," Eugene said absently. "Tank explodes, water might put out the fire before the house blows. Ain't fair for the fish to die, neither."

Little Ray started filling a bucket, making trips to the sink. Eugene chased critters with a net, dumping them into another bucket.

It took nearly fifteen minutes to get most of the water out, most of the fish caught. Little Ray made several trips down to the stream to release them.

It was long enough for Eugene to share the secret, to explain what he needed—just in case.

Just in case.

Little Ray didn't like hearing it, but he promised he would do his part, no matter what.

No matter what.

"So the aliens ain't really comin'?"

"No. I never got a chance to answer the call."

*   *   *

"Offer no resistance," Jake Coleman instructed the group gathered in the cave. "When they come in, surrender."

Several people tried to object. Jake held up his hand for quiet.

"We can't win this one. All we can do is get killed, which is probably what they want. That would shut us up."

"But we'll wind up goin' to *prison*—"

"Most of you—no. Don't be holding any weapons when they come in. They can't prove you did anything illegal and none of you had warrants. Eugene and me's the only ones left—"

"Where is *he*?"

"Destroying evidence. I'm not gonna say no more."

Jackie Blounten asked, "How do we handle the arrests?"

"Nobody say nothin'. Stand mute. And don't sign nothin', neither. Just let 'em process you. Our lawyer will arrange to get private attorneys for everybody who's taken from the compound. You may have to spend some time locked up until it gets sorted out, but it'll be okay in the long run. Just don't start telling your story until you're out and safe. Then you can tell anyone who'll listen."

The cavern's low ceiling hung ominously above their heads, odd shadows playing across the rocks, dozens of faces glowing in the light of several fluorescent tubes. Most looked worried, unsure, a few still defiant.

"Don't seem right, Jake," one of the men said. "Patriots oughta be willin' to fight and die for our rights."

"But fightin' and dyin' today won't preserve 'em for *you* or nobody else. *Survive* today, then fight again later, on their own battlefields of public opinion, with ideas that break down their power. You *die* here today and they'll say whatever they want about you and everybody'll believe it." He looked around at all the faces, then added quietly, "And don't ever let 'em forget who did give up their life for us."

Leroy Carter stood up. "Mr. Coleman. I'm grateful for what you done—and for tryin' to help my daughter—" He cast his eyes down, sadness creasing his face. "It is true about aliens and all?"

"I don't know, Mr. Carter. I really don't know. But everybody's got a right to believe—and to be left alone. If we refuse to let government run our lives, won't matter if they's aliens or just people. We'll still be free."

*   *   *

"FBI and state police have about four blocks shut down. We're tight for now," Poole was explaining frantically.

"Lieutenant Colonel," Four-star hurried, "You are hereby assigned as commander, *Program Invigil.* Any other damage there?"

"Just that McGovern's confirmed to have boarded the chopper. It's down and ain't no pieces left of it bigger than a yo-yo."

"Proceed as planned without him. I see in the strategy brief that he was going to send only Weisman to quarantine. I think everybody in the compound should go. Get that changed. All prisoners to be processed at Redstone Arsenal."

"Is the doctor there yet?"

"Whole team's getting set up now. All they'll need is thirty minutes for each prisoner—it's some new kind of way to calibrate an MRI—then each'll be cleared and can be transported to the holding camp."

"All but Weisman."

"Of course."

"Did you get—?"

"Wait, let me check. You had no trouble making the switch this morning?"

"Naw. McGovern was down the hall in the bathroom."

There was a pause, some noise in the background, voices off-phone.

"Yes, it just arrived. I have the real black box here."

*   *   *

Anesthetic-gas canisters were lobbed in first, followed by several softball-sized emitters squealing bursts of ultra-high frequency pitches to temporarily deafen, disorient, inflict pain. A remote armored module tracked to the cave entrance and started firing hundreds of wads of exploding sticky-nets designed to ensnare and entangle anybody trying to move around inside. Bright spotlights shone in, wand camera lenses revealing that the area was unoccupied.

A team of explosives experts and bomb-dogs moved in next, advancing slowly, studying the area for traps. Within ten minutes, more equipment was positioned inside, the armored module winched down onto the lower floor so it could advance to the next cavern, netting cartridges reloaded.

The path through the crack was too zig-zagged, dropping several more feet, so two small remote "buggies" like children's radio toy cars were driven in, camera signals fed back. No people, just boxes of supplies, light fixtures, some portable toilets. They repeated the scan and search.

The third cavern was at the end of a long passage that required climbing concrete stairs. They found a sign at the entrance, a sheet of cardboard with Magic Marker:

We are in next chamber.

We surrender.

*   *   *

Jake hurried from the control bunker over to the house, a crate of exotic weapons in his arms. He found Eugene and Little Ray catching fish and emptying the tank.

"They're inside the cave! I'm leaving these here for the burn because they're things Durbett wouldn't want 'em to find out we had. Ray, you get back to the cave now!"

"Almost done!"

"Jake!" Eugene stopped him. "There's something you need to know for this to work," he explained. They talked quietly for a minute.

"It's not gonna come to that," he argued. "Hurry, we'll talk about it later."

Jake hurried back to the bunker.

*   *   *

Eugene was breathing hard, that infernal pounding of his heart, wiping sweat from his brow. He couldn't seem to catch fish fast enough. Down to the pair of young bass. Eugene patted his jeans pocket, feeling the vial of ricin.

"You run these down while I catch the last two. Then make sure you let 'em go before we burn." Eugene was trying to project calm, assurance, trying to hold the net steady.

Little Ray looked up at him, studying his face.

"Hurry now," Eugene said quietly. "Remember what I said." He put his hand out to shake the boy's, but Little Ray put his arms around him, a bear hug between friends. Eugene held tightly for a moment, then pressed a small box of wood matches into the boy's jeans.

The sound of armored vehicles on the gravel road.

"Hurry, Ray! Remember, do what's right. No matter what. Always . . ."

*   *   *

The little boy raced down to the stream, released the fish, and hurried back. He paused in the doorway. The house had fallen silent, choppers loud in the air, armored vehicles moving in.

Eugene was lying on the floor next to the bucket, the open vial in his hand.

"Eugene! Eugene!" Little Ray tried to rouse him, shaking, touching his face, fighting back tears.

But it was too late.

"Little Ray!" Jake hollered from somewhere outside. "C'mon! Now!"

The last two bass, Eugene's favorites, swam in the bucket.

Let 'em go, then burn.

He hustled the bucket down toward the water, the crescendo of choppers deafening. He could see them circling the compound, closer with each pass.

Plop! Plop! Plop! Gas bombs landing everywhere.

"Ray!" Jake running toward the boy. "Get down! *Down!*"

Ray stumbling, tripping in the rocks and mud, dumping the pail into the stream. Scrambling to his feet. Gotta get back to the house. Gotta light that fuse. Fumbling for matches. Gotta burn it for Eugene.

Plop! Plop!

Pfoom! Pfoom! Scattershot. *Pfoom!*

Jake running toward the boy, M-16 in hand. Tackling Ray, holding him down, the boy struggling.

"Gotta burn the house!"

Toop! Toop! Toop! Toop! Sticky-net from a chopper, tangled, unable to get up.

Armored vehicles tracking down the slope.

Jake twisting to aim his RPGL.

Psooo . . . Boom! Direct hit.

Boom! Boom! Gas, dynamite blowing.

Ka-Boom!

Huge fireball, cloud of black smoke rising into the sky, debris raining everywhere.

Jake squirming to cover the boy, Ray lying still, shivering, crying softly.

One chopper banking off with a trail of smoke, the others pulling back. All advances stopped.

Debris still raining, a small grass fire.

Foot troops moving again, debris pelting trees, splashing the stream, smoke drifting everywhere, hot flames licking the sky.

The house collapsed into a flat pile of debris and embers, burning blue-hot, crackling and spewing fumes and soot and ash, the stench of death.

Jake pushed the rifle away as far as the net would allow, pulled the squalling child close, wrapping his arms around him and holding tight.

"We surrender!" he shouted over the flames.

Little Ray buried his face and cried hard.

Surrounded by soldiers, Jake whispered, "You *did* it, son, for *Eugene.*

You helped save the world."

Chapter 16

A.D. 2000

"Mama, when's Unca Jake gonna get here!?"

Little Genia was growing impatient after two days of excited preparation.

"Any minute now, sweetie!" Licia swept her little girl up into a big hug. Though not quite five years old, she looked so much like a cherub version of her father it still sometimes brought tears to her mother's eyes.

Figuring about two hours' drive from the federal prison, Uncle Flynn was overdue with the newly paroled guest of honor. It would be a party like none other, dampened only by Ray Blounten still having another eighteen months to serve—owing mostly to all those unproven rumors about his involvement in the attempted federal-building bombing.

Lena steered Tracey away from the refrigerator. "Girl, you done checked those drinks a dozen times now—you're lettin' the cold air out."

"I'm a nervous wreck." Tracey smiled. Lena grinned with her, then pulled her into a hug.

"She's gettin' ready to start her honeymoon!" Leroy Carter teased from his vibrating recliner. "Of *course* she's nervous. Bein' married near five years now and just gettin' around to that honeymoon—these young'ns sure do like to take it slow." He chuckled. Nearly blind, he was still sharp as a tack and could hear every little sound.

"Now you hush up, Leroy," Van sparred from another recliner. "Don't make me come wrestle you down." Recent heart surgery made that highly unlikely, but it was a way for them to engage in some good-natured banter while they passed the time waiting for Flynn and Jake.

Tracey needed to keep her hands busy, so she started adjusting and fiddling with the decorations, Licia and Lena standing off to the side shaking their heads.

Little Genia decided to help, her assistance enough to keep Tracey more than busy for a while.

Watching Genia climb up the back of a couch, giggling every time Tracey tried to hold her, Licia imagined how Eugene must have looked at her age: the same fine sandy-blond hair, cropped shorter than the little girl's he'd never lived to see; freckles dotting her nose; big bright eyes that missed nothing; smart as a whip, a little hellion when she could get away with it and a charmer when it suited her purposes . . .

A tyke who liked to question authority, but could always be counted on to behave when it really mattered.

*   *   *

Genia had been wondering about her daddy since she was old enough to ask. She didn't know yet that he'd had a brief, though ignominious, brush with fame. But she did understand that he'd been a fine young man and all the important people in her life—Unca Flynn and his wife Aunt Lena, Aunt Tracey and Unca Leroy and that silly Mr. Van who always brought her something fun when he came to visit—they all loved her daddy and reminded her she should be proud of him. She absolutely adored Little Ray, always looked forward to his visits. He'd told her Eugene was his best friend, and that when she was old enough, he was gonna marry her!

All the grownups had laughed, but she liked to think just maybe that might really come true.

*   *   *

Flynn and Jake tooled down the highway toward Dickson, their first private conversation since the siege.

"You understand the lawyer couldn't tell me what you wanted me to know," Flynn tried to explain. "There was no confidentiality of what would be said between us—only between you and him."

"I just hated havin' to wait so long—taking that chance."

"Well, it was all for the best, I think. You told me enough to figure out what I needed. Now that I've heard all the details of what happened in the compound that day, I don't think you oughta repeat it to Licia and them. Let's just leave it that Eugene was a hero."

Jake agreed. They rode on in silence a few minutes. "I can't believe you done settled down, not only with your wife, but sharing a home with Tracey and Licia and that young'n." Jake chuckled at the thought.

Flynn just grinned. "Sometimes I have to go out and drink beer and cuss and shoot something just to keep from wantin' to play dress-up or do my hair with the girls. I been plum *overrun* with women."

"Are you workin' at all?—I mean, you know."

"Twice a year—only because I owe the man that helped us put it together. It's safe and easy and keeps filling those trust funds I set up. By the way, you got a real big one comin' soon as you're off parole. Didn't want the feds to be able to get their hands on it."

Jake looked awkward for a moment. "I can't thank you enough for paying for everything, the lawyers and what-all."

Flynn waved him off. "Tracey done paid it off with good cooking." He patted his gut for emphasis. "Lena can't cook toast."

They chuckled some more. Flynn couldn't help notice the lines in Jake's face, the hardened look in his eyes, the determination of a man who'd struggled to maintain hope and dignity in the worst of worlds. "There's another surprise, too. We got an exotic honeymoon booked all next week for you two."

Jake was surprised, then concerned. "I can't leave Tennessee for a while, you know."

"That's why Tracey picked Gatlinburg."

"Eee-ha!"

Jake showed surprise at the new blacktop road, duly impressed by the fully rebuilt mansion that had replaced the old Emery farmhouse. He got mobbed with hugs and kisses all around, Tracey in tears, Licia not far behind. Little Genia acted shy at first, then wanted to join in when she saw him hold her mother for such a long time.

Presents and food and music and stories, it was almost too much. When Tracey presented Jake with a new hat, blue-jay feather and all, he got choked up.

"Don't you think you oughta try it on?" Flynn asked quietly, breaking the tension.

A round of applause because it fit, more laughs followed as he cocked it and tilted it and tried it every which way.

A dozen more people stopped by for a while, a late wedding reception, a welcome-home, a thank-you from friends, a celebration of survival.

*   *   *

Later that night, Genia didn't understand why she was sleeping with her mother on the first floor in a back bedroom.

"We're giving Jake and Tracey the whole upstairs tonight so they can be by themselves. It's their first time together since they been married."

Genia cuddled up next to her mother, Licia gently stroking her hair, a slash of moonlight sparkling her eyes, the sound of spring crickets and peepers chittering through the screen.

"Mama. Did Unca Jake know my daddy?"

*   *   *

It proved a glorious day for a memorial service, warm morning sunshine, dogwoods in bloom, the scent of crabapple and honeysuckle, birds singing, the frantic gurgle of Little Richland Creek at springtime flow. Several ducks swam lazily in the small man-made pond, fountain spray in their faces, shifting rainbows refracting in the mist. More than two dozen people gathered at the meticulously landscaped cemetery along Highway 13.

Shiny marble headstones marked graves old and new . . . the Watterson family; Willow Weisman, Eugene's mother, Eugene Weisman beside her; Mr. and Mrs. Emery, son Marshall at one side, cousin Lloyd Stewart next to him; Jolene Carter off beside her own mother, a triple marker with room for Leroy when it came time for him to join his family once again.

Genia squirming impatiently, everybody listened while Jake spoke of heroes and honor and commitment, of family and friends lost, of loved ones they'd left behind. He praised Jolene Carter for risking so much to follow her conscience; told stories about Marshall, tribute for a soldier downed in the line of duty; of brief acquaintance with Lloyd, giving his life in a desperate attempt to stand by his family; of Eugene, barely a man thrust into responsibility for all men, bravest of all, making the ultimate sacrifice to leave a better world for the child he would never touch.

Eugene Weisman, hero, Flynn Durbett's fallen friend . . .

There were tubs of cold soda and fruit juice, card tables of sandwiches and snacks, bouquets of flowers here and there, Genia feeding pretzel sticks to nervous finches and daring sparrows.

As people drifted away, Flynn and Jake carried a cooler down to the creek, Van and several others standing around casually, watching every direction. Flynn removed the detector taken from the agent who had searched the Watterson home. Jake sighted the location, leading Flynn along a ridge of rocks, the undergrowth of heavy shrubbery.

Blip!

A collapsible shovel quickly revealed a dirt-caked black box, not much bigger than a bar of soap, hidden more than five years before by a scared, teenage girl who was confused but understood at the last minute whom she believed, whom she trusted.

Jolene had told Eugene where she hid it, then died trying to retrieve it. Eugene had told Jake during the seige, then died fooling the agents into thinking it was destroyed in the conflagration. Jake had carried the secret through years in prison, no safe way to tell Flynn, waiting for this day.

Flynn Durbett nodded confirmation to the others, the box disappearing somewhere about his person.

"Sure don't look like much."

*   *   *

Leroy out visiting at Van's for the day, Jake and Tracey had the place to themselves, packing and planning to head for Gatlinburg the following morning. Flynn and Lena Durbett, Licia Emery and little Genia Weisman were off to spend the day with the Blountens at their place along Mill Creek, Guntersville Lake.

"Uncle Flynn! Aunt Lena an' Miss Emery! Hey, Sweet Genia!" Little Ray, at fourteen, could more appropriately be called at least *Medium* Ray.

Genia waited long enough for the guys to bear-hug and wrestle a bit, each trying to cause the other to lose his balance. Ray was years away from matching the older man's size and cunning, but he wasn't embarrassing himself, either. Once they'd settled down, the little girl climbed up to hug Ray's neck. By then, Jackie had come out for another round of hugs.

"Can we see the minners, Ray?" Genia wanted to know.

He took her around back to a series of concrete tanks teeming with tens of thousands of shiners and tuffies and goldfish and shad fry. Raising them had been a hobby, a commitment, even a small-business venture. He let her carefully spoon in the right amount of food, netting some of the little fish up for her to splash her hands through. She always enjoyed touching them, holding a wiggler for a moment before returning him to his watery home.

"Can we feed the *big* fish?"

"Sure! But let's see what Uncle Flynn has to say about it."

Jackie and Lena were unloading cold drinks from the boathouse refrigerator. Licia was standing on the pier gazing across the water, Flynn behind with an arm around her shoulders. They were watching a heron step gingerly through the shallows up in the cove, head darting this way and that, waiting for a tasty meal to swim his way. Chipmunks and silver-tailed squirrels scurried around tentatively like they knew company meant somebody would break out peanuts and feed the twitchy-tailed critters who called the

Blounten place home.

"Haven't fed 'em yet today," Ray told Flynn.

The mercenary nodded. Genia dutifully helped—got in the way mostly—while Ray loaded up a bucketful of minnows. Licia retrieved her daughter's arm floaties and swimsuit from the car, taking her inside the boathouse to change.

The little girl walked down the steps into the water, sitting with her feet submerged. Ray retrieved a scuba diver's flag on styrofoam ring and set it afloat, tying it off with a rope. Several dozen fish who had learned the signal for feeding time schooled along the pier. Ray started dropping minnows to the hungry mob, letting Genia toss a few herself.

The little girl submerged her hands, confident that at least one would come up and let her pet it for a moment or two before swimming away.

Flynn sat beside her, the black box appearing from under his vest. He held it just below the surface, swishing as if to clean it off, watching the refracted light play designs across its smooth ebony surface.

A big old bass circled around, getting closer with each pass. Finally, in a bold move, it eased between Genia's hands and let her stroke it gently.

"Oh no! She's sick!" The little girl was distraught, the bass slowly rolling to its side and floating away from the pier. Ray kept feeding the others. Flynn put the black box away.

Jackie directed Ray to fire up the barbecue for an afternoon of sirloin tips and hotdogs, potato salad and watermelon and cold soda, pesky chipmunks raiding the table, sparrows flying sorties. Genia never got far from Little Ray; she thought he was a pretty good feller indeed.

Jackie had reserved a pontoon-boat rental down at the marina, so they all went for a leisurely cruise through the lake, watching a pair of eagles overhead, geese and coots flocking still waters, fishermen casting among stumps, the smell of springtime in the air. Genia found herself enthralled by the *Mississippi Queen* paddlewheeling by.

They eased the pontoon into Town Creek cove, just a few miles below where Eugene had given his life in the Sand Mountain Patriots' compound.

Genia pronounced, "I'm a *girl!*"

Everybody was watching her; nobody spoke. She climbed into her mother's lap.

Each of you got it in you to be salvation.

"Lots of fish and turtles and birds all over the lake got aliens," she said matter-of-factly. "The good ones. They all know. Of course, only one is fully mature now."

"A smart plan," Flynn said. "Especially using the bass."

Persevere, no matter what, and wait for your chance.

"What happened to McGovern and the doctor?" Genia asked.

"Both dead."

She looked satisfied. "Was that the box?"

Flynn produced it, handed it to the little girl.

She caressed it gingerly. "He says for me to answer the next call."

Little Ray moved closer. "That's what your daddy wanted."

"So did Mr. Watterson," she reminded.

Flynn nodded. "We'll take care of you, keep you safe."

"We believe in you, Flynn." She meant it.

"And we won't tell nobody else," Licia promised.

"Just us," added Ray.

Be careful, little one.

Genia looked determined. "And Daddy."

You will be captured or killed.

More Books by Stephen Geez

General Fiction
Dance of the Lights
What Sara Saw
Papala Skies
How It Turns Out

Media Thriller
Fantasy Patch

Mystical Adventure Series
Rich Mr. Fixx: *Crystal Clear* #1
Rich Mr. Fixx: *Spider-Boxed* #2
Rich Mr. Fixx: *Hot Doggies* #3
Rich Mr. Fixx Graphic Flashback #1: *Shell Game*

Science Fiction
Invigilator
Zhasou Pure

Essay Collection
Been There, Noted That

GeezWriter
How-to Series for Writers

The Fresh Ink Group

Publishing
Memberships
Share & Read Free Stories, Essays, Articles
Free-Story Newsletter
Writing Contests

Books
E-books
Amazon Bookstore

Authors
Editors
Artists
Professionals
Publishing Services
Publisher Resources

Members' Websites
Members' Blogs
Social Media

www.FreshInkGroup.com

Email: info@FreshInkGroup.com

Twitter: @FreshInkGroup

Google+: Fresh Ink Group

Facebook.com/FreshInkGroup

LinkedIn: Fresh Ink Group

About.me/FreshInkGroup

Invigilator's Flynn Durbett teams up with Danté in Fantasy Patch

FANTASY PATCH

By Stephen Geez

Picture This!

Danté Roenik creates ad campaigns, reveling in the fine art of rendering his concepts on million-dollar canvasses financed by big-budget clients. Intoxicated by the sheer power of directing public opinion, he dares wage war against the conglomerate behind a worldwide anti-depressant increasingly associated with sporadic violence. To juxtapose his images with reality, he enlists a mixed palette of business tycoons, his fiancée/attorney, a team of corporate-spy soldiers of fortune, one resurgent news anchor, and the best TV-production crew in Chicago.

But the sharp lines dividing perception from truth begin to blur when the darker motives shaping mass media come to light. Forced to re-examine the ethics of designer pharmacology, Danté is painted into a corner, his future about to be erased as patients die, clients lie, and unhealthy doses of murder prove too hard to swallow.

Too late to whitewash the stain of deceit, Danté must decide who deserves to appear in his picture, the true subject an unfinished self-portrait way past its own deadline.

It's not what you see, not what you get . . .
But all you could ever imagine.
Let Danté show you how . . .

With a Fantasy Patch!

www.FreshInkGroup.com
ISBN: 978-1-936442-06-5

ZHASOU PURE

By Stephen Geez

How can I kill my own kids? Purple-skinned Sullrob could never imagine taking his loved ones' lives, be they racially contaminated or not—but others prove all too eager to seize that honor.

Am I risking my children's future? Peach-faced widower-dad Brog Pawligan tries smuggling to build a better life ground-side for his own "orbiter brats"—but what will happen to them if he gets caught . . . or worse?

"Abig big big peoples an' li'l peoples," says big brown-bodied Heilen Hewed about his burgeoning community, *"peoples of ev-ree colors, afrom all over th'galaxy!"*—but will the lethal aspirations of an interplanetary corporation steal this stellar chance to reclaim his wife and boy?

There where fuzzy weenshuggers sing in the pink light of dual moons, where prejudice and fear threaten to out-kill a deadly global plague, how can the ascension of one squeaky-voiced little Seeliot lad save billions of souls scattered among the stars?

It might just be time for a new breed in myriad colors to transform the ancient Celebration of Life—the recitation, ritual water, and tiniest pinch of pungent sweet granules from the exquisite purple plant that everybody adores served up . . . *Zhasou Pure!*

www.FreshInkGroup.com

ISBN: 978-1-936442-04-1

PAPALA SKIES

By Stephen Geez

Chicago native Rochelle DuFortier likes to imagine the future, her world a series of picture postcards so vivid they sometimes seem real. When a foolish mistake at thirteen causes her mother's death, she's sent to a secluded Hawaiian valley, an outsider "haole-girl" among pidgin-speaking boys who hurl flaming papala spears under the full moon to summon her mother's spirit. After boarding school and a prestigious university back east, the ambitious young woman is torn between chasing new career opportunities, discovering her mother's heritage in a remote French village, and meeting obligations pulling her back to Hawaii.

On this island steeped in ancient mythology and modern superstition, Rochelle tests the possibility of sharing pieces of her life with those whose beliefs she barely understands and never intends to embrace. She dives the depths of a pristine coral lagoon, conceals bodies in a subterranean lava tube, and challenges the eruptions of a living volcano, even as she deciphers the truth about her mother's death and struggles to satisfy new debts born of old betrayals.

Papala Skies is the story of a young woman who makes all the right choices, only to find herself living an unexpected life. It is about the need to belong, and seeking one's own version of truth amid such differing cultures' responses to wrenching loss and abiding grief. It is about yearning for a sense of place, yet having to confront new ways to honor the love of family and friends.

Will Rochelle lose what matters most, or might she learn what the smart octopus already knows?

www.FreshInkGroup.com

ISBN: 978-1-936442-07-2

DANCE OF THE LIGHTS

By Stephen Geez

Frank relishes fast success and early retirement, but struggling to preserve his life's work thrusts him into a desperate battle to protect the people he cares about most.

Beverly seeks a new beginning in Tarpon Springs—until those she trusts steal control of her destiny, forcing a fight for her very survival.

All twelve-year-old Kevin wants is attention from the only man he respects, yet murder and the wrenching indifference of a callous legal system toward one vulnerable child proves even friendship might never be enough.

Riven by tragedy, consumed by grief, all three must confront the wondrous possibility that our indelible bonds may somehow transcend even death, that a cherished soul truly can find the way back.

Only together might this improbable family dare embrace their own brand of unexpected love, that infinite potential to achieve more than any one person can alone. Through it all, they are teased by the mystery of those dancing lights, a million pinpoints in every imaginable color swirling to form brilliant images of extraordinary lives.

www.FreshInkGroup.com
ISBN: 978-1-936442-00-3

BEEN THERE, NOTED THAT:
Essays in Celebration of Life

Observations, Inspiration, Remembrance,
& Noteworthies To Share

By Stephen Geez

The simple lives of everyday people in a mundane world prove extraordinary in this collection of 54 personal-experience essays by novelist Stephen Geez. The eclectic mix of memoir, commentary, humor, and appreciation covers a wide range of topics, each beautifully illustrated by artists and photographers from the Fresh Ink Group. Geez catches what many of us miss, then considers how we might all share the most poignant of lessons. *Been There, Noted That* aims to reveal who we are, examine where we've been, and discover what we dare strive to become.

www.FreshInkGroup.com
ISBN: 978-978-1-936442-05-8

www.ingramcontent.com/pod-product-compliance
Lightning Source LLC
Chambersburg PA
CBHW030637020726
47493CB00006B/1757